THE

BEST

AMERICAN SHORT STORIES

1964

THE
BEST
AMERICAN SHORT STORIES
1964

and the Yearbook of the American Short Story

EDITED BY

MARTHA FOLEY and DAVID BURNETT

HOUGHTON MIFFLIN COMPANY

The Riverside Press Cambridge

1964

"The Broomstick on the Porch" by Frieda Arkin. First published in *The Kenyon Review*. Copyright © 1963 by Kenyon College.

"Mr. Iscariot" by Richard G. Brown. First published in *The Literary Review*, Summer, 1963. Copyright © 1963 Fairleigh Dickinson University, Teaneck, New Jersey, U.S.A.

"To a Tenor Dying Old" by John Stewart Carter. First published in *The Kenyon Review*. Copyright © 1963 by Kenyon College.

"A Story of Love, Etc." by Daniel Curley. First published in *Epoch*. Copyright © 1963 by Cornell University.

"The Woman Across the Street" by May Dikeman. Copyright © 1963 by The Atlantic Monthly Company, Boston, Massachusetts.

"A Long Day's Dying" by William Eastlake. First published in *The Virginia Quarterly Review*. Copyright © 1963 by William Eastlake.

"Figure Over the Town" by William Goyen. First published in *The Saturday Evening Post*. © 1963 by The Curtis Publishing Company.

"Black Snowflakes" by Paul Horgan. First published in *The Saturday Evening Post*. "Black Snowflakes" also forms part of Mr. Horgan's novel *Things As They Are*, published by Farrar, Straus & Company, Inc., in 1964. Copyright © 1963 by Paul Horgan.

"The Pump" by William Humphrey. First published in *Esquire* Magazine. © 1963 by Esquire, Inc.

"Birthday Party" by Shirley Jackson. First published in *Vogue* Magazine. Copyright © 1962 by The Condé Nast Publications, Inc.

"The Power" by Edith Konecky. Reprinted from *The Massachusetts Review*. © 1963, The Massachusetts Review, Inc.

"Mule No. 095" by Kimon Lolos. First published in *The Carleton Miscellany*. Copyright © 1963 by Carleton College.

"The German Refugee" by Bernard Malamud. First published in *The Saturday Evening Post* under the title "The Refugee." Reprinted from Mr. Malamud's book *Idiots First* by permission of Farrar, Straus & Company, Inc., and Eyre & Spottiswoode Ltd. Copyright © 1963 by Bernard Malamud.

"Sucker" by Carson McCullers. First published in *The Saturday Evening Post*. © 1963 by Carson McCullers.

"Simple Arithmetic" by Virginia Moriconi. First published in *The Transatlantic Review*. © Joseph McCrindle, 1963.

Acknowledgments

GRATEFUL ACKNOWLEDGMENT for permission to reprint the stories in this volume is made to the following:

The Editors of *The Atlantic Monthly, The Carleton Miscellany, The Colorado Quarterly, Epoch, Esquire, The Kenyon Review, The Literary Review, The Massachusetts Review, The Saturday Evening Post, Shenandoah, Southwest Review, The Transatlantic Review, The Virginia Quarterly Review, Vogue;* and to Frieda Arkin, Richard G. Brown, John Stewart Carter, Daniel Curley, May Dikeman, William Eastlake, William Goyen, Paul Horgan, William Humphrey, Shirley Jackson, Edith Konecky, Kimon Lolos, Bernard Malamud, Carson McCullers, Virginia Moriconi, Joyce Carol Oates, Reynolds Price, Vera Randal, Harvey Swados, Robert Penn Warren.

Foreword

THE PAST YEAR has been an important one for both the readers and
writers of American short stories. For readers it has been important
because for the first time those who have access only to the mass
circulation magazines have been given the opportunity to see stories
of real literary merit. Many who have been inured to the old kind
of "slick" magazine fiction have been startled to find that with the
exception of a few dullard periodicals — or shall we be kind and
call them "slow starters"? — editors generally have lifted their short
story sights and are treating their readers as mature men and women.
No longer is the impact of a story measured for that mythical reader
with the mentality of a twelve-year-old who dominated too many
editorial decisions for too many years. After all, millions of Americans now have been to college.

Reading a short story should be an emotional adventure. It may
be an adventure in joy. It may be an adventure in sorrow. Sometimes it may be an adventure in both. But to deserve the time
spent in reading it, it must not be a soporific, a drug shutting out
life. Good short stories must have a springboard of reality, no matter how high the authors' imagination may afterwards soar, and at
their end they must leave the reader in one way or another revital-
ized, even if it be only with anger. Such fiction can be a greater
challenge to the reader than any other form of writing, except
poetry. The man who says, "Oh, I never read fiction, only serious
work, factual stuff," is, if one can be excused a hackneyed quotation,
"more to be pitied than scorned." He does not know what he loses.

For writers of short stories the past year has been important because their field of publication has been widened. Paradoxically, what used to be called the "quality" magazines, *Harper's* and *The Atlantic,* have continued to narrow the space they give to fiction. (There was a time when *Harper's* published as many as eight short stories in an issue!) Simultaneously both magazines have inserted more and more advertising in space once given to excellent reading material. Only a year or so ago no serious writer would have dreamed that magazines such as *The Saturday Evening Post* or *The Ladies' Home Journal* would publish more and better fiction than the "quality" magazines. But it has happened. The names of authors once found only in the "little" magazines, in the literary quarterlies and the more esoteric publications are now being boldly featured on the covers of the "slicks."

May the day of boy-meets-girl, boy-loses-girl, boy-gets-girl-back-and-job-in-the-bank never return! It is amazing that in the country of Poe, Melville, Crane and their long line of magnificent literary descendants the formula could have survived as long as it did.

The acceptance, at long last, of short stories of permanent distinction we owe in large part to the "little" magazines and literary quarterlies, to their long struggle for really good writing and to the sacrifices, financial and otherwise, of their editors. And it is to these journals, moreover, that we must still look for the new frontiers. With advertising pressures being what they are, they must still be thought of as the places to which those who want to be the first to savor good new writing must turn. No matter how the big publications have improved their standards, only the less commercial magazines can afford to be the daring ones, the first to hail a Joyce or a Genet abroad, a Faulkner or a Baldwin at home.

This year two of our finest literary magazines celebrate anniversaries. One is *Epoch,* edited by Baxter Hathaway at Cornell University, and not nearly as renowned as it deserves. It has just published its fiftieth issue. The other is *Kenyon Review,* renowned and deservedly so, which marks its hundredth number. For years it was edited by John Crowe Ransom, whose recent seventy-fifth birthday drew tributes from writers all over the world.

In his overly modest foreword to the anniversary issue of *Epoch,* Mr. Hathaway writes:

For the sake of the writers it has printed and for the well-being

of the American "spirit" (pardon the use of the "noble" word)
Epoch *has wished over the past sixteen years to capture a larger
public than it has succeeded in doing. This is not to attack* The
New Yorker *or* Esquire *for having succeeded; they need support
even in their relative success. If we are envious, our envy takes the
form of thinking that success in those places is the result of an* impure *alliance between sheer excellence or power of literary art and
something else, whereas* Epoch *has not succeeded in th same way as
a result of being too pure. Pure in focusing upon the writing itself
and not, on one hand, upon the critical essays and literary cud-
chewing that one large part of our potential readers have always
let us know they wanted and, on the other hand, the perfume ad-
vertisements, the calendar of available entertainment around the
metropolis, the projection of sophistication or stag-party naughti-
ness, or the projection directly of informing ideas. A* haute culture
*is ultimately informed by ideas and not by literary art products,
even though ideas may find their richest and most potent forms in
the art products. But to present the art forms without impure
amalgam with the detached ideas is to court disaster. This kind of
disaster we have always somewhat consciously courted and we
should be willing to reconcile ourselves to the consequences of our
"purity."*

In contrast it may be interesting to quote from *Kenyon Review*'s
anniversary editorial:

What the Review *stood for was always perfectly clear. It stood,
first of all, for the discussion of values in literature. As Mr. Ransom
said, "One of the saving gifts of our age, against the many ways it
has devised for being wretched, is its turn to literary criticism, and
for a literary criticism evidently so surprising and acute, and so
grounded in good conscience, as can scarcely be predicted of the
other periods of literary history." He thought of the era in which
this magazine appeared as one of evaluation and critical compre-
hension rather than one of high creation; it was a time of literary
conscience rather than of literary passion.*

Fortunately, Mr. Ransom failed. He was too good a poet and
creative artist himself to have succeeded. The *Kenyon Review* has
published much of the finest fiction to appear in this country and
what Mr. Ransom hoped would be *Kenyon*'s main influence, the
so-called "New Criticism," long ago started to fade.

So to Mr. Hathaway, whom we met only once, our sincere congratulations on what he considers his failure in trying to be "pure." And to Mr. Ransom, whom we came to admire greatly as a person one memorable summer at the University of Utah where our chief extracurricular activity was trying to keep his pipe supplied with matches, our equally sincere congratulations on his failure to be "impure." Both men have greatly enriched our country.

To return to the more general aspects of the short story situation today, we wonder how many readers of what are called novels appreciate that they are really reading collections of short stories. It is a publishing phenomenon attracting less attention than it should that the short story and the novel have been married. Once the novel — think of practically any of the eighteenth or nineteenth century novels — was as complex as a symphony or an intricately woven wall-sized tapestry. The short story was more like a song or a framed painting. Some twenty or so years ago collections of short stories developed — for marketing purposes, perhaps? — what we might call the "protective coloring" of novels? One has only to consider the work of Bellow, Cheever, McCarthy, Porter, to name a bare handful. Nearly every magazine we have read this year has published as a "short story" writing which is labeled "from a forthcoming novel." So much for the vagaries of both literary and publishing evaluation.

Anyway this book *is* a collection of short stories, labeled as such. Sifted from many magazines, they represent a kind of writing in which America has excelled. We hope you will find each of them an emotional adventure.

We are grateful to the editors who have kept us supplied with their magazines and to their authors for generously granting reprint rights. We welcome copies of any new magazine.

The editors and staff of Houghton Mifflin Company are also entitled to gratitude for their help. Finally, tribute is paid to the memory of Edward J. O'Brien, who founded this anthology.

Martha Foley
David Burnett

Contents

THE
BEST
AMERICAN SHORT STORIES
1964

FRIEDA ARKIN

The Broomstick on the Porch

(FROM THE KENYON REVIEW)

LOUELLA, having come all the way across the state in the Trailways
bus, passed, for the first time in her life, nearly a whole day without
the sight of a face she knew. She smiled at everyone, though, and
quite a few smiled back. And, when she rose to get off, the red-faced
woman with the knotted nose beamed deeply at her and got up too,
helping Louella pull the straw hamper down off the overhead shelf.
The bus driver was a man named Mr. Simpson who had quite a few
folks, he said, in Berkham County, nearby her own, and he patted
Louella on the arm in a fatherly way after extracting her old patent
leather suitcase from the bowels of the bus. "Have a good time,
honey," a few people called out to her as the bus moved away. They
thought, probably, that she was starting on a vacation.

"I'm from over Dorloo way," Louella told Mrs. Austin a week
later, settling herself comfortably onto the fat, down-stuffed cushion.
She sat in the blue-carpeted living room in a wing-backed chair facing Mrs. Austin who, a child on each knee, stooped now and then to
nuzzle the blond one in the back of the neck.

"Dorloo?" Mrs. Austin murmured, and suddenly bent to kiss the
other one, the boy, who was staring intently at Louella. "Dorloo?
Now where is that?"

"Kellem County." Louella answered absently, looking around at
the walls — a painting of a countryside, another of a woods with
purple trees, real purple, and a long one, above the piano, of a furiously boiling river, the white water going every which way. She

looked at the black grand piano which stood nakedly, not a photograph or a scarf on it. Not a photograph or a picture of a person anywhere. "You got folks?" Louella asked politely.

Mrs. Austin shifted the blond one, the baby, a little. "What we're looking for, Louella," Mrs. Austin said, "is some nice young person who loves children. That's the most important thing with us, who loves children. The housework is secondary. You've had experience with children?"

"Took care of all my brothers and sisters," Louella said. "We was eight. Ma never could stand the noise. Kellem's over at the right-hand end of the state. You from these parts?"

Mrs. Austin's eyes were a surprised pale blue, like the boy's, and she turned them now quietly on Louella. "No," she said, "we've only just moved here. We're from New York. But we expect to be here about three years."

"Three years." Louella looked down at her strong young hands where the white half-moons showed, clear and forthright, under her nails. It had taken months of scrubbing and pushing back the cuticles to achieve that elegance, and she clasped her hands together and smiled brightly up. "That'll be all right, I guess. I expect I should be gettin' married about then."

"Really?" Mrs. Austin said, startled. "I didn't know. You look so young."

"Oh, it ain't nobody yet. I'll be twenty-one then, is all I meant." She pushed a wisp of sunny hair back behind her ear, beginning to look a little frightened, and Mrs. Austin laughed. The telephone rang suddenly from another room and Mrs. Austin deposited the boy on the floor and carried the baby out with her into the hall. The boy looked to be about four, unusually silent for one of that age. Louella smiled down on him charitably.

"I know a story," she said to him, and rose up from the chair to crouch close to his level. She gave him a great wide smile as his round eyes opened at her. "It's all about a broomstick."

"Yes." Mrs. Austin's voice sailed in, high and pleased, from the hall. "I can't say for sure, but I think so."

"You see, this here broomstick was stuck up against the wall on the porch, and one night there came a knock at the door. Just like that, in the middle of the night. Three raps on the door. You know what happened?"

The boy's mouth was open. Louella's face darkened portentously and she pushed her lips out until her mouth was a small black O.

"And you know what happened? They opened the door, and there was only just this broomstick, layin' on the porch, and nobody there. And the next night it done the same. Each time they stuck the broom back up against the wall and closed the door. For three nights it done that. And, on the third night, there was this girl, see, sick in bed in the house, she had an awful sickness, and on the third night they picked the broom up and then they went upstairs, and there they found her, alayin' on the floor, dead. And — "

Mrs. Austin's footsteps, clicking in from the shining wooden floor of the hall, were abruptly silenced by the carpet. Her voice was sweet and bright, like the sunlight outside.

"Shall we give it a try, Louella? You can start right in today, if you want to. Where are your things?"

The boy was watching Louella raptly. Her own lips were smiling now, wide and pink with tenderness, and she turned her head to look up at Mrs. Austin. "They're over to my aunt's, over to Greene Street. I come to live with her last week. Ma says another mouth less to feed. You want me to move in today?"

"If you'd like to, dear, I hope you have the right clothes — you know, housedresses and things of that sort." Mrs. Austin's light eyes rested on the froth of pleated chiffon which Louella wore at her neck. Louella smiled and looked down on it and touched it with her hand.

"This here's Ma's jabbo. She give it to me for the bus journey. Says she don't have no more use for it, she wore it to church and all, the times she was carryin' the babies inside. Said it kep' folks eyes up where they belonged."

Mrs. Austin was laughing again. Her reddish hair, fine as Louella's own, seemed surrounded by a golden halo as she stood with the window directly behind her. "But you do have housedresses and aprons?"

"Yes, I do have." Louella rose up full on her feet. "I can go over right now to Aunt Nellie's and get my things."

Mrs. Austin had begun nuzzling the baby again. "This is Cynthia," she said. "I see you've made friends with Robbie already. I know you'll all get along fine with one another." She was walking toward the hall again, smiling back over her shoulder, and Louella hesitated, then leaned down once more to the boy. "I got seven aunts dead," she whispered to him, and gave his head a tousle and stood up and walked to the hall.

On the porch she shook Mrs. Austin's hand languidly. "I know about the bus back," she said. "Aunt Nell drilled me good." She brushed at the hair which rose back from the light springs at her temples. To Mrs. Austin she looked vulnerable, very clean, and very young.

Louella received her first letter from home when she had been with the Austins about a month. Her mother wrote in pencil in her large Palmer Method hand, on lavender dime-store paper, and Louella bent to the folded sheet in frowning concentration and cried out when she turned the page. Mrs. Austin looked up from her sewing basket. "Not bad news, I hope, dear?" Mrs. Austin said.

"It's just that Charlie Ryder's dead," Louella told her. The look in her eyes was far from the quiet spring afternoon, and Mrs. Austin, noting it, murmured something and bent to her work again.

Louella would never forget old Charlie Ryder. He used to work for the railroad, but to her recollection he was always at home, sitting in the black Morris chair near the window, his left arm bent at the elbow, hand cradled tenderly in his lap. The nail of his pinky finger was a good three inches long (he swore he had never in his life cut it), a horny, gray-yellow saber. Because of it he had never been asked to lift a hand around the house.

His wife's tastes also ran to length. Mrs. Ryder had thick, glossy, black hair, coarse and resplendent as a horse's tail. It hung down as far as her big white behind, which was full of dimples and the color of pale marble. Mornings, daily, Louella used to come into the sun-spattered front bedroom and for two cents a day brush and comb and curry it, using two men's hairbrushes. Then she collected her pennies and took them home to cache with the others in the tumbler her grandmother had once used to keep her false teeth in. Louella still had the pennies, tied in a blue bandanna handkerchief in a corner of the bottom drawer upstairs. They must have weighed two pounds, easily.

In her room, remembering Charlie, Louella cried a little. She would have liked to be at home to see him laid to rest, the coins on his eyelids, his spear of pinky nail intact, in one of Mr. Baumbart's satin-lined coffins. She enjoyed all funerals, but missing Charlie's she particularly regretted.

She always got along with children. Mrs. Austin's two were the usual — the baby suppliant for love or a smile, ecstatic at a word from her, too young yet for mischief. That Robbie was a quiet one, though, with eyes too large. She expected murder from him, maybe, in six months. Louella could keep them both quiet with her stories. The boy would listen for hours on end, if she had a mind to go on. She gave him the tales she'd been raised up with, having heard them in every odd corner of the village . . . down by the railroad tracks told by rough boys . . . in the park, crooned mysteriously, sometimes, by one of the older girls . . . sitting on the hot noon sidewalks of Main Street; stories whispered, denouements hinted at, curdling matters having to do with bats and giant darning-needles and the deaths of children. To the baby she could say anything, who would listen owl-eyed to the two-times multiplication table clear up through to forty; she'd tried it.

She rose early, mornings, each day noting the path of the slim figure of sunlight which advanced across the grass of the yard outside her window, earlier and earlier as the spring came on. She was used to rising at any hour, and when one of the children cried out in the night was at the bed before Mrs. Austin had time to put a bare foot to the floor.

"Now, Louella, you work hard all day; you let me get up at night with the children," Mrs. Austin would tell her time and again; but Louella shook her head. She took her work seriously. The children were hers to tend.

Mr. Austin was something else again.

Louella didn't lack for ideas about men and boys. She had more than she needed. But for the matter of size, she drew a distinction the width of a hair between the two. Boys were present or incipient troublemakers; all anyone could hope to do was postpone an eventual misbehavior as inevitable as the sunrise. Men were little different. She hadn't the slightest doubt that when the time came she would be perfectly able to cope with the larger edition.

There was something about Mr. Austin that kept bringing Charlie Ryder to her mind. Not that he displayed any remarkable adjunct like Charlie's fingernail, which was as attractive in Charlie as a ribbon in a girl's hair. (Even so, her admiration of Charlie had never really misled her about him: his wife, to the rhythmic accompaniment of the hair brushing, had elaborated with earthy relish on other of Charlie's traits, hidden to casual visitors. Charlie fitted comfortably into the world of men Louella had constructed from her own observations of her father, of two uncles, and a grown male cousin. All you had to do, Louella sagely knew, was let them think they ruled the roost. Women managed.)

Like Charlie, Mr. Austin was a quiet man. He had only recently been brought in to set up and direct a factory where they made radio parts, this Louella knew; and he arrived home each day punctually at six, ate with Mrs. Austin, played with the boy, and generally retired to the living room afterward, a book in his hand. But she never knew him to read it. He sat hour-long, evenings, beside the window, looking out at the blue which descended later and later, but seeing — Louella knew — nothing whatever out there. Walking furtively past the doorway she would throw small, covert glances at him sitting there with his eyes turned inward. "He has nothing else to listen to but the sounds in his head," her mother would have said. But Louella found it worrisome.

He spoke so little. Louella tended to flatten her body against the walls when she passed him in the hall, in the rooms, her eyes always a little off to the side. Only on the first day, when he spoke to her and shook her hand, had she looked, once, straight into his mild gray eyes and found no self-appointed god there. But he accepted her as he might the wallpaper, and she was relieved, finally, to be allowed to merge herself with the children and not be forced to whittle away at Mr. Austin and trim him into familiar shape.

The boy was beginning to become fearful over the possible loss of limbs. He had a nightmare, a few weeks after Louella's coming, shrieking out in high terror that a man was trying to cut off his legs, but by the time Mrs. Austin had come tearing from her room Louella had already reached his bedside and enfolded the small, quaking form in her arms, speaking soothing, meaningless words, gentle sounds like the soughing of quiet winds. He subsided into faint whimperings, gave a long, tremulous sigh, and was asleep in no time at all.

"They get that way, this age," Louella explained to Mrs. Austin kindly. "All my brothers were the same. See? He's asleep already."

Mrs. Austin rubbed her hands worriedly. "You haven't been threatening him, or anything like that, dear, have you? About sucking his thumb, I mean?"

Louella stood beside the small, silent bed and pinched her cotton flannel nightgown to her neck. She smiled gently and shook her head. "I wouldn't do a thing like that. My Ma, she always said they was afraid of losing their little peewees; it comes round about now. Nobody has to tell 'em anything. Now you go back to sleep, Miz Austin, you don't know about little boys, is all."

"I just can't get over how the children take to you," Mrs. Austin said to her. It was evening, and Louella had come in with them through the back door. For the past half hour Mrs. Austin had hovered at the window, peering out at where Louella sat on the grass in the dark of the maples, holding the children in her lap, talking. And they, quiet as mice.

"How they do love to listen to you. What *do* you talk about, dear?"

"Stories," Louella said, and swung the baby up on her head. "Time for baths now. You run up, Tukey." She had her own names for them. They took the stairs in a rush, leaving Mrs. Austin with a faint crease between the eyes.

Louella took the boy downtown once. "We'll go to the train station," she said to him, and dressed him in his Eton jacket for the occasion. "We'll go see trains, Tukey. Round and round the wheels go. Swish, swish, and the smoke," she said, holding close the picture of the town depot at home, and she let her arms drop down from him and sat on her heels, smiling. The five-o'clock hoot of the through train had used to bring her when she was a child — all of them who lived within sight and smell of the track — to watch it slow and throw off its mail sack and the small bundle of city papers, then pick up speed again, the black pistoned beast pulling the three, four, five coaches away, away to the northern mountains. Homesickness grew thick in her throat and nose for the hot cinder smell and the swirl of steam and smoke. Louella cried a little, and buttoned the small jacket firmly.

They took a bus to the station, and when they alighted and stood facing the high gray stone of the place she wanted to cry again, for it was not at all as a depot should be. Too large for assimilation, it would have crowded them backward if she had not refused to give way. She grasped the boy's hand and took him through the thick glass doors.

It was wrong, too wrong for them to stay. The air of the huge vault shook with calls and echoes and the trundle of luggage-heaped carts, and the ground beneath their shoes trembled. Alone, scared, she strained the boy to her and turned to reach the street again.

Train stations were meant to have thin-paneled wooden walls like the brown, sticky-varnished walls at home, glistening under the big dim bulb in the center of the ceiling, where the swift, bronze roaches ran to the occasional sudden loud chatter of telegraph keys. Quiet, for the most part, with the dusty inside smell of country silence. A place for dreaming in.

"I want trains," the boy said with insistence, and Louella clasped his hand more tightly. "We'll go overstreet," she told him; "we'll find us an eatin' counter, Turkey, and have something good. And we'll look in all the store windows, and buy you and Sissie a balloon, one apiece. You come along with me, now," and she made him leave the dreadful place behind him.

Half leading, half dragging, she crossed streets and turned corners, a sure sense taking her where she knew she wanted to go. The station-adjacent streets gave way gradually to broader ones and cleaner ones, and eventually they came to where the big stores were, and small bright shops, and people. Louella and the boy stopped in pleased wonder before the resplendent windows.

"This here is where your Ma buys her clothes," Louella told him positively, seeing the dresses inside and the air they had, and both of them smiled in recognition. She pulled him from a tobacconist's window where his eyes had fastened on Dutchmen's pipes, and she cautioned him against filthy smoking and chewing, recounting to him episodes from among her dead uncles.

At the end of the second block the boy stopped short before a store window, and Louella laughed through the glass at a real live man who winked at them, and was fitting black shoes to a manikin. "See?" she said to the boy. "That's how they fix up them windows. That fella has a right good job, dressing ladies and all, for all the world to see."

The boy had not moved, and, with her tender smile, Louella

looked down on him. There was that in his eyes which pulled her
own up once more to the window, and when finally she saw the direction of his look she took him smartly by the arm and led him back
up the street.

"That lady in there ain't *alive,*" Louella said to him almost angrily. "The man took off her arms because otherwise he just can't
get that dress down over her shoulders. Don't you think none about
it, now. The arms fasten back on, it's just like a big doll; you know
that." But she quickened her steps and looked desperately to both
sides of the street for a small eating place, the boy stepping squarely
along in silence beside her.

He had another nightmare that night, much worse than the last,
infinitely worse than anything she was used to. His initial scream
into the black rose so high, pitched so to the moon like the fire siren
at home, that she sat up stiff in her bed, unable at first to place herself in her surroundings. And when she reached his bed the boy was
gone, the high, steady screaming rising to her from the stairwell,
where she found him running in a complete abandon of terror. Nor
did he wake when she flew and caught him up in her arms. She held
him, sitting on the step where the light from the outside streetlamp
flowed in on them through the downstairs door, and she crooned her
old balms and sang to him of safety. But the boy's eyes were mad,
and his body stiff. She felt the fear rise up through her own body,
from the place where she sat, up her backbone to the nape of her
neck, and prickle there. The terrible crying continued.

"What is it, in God's name what is the matter?" Mr. Austin came
pounding down the stairs. He snatched the small, convulsing figure,
like a marionette, from off Louella's lap. "Robbie! Robbie!" the
father shouted, and shook the child with fearful vigor. "Wake up!
Do you hear me!"

The boy gave a gigantic shudder and then lay inert on his father's
shoulder, eyes opened and looking down on the stair carpeting as
though musing. "I don't *want* them to!" he suddenly shouted, but
now the realm of his fear was normal to them, and sobbing noisily
he was carried upstairs and into his room.

Louella pulled herself up slowly and turned to face the top of the
stairs, her hand on the banister. Mrs. Austin stood there, frozen,
and they looked at one another in silence. Then, slowly, Louella

walked up to the top, her body feeling old as her grandmother's. Mr. Austin appeared in the gloom beside his wife. "Where did you take him today?" he demanded of Louella, and came forward and shook his fist crazily under her nose, almost touching her face. Enough light filtered around them for her to see how the strands of his sandy hair fell forward over his eyes, jigging up and down with the fury of his bobbing head. She could almost have laughed at the comicalness of it, frightened as she was to the marrow of her bones.

"Just down to the train station," Louella said, and she looked at him obliquely, then away, then down to the floor runner. "An' on into town, over to the main section. The stores and all." She threw a quick look again at his face and saw further fury beginning to gather inside him. Hastily she spoke on. "An' we stopped in at that little Sunflower place they call it, and I ordered a piece of lemon moran pie, and he ate the point off it, and a glass of milk. Maybe it's that, somethin' he ate," Louella said, and the thought was a shaft of sunshine to her. "Somethin' he ate," she said.

Mrs. Austin had put a hand to her husband's arm. "Stop it," she whispered. "This isn't going to do you or anybody any good. It's over. Let the girl go back to bed." She pressed him aside, and Mr. Austin turned, undecided, unspent.

Louella crept silently to her room.

Sometimes, in the middle of the spring nights, Louella would wake and listen, though the only sound was the scraping of tree branches against the dormered roof of her window. On those nights she would open her eyes calmly as though she had not been sleeping at all, and look at the flower-papered wall opposite, ears alert. It was always hard for her to fall asleep again, and she had to call to her mind all the people she knew or had ever known at home, bringing up their faces, ticking each one off with a little nod into her pillow. Eventually, a particular face would start the memory of a chain of events, and, recalling it, and smiling, or frowning, or pursing her lips, she would fall asleep as gently as she had wakened.

On such nights, Charlie Ryder often returned; but now it was in Mr. Austin's chair by the deepening window that she kept seeing him, and she would turn her head against her pillow and pluck Charlie out of the wrong chair and the wrong room and settle him back where he belonged. But the shade of Charlie seemed to have no other mission, and Louella had often to scold him in her thoughts.

It began to rain, days without end it seemed, and the real and fancied sounds of the nights drowned themselves in the poundings against the eaves and roof. Even in the lulls she could hear the rain coming on through the air, and now when she woke she knew there was no point in straining her ears for anything. Maybe it was Charlie, coming in where he wasn't wanted, that she kept listening for.

It seemed a natural consequence of her struggle with Charlie, the night she heard soft, scuffing sounds in the hall outside her door. Louella sat up quietly in bed, swung her legs out and was on her feet as swiftly and surely as though one of the children had called.

She found Mr. Austin there, in his blue-and-white striped robe, shivering and leaning against the wall. "I think somebody's sick," he said blurredly when he saw her, but his eyes in the pale night light were glassy. With no thought or hesitation Louella walked up to him and placed her palm to his forehead. He was unbelievably hot.

"Come," Louella said to him as he stood, and she took his burning hand and led him down to his room. She knocked on the door, and, when she heard Mrs. Austin's muffled query, pushed her head around the door jamb, still holding Mr. Austin by the hand.

"Mr. Austin's sick, ma'am. Real sick; he's hot as blisters." And she gave his hand to Mrs. Austin, who took him over and with a little struggle got him arranged in the double bed. The two of them watched him shuddering beneath the blankets.

"I'll make some hot tea," Louella said. "You get him to drink it, Miz Austin. You got some lacin's for it?"

"Yes. No. I don't think we ought to, Louella. Some aspirin would be better. Perhaps we'd better call the doctor."

Louella scoffed. "It's only that there cold he has, that he wouldn't take care of. Goin' out in the rain two days running, and no rubbers or nothing. They're like that." She gave Mrs. Austin her young, wise look and ducked her head positively. "You just got to keep him warm. Sweatin's good. I'll get the hot-water bottle."

Fever like that in a grown man. Louella stopped momentarily with her hand on the knob, thinking, suddenly, of Charlie's insistence on getting into Mr. Austin's chair, and she settled her lips in a firm line. She didn't like it, not one little bit. Her thoughts brought a feathery feeling to the back of her neck and she had to shake her head. Not one little bit, she didn't.

They did have to get the doctor, in the morning. Mr. Austin kept throwing himself about amongst the bedclothes, muttering about people who would bring tractors into a man's bedroom. Louella hadn't known about his having a bad heart, and when the doctor named pneumonia to them she went to her room as quickly as she could get away to it and sat on the bed and spoke fiercely to Charlie.

"Now, you git," she told him. "This ain't your house and these ain't your people, and you just git, Charlie Ryder; don't come in where you're not wanted. You make trouble here and I'll go back home and I'll pull the headstone down off your grave, I will." She said things like that to Charlie and a lot more, so that Mrs. Austin had to come rapping at the door in order to explain that because of the rain and Mr. Austin's heart they couldn't move him to the hospital, and were going to have to care for him at home, and how she was putting all her love and trust in Louella.

Louella did as many things by threes as possible, counting steps from the stove to the table, setting down the plates and silverware. There were portents in a thousand things. The children she handled swiftly and quietly, and it was almost as though, all during that time, there were no children in the house at all. Mrs. Austin, far gone as she was with worry, had to shake her head again and again with marveling at it.

A nurse, quick and starched, came in for the nights, and the bedroom looked more and more like a hospital room with each passing day. Once, Louella stepped unthinkingly on the white border of the bedroom rug instead of over it, and in silent panic she walked softly over to look down with gloom at Mr. Austin's blue-flushed cheeks, sunken now almost out of recognition. The children, Louella thought, those little, little children.

When they brought in the oxygen tank Louella went fearfully to the kitchen, speeding the children before her, and she sat with them on the back kitchen stairs and told them stories. The boy wanted the broomstick again, and she shushed him quickly, and went on to others. She told them stories straight through from two o'clock until five.

That night was the bad time. Through the door she could hear the slow shuddering sound of Mr. Austin's breathing from inside the little white tent they had buried his face in. And for the first time since he took to his bed Louella wept, great, silent tears coursing down her cheeks and nose, and she wiped them away with the back of her hand, uncaring.

Late in the night she awoke when she heard, again, the rain sounds, and turned in her bed consciously seeking Charlie. When he would not come she rose and walked immediately into the hall on her naked feet. There was no slightest sound. The door to the Austins' bedroom, slightly ajar, streamed a line of amber across the hall floor and up the wall. Louella stopped and listened and then, very slowly, she sighed. With quiet purpose she went back to her room and stood in the near blackness, the sounds of the rain all about her.

"All right for you, Charlie Ryder," Louella said grimly. Then she walked to the bureau and, stooping down, noiselessly pulled open the bottom drawer.

She came back down the hall, the hem of her nightgown flapping at her ankles. She reached the Austins' door and, gentleness in her fingertips, pushed it open.

Mrs. Austin and the nurse were sitting quietly beside the bed, facing one another. The oxygen machine was stilled. Louella had come in without a sound, but Mrs. Austin rose up in her chair, staring, startled. Then she smiled.

"Come in, Louella," she whispered, and the nurse, roused from seated sleep, smiled warmly too. "Come in, dear. Mr. Austin is doing fine; he's out of danger. He's been sleeping like a baby most of the night."

Louella bent her head and gazed upon the floor, studying the white border of the rug. Her hands had fallen to her sides. She said nothing, then walked silently over and stood beside the bed looking down on Mr. Austin. The blanket over his chest rose and fell gently and peacefully to his breathing, and he looked to her like any other man, sleeping.

Mrs. Austin leaned over and snapped off the lamp on the night table. Pale blue light shone in between the slats of the venetian blinds.

A child called out in a bright morning voice, and Louella turned quickly and walked to the door, her nightgown billowing. For the moment she wasn't sure what to do with the two copper pennies she carried in her hand; then she reached up and laid them on top of the high bureau near the door. She never liked leaving small things about, not where the baby might get at them. Mrs. Austin found them there the next day, when she was dusting.

RICHARD G. BROWN

Mr. Iscariot

(FROM THE LITERARY REVIEW)

AT 2 A.M. in the black dark night Mario Alejendro de Valera y
Guerrero rolled nonchalantly up the white-powdered driveway to
the white powder-covered '61 deluxe robin-egg-blue Caddy, that he
would have walked up to nonchalantly but bulky chest-torso on
squat little body-legs made him roll instead of walk and as he rolled,
nonchalantly, deceptively rolling in the black dark he squinted cun-
ningly at the dark house. He was not afraid of Big John Sanchez.

He had been waiting the two hours pulling at the white
port hidden in the bushes across the road. Waiting for the house of
Big John Sanchez to quiet; Big John's Caddy he was snatching. Re-
possessing, technically. Big John a "leetle beet" behind in payments
to Credit Finance Ink (like he wasn't-gonna-pay-what-ya-gonna-do-
about-it). But it was a difficult snatch. Impossible they said. And
then asked him to do it. For three months then coming by
Big John's house, here, a mile across the border what they called
skunk hollow casing this snatch. And only tonight for the first time
in three months was the Caddy not parked way up in front of the
garage, with the chain on it, and the big truck in back tied to the
chain so it was impossible to get out but now instead halfway out in
the white-powdered drive yet still right beside the ominous quiet-
dark house of Big John Sanchez. Who was the local chicano gang-
ster who had the smuggling, prostitution and pornography of this
border town sewed up in his chicano pocket with a reputation of el
desarmados but mostly because of the 'marican magnum he'd somehow got hold of, as he walked across the white-powdered drive, and

he was not afraid of Big John Sanchez. He did not want to die. But he was decidedly not afraid of Big John. Nor of the magnum.

It was only the other . . .

He took the first key of the fifty on the ring bunch he'd held in his hand, tight, all the way up so it would not sound and carefully, very quietly, tried it to the doorlock. The dog immediately started barking and he walked nonchalantly back across the road and sat down with the white port bottle. He looked up at the black night and wished it was dawn and drank the white port. Credit Finance Ink was a job, he thought but bitterly, the first bitter thought he'd had all night and so it was a job even though he only snatched couple times a month. And all chicano's cars he thought.

The dog had quieted and he got up, padded across the white-powdered drive in the dark with the second of the fifty-key-ring bunch and he was not afraid of Big John Sanchez still. Nor his guns, nor his rifles, nor his knives, nor his Tarzanes then thought again of the recurring dream, his mother with no clothes and looking like a *homo* and him wakening just before he could ask why, the second key did not work and the dog started barking and he walked nonchalantly back to the white port.

While waiting the light came on once in the house and a voice yelled at the dog and the light went out.

It was she who had wanted to go to Los Angeles fifteen years ago where his father had died trying to be a CHICANO SUCCESS in Los Angeles and finally from where he and the mother returned to the border town with Chana, fourteen years old, from the anglo wife he'd married while in the navy who chipped on him and he'd beaten up and taken the girl back with them.

After fifteen minutes he got up to the dark silence again to try the third key thinking if it's fifty it'll be all night he should've got the right one at the office instead of using his whole master fifty-key-ring set except he did not like to go to the office. *They* would see him.

On the fourth key he thought the dog would not bark and he could try the fifth but at the last minute the dog barked and he had to go back for another fifteen minutes but the fifth key did work and it was time and he ripped open the door dived for the ignition roared three fast times, first, loud as he could get his foot smacking the accelerator and revvied out of the white-powdered drive, roaring let the door fly shut as he geared forward and away picking up

speed to 60 in 8 seconds with a cold engine thinking it was a
big good motor for that in the black dark.

He was heading home, after he'd crossed without trouble feeling
warm wheeling the big robin-egg-blue Caddy that wheeled so mar-
velously easy that he was jealous of Big John Sanchez for that, but
taking the back streets because he did not want to be seen waiting,
reminding himself to get another white port bottle to the gate
where he'd forgotten Credit Finance Ink was closed, the gate would
not be unlocked until six-thirty, knowing now the one hour at the
most he could expect before Big John would have the Tarzanes out.
So he headed home, too shrewd to leave the car on the street but almost out of town remembered the white port, turned when he was
almost out of town, almost home and came back in using the side
alley that paralleled the main street, feeling the good warm easy-
power of the big Caddy wheel in his lap.

Three houses away, in back, just around the back alley corner he
rolled in dead motor without lights between the high view-shutting
sumacs and widow Tomas' garage side, got out and walked, roll-
ingly peaceful down the alley around to the liquora beside the cantina that fronted the main street. It was here while he was standing
in front of the liquora entrance that he saw the first Tarzane tor-
pedoing wide open the main street leaving dust funneling behind
in the dark, him standing for a moment, placidly watching for a second hardly even curious before he turned and went in to get his
white port which was of more serious business — because he had to
decide whether to get a small or a large bottle; the small would not
last until dawn unless he was exceptionally frugal but the large
would make him drunk. But he did not have money for a large bottle as he watched the owner speculatively; he would not get paid for
the snatch until the end of the month. And the owner was in a bad
mood so he did not mention the end of the month and finally got a
small bottle. Then he had only come out when the second torpedo
came barreling after the first easy to recognize by the 'marican fins,
chrome, duals, off-color-luminescent-chartreuses-and-fuchsias and he
rolled back to the Caddy that at least had taste (gave grudgingly
Big John that) and threw the white port in the seat and had an idea
and padded back down the alley to the street, the first torpedo returning in front of his funnel which would have made him think

of keystone-cop movies except he was no longer interested and he went into the cantina.

There was little business. The old man at the end, and Gonsalez sitting . . .

"Mario, my friend," Roberto Gonsalez opened his arms. "A drink señor bartender for my best friend."

"Hiya Bob," he grinned. "Como'sta?"

"Ah, what chickencrut luck. They —"

Several chicanos came in. Hey, Mario, you working yet? Catch me, man, grins, laughs. Hear the U.S. Testing Station open for jobs. Ah-choorguy, I theenk I try mañana, laughs, they pass down the bar.

"Maybe I'll go out there tomorrow," Bob Gonsalez said. "Want to go?"

"Choorguy," Mario grinned gently. They laughed.

"Ah, what chickencrut luck," Bob swore. "They come took my Rosita's new kitchen set."

"Who?"

"Credit Finance. Canbronnes. I can't go home, she — Stove, washing machine, everything. For two lousy payments!"

Mario looked away.

"They find out I was working part time 'cross the border. How the hell they find out?"

Down at the end the old man was hitting a string, Mario took his drink, moved off "see ya Bob." He did not look back.

"They get your stuff?" a chicano called to Bob.

"How the hell they find out?" Bob swore.

"They find out. Somehow they know because last time I work, man, they —"

"There is a Judas," somebody said loudly. "A Judas . . ."

Viejito Don Marquez pulled his soft grey goatee hair before each time someone else tossed off their snifter of tequila or wine. Out of the corner of his eye he followed Mario's advance like an ancient turkey buzzard.

"Salute Mario Alejendro," and then settled the old guitar behind him. "How is your family?"

"My father is not well," Mario grinned.

The old man ignored the witticism.

"Not very well at all," Mario repeated.

"I knew your father when he had cajones."

"You never knew him after he left for Los Angeles."

"No, I never saw him after that but I knew your father before, when he had cajones. Before he married Chana Christobal Samie-nego."

"He never married Samienego. He went to jail in Samienego." Mario knocked off the remainder of the snifter clean.

The old man shifted his guitar in front. "He was not a warrior like your grandfather. Like the Guerreros. But he never worked for anybody just the same."

"There is no middle class in Mexico," Mario said.

"No, there is no middle class and you must either work for a grandee or you must be a grandee. But your father never worked for anybody. He traveled on the oceans or he went for long trips. If what I hear is true he once owned a cattle ranch in Argentina. Even the warriors worked for somebody else."

"A conquistador?"

"No, a conquistador conquers for somebody else. Although he also is very lonely."

"Would you like a drink, old man? I would be very pleased if you would accept a drink in my honor."

"I would be most honored Mario Alejendro."

"Señor bartender. Please. A drink of your best tequila for my good friend Viejito Don Marquez."

The bartender glowered at them but made no move.

"Come, señor bartender. Is it not a point of respect and friend-ship that I should offer to buy the very best friend of my father a small drink?"

The bartender finally came over. "Come off that, Mario. You know he's cut off. Doc said one more drink his ticker'll explode like a bomb. Just lay off," he grumbled sourly as he left.

"Yes," Mario said earnestly. "It is true. That last heart attack was a very bad one, Viejito Don Marquez."

The old man sighed and pulled at his goatee hair. "Perhaps you could, ah, obtain a certain substance at the liquora next door?"

Mario speculated. He had three cents left in his pocket. Most certainly not enough for a large bottle.

"Why, old man, why is the Gumuchíl on top of the hill in back of the town growing there? So far north?"

"I do not know. Nobody knows."

"I heard my father say it is an underground spring."

"Nobody knows," the old man repeated fingering the glossy guitar neck.

"Somebody knows," Mario said.

"I do not know," the old man said.

"Who knows?"

The old man replied in very formal Spanish. "Why do the young always expect impossible answers from the old when the only answer is time. Which is the one answer the old do not have. Oh, yes, they say it. They say it to boredom but both know they do not mean it."

"What was my father like before he became emasculated?" Mario asked in Spanish.

Viejito Don Marquez softly fingered some strings and did not answer. Mario smiled sweetly. He did not believe the old man would speak again. He acted like that sometimes.

"Emasculated," Viejito Don Marquez said slowly. "Yes. For the sake of this new modern thing that is very strange and of which I do not understand."

"What is that, old man?"

Viejito Don Marquez shrugged.

"Security?" Mario asked.

The old man shrugged.

In back of them the news of Big John's car had exploded in the room. Who did thees? when did thees thing happen? incredulous! disbelief! Por Diaz, that poor hombre that took eet! A Tarzane had come in, looked evilly around and tramped out again. Mario was bored. It was only the Gumuchíl tree that he could not get out of his mind.

"Perhaps I could get a bottle," Mario said kindly. "But unforunately, it is terrible. I have no money."

"I have money," the old man said very simply. But quickly.

"But your heart, por Diaz . . ."

"An old man has not much," Viejito Don Marquez sighed. "He has not love nor family nor servants. Nor work. Perhaps a bottle is better than a heart? You think so?"

"Perhaps. If two bottles are better than two hearts, then."

"Of course," the old man smiled.

Mario went back out into the dark night, onto the comic opera stage again which was very funny now and he wondered why he was

not amused before when clearly it was so very ridiculously funny.
Up one street, down another, zing, wham, whoosh, torpedos to the
right of you, torpedos to the left of you . . .

Placidly, letting the Gumuchíl tree sink back into the darkness of
his subconscious, he went into the liquora with the old man's grimy
wrinkle-hidden bill thinking the crazy bastard will kill himself, but
he'd get it somewhere, and met him back in the darkness behind the
liquora to give him his bottle, the greedy old bastard, he thought
angrily, and nipping at the white port slowly, placidly wheeled the
big robin-egg-blue Caddy out of town by the alley that paralled the
main street . . .

"Go away!"
"I wanna come in," he kicked the door.
"Get out! Go away!"
He kicked the door again, louder.
"What do you want? Go away!"
"It is no more important that you are a mother to let me in," he
screamed in Spanish.
"Why don't you get a job?" his mother screamed back. "I work
hard all day. I feed you and your daughter. I tired and sleep little
you banging all night this door."
"Let me in you blank old woman." He kicked the door again.
"Go away. My back is sore, my legs ache from working hard all
day. I go to sleep now."
"Let me in you dirty old woman. My bed is in there on which I
want to sleep. In order to keep me out of my bed you think you
have a perfect right?"
"Why don't you get a job and be a decent man? All you do is
drink," she screamed.
"Let me in you black mammyjammer." He kicked the door until
his feet hurt and he stopped.
"Drunk! Every night drunk. Go away! You will not come in my
house on my dear dead husband's name!"
"Oh, you dirty old black mammyjammer," he yelled. He kicked
the door but his foot was too painful and he started beating with his
fists.
"I will now call the police," his mother threatened.
"Mieda on you," he yelled.

"Oh, el monstro!" she yelled. "El monstro!"

Finally his fists also hurt and he stopped beating on the door altogether. The sudden black silence twisted at him inside.

"Where is Chana?" his mother scolded him. "Why she no come home tonight? Fourteen years old."

"Whatdya mean, not home? Where is she?"

"She no come home I told you," she screamed. "Go away! Go find your daughter."

"Where is she?" he roared.

"How do I know? She never tell me anything. Every night all this week she stay out almost all night. Why you no get a job? Take care of your own family."

He did not say anything. He did not know Chana had been staying out so late. Or so often.

"I'm tired, my back aches. Go away! Get your daughter and find a job. Goodnight!"

"You black mammyjammer," he yelled half indifferently. "Where is she?" He kicked the door again. Not hard because his foot hurt.

"My legs are aching standing here all night. Go away! Goodnight!"

"Well, to hell with you," he screamed. "Chinga a tu madre!"

"Oh, el monstro. EL MONSTRO INFAME! !"

He walked away and then came back and beat and kicked on the door again. "On your grave when you die I will cager and miar on your grave," he yelled. And then had to trudge back again completely across the long crop field in back of the house to get to the Caddy he'd hidden there. He actually didn't know how he made it and he was so exhausted and out of breath that he had to lean on the car to get his breath back before he could even open the door and get the white port.

On the hilltop above the town with the rare Gumuchíl tree growing where he came and parked waiting for the dawn was a place he had come many times. It was really because of the Gumuchíl he thought such a very strange wonder for this semi-arid border town in the north but also from here on the hilltop on a dark clear night he could look down across the lights of the town, deep across beyond that into the heart of the Sierras and big Mexico beyond (Méjico is masculine he thought), and sometimes if he did not drink white port until he passed out he could see the dawn rising clear and very golden and beautiful lighting up the face of this golden homeland across where he and his father had come so many years before. When he was too small to even remember.

But the Gumuchíl with the impossible-to-climb thorns studding out at every branch fork, yet very large branches grown for a shade tree on the central plateau and Mexico City where there was adequate rainfall but so rare for up here that no one knew why. A spring under the hill, he thought (also thinking although he couldn't remember the gender for Gumuchíl, the word tree, arbol, is masculine) because the sucker needed such a *fantastic* amount of water and he wished the sucking dawn would come.

He wondered if the Tarzanes were still down below, leaving their broads for this long a time which was a very long time for a Tarzane, even for the robin-egg-blue Caddy of Big John Sanchez and was glad he had also the large bottle with him instead of just the one little half quart already dead and wondered how the old man was getting along . . .

Boredom, leaning back bulky-torsoed, deep into the matching blue cushions, thoughts. An idle idea, curiosity, hah! As though the car of Big John Sanchez had suddenly become a personal thing, he started rummaging around, in the glove compartment, behind the sunshades, under the seat, climbing over the back (searching for private treasure, ha!), back in front, feeling very personal, inhibited personal, like searching with your hand in another man's pocket, finally finding something under the floor mat beneath the front seat. A white envelope with photographs, giggling hilariously at his cleverness recognizing with delight the rooms of the house, the beds, even the broads, even some of the Tarzanes (laughing because these were Big John's exports for norteamericanos) and of course the positions and seeing Chana suddenly in the fifth or sixth shot.

He laid the photographs carefully on the front seat, very surprised that he felt no anger at Chana whom he loved above anyone, really no anger at all although of course he was no longer chuckling at his own cleverness and wished more desperately now as he looked out the window eastward much more desperately now for the dawn to come.

But then he could even smile sadly thinking my dear-own-loved-more-than-anyone-Chana had returned more than he and she not even full blood he thought wonderingly. And all this still with the sad smile realizing, completing this whole picture-story, what he had done to his own self-strings. But not to her.

But to the tree, he thought looking northward to the great giant eucalyptus-like Gumuchíl that covered the car like an eagle. It is the tree and the tree he thought sucking the white port. The tree. Yet there is a tree of Buddha he remembered called the Bo tree. And there is a tree of knowledge, also a tree of knowledge of good and evil, and a tree of life. A tree of porphyry, a tree of heaven, a tree of the sun, a trembling tree and a Tyburn tree. There is also up the tree, he thought. But not the Gumuchíl because you can never climb the Gumuchíl.

Them . . .

He opened the car door and stepped out hoping against hope to see the dawn he was so desperate for now looking off to the Sierras and the east beyond that mountain range across the face of which the red golden would come and not seeing it. He thought it must be dawn time yet he could not drive into town before that and he got out to *see!*

But out in the cool blackness of the hilltop it was as black as the coffin tomb of a womb . . . not even the light before the dawn and he realized not with scaredness but with sickness of the night darkness and he would not even look at the lights of the town. He clambered up on the fender of the robin-egg-blue Caddy and balancing himself bulky-torso-clumsy but one hand holding the white port up onto the roof of Big John's car searching the face of the faraway Sierras for that gold, thought he saw it but could not find it again. If only he was tall enough, him already stretching tiptoes on the car roof, just high enough to see over the Sierras to the broad central plateau in whose nestling, comforting apex was Mexico City. He clambered down awkwardly and opened the trunk of Big John's car looking until he found what he wanted and carried the rope back up to the roof and threw the end over the large bottom branch of the Gumuchíl who he thought he'd cheat after all, wanting to get up in its branches which were unclimbable but knowing *the rare Gumuchíl could see* . . . catching the rope end, securing the navy hitch, drawing it up and fastening the noose knowing all along it was not true, you could not cheat the Gumuchíl.

He took the last long drink of the white port he'd at least outfoxed that sly one thinking last of all that Chana was right and he was wrong before he put the noose over his head and stepped off Big John's robin-egg-blue Caddy, swinging, jerking, thinking, twisting . . . *He had to do it, he had to go with that. Yes, obviously. He did it, so it had to be . . .*

JOHN STEWART CARTER

To a Tenor Dying Old

(FROM THE KENYON REVIEW)

A FEW YEARS AGO I began to see a picture in my mind's eye, and
for a long time it puzzled me because I could not tell where it came
from. I might have seen such a picture in a gallery somewhere. It
may even be a relatively well-known painting, for I see it in oils, as
it were, and very distinctly. But I could not have seen either the
actual occurrence shown or any of the details. What I see, I could
not have remembered, even thought it hovers uneasily on the fluttered edges of remembrance and is more real than much I have seen,
much I have remembered.

It is a big impressionist picture. A careful one. It shows the
vaulting height of the Galleria in Milan. Bars of bright, wintery
sunshine drift from the open wings and end, illuminating the canvas to the point where the shop windows begin along the sides.
These windows — of antique stores, picture galleries, goldsmiths —
are done with jeweled strokes of high color and are lighted by the
lamps within rather than by the filtered sun from above.

The Galleria is crowded with loosely indicated shoppers — some
in a hurry, some strolling — all done with a sense of flow, of movement. Although the figures are smudged in blue-murked grays, it is
clear that they are dressed in the fashion of 1913 or so — a fashion I
must remember from the frontispieces in E. Phillips Oppenheim,
summer-cottage books. Long draped dresses, big plumed hats — that
sort of thing. The men are in skirted overcoats and either wear caps
or tall silk hats which catch the light from time to time and help define the smeared, reflected colors that dot — pointillist, although

that is not the technique — the blurred darkness of the central flow.

The odd thing, the haunting peculiarity of this, is that I am perfectly aware that one of these scarcely suggested figures is that of Edward Sciarrha as a young man. His face, if I could see it, is beaming, so full with happiness and well-being that the flesh of his later years is made probable, and what was to become a pouter-pigeon chest is already foreshadowed. But here those tremendous, sustaining lungs seem filled with pride and joy and triumph. The cheeks, the visage which I and the rest of the world were afterward to know as saturnine, if not actually sallow, are suffused with an almost russet, Tuscan, even Venetian glow, for his skin was always transparently fair and his eyes blue — though his hair and the shadow of his beard were black. Here his hair clings in moist, jet, very Italianate curls as a thick cap to his head. I never knew him when he was not balding, and he always had to wear a wig on the stage. It is odd, too, that of all that crowd he is the only one who is hatless. In 1913 it is almost impossible that he, a singer, should be so. He is wearing my grandfather's black broadcloth, sable-collared coat.

I learned a great deal from Edward Sciarrha during the course of my life, and the appearance of this picture suddenly a few years ago was a source of wonder. It would come upon me as I walked the dog late at night, as I lay in bed waiting to go to sleep. I even went out of my way once when we were driving from Locarno to Venice to stop off at Milan, where all we did was to walk up and down the arcade for twenty minutes or so.

"Well," said my wife, "that's the silliest yet"; and when I said something about wanting our daughters to see it since they never had, they chimed in with: "Really, Daddy, we could see it sometime when we were coming to Milan. What's so special?"

What was so special of course was the compulsion I felt. It was as if I were being pulled back in time to the point where the involuntary memory would take over and where something that had happened would happen again with all its original emotion. This time, somehow or other, I expected that the emotion, the passion, would be understood. Yet it could not be like that. I could not have been there in 1913. Or in 1923. I was never in Milan until December 1928, thirty-odd years ago.

I was there then with my mother and father, my next younger brother, Gordon, and my cousin Corinne. We had come to Europe in September because my father was giving a series of lectures at Guy's Hospital in London. My brother and I were at school in Paris — I was fifteen and he nineteen months younger — and my mother and Corinne, who was six years older and had graduated from Smith, stayed with us there, my father returning to London when he had a lecture to give. Corinne was with us that year, for those who like the *autre temps, autre moeurs* bit, because, in supposedly roaring 1928, it would have been considered impossible for her to come to Europe by herself, even though she had the excuse of wanting to study the piano.

Corinne was with us often during the '20s and today explains our relationship with: "We spent the twenties together, you know." Her mother left my Uncle Frank when Corinne was about ten. I was too young to have heard anything about their divorce and have only one strong recollection of my Aunt Louise. She had been in California and was on her way to Europe. It was arranged for Corinne, who was then twelve, to stay with us. Actually, she never returned to her mother after that. Anyway, I can remember inquiring of my mother when we knew they were coming whether I should call Louise "ex-Aunt Louise" — probably from having seen "ex-wife" and "ex-husband" in the newspapers. I was told that plain *Louise* would be *just fine* and to try not to stare.

"Don't be so *interested,* darling," my mother used to say. But of course I always was and still am. I must really have stared, because I can still see Louise and Corinne when they came in from the train, Corinne with the long sausage curls of the time, a beaver hat, probably even braces. Louise was in black, a dress so tight that Gordie and I decided she had to take it *all* off to go to the toilet. She could scarcely walk. She teetered in, and a long panel swayed at the side. That night my brother and I put both legs into one side of our pajama bottoms, letting the empty leg fall as the panel. We buttoned the pajama tops on each other backward, and then each took a down quilt in mock of her exaggerated furs and bunched it around his skinny neck. With hands on hips we waddled, waggled, wiggled, giggled back and forth.

" 'Oh Doc, you smell so wonderful, so completely *ether.* Just like old times,' " Gordie quoted.

"All bloody bandages and pus," I contributed.

" 'You are *not* to do a *thing* for us, you understand. Corinne and

I have had to look out for ourselves, you know, and just the tiniest bit of coffee, and a morsel of toast in the dining room. *No trays!'* "

"It was *morceau* — that's French — of toast, you stupe."

"It was not. It was morsel — "

Then I think we probably beat each other up out of pure joy, because that's what we usually ended up doing when we got anything as good as this to work on.

The next day I heard my mother on the phone to her sister: "Frank's bracelets in the afternoon. How she got down off the Pullman, I'll never know. Dumping the child like that for God knows how long and then that about trays. I should have them keep the dining-room breakfast going until eleven o'clock. As if trays weren't easier. Well, she got a tray, you may rest assured. *Just* as she expected. But why mention it? Of course it is terribly hard on big Gordon. He's so fond of Frank. We all are, I know. But Gordon was as white as a sheet. He was the best man at their wedding. Remember? Such simpering dresses, the bridesmaids. Well, Gordon and he went on that hunting trip together. Then, oh I must tell you. Without a word of warning she turns on poor Gordie. He's so proud of his new trousers because they have a buttoned fly. Yes, I know. Sweet, really. So I let him wear them yesterday because they were coming. Well, she turns on him and says how he's grown. Then her hand to her mouth and great rolling of great eyes, she says, 'And the dear, he's got a fly.' Corinne is sitting right there so I say *'Pas devant.'* Naturally. Oh, I know, I know. You don't have to tell me. It's the only place she ever does look."

I can probably reproduce any telephone conversation my mother ever had — domestic wisdom, a kind of acid wit which was not at all good, clean fun, and a dazzling irrelevance, an externalized Joycean monologue. We heard — often — "And the dear, he's got a fly" because it delighted our father, too. I put it in a telephone conversation because that's where I'm sure it belongs. I have no idea where this next belongs. It's isolated. But I know it is there. Sometime in that day and a half while she was at our house Louise must have said, "You and Doc are so much better equipped than I. Your household is so much better sustained . . ." It is out of character for the Louise the family talked about, so it isn't likely I would imagine it. I don't suppose my mother heard the pleading in it. I certainly couldn't have then, and it is only now that it drifts back — the strangeness, the exactness of the words. It was Louise who knew "how to handle men," but it was my mother who went on living in her own houses while Louise went from hotel to hotel until she died. It was Louise my mother cast in the role of *femme fatale*, but it was my mother who had a rich, good-looking husband — who was independently famous even aside from his name — for all of his days.

Edward had written us in Paris that he was opening the season at La Scala with Mazzini in *Tosca*. It was his biggest break — the biggest he or anyone else could get. We had known him in America for more than fifteen years and he had already sung at the Met, in Chicago, and all over South America. But this was the opening of La Scala and was equivalent to saying that he was the foremost lyric tenor in the world. We had planned to go to Athens for Christmas anyway — to get warm, my mother said — so my brother and I left school early, we closed up the apartment, and arrived in Milan the day of the performance. Both Corinne and my mother had new Paris evening dresses — *frocks* was the word then — and my mother even let Corinne wear some of her jewelry so she wouldn't look too *jeune fille*. One of the reasons Corinne was with us was that she had abruptly decided that she would not, could not, marry Bob Patterson who had been her best beau — that still was the word in 1928 — ever since she came out.

"You dance with your eyes closed and that means that nobody — nobody — can cut in, Corinne?" I asked her because she was my final authority on the great world. Even better than F. — I still gave him his "F." — Scott Fitzgerald, because there you had to look for the answers, and Corinne you could just ask. Fitzgerald was all right for things like how horrible it was to wear a made-up bow tie with a dinner jacket, but I never saw a made-up dress tie until I came under the democratizing influence of Eliot House, so I had to ask around to find out what it was.

"It sure does, Enoch Arden. You like the arms you're in." Corinne had the advantage too of being slightly shopworn in my eyes. After all, she had been out for three years and had graduated from college. But she was what I called *svelte*, and even in Paris college boys called for her and took her out dancing with onion soup in Les Halles and all. But she called them "college boys" — which is what I yearned to be — as if it were a term of reproach. She was on edge a great deal of the time that year, and once I came home to find her with a cocktail shaker — cocktails were still shaken and no one had heard of "bruising" gin — livid with rage at some youth.

"Give me those tickets," she said to him.

"What the hell. If you don't want to go, just say so. But why do I have to give you the tickets?"

"Just give them to me, that's all."

He handed them over, and she walked across the room to me, amazed in the doorway.

"Now here, Il Penseroso, is one for you." She walked back across the room and said to him, "And here, L'Allegro, is yours. The two of you can go to the Folies Bergère and drool. I won't be there. Corinna's *been* a-Maying long enough. Chicken-licken can teach Ducky-daddles how to be a college boy. Oh, get out! The two of you. Go — salivate."

I never did know my unexpected benefactor's name because he never came to occupy the seat next to me, and it stood empty until the intermission.

How shall I tell about the Folies Bergère of an American in Paris at fifteen? At fifty, it still seems to me one of the great national monuments, the equal of Mont St. Michel and Chartres; at fifteen, I had not even known it could exist. The year before, I had been to the Star and Garter in Chicago, but this had just resulted in a sniggering match with my cousin Georgie. On this trip, I had been to the Rue St. Denis one night, not as client but as tourist. It was still in 1928 lighted by gas, but the strolling, stylized, bedizened whores, and the great mass of shadowy men moving like ghostly phalanxes from the lost armies of Gomorrah between the soot-soaked gray of the Paris houses frightened me. I had gone to bed with a clammy unease from which mushroomed nightmare terrors of fungus growths that withered sticky-wet even as they limply failed of bloom.

I came upon the Folies at the precise moment when I needed it most, for here before me stretched golden women, their breasts proud-eyed, their muscled softness polished by a dazzling light, their bellybuttons — oh — beseeching tongues, their thighs wanting hands and lips. I sat in dazed ecstasy, reeling not, I think, with immediate desire but with thankfulness that they just existed. Even the bronzed and gilded men in the grouped statues seemed gods, not hairy waifs, for their legs were smoothed and they were shaved under the arms. Gone was the locker-room stench of sweated gym shoes, yellowing, twisted jockstraps, the somehow even sexier mat of cotton stiff with brownish stain upon the feet of white, misshapen socks. These were men worthy of the flesh with which they postured.

The first half of the show always ended — it still does — with an "international number." The girls come down to the lights, lean over the frantic orchestra, shake their darling rumps, dangle their lovely breasts, and sing in French, English, German. In 1928 it was a song about millionaires and ended with their asking time and time again of the bald-headed rows, "*Êtes-vous*, are you, *bist du, Millionai — re?*" There was a bump on the final "e." The last stanza ended with their leaning back, arching forward their G-string clouded — a word I had until then not even dared to use to myself — shaking their hands and bodies: "*Êtes-vous, bist du,* are you, *Millionai — re?*"

I rose in my seats, for I had two, threw my hands over my head in a jittered echo of their waving, and cried, complete with bump, "*Oui. Moi, je suit millionai — re.*"

Now I know perfectly well that I did this in precisely the same spirit as a fifteen-year-old might rise at a revival meeting when implored to come forward and be saved. Goddamn it, it was a spiritual ecstasy. Maybe you didn't know, oh Henry Adams, but it really is Mont St. Michel and Chartres.

Let me prove it. After the intermission I had company in my extra seat. A girl in rose taffeta picked me up in the lobby and asked if she could have the seat beside me since she had paid only the promenade admission. Of course I said "Yes," but I was so enchanted by the continuing vision of what I had seen that it didn't occur to me that I was being picked up at all, that my confession of riches had been heard, that I was supposed to notice — although of course I did notice — the pressure of her breast as she took my arm when we went back to our seats. I never made the connection between the rose taffeta at my side and the golden nudes before me. Not even when she let her hand fall to what must have been my plainly tented lap. It wasn't her hand I wanted. I didn't even notice it, honestly, really, until I got home and looked with unflexed wonder on my own spread and glistening fingers. In the theatre, it wasn't release but communion with the gods that I sought. The ecstasy had come to me at last, and it was not at all more than flesh could bear. It seemed to me what flesh was made for.

In the finale, the girls descended — they still do — from the roof. This summer it was called "The Descent of Venus"; in 1928, they were the "Happy Balloonists." A kind of revolving platform is let slowly down directly over the audience. The girls are smiling, chalk-white with only powder over their nakedness, and in 1928 each held a dove aloft by a blue, blue ribbon which fluttered across their breasts. The mirrored balls turn shooting darts of glitter, the house lights come on full, the blare of brasses in the orchestra is orgastic, and the revolving girls are drawn up again to the gilded sky. In 1928, the girl in rose taffeta had fled.

At the holiness of my fifteen-year-old vision? Maybe. Maybe because she was French and knew. Maybe just because she had to get back to the promenade.

I told Corinne about it the next day, as well as I could, but the metaphysical vocabulary of fifteen is limited. What got across, though, was that, while I loved the girls, I had been able to fall in love with myself. I had been able to know myself as a lover. I would never again, I thought, fail of bloom. With this knowledge I could wait.

"That's nice, Porphyro," Corinne said. "But there are lots of things nicer about being a man — even a college boy. And hairiness, you goof, is one."

Edward had sent great baskets of flowers to my mother and Corinne at the hotel — "How *wop!*" Corinne said — but we didn't see him until we saw him on the stage, and he didn't see us until the first-act curtain calls when I waved. (I'm a great waver, you can tell.) He was in magnificent voice, and as I said about him in a poem I tried to write when he died, "He spun tenderness to song for me." It was another face of love I was seeing here — learning about — and the thunder of applause as he finished his last-act aria about the light of stars was deeper, more resonant, than any at the Folies. I don't mean to say that I made the observation in those words at the time, but I certainly felt it in my heart, which crowded to my throat. Poor Tosca — who lives for art and love in a world dominated by church and politics and ruled by a man who says he has to have an unwilling woman.

Edward gave a large dinner for us and the principals after the performance. It was in one of those incredibly lush, red-and-gold Italian restaurants with mountains of highly decorated food and great sheaves of wired flowers. It was closed to the public — actually, it was the main dining room of the hotel where we were staying — by the time we got there, and a kind of Aladdin's cave had been created with marble serving tables and gilt screens upholstered in watered, scarlet silk. These circled the large round table at which we ate, which was placed directly underneath the first of three enormous ormolu and luster chandeliers, diminishing in splendor down the mute, heavy magnificence that throbbed darkly behind us. These were not lighted, but rustled with the prolonged flames of the candles reflected from the dinner table.

Edward and the rest of the cast were wild with excitement, glistening with happiness because they knew that they had been superlatively good.

"You were good, good. Very good. Say that 'Tutta Roma' again. And so beautiful." This was Edward embracing Tosca.

"Tutta Roma" — that wonderful, rolling triumph that had chilled the audience to panic.

"Oh, how good to be good." Edward sat attentive at the head of the table and kept the conversation in English for us as well as he could. But even so there was much Italian, much flirting, bare shoulders, wine and more wine. I was all eyes, of course. It was like the first act of Traviata, and the surprising thing was that my mother and Corinne seemed perfectly at home. Corinne so svelte, her hair with its plastered, jet-black curls nodding this way and that like a garden flower, my mother full-blown but soft and beautiful, gay, flirtatious as I suppose I had never seen her. When I was fifteen, she was thirty-seven, but I don't remember — and my brothers don't either — ever having thought of her as a sexual object at all. She and my father went out a great deal, and she always came in to kiss us goodnight, heavy with perfume, glittering with diamonds in the dark, rustling with silk. I can remember her loosening the skinny arms I had thrown around her neck and murmuring, "Oh, darling, my hair. You really mustn't," but I still cannot even summon up a sense of rejection. Sex, for me, was Swedish maids, cotton slips with drawstrings, stained, cotton corsets flapping on the line on washday. When our mother kissed us goodnight, she ceased to exist. She certainly did not occupy our imaginations as did the odorous lives of the unmarried maids who slept above us on the third floor and who also kissed us goodnight — but with wet-mouthed abandon — and stroked our hair and sang us lonesome, tuneless songs in a strange tongue.

I suppose it was that night in Milan, beneath the enormous bunches of polished glass grapes lustrous with shadows, that I caught up with her. At any rate, to see my own mother smiling so sweetly, so poignantly — for that was her style — at the man who played Scarpia was a revelation. It may be obscurely significant that my mother's behavior I excused, but that I thought my father an old goat because of his interest, which he did nothing to conceal, in Tosca's fantastic — by American standards — décolletage. My mother and father were the same age, and Tosca herself could not have been much younger and certainly did everything in the world to provoke him. I was to learn years later from Edward that her lover at the time was a much younger man, a Roman count.

"Alfredo and Violetta, you understand? Except that she was a great artist and she gave him all her money and he was nothing nor ever would be. She did die, you know, in Rome. So Roman, so prodigal, so sumptuous she was. It was T.B., too. But there was no letter scene, no arrival. Just death."

You will see as this goes along that Edward always described people, situations, attitudes in terms of their operatic counterparts, as if the real world were in the preposterous librettos and the unreal world was where he lived. His own wife-for-a-time's name was Sophie — the Sophie of *Rosenkavalier* — and he came to grief trying to figure her out in Strauss's and Von Hofmannsthal's terms rather than in terms of Chicago Back-of-the-Yards where she had her being. *Alt Wien* rather than the hog butcher of the world.

The party was a great success, and Edward was consistently kind even to my brother and me, throwing us questions, trying to get us into the occasion. Of course, our dinner was very late indeed — even by Italian standards — but when our mother suggested that my brother and I be excused to go upstairs to bed, Edward jumped in with: "No. No one is excused, madame. Tonight I am making a speech. In America maybe you do not make a speech, but in Italy I do."

Everybody clapped and laughed, and Corinne put up her white, white arms and little hands and called *"Silenzio."*

Edward rose. "Thank you, signorina. Thank you, my friends." It was already clear that this was really to be a speech because you could see him take the kind of breath under his white waistcoat that he would take to sing. "At times like this you think long thoughts, and for many days I have had these thoughts, and I have made up in advance what I am going to say because these people I love so much are here." He named us all, and there were little firecrackers of applause after each of us half-rose in his chair to bow.

"The trouble is, I am a great liar, and the newspapers are even greater liars. In *Who's Who* I do not put any date for my birth. I do not even know it myself anymore, but these weeks I have had to think, who is that Cavaradossi who is to open La Scala? Claudia, do not think, Maestro, do not think I do not know you — more than I — open La Scala, but you, Maestro, for many years, you, my Claudia, for three years have done this. Tonight is first for me. There may not be a second. If there is, I promise no more speeches."

Everyone laughed, but he was so obviously, so sweetly in earnest that we weren't embarrassed for him, or restive at having to listen.

"Tonight it will be the truth — except maybe for some little lies I cannot help because they make things more interesting for you and for me, too." There was one of those breaths as if the next phrase were long and intricate.

"I was born, the Cavaradossi was born in Tuscany, the village so small that even if you have been there you will not remember. There is not even a statue in the village square. Just a well, and dust when it is dry and mud when it is wet. There are sometimes a few sheep, a few goats, a few pigs, two or three geese and some hens. That's all. My father was cobbler in this village. *Ich bin nicht Lohengrin genannt.* Or at least he was until one night a robber even poorer than we took his tools. And then he was nothing. From being meat only Sundays, there was now never meat, and my father went away. I think he must have worked very hard away because he was in Genoa and sent word that he was going to America where an uncle of his was. He would send us the money when he could. He must have been a kind man, because my mother was a plain woman, and what is a boy of six? I was twelve before there was enough money, and there were new boys he could have had in America by softer women. My mother, I think, was rock. Not marble. The brown, clayey rock of Tuscan hills, crumbly on the edges but with veins of dirty gray hardness. Azucena, except she is Sicilian, and there is some excuse."

The Sicilians all laughed. You could tell he was trying to be very exact, very just. That this wasn't part of the speech he had prepared. That it had just come upon him with bitterness. Suddenly, in the gilt magnificence of this room.

"She made us wait a year. I read the letter to her. She could not read and she made us wait a year, a year before she could bear to use the money for our passage. And when we got to New Orleans there was a letter from the uncle. And I read that too, standing in the Customs House. My father" — he spread his hands palms outward in the most Italianate of gestures, the thing you see in pale, primitive frescoes of badly drawn saints — "was dead."

The Italians were weeping. It was the kind of sorrow they liked. The *"Piangi, piangi"* of their operas. I could only feel the uneasiness of fifteen mixed with an immense longing to be taken in my own redheaded father's arms which now I could scarcely remember, it had been so long. Corinne looked up at Edward in undisguised wonder. He let his hands fall to his sides. I don't suppose I ever was able to tell when he spoke or sang how much of it was *timing*, how much of it was instinctive. He never held his audience a moment too long. He relinquished them — I'm sure that's the word —always. They were there then when he wanted them again.

"I tell you this not for tears, but so that you, dear Maestro, will know that your Cavaradossi was a revolutionary by the time he was eight. That he is not now makes not so much difference. And you, Marcella, so beautiful a shepherd boy. I listen to every note as you sing backstage even though I know you are already *en grande tenue* to come to this party. I listen because I try to remember something kindly. My voice must be kind when I write my letter by the light of Roman stars. Of course such songs I sang in Tuscan hills and just so beautifully too, because always I could sing. But let me tell you something strange. I never remembered at all. I did not see in my mind's eye or in my thoughts or anywhere, ever, the wild flowers of spring until I came back to Italy and saw them for the first time in the paintings in the Bargello." He looked up then as if to ask us if any of us had had the same experience.

"Does this make sense? I lived in those fields, sang there. I had never seen the flowers at all. Oh, bougainvillaea, crape myrtle — these I saw, you have to see. But the tiny flowers — daisies, wild tulips, primroses, violets, asphodel that sprinkle like stars the Botticelli lawns — these were there all that time, but I never saw them until I saw them on a palace wall. I saw them tonight when you sang your shepherd's song, Marcella, and I thank you."

Everybody began to clap, but he silenced them.

"We will have some more wine" — he motioned the waiters and they moved almost like a ballet with the dark green bottle heads in their white napkins pouring the pale, fizzy wine in that red-and-gold room with the crystal grapes heavy above. Fitzgerald says somewhere that the rich enjoy life young. I don't know. Maybe it was like Edward with the field flowers. I was certainly conscious of the room that night, of Edward's charm, and I was young to *enjoy* it. I even feel guilty that, having been given what Nick Caraway's father would call the "advantages," I can't do better by them. But I don't think I was conscious of *enjoyment* before that. I had other things — *vide supra* — to bother me. But, from that night on, I began to see what had happened to me in a different way. Oh, the change wasn't all at once. It took a long time happening and is still happening in a way, but it was because Edward saw my world as beautiful that I was able to see it so, too. Of all my enormous family, I don't suppose a half-dozen of us have the trick, and, since this has a great deal to do with the way this story is written, I mention it here. To get back to Fitzgerald, it didn't begin by my enjoying. I was just there at first, but later I had much to remember, much to *enjoy*.

I had sat in opera boxes from the time I was very little. I have the old Ricordi librettos with crayon markings on them, for my grandmother always took all available grandchildren to Saturday matinées, even though the family as a whole had the box for every performance. We were "Odd Thursdays," and every time I went, I would look us up in the program. Since my grandfather's death, the opera had been what she would have called her "big outside interest"; not only was she one of the principal guarantors, there were always opera people practicing about the house in town where she let them use the old-fashioned, third-floor ballroom with its gilded concert-grand Steinway. We were seldom at the house in town; she more often came to our houses. But we were often in the country, and that's where Edward became our friend.

"Hit me a B-flat real loud," he would call to anyone near the piano from any place in the house or along the terrace. He had relative, not perfect, pitch. You could give him a C, and he'd begin, beautiful golden notes floating over those beautiful gardens as effortlessly as the curtains, pennons at the long windows, floated up in the sun-bright breeze from the springtime lake. Those windows were not french, but enormous sash windows reaching from the floor toward the heights of the ceilings. It took two men to raise them. After a phrase or two, he'd know and come rushing in.

"Villain, villain. I'd choke myself up there. Please, please, bébé, no tricks. I can feel it coming in my lungs."

We thought this very funny, and said so, but he pushed us from the piano bench and began playing for himself very badly — real loud, as singers generally do so that they will be sure of the notes. Corinne came in then — let's say she was fourteen — and said, "I'll play for you, Edward."

What he sang was, I know, *"Il mio tesoro,"* and it was as ornately perfect as it was ever going to be. I said, "Oh, Edward, that was wonderful."

"Yes, it was. You know Caruso cannot hear himself sing? But I can, I think, and it is a great pleasure to me. Particularly when you are so pleased." He was always like that to us, even when we were little, but then he said something strange. At least I was unable to make the connection. "I'd rather sing Almaviva or the Don than Don Ottavio."

I know now that this was said to Corinne, but I didn't then, even though she blushed and said, "But they're baritones, basses even."

"Of course they're baritones, basses even," he answered.

The rest of Edward's speech was about his life in America. His father had been killed in a construction accident, so there were a few thousand dollars of insurance from the company, which made them rich in the eyes of the uncle and the neighbors in the Italian-American section of the West Side of Chicago. He had gone to the public schools, learned English.

"Dago, wop, I was. But that was not bad at all. I was not hungry, and I could walk to the grand hotels on Michigan Avenue and sit there clean and warm and the scent of women's furs and perfume. I could not sing because my voice had monstrous cracks in it, but in my heart I think I sang. I know no Giotto, no Botticelli had to tell me later that marble pillars, ostrich plumes, overcoats with sable collars, the trickle of water in an alabaster fountain were beautiful. I just looked and looked, and when the time came, I knew many things I might not otherwise have known."

There was a general sense of loneliness about what he said, and he did it very well. He'd seen Caruso once in the lobby of the Auditorium Hotel and had spoken to him in Italian. Caruso himself had been young and "only had an astrakhan, not a sable collar," but he had felt, he said, "the difference which was my difference too."

He began to sing again in his last year of high school, having discovered for himself a kind of baritone falsetto with which he could negotiate "Where e'er you walk" and *"Una furtiva lagrima."* With these he had brought down the largely Italian house at his graduation.

"It was terrible and anguish-sweet, and I knew it was terrible, but I also knew it was so much better than they who liked it would ever know."

His high-school music teacher had got him a scholarship with the music critic on one of the papers who taught at the Chicago Musical College. He seemed to remember none of these people with affection, but the scholarship led to various church jobs, funerals, weddings, and solo parts in oratorios. He actually earned his living by singing very early, when you consider the tenor voice, and left his mother's when she married again "oh late in an always too late life. A cruel man, not a kind one."

Somewhere along the way he had met Alta Swanson, who was ten years older than he and a Swedish mezzo with, he said, an intense musical understanding. Later he was to tell me much about her, but that night in Milan it was only that she taught him more about phrasing, more about character than anyone else. It was she, too, who had got him into the quartet of the church my grandmother attended after my grandfather died. Of Grandmama, he said: "Sables, black velvet, pearls that had once been the Empress Eugénie's. She was the Marschallin come to life."

"A little old even for the Marschallin, don't you think, Edward?" my father called out. I tried to do the arithmetic in my head. She was probably forty-five, the second wife of my grandfather, who was twenty years older and had married her when she was eighteen — a circumstance we were brought up to consider romantic.

Edward laughed, and from what he told me later said less than he had planned, but he did go on.

"I was buying her a pair of gloves for Christmas once, and the girl who waited on me was so young, so blond, so downy soft that I said 'I'll take these, Sophie,' and that turned out really to be her name, so she was amazed. Oh, there was no silver rose, and her father was a Polish stockyards worker, not a rich merchant, but I was used to providing the appurtenances for myself. I married her."

I don't remember how he glossed the next. The fact was, I knew, that he spent little time at Sophie's and that they never even had a flat of their own. Most of the time he was at my grandmother's in the country; we even called his room in the west wing "Edward's room." The speech was arranged to do honor to us and how kind we had been to him, so he didn't have to mention that the marriage had lasted less than twelve months and that he had left for Europe for his final years of study even before his son was born. The silver rose tarnished quickly.

"I was never Rodolfo, thanks to these people, but I was always afraid of becoming Rodolfo so that I knew him, hungry and cold. *Ché gelida manina.*"

The party broke up after that. It was dawn when we walked across the lobby to the elevators, but I was still as alive as I had been at the beginning. And I heard him say, as he helped Corinne into the white broadtail evening coat with its sparkling white fox collar that Grandmama had given her for graduation, "The butterfly returns to its cocoon."

I also heard and remember my father's, "This only is the witchcraft I have used?"

"I want you to watch your bill. I'm willing to bet that dinner's on it," was what my mother said. But my father, even if he had noticed it, would never in the world have told her. While perfectly capable of being enchanted behind the velvet curtains of the dining room, my mother saw things by the light of dawn in what she was always calling "their proper perspective."

The trouble with the "proper perspective" is that you never have all the pertinent facts, and I didn't have all the facts about Edward until after he was dead. My father would have said — did say, really — that the only pertinent fact was that Edward was a man of talent. I too became an artist, a writer, and three years after the dinner in Milan Edward made an important distinction for me. He was in Boston with a post-season *Lohengrin* and took me to dinner — for which he did pay — at Locke-Ober's. I had by this time seen a made-up dress tie, but I was still technically a virgin, still content to wait.

He asked after Corinne, and I told him that she still saw a lot of Bob Patterson.

"People say, you know, that he married Marge Lawson on the rebound. I think they'll get divorced, and Corinne will marry him. Before she died even, Grandmama gave Corinne the gardener's cottage. She's added a wing, and there she is. Corinne seldom comes into town. Everybody's very poor, of course." This was 1933.

"Do not tell me, bébé, that Corinne is poor. In a cold-water flat with one toilet for the whole floor, Corinne is not poor. Starving to death, Corinne is not poor. She is never poor because it is not something she can imagine. What you cannot imagine, you cannot be."

"Well, you know what I mean, *poor.*"

"You want to be a writer, you say. Let me tell you something. This is different from me. I am a performing artist. If you are good, you will be a creative artist. It is not the same thing. Not the same thing at all. You are not obliged to become someone someone else has created."

"Shakespeare played the ghost in *Hamlet.*"

"Ah, you take my point. The ghost, not Hamlet. Hamlet is for someone else, for the world, even. He is given away. I think it is like having a child. Flesh and blood — genes, is it? — you give him. But the lungs, the lungs must be filled with someone else's breath. After he is created, even Hamlet is no longer Shakespeare's."

"But Corinne knows about being poor. I do, too."

"About other people being poor. Not about yourselves. You can create me a poor boy in the Tuscan hills, on the West Side of Chicago. But you cannot create yourselves poor. You cannot be poor. I sing Lohengrin. My father was not Parsifal. I do not believe in Parsifal. I am not holy in any way. I have never been holy. Holiness is not my métier. But I am a performer, and as long as someone imagines Lohengrin for me it is all right. I sing, Magda sings. In the action we become. We follow someone else's notes, and it is for us heavenly music. We are what we perform.

"Let me tell you. In bed even, always I perform. I am conscious of the cat curled up on the chair, the eyes in the photograph if there is no cat. The crash of cymbals at the height is not within me, but without — as if other people had burst into opera house applause.

You are a great noticer, bébé, and you see my cat on the chair, the eyes in the photograph. But you note them only. It never occurs to you that they can see you."

Of course, when anyone talks to you like that, you remember it all your days, and you always wonder why. There is no use trying to figure it out. There is no use, even in a story, trying to make it credible. It just sometimes happens. It simply is there and, if you are going to write at all, you have to write it. I suppose that it was the attempt to make it credible to myself that led me to say to Bob Bonney, who was studying in my room when I got back to Eliot House, "I had dinner with Edward Sciarrha at Locke-Ober's."

"For Chrissake. How the hell do you know him so well you have dinner with him?"

"He was my grandmother's lover once."

"Wow!"

I practiced a great deal on Bob. Sometimes I told him lies of great circumstance, which he usually believed. Sometimes I told him unadorned truths, which he found incredible. I hadn't at all turned into the Charles Macomb Flandrau college boy of my dreams of a few years back, and the truth is that I had no pattern at all for what I did become — half-truthful lies, half-lying truths. Coming home one night I had related so minutely to Bob my supposed seduction by a Boston second-year girl, who had merely let me feel her up a very little on the front steps, that his "Wows!" took on the awe of "O rare for Anthony!" In honesty I should add that the odorously imagined scene became, without change, my own bedtime and completely satisfactory fantasy for the months that remained of my virginity, and that I have even had occasion to use it since. My own actual seduction I later gave — in Edward's sense — to one of my characters, and though I know it is all true on the page as I read it — I can, like Dickens and Christopher Isherwood, even weep — it no longer belongs to me in the sense that the unpublished, nonexistent, second-year girl does.

When I said that Edward had been my grandmother's lover, I had no idea that it was true. It was an uneasy intuition made swiftly conscious — but not necessarily true — by the necessity of explaining to myself the intimacy, the honesty, the seriousness of Edward's tone. It was this far more, I am sure, than the touching, grandiose homage he had meant to pay us in Milan when my father — whom I

never before this moment had ever suspected of any overt social
sense — stopped the reference to the Marschallin.

I don't want to make a big production about my true lie to Bob
that night. I don't think I thought about it at all after I uttered it.
It came back only at the time of my own wedding, when I suggested
that I could ask Edward to sing.

"I don't think so, darling," my mother said judiciously. "It's so
much like asking for the return of past favors, don't you think?" It
was said with the aplomb of Madame de Sévigné, but I understood
my mother by this time better than she thought, and it only took a
moment to remember that he had not sung at my grandmother's
funeral or at any of my cousins' weddings. He hadn't, literally, been
in any of our houses for twenty years. I let the matter drop. He
sent a score of *Tosca* inscribed to him by Puccini in a magnificent
Rivière slipcase — I looked up the spelling of Cavaradossi in it when
I came to use it here — but he didn't come to the wedding.

Edward's voice lasted through the '30s. The last time I heard
him was as Don Ottavio in *Giovanni*. He was fat — almost a hay-
stack in the black cape — but the notes of *"Il mio tesoro"* floated in
the same way as they had the day Corinne had played for him at
Grandmama's. Of course, I couldn't remember to compare. The
youth must have gone, surely, but the big windows at my grandmother's that gave so largely on the sunny gardens and the blue lake
opened once more, their curtains blown pennons in a springtime
breeze.

The war came right after that. Edward was caught in Rio and
sang there for a few years, but toward the end, he told me later, "I'd
look up and see those people in the galleries and know that many of
them had done without lunch. I just wasn't that good any more,
bébé, and there wasn't any chance at all that I'd get any better. Oh,
I would have liked to sing *'An die musik'* as a last encore at Town
Hall, but I just climbed into my swan and rode off into the wings. It
was the end of the season, and I never went back. *Im fernem Land.*"

At the end of the war, he didn't come back to the States, but for a
time he was in Lima as artistic director of the opera there, and from
time to time he'd meet his old friends — "All on the way down,
bébé, all on the way down. — It was too sad." After that he lived in
Mexico City, which is where I saw a lot of him.

One day shortly after Nan, my Uncle Tom's wife, died, Tom called
me and asked me if I'd go down there for him.

"Edward Sciarrha's there, and I don't want to give him the idea we're checking on him, but I'm curious. It isn't money. He has $8685 in his checking account here" — you could tell Tom had had the records brought to him and was looking at them — "and he hasn't drawn on it in over a year. Then he has $37,000 in bank stock. The dividends are deposited on order. He must have some other stuff, but, even if he hasn't, it isn't money. I could understand if he were in Italy or California . . ." His voice trailed away.

"Why don't you go down yourself, Tom? You ought to get away."

"No, he'd smell a rat. You take the kids and all. You can say you're down there writing."

"But what am I supposed to do?"

"Come off it, kid." He laughed and I laughed too, but he went on: "You're supposed to find out something. I don't know what, just something. I got to thinking he might be sick, alone, just lonely. You could find that out and anything else." He must have swallowed a couple of times, because his voice shifted from its speculative melancholy into the defensive good nature required for "Snoop, kid, snoop. I talked to your dad, and he didn't see any reason why not, and don't you tell me you wouldn't like to know."

The picture of the Galleria had already begun to haunt me for no discoverable reason, although neither Papa nor Tom knew about it, so I suppose I was less honest than Tom — snotty, even — when all I said was, "Well, I'd love to go to Mexico, of course. Sure, we'll all go. Thanks a lot."

Tom was always quick at picking up things. It is hard to explain, but, even though we were talking over the telephone, it was as if he put his arm around me when he said, "You don't have to tell me, you know. It's not knowing like that that I care about. Just so one of us knows, and if anything can be done it's done."

As it turned out, we didn't all go. Measles. I went by myself and saw a cake in a shop evidently for someone recovering from surgery. A spun-sugar operating table with a spun-sugar patient, complete with red abdominal gash. A couple of spun-sugar bearded doctors, and nurses in sugar nun's habits. A pail full of scarlet sugar slops had been artistically knocked over, and there were spun-sugar bluebottle flies glutting themselves on the offal. I ordered the cake sent to Edward with my card and ordered another set of the figures for my younger daughter, who has a fine taste in these matters.

Edward called the hotel in ecstasies and sent his Chevrolet with a villainous driver for me the next afternoon. The driver spoke no English and assumed that I was speaking Italian, because he agreed violently with everything I said — *"Si, si, signore."*

"How long have you been with Mr. Sciarrha? How far is it to his house?"

"Si, si, signore."

Mexico City has some of the most beautiful private houses in the world, and often they are set to take advantage of the spectacle of an enormous city spilled beneath the sumptuous rise toward the bluish heights. Edward's house was ordinary on an ordinary street. An apothecary's house, he called it. There was a small, lush, ill-kept garden where a cock strutted, and an upright majolica fish dribbled water from his chipped mouth to a small, shell-shaped pool. This in turn overflowed in a trickle that merely damped a darker vein in the hard-trod sand of the walk.

He heard us arrive and came out to meet me, kissing me, Italian fashion, on both cheeks.

"Bébé, no longer bébé." His eyes were shining with pleasure, which is always endearing, and he patted me toward the living room, the salon, which had been devoured by the enormous black bulk of the Steinway. There was literally only room for a hard, Spanish couch of powdery leather under the three high, flawed, leaded windows, and even that had a pile of age-brittled music on one end, the overflow from a large table that was stacked high, and under which was a portable phonograph and a half-dozen books of recordings.

"We sit here now. Afterward there are more comfortable places. But we must be formal for the sake of Conception." Conception was evidently the barefooted Indian woman with the condor beak who brought us a bottle of rum and three glasses that, for lack of room any other place, she put on top of the piano.

"S'il vous plaît, madame." Edward bowed to her. She bowed to him in Spanish and did not speak at all, but poured out three glasses, handed us each one, and then retired to the other side of the threshold where she bowed — again in Spanish — to me, raised her glass to her lips with ceremonial unction, and departed toward the kitchen.

"Pique Dame, I call her." Edward was laughing at my pantomimed bafflement. "She is from the third act of *Carmen* and looks with horror through the electric firelight as Carmen tells the cards.

La mort. La mort. Toujours la mort. It is good to grow old with
such a one around. Far better than Zerlina."

His mood was by no means elegiac. He was witty, urbane, his
wit sharpened by the excitement of the occasion. He opened himself
up, as he always had to me, and there was no constraint, no groping
for suitable topics of conversation. We talked on and on. That first
day it was mostly vital statistics. The deaths among my uncles, their
wives, my cousins. Pete and Harrison had been killed in the war, as
had Bob Patterson, Corinne's husband. He wanted to know about
Corinne, and I told him that she still lived in the country, showed
no interest in remarrying, and had gone rather to fat.

"The sleek Corinne?"

"Yep. *Gemütlich,* I think, would be the word. She even cooks
when you go out. Marvelous dinners, course after course, flour on
her hands."

"The brittle ankles, the tiny feet, the glitter of those perfect
calves?"

"Skirts are long now. Her eyes are still beautiful. I suppose I
notice them most when she plays the piano for you — for one —
after dinner."

"How is that?"

"Very good. Real authority, you know."

He seemed surprised and said, "That, I never heard."

"No, I suppose not. She's only had it for a little while." The two
of us went on like that. I was rather piecing together these people I
knew so well and had had little reason to think of or to try to bring
up to date. "They never had any children, but she's fond of Bob's
son by Marge Lawson. He'll get all of the Patterson money,
of course."

"Maybe that's why she's fond of him. Because he doesn't need
her." He looked at me shrewdly, and a whole set of relationships began to shift and re-form in my mind, as if what Edward provided
were a kind of moral kaleidoscope which, when it was tapped, sent
prismatic chaos scurrying into nonprogressive, geometric form.

The visit was so successful that I left the hotel the next day and
went to stay at Edward's. He insisted on giving me his room because
it had a large table in it for me to work on. The villainous driver
carried the bags up and Edward said, "I've left everything just the
way it was. At this late date there seemed no point." He waved me

in, and I saw immediately what he meant. There was a Boldini drawing of my grandmother in a black net evening dress seated, very *femme du monde* — as she herself would have said — on the foot of a Louis Quinze chaise. She has her diamond astr and a black aigret in her sooty hair and is leaning forward, fingering her pearls. The length of the chaise, which is on a slant, is exaggerated, and its back is scooped out to repeat the curve of her body. What you have is a pair of arched wings fluttering into flight. She herself is seen as an exquisitely elegant bird, white-throated, with acquisitive eyes. I had never seen her anywhere nearly so young as that, or in that way at all. I mentioned the eyes to Edward, and he said, "*Appraising* would be kinder, perhaps. A kinder word. They're your eyes really, you know, whatever you do to disguise it. It is best to be kind."

"They're in the Paul Helleu that Tom has, and in the Sargent we gave to the university." I could not take my eyes from hers, and you could tell that Edward too was looking at the picture for the first time in a long while, but he drew himself together and stroked the signature and its date, "Venezia, 1913."

"The winter before you were born, bébé. The first year I was with her." He moved toward the door, but he wasn't afraid of my eyes, nor I, strangely, of his. "Octavian to the Marschallin. Will that make it all right?" His smile pleaded. His hands turned outward in the Italian gesture I had seen that night in Milan, and it occurred to me that the only possible answer was the kiss on both cheeks. I had even stepped forward when the room was invaded, the sky was rent, with the clamor of tuneless bells from the nearby church steeple. Bong! Clang! Cling! Bang! The house shuddered under the demon assault of iron clapper tongues lashed into furious discord by the whirred, wheeled descent of the turning bells. There was nothing to do but to stand there, scourged by the obscene whips of sound gone mad. Edward was used to it, may even have expected it. At any rate, he was able to laugh as the assault diminished, and to absolve me from the awkward kiss on the cheeks with, "That's the veritable voice of God, bébé. It calls me to a kind of prayer, too, for now I have a student." He patted me on the side of my arm. "Come down when you like. Neither *Pique Dame* nor Spoletta knows about such things, so you will have to unpack for yourself." He closed the door behind him.

I did unpack, hazy in my mind, my feeling unfocused by the flay-

ing of the bells, the moral kaleidoscope lashed from my hands at the
moment its radiance might have assumed the proportions of bloom.
I was incapable of either surprise at what Edward had said or relief
because he had confirmed what I had suspected for a long time. Usually, I think the detail of revelation rather than the revelation itself has the power to move, to give the turn of the screw, and I suppose Henry James knew this, but the brutality of the bells was an
outside force, was completely accidental. It had nothing to do with
Edward or me or my elegant grandmother. In the interest of art, in
the interest of achieving the well-made tale, shouldn't I exclude it?
Temperamentally, I can't. The blows were real; they happened.
The insane clangor of their derision made it possible for me to look
with both my eyes instead of squinting through one at bits of glass
arranged in specious order at the end of a confining tube.

I was made aware of this change of view almost immediately, for
I think the dissonances still clung to the room when I first saw on
the dresser the incredible array of gold-backed brushes, gold-topped
boxes, bottles, picture frames, clock. Everything was gold, and each
piece was decorated with raised, scaled, twined, even copulating
snakes twisted into the initials "E.S." Suddenly, I saw even more
distinctly than the brushes, bottles, boxes of the dresser top the
grandmother of the Boldini, the woman I never knew. There she
was at a Venetian goldsmith's, in re-embroidered lace, the pigeons
of St. Mark's rising in fluttered chaos from the dazzling marble of
the square. I stood there for a moment, dizzy with vision, but I
didn't see Edward at all until I picked up one of the hairbrushes and
saw the soft gold dented, the bristles sapped by time, and the "E"
and the "S" worn smooth with use.

I lay down after that and slept a warm sleep, a soft sleep without
dreams in the waning Mexican afternoon. Waking too was pleasant
— as if knowing fingers were folding back one by one the layers of
silky sleep to free me for a known happiness. What really happened
was that I became conscious of Edward's pupil singing *"Allerseelen."*
It would hover in the air a moment, then fade, return. A phrase
would be repeated, the piano might insist, reiterating strictly a note
that had been blurred, but none of this was unpleasant as practicing
usually is. Instead, it was as if the song itself were opening up at the
same time, in the same way as I was regaining consciousness. It was
getting dark, but, as I twisted with enormous comfort to yawn upon

the bed, my grandmother's eyes caught mine, and I smiled to her as
I might have when I was a little boy and we shared some delicious
secret.

When I went into the upstairs hall, Edward was standing with his
student below and called up to me.

"Come down, bébé. José is going, and I would like you to meet
him."

José was a spectacularly handsome boy in a flamingo silk sport
shirt. He shifted his music roll in order to shake hands with me, but
he cast down his eyes and perceptibly drew his body back in an exaggerated bow.

"I am trying to tell him that in Austria *Mai* is really May. *Im
Prater blühn wieder die Bäume,* and not at all like Mexico, so he
must sing once with the bloom on and young, '*Wie einst im Mai.*'
He has the voice but he does not know about *Mai.* And already it is
with him *Mai.*" The boy looked up then, and I saw his great, lost,
tragic eyes.

"The man who begins the song is old, and it is All Saints' Day —
November — but he is capable of remembrance." Edward lifted his
hands in an operatic gesture, as if they held all the Austrian spring-
times and he was afraid of the apple blossoms spilling over. He let
them fall then slowly, and, even though he did not sing, he made
love to the phrase, "*Wie einst im Mai.*"

When the boy left he said, "He is queer, that boy. You got that?
And it is very sad. Mostly I do not think it is sad, but this time I do.
So beautiful himself, such a beautiful voice. Real talent. Real understanding. But he is afraid, and he says he is going to become a
monk. His father is a rich man and does not want this, naturally.
A priest maybe. At least they have to say so because they are devout.
But a monk is nothing. So silly. So stupid. I cannot say to him 'The
opera houses of the world are full of accommodations. It is nothing
so terrible. You will be happy or at least as happy as anyone else
ever is.'" He was silent a moment as if considering the effect of such
a statement on the boy. "No, I cannot say it. It is all wrong that I
cannot. He would wither before my eyes. So cruel, so deep the
shame. Already his eyes are haunted. He cannot even in May imagine May. Oh, bébé, there is so much shit in this world. So much
shit. Maybe it is better a monk, a nothing."

Pique Dame came in then with the rum, and he looked at her startled. "In the garden, *s'il vous plaît,*" and we went out there and sat under a patch of sky still too light for stars.

We talked for a long time that night and in the nights that followed. I was supposed to write during the day, but apart from taking notes I could get nothing finished onto paper. The notes I'd shuffle around aimlessly while I listened to Edward's pupils downstairs. Faust, Rodolfo, Cavaradossi, Pinkerton, Rhadames, Tonio, the Almavivas. It was like the Victor ads in the Christmas magazines of my boyhood. The whole company was spread in an arc across the top of the double, glossy page. Melba was at the lower left, larger than the others, with a pocketbook on a chain around her waist, as Marguerite. Caruso in what I thought were Boy Scout boots as Rhadames; Scotti as Scarpia, elegant with lace cuffs; Da Lucca — was it? — with mustaches as God knows what. Only John McCormack was in evening dress. I was too young to have heard or to remember having heard any of them in the flesh. In fact, I haven't any idea who Da Lucca was, but I remember the name and the mustaches. I hope somebody else does too. I heard them all on records, of course, but mostly I remember looking at them spread before me as I lay, belly down, legs in air, on the Persian carpets that flowered softly for my youth.

Well, this was like that. The pupils were like the people in the ad. I listened and listened, just as I had stared and stared, but they had nothing to do with what I had to write, and the only relationship between the notes that I scribbled and the understanding that I had somehow to arrive at was narrative and not, from my point of view, important. Here is one.

"Went to bullfight with E. Neither of us interested. Could possibly do something about color, circular crowd, blood and sand but *moment of truth* pure crap. Maybe poem."

Here's another.

"Struck by fact that E. has *never* called Gm. *mistress.* He is always her lover. I am *bébé* because they spoke French together so that he could learn it. I was much around then. Never *tu-toyer* between them. Never *Barbara* even. Always *Madame.* Two forces operating in conversation. Regard for me then and now, and love for each other. Try to describe *eloquent hesitancy* in E.'s eyes as he tells me story."

And a third.

"E. remembered dinner in Milan down to last detail. On Papa's silencing him on the Marschallin bit, 'How swift you people are! How sure! The *grand seigneur* as well as the surgeon wielded that knife. It was over before it could be said. I could not say it then. I have kept silent over twenty years.' "

I knew I had to put these notes in order. "It is your métier, bébé," Edward kept saying. "Without this you cannot really write. It is your subject matter. You cannot help that, but I told you once it is not enough for you to *be,* you must imagine what you are."

The narrative facts are simple enough. Most of them I have already given, have come to terms with. When he was nineteen, Edward had been seduced by Alta Swanson, who had indeed later sung Octavian. He had led a strange and violent life with her, for, as he said, "She knew everything there was to know about music, and a good deal about love, but nothing whatever about life." It was she who taught him how to work, how to study, how to hear a phrase. She was quite merciless, and made him practice at half-voice until his own should be stronger. She was professional in the best possible sense, and determined, in the worst possible sense, to keep him for herself. She would make him lie on the floor and then sit on his diaphragm. "Surely the goddamnedest exercise you can imagine" — and tears of laughter would stream down his cheeks — "with both of us naked. Half the time I was dizzy with fulfillment, and sitting next to her in the quartet on Sundays — that beautiful voice, my own beautiful voice, the sunlight through the stained glass, the great bouquets of expensive memorial flowers — I was very happy.."

They had lived together for over two years when a series of violent quarrels began: "But I knew my *Bohème,* and they were to be expected." One night he had awakened to find her over him with the butcher knife — "It was castration I feared, not death" — and she had begun to cry "Kill me. Kill me. Murder me. Murder me," in the extremities of her pleasures. This was not *Lucia.* She was quite mad by the time Edward arranged for her to be taken to a sanitarium. My grandmother paid for her there for over a year, and then the doctor told them that she had no idea of her surroundings and that she might be better off in a state hospital. People are always telling the rich things like this, and they are happy to believe them. The poor, however, are customarily bled of their last sou.

Edward and Grandma went out to see her there at Christmas,

when she was performing in a program. She sang the Gluck *"Divinités du Styx"* without accompaniment to the thunderous applause of madmen.

"The voice was still prodigious, the phrasing exact, the plea for pity heartbreaking. And all contained in perfect classic form. Not a shade too much. Not a shade too little. The ornamentation exact. It was that day that I knew about the independent life of a work of art, for how could Gluck have ever foreseen, even for a moment, that moment? A madwoman in a madhouse to a mad audience singing that aria with such exquisite precision?" He stopped a moment and knew my quietness.

"Well," he said, "I have had that scene for many years to haunt me. Your grandmother had it too, for soon after we were lovers. Now it is yours. See what you can do with it."

Edward will never see this now, and I don't know if he knew then, but, in his saying "Your grandmother had it too, for soon after we were lovers," he told me a great deal more about their relationship that he would have had he provided me with the most circumstantial account of their lovemaking.

They had been very circumspect and very careful, and there had been, he thought, no talk because the house was usually full of chaperons in the form of children, grandchildren, and other visitors. Even though it was well known that a room was kept for him, it was in the west wing, far removed from Grandmama's, and when they went to Europe they went on different boats. My grandmother had returned from Italy shortly before my birth, but Edward had stayed in London, where he had a contract for minor tenor parts at Covent Garden. He described his first meeting with my grandmother on his return almost a year later. She had not come into the hall to greet him, even though he was expected. Indeed, he had been announced as if at a party at the drawing-room door. It was a November day of icy rain, and Grandmama had me in her arms. She was wearing what was then called a tea gown of sulphur velvet, and my mother, who had evidently just come in, was standing by the fire, still in what would have been called a *tailleur,* hat, gloves, furs.

"It's so nasty, why don't you stay all night and hear Edward's news," my grandmother had said.

" 'No, no. I just thought you'd like the baby while I was at Maud's lunch. But now I must fly.' " Edward did my mother very

well. "Oh, it was interminable, bébé. I did not know where I stood
at all. I wasn't used to this endless talk as I became later. That
dead-white skin, that blue-black hair, that sulphur-yellow dress with
point de Venise across the breasts. But you in her arms so that she
could not press my hand, could give no sign, could not even look
into my eyes until your mother was gone. Then it was all right. I
knew. But you know, bébé, we could not even eat by the fire that
one night? The dining room. Two men handing dishes."

During the first war, Edward had been a sergeant — "The Singing Sergeant, bébé. No college degree. Clearly not a gentleman. But
I sang 'Keep the home fires burning,' 'There's a long, long trail
awinding,' 'We'll be waiting when you come back home' to Liberty
Bond rallies, and God could I wallop them with 'Mother Machree,'
the last phrase in my most expensive voice. Not a dry eye in the
house."

The affair had dwindled during the war — "A balding sergeant is
no longer Octavian" — but in 1920 they had spent the spring and
early summer in Venice again and had been "softly happy." After
that there had been nothing, even though he continued to stay at
my grandmother's house whenever he was in town. Later, Corinne
was to tell me what I suppose I could have figured out for myself,
that "Grandmama traded him in on Charlotte Payne." My Uncle
Tom had fallen in love with a girl who was taking care of my
brothers and me one summer. My grandmother, thinking this "un-
suitable," had stepped in and "put a stop to it." My older cousins
knew all about it, but I was only six at the time and didn't hear the
story until later. Corinne's theory was that Grandmama, having
taken a "firm line" with Tom, took an equally firm line with herself.
Neither Edward nor I knew of this complication at the time we
spoke, and Edward's explanation was that he had become too well
known and that the grandchildren were older.

"But we just did not love each other anymore. It was sad to me,
but now it seems that even while I loved her I did not really know it
was she I loved. I know now that everybody, always, creates the image he loves, but I don't know that I knew it then. If I tell you this
you will not hold it against me? Many times when I have had other
women, it has been *Madame* in my arms. I do not know. I cannot
say it. With Sophie this was most true, and I thought, 'She is peasant. I am *snob*.' So *snob* that she was dough, and I could not, ex-

cept with other visions — Alta, your grandmother. Oh bébé, you will have to create me. I am an old man, and I do not know. I hope to know. I think I am honest with myself. And I am glad you came because you make me be so, and I can listen to the words I speak just as I could listen to myself sing."

The day I left, Edward played me some records of himself at his prime. I had never heard these because they had been done in Buenos Aires. He and Borghese sang the duets from *Bohème* in Spanish to the thinned, wheezing orchestra of those thin old recordings. But the voices were full, passionate, sure, and the accommodation that each made to the timbre of the other was in itself an evocation of love. (In the old Garbo *Camille* there is an example of this sympathy made visual when Garbo and Robert Taylor walk toward the bed and Garbo corrects her step to fall in with his.) Puccini could not have written what they achieved into his score. There is no system of musical notation or guide word to scrawl across the page to encompass such performance. It was something they did on their own out of their own hearts, out of their own lives, for the people they played.

I watched the thin tears of age gather in Edward's eyes and spill to his fleshy cheeks crisscrossed with minute veins. His ageless hand with its still swart hairs moved, beating time, in and out, in and out of a shaft of sun that dazzled with light the drifting dust of the Mexican afternoon. Then it fell upon the piles of scores, their spines long since torn naked and splayed so that you could count their gatherings, the very strings of their bindings now raveled until caught in brittle, still faintly opalescent daubs of long-dried glue.

Critics speak of the moment of revelation or understanding as if all of a sudden everything became clear, as if the dramatic incident — Isabel Archer coming upon Madame Merle — could exist without what had gone before. As if the catalytic moment alone, however underwritten, however underplayed, were in itself sufficient. I can tell you with Edward that nothing like that happened. There was no one "moment of truth." He puzzled me, stayed in my mind until he died, and even though there were important incidents in his life that he did not tell me about, at the moment when I learned of them there was no sudden realization that here at last was the key. He had told me to "create" him, and you might argue that I was free — indeed duty bound — to invent the dramatic incident that would show him in his entirety, as he really was. But the moment I do this the relationship we had will vanish.

I could "discover," for example, that he was in truth my father and that my supposed mother had agreed to the deception with her mother-in-law. Believe me, there is nothing in the character of either woman which would have made this impossible, and the dates as I look back, would take little or no juggling. Whenever I am tempted to write the scenes involved, oh Edith Wharton, I run into myself. My relationships to my own father and to my Uncle Tom, the men of my family I was closest to, were entirely different from my feeling for Edward. They were a part of me. The feeling of consanguinity was there and was very strong. I knew, really knew, my father and Tom as men. Either one of them could have been me at the Folies Bergère, and I never looked at them or thought of them as figures on the glossy pages of the Victor ad. When their pictures did appear in the society columns of the newspapers, there was never any *wonder* on my part. I knew who they were, how they lived, under what black marble they would molder when they were dead. I loved them, even though I was sometimes oppressed by that love which was not something apart from myself but as intimate as the stirring within my own heart.

And this is strange. Strange because Edward's continued, probing concern with the artistic process was, in truth, central to my own life and of far more immediate importance to my existence, in the philosophic sense of the term, than the often vague but constant identity I felt for the men of my own family — sons, certainly, of Edward's *Madame,* but fathered by the blind Titan of another myth. Corinne has tried to tell me that I never really knew Edward, that by the time I was six or seven he was no longer "lover-in-residence" but merely a voice in the house. "After all," she pointed out, "the twenties were only your boyhood. The thirties were your youth, and apart from seeing him on the stage, hearing him sing, you seldom saw him."

What I would like to think, what I am sure Edward would expect me to think, is that hearing him sing was the final intimacy, an intimacy stronger than that of blood, an intimacy still not explained even if I were in the interest of art to make him my veritable father. What existed between us was a creative sympathy, and we met each other outside of ourselves on an intensely imagined but never, I think, intuited plane. Any one of the incidents I have told you about could be used artistically, even in the good sense of that term, as if it were the catalytic agent which would bring Edward to life. But in the end there would be no Edward, no me. What Edward had said when he said, "But there was no letter scene. Just death." I know what I have to do, and it is nowhere so easy, so sure of success, as a dramatic incident would be. I have to modulate my voice as Edward did in the duets from *Bohème,* giving much of my own that his voice may become purer, but at the same time taking the timbre of his that both voices may well sweet with unwept tears.

In the years that intervened between my visit to him in Mexico and his death, I don't suppose there was a day I did not think of Edward. Not sadly, as you would of a lost lover, but with wonder. He might cross my mind only for a moment, or something might remind me and I would puzzle for a long time. I know I never wrote anything without considering the effect it would have on him. What I was trying to do all this time was to reduce to poetic terms feelings of his about art and love, feelings of mine. Some of the poems had direct quotations from him, and I'm sure that the rather peculiar rhythm of his speech is responsible for what one reviewer called my "un-English line." Since I think, feel, speak, even see in terms of a five-foot line — you can scan whole pages of this — I was amused, but I saw its justice. Edward never appears in the poems as Edward. No one but me could feel his presence, the pressure of his still "uncreated" being, and he himself never mentioned any of the poems I sent him. It may very well be that he had no idea that he appeared at all. He had "given" himself to me — as he used the word, as indeed I used it myself to myself and have used it here in speaking of my own seduction. Apparently, he had no further interest in the Edward who was becoming a character. I used him shamelessly as he used Puccini. I was in danger of losing my own identity even as a poet, for I would ascribe to myself as speaker of a poem a virtue and sensibility which were not mine but Edward's — yet, even so, even now, the result does not ring false in my ears. If Edward emerges from these pages, it will be because I have given him blood of my own store. In telling me to create him, he had said, "I can give you the lungs, bébé, but the flesh and blood must be your own." The most successful of these poems were three longish pieces called "Conversation," "Mr. Di Paolis and the Shades," and "Triptych." Even today they seem to me skillful in the blending of the two of us. Only because I am the author, the ultimate authority on my own Road to Xanadu, do I know when Edward speaks and when I answer. It's like the time when people wrote in from all over the world to the Victor company to settle arguments as to whether Caruso or Scotti sang the first phrase in *"Solenne in Quest'ora"* from *La Forza*. I "gave" him some of my best lines, and "took" in return many of his. His low voice so overlapped my upper register, as it were, that it is impossible to tell the difference. Maybe it will help if I say that if in schizophrenia you have the division of a single personality, here you have the coalescence in one personality of the traits of two.

At any rate, "Triptych" uses the famous passage from Freud about man and the stars as its epigraph and has the figure of "Icarus lashed to Ixion's wheel." The phrase had been written for over a year before I, who wrote it, knew that it had really come from Edward's dependence on my family. Just how deep, how tragic, this was I must now try to tell you. There was no "revelation," you must understand, for although I had no idea of the precise detail I had, as Edward said when we gave him C instead of B-flat, felt it coming in my lungs.

Corinne had me out for a few days one May when Mary, my wife, and my daughters were visiting with her father. "Come and sit under my leaving, surgeon-tended trees," she had said, and I had gone. When I arrived, she was in the kitchen with the most fantastic chaos of dirty pots, smeared bowls, beaters stiff with cream, broken egg shells, butter papers, peapods, lobster claws, strawberry hulls, flour-smudged wine bottles that I had ever seen.

"What beautiful, expensive garbage!"

She laughed and kissed me, giving me a chocolate finger to lick.

"I throw a pound of butter out the window before I begin to get into the mood. Alma, I'm sorry" — this was to the maid who had let me in and who would have to clean up the mess — "but I do get carried away."

"Modom can do as she likes in her own kitchen."

"So I can." There was no ice, no steel in her voice. It wasn't nasty; it wasn't good-natured. She even resisted the inclination to say "So *modom* can" as she walked out and up the stairs with me to show me my room. "There's a dinner jacket of Bob's in the closet. Try it on. If it fits, take it home."

It did fit, and I was glad to have it. I kept it on to show her even though I had no tie, and when I came down I saw that she had dressed, too.

"How elegant we are!" I said. "Wouldn't Grandmama be pleased?"

"The suit's fine. Turn around. I don't see how it could be better."

"Much nicer than mine. Thanks."

She seemed really pleased and said she thought there'd be a tie in the pocket of the jacket she kept for the man she had sometimes to wait on the table. In the interest of Emerson's all things hastening back to unity, I have to report that it was a made-up tie, but I put it on anyway. You couldn't tell.

After dinner was when we really talked. When I first got back from Mexico, I told her about Edward, the gold brushes, the Boldini, and when I first began to be haunted by the picture I had told her about that, too.

"I felt a little funny — a wisp of shame — at giving you Bob's jacket. Like Edward in Grandpapa's sable coat. It wasn't just a collar, by the way. The whole thing was lined."

"It crossed my mind, too, as I came down the stairs. It's a funny thing. Neither of us really knows she gave him the coat. It's just there in my picture. I never saw the coat, even. He was dead before I was born."

"Oh, you could have seen it in snapshots, newspaper pictures. But I didn't remember it until you saw it in your goddamned picture."

"The only thing I can think of is that I picked it up from the reference to Caruso in an astrakhan collar. But how the hell would I have remembered that detail unless the other detail were there to make it significant?"

"You know, don't you, Marcel, that the trivial persists when the significant is gone?" She put her hand to the flexible diamond-and-sapphire bow she was wearing. "Grandmama's been dead under a black marble slab since 1932. I've still got the pin, but I have no idea when it was given to her. What sentimental occasion? With what special fervor was Grandpapa thanked? You want to know about the suit? I ordered it for Bob when I thought he would be coming home and he hadn't had a new dinner jacket since college. Now it hides your hairy ass, not his."

"Not to worry, darling, not to worry."

"Oh, I don't worry. It doesn't even make me sad any more. But, God, I patted it, rubbed my cheek along it, sniffed it, and when I gave all the other stuff away I just left it hanging there. It couldn't even smell of him because he never had it on. He never even saw it."

She talked on like that for a while, and I asked her in what I thought was an oblique manner how much she really loved Bob.

"Johnny-jump-up, Johnny-jump-up. No one would believe you. How would I know? How do you know what love is, especially at fifty? I wasn't frigid, as they say on the Women's Pages now, but when you think what was done to girls like me, the way we were brought up. There weren't books to read. There weren't even people to talk to. I used to wonder about myself, 'Am I really sexy?' " She laughed. "Remember you at the Folies? Well, I didn't get any kick out of it. None at all. I'm not really a looker, a noticer. I had no yen, as a yen, for Bob at all. There was my mother, of course. Look at where it landed her." She stopped, considered, and then went on, "And Grandmama."

"But you didn't know. You said you didn't know. That you thought none of them but Tom ever knew."

"Knowing? What the hell is *knowing*? Did it make any difference when you knew? Knew that *the* act took place?"

"No. I suppose not."

"You're one of us, George Gordon, Lord Byron. There's not one of us who hasn't admitted the possibility, even the probability. But how loyal do you think our aunts by marriage were with their families? Your mother and her sisters? As long as nothing is said to those involved, such things can be arranged. It was just Edward who didn't really know the rules, so even the inlaws could be affronted, and we slammed all the doors in his face."

"I don't know how you can say that."

"Come off it. Come off it, Little Nell. We never let him establish his claim, his kinship."

"And that's what he wanted?"

"Certainly. Always. Even now."

"You don't think I love Edward?"

"You can't just gaze and gaze and gaze. You've got to be able to look with someone else's eyes. At least, that's what I've always gone on. When you do that, then I think you love."

The next day we walked up to the house. One of the reasons I'd come out was that it was to be torn down, and I wanted to go through it again. There, if anywhere, I should be able to find Proust's uneven flags. As we took the turn in the drive that brought it into view, Corinne said, "It's certainly not the House of Usher."

The day was bright with May, and the rosy gray limestone house looked as it always did to me, beautiful. Sturdy, contained, gleaming with hundreds of big windows. It was in the French style, balanced, formal, restrained. The main block of the house was flanked by the two wings which formed a forecourt. A balustrade ran around the flat roof, and there were great stone urns of stone fruit, six of them, on the long front. Over the ground-floor windows and the front door were swags of limestone flowers. From a distance, the house looked as lived in as it ever had, and the builder who had bought the property had even, after a fashion, kept up the lawns. The brass and wrought-iron gates that had closed in the court were gone. "Sold," Corinne told me. "You'd be amazed. The urns are sold. Almost everything had a buyer."

At the front door the brasswork was all gone, and we had to let ourselves in by removing a big padlock to which Corinne had the key. I remembered how I used to wonder just when I would be able to reach the big dolphin knocker, and I told Corinne how that was all I was able to think of the year we came back from Edinburgh.

"All the tugs, the bridges, the skyline, the Statue of Liberty, and that's what I thought of. Can I reach the dolphin now?"

"Could you?"

"No. I don't know that I remember that. I do know that all the doorknobs were so high. So much higher than at home."

The hall was cavernous before us. Emptier than merely empty. The fireplaces were just holes, and even the bronze stair railing had disappeared, so that the steps seemed to slant drunkenly to the outside. The big rooms ran along the lake front, the back of the house, and that's where we went first. These rooms too were stripped. Plaster dust, bits of lath, bent nails strewed the floor, but the rooms were still beautiful, just as a tree is when it has lost its leaves. You could see the essential proportions, the architecture, the magnificence of the conception that took into account not only the rooms themselves but the sweep of the three planted terraces that descended to the bluff above the shifting blue lake where today whitecaps rolled toward the shore and brought the eye back from that immensity to the lilacs drunk with sun, rumpled by the wind that tossed pale blue across lavender, purple, wax-perfect white. The two of us stood looking out for a while and then turned together to look up at the wall where the Sargent had hung. The claws of the toggles that had held it in place were still there, and the brocade of the panel which it had hidden was a brighter, harsher gold than the warm, pale yellow that was all I had ever known and that still clung, tattered, to the rest of the walls.

"Even if you'd had room for it, would you have wanted it?" I asked.

"No. It wasn't just the room in a room. It's room in a life. God knows we live in a cherry orchard as it is." I poked my finger into the damask and tore off a strip which I wound around my finger as a kid will wind a string or a rubber band tight so that the blood stops and the lines leave welts. It was difficult to arrange our voices as we walked through the empty rooms. Sometimes they came out too loud, and sometimes the emptiness reduced them to mumbled inconsequence, but I don't think that was the reason we gave up trying to say anything. The six years difference in our ages just meant that we had different things to remember and to not remember. The rooms along the sides of the ground floor were lower ceilinged and had always had more comfortable furniture than those at the back, but strangely we had not used them much. When I mentioned this to Corinne, she just said, "What are you twisting that damned cloth around your finger for? Look at your hands. They're a mess."

I looked down at them and saw that the damask was now just strings and that the dried paste had melted to a gritty stickiness.

"Freudian. Downright Freudian." She laughed, but there was still an edge to her voice.

We crossed the big hall then to the dining room, and from there went on to the pantries, kitchen, and servants' quarters, where the whole machinery of the house was laid bare. Although at home we spent a great deal of time in the kitchen, at Grandmama's we were only allowed in this part of the house when Grandmama herself was there. At home we were never allowed to ring bells for servants, but at Grandmama's we were *supposed* to — "Your grandmother runs her house the way she wants. I run mine the way I want," our mother said firmly. "If you want a glass of milk, go ask them for it in the kitchen. And drink it there." As children, of course, we would have liked to reverse the rules, to have been able to ring at home, not to have had to ring at Grandmama's. Something of this must have been going through Corinne's mind because, when we came to the back stairs which we were never supposed to use, she said, conspiratorially, "You think we dare?"

"I dare ya. Double dare."

"You know why it was done, don't you?" She stood with her hand on the newel post, her eyes laughing at first, but then a kind of haze came over them.

"Oh, there might be people coming up or down with trays, their hands full?"

"That, I guess. But do you know what I was told, Karl Marx? Do you know what I heard with my own ears? 'You must always show the most exact consideration . . .' "

"For the servants."

"Oh no, Karl. That was *your* mother. Think again."

"Don't tell me it was the lower orders. That I can't believe."

"Come again, Karlie-boy. I think maybe it's worse." She looked at me and saw I couldn't get it, so she turned and stomped the syllables out, one to each step, as she went up the stairs: *"For those who are de-pend-ent on you. Chee-rist. Je-sus H. Chee-rist. Je-sus. H."* — and then she ran out of steps.

Upstairs, a kind of numbing loneliness set in, for there every room was associated with a distinct person, but even Tom's room was no emptier to me than Edward's, and my own room in the east wing was just another kid's room as we went methodically from one to another. I looked out from my window, kneeling on the now padless seat. The apple tree that had bloomed popcorn was gone, and the landscape was strange with new roofs where once there had been woods. I must have been there longer than I realized, because Corinne asked me from the doorway, "You've had enough?"

"Oh, sure."

"Should I have let you come alone?"

I looked into Corinne's honest, inquiring, kindly eyes, and my heart gave a tremendous thump. "I don't know why everybody's always so goddamned *nice* to me. You, Tom, Edward, my own father. As if I were the only sensitive plant around. You know, don't you, that I know what has happened to you here?"

"Do you? Do you really?"

"The enormous, fantastic machinery of a place like this. Moral, emotional machinery. Not just physical."

We were back in the big upstairs hall that we called the lounge, and the May sun was pouring in through the skylights, washing back the shadows into radiant emptiness. The memories held back by the unconscious will because they really could not be used then and there flooded as tears to my eyes.

"You, Horatio, are our only chance. Report our cause aright. We're the shades that beg Ulysses for the cup of blood."

I started perceptibly. I had already written but Corinne had not seen "Mr. Di Paolis and the Shades," which begins:

> *Of all the blood Ulysses shed*
> *with his broad sword to clot the parched*
> *and during dust of storied plain*
> *or flow in dilute crimson through*
> *those far refracting sky-impacted seas*
> *where thought like restless dolphin*
> *darts with gleaming back to breed,*
> *he could not spare a little cup*
> *for those poor shades who cried aloud*
> *to feel again — remembered pain?*
>
> *Those shades are at me now for life*
> *and I am no Ulysses who*
> *could stand upon the bourne of world*
> *to shake a brine-encrusted beard*
> *in high rebellion at the graveless dead,*
> *but am suppliant myself*
> *whose one day's stubble with due rite*
> *is sacrificially removed*
> *before a porcelain altar*
> *by priest emasculate in Jockey shorts.*

What was even more remarkable was that — again after I had written the lines — I had come upon the idea in a letter of Proust's.

Here in the sunlit emptiness was the idea again from one of my own "characters."

"We're the eyes of Edward's cat. The eyes in the photographs. We can see you better than you see us. Our eyes are wide, wide open. There's no aesthetic distance. We don't even blink. But we're mute." The house had come crushing down on us both.

I stared at her, this fifty-year-old cousin-sister of mine in a tweed suit, and wanted her. I felt strong and sure and young in the wanting, and I put my arms around her, but there she became old, and I was old, for coming toward us up the stairs were two women I had never seen. It wasn't necessary that they had seen the embrace. You couldn't tell. They hadn't known that we would be there, and our lips had scarcely touched before I was aware of them and had broken away.

"Oh, Mrs. Patterson, I'm Sharon Ober, you remember?" In the reverse snobbery of the day, she was in blue jeans, loafers, a sweater and a nasty add-a-pearl necklace.

"Mrs. Ober? Certainly." Corinne was sure of herself, but I saw the appraisal in her eyes.

"I would like" — Mrs. Ober indicated the other woman, who was in city clothes complete with heels and gloves — "to present my husband's sister, Brenda Burns."

I thought, "Christ, the woman's going to curtsy," but Corinne stepped forward, offering her hand as she had always been taught to do at Grandmama's — "You girls are at home here. When you're here, it's your house, and you must shake hands with guests, just as I do." I could remember Edith at thirty standing when even a younger man came into the room.

"How do you do, Mrs. Burns? This is my cousin. He and I have been having a last look around." Corinne, I thought, isn't sure. She didn't give them my name — that was characteristic enough — but any kind of explanation was totally out of character. I looked to the women to see if it was noticed, but I think they were still flustered at having been caught where they had no business and amazed at Corinne's exactly modulated courtesy.

"This was Mrs. Patterson's home, Brenda. I bet they have some tales to tell." The archness of this was so out of date, so remembered, as it were, from women of her mother's generation that I knew it sprang from embarrassment — whether at having been

caught themselves or at having caught us, it was impossible to tell.
"Did you come out here?"

"No. My grandmother did give a tea dance for me that year,
and I was married in the drawing room downstairs."

"What a fun thing." Mrs. Ober was back in her own generation now. "Brenda and I have just been decorating those rooms in
our mind's eye. We bet each other you used those darling rooms to
the west and scarcely ever went into the big rooms at all."

This would have been too much for Corinne even had we been
caught in *the* act, so she said, "I think if you knew us you would
find us essentially formal people."

"Oh, you can't say that, surely. I never knew anyone her age so
completely *fun* as Edith." She must have felt Corinne bridle because she retreated to "your cousin, I mean, for her years." Mrs.
Ober was lost, but Corinne was merciless.

"Mrs. Atwater is coming for dinner tonight. I'll give her your
compliment."

"What I meant was a fun-grandmother is something rare."

"You see, you didn't know ours." Corinne's smile was her social
smile, interested, attentive, polite, the head at a scarcely percepti-
ble slant. "Mrs. Ober, Mrs. Burns" — there was a nod to each, and
each was looked squarely in the eyes. Then, I swear to God, Corinne gathered her short, rump-sprung tweed skirt as if it were trailing, sulphur velvet and stepped by them to sweep with remembered
grace down the suddenly recarpeted, rebalustered stairs.

The Corinne who became Grandmama on those stairs was, of
course, the same Corinne who not half an hour before had stomped
with such violence up the back, just as the Corinne who lived in
the gardener's cottage and had no room in her life for the Sargent
was the same Corinne who over the course of the years had spent
$100,000 doing the cottage over. She laughed when I mentioned
this to her and said, "The trick now, Thorstein, is *inconspicuous
consumption*," and of course I knew she was right.

The two of us stood at the turn of the drive which would take
the house from sight and looked back. It was awash with a vast
emptiness that seemed to flow from the distant windows which by
some trick of light had caught the blue lake where the white, returning breakers moved.

"No, it's not the House of Usher, Edgar Allan. There's no crack, no fissure. It will take the bulldozers, the iron ball swinging on a chain."

I got a poem out of the ball swinging on the chain, but I didn't get the rest of Edward, or as much as I ever was going to get, until five years later. It was just such a day, blue as heaven, but late in June, and Corinne was with us. She had let her hair go completely gray, but she had looked very elegant the night before at the dance we gave for our daughters and which was the reason she had stayed over. We had been very late at the party, and although it was noon no one else was down but the two of us. Bob Patterson, who was indeed a nice boy, had got very drunk and had had to be put to bed. This worried Corinne; when I reminded her of how much really heavy drinking we'd done at twenty, she countered with, "Aren't you afraid for the girls?"

"Oh, God, yes. I stay awake and all that. But how else do you grow up?"

"Well, I was a bitch, and I just don't want Bob to end up Tom Buchanan."

"He won't. Remember, he had to get into Princeton. And stay there. Things are different now. It's no longer *droit du seigneur.*"

"I was pretty goddamned bright myself. It's no guarantee."

"Not at the moment, no. But in the long run, probably. Anyway, you're not so bad."

"Okay, professor."

"Are you going to mention it to him?"

"Should I?"

"I think the Tom Buchanan bit might be pretty good, but then I believe in Gatsby and art."

"What chance has art — upper case — got when he'll have three million next year and the rest when he's thirty?"

"That's been the problem all along, hasn't it? The history of America."

"The history of America is the history of us?"

"Well, that's what we were taught, and it's easy enough for us to look back and see it, but they teach them something different now, I'm sure."

"But what chance has the teacher got, what chance has even art got against that much cold cash? Doesn't art always lose? Look at Edward, the dinner in Milan. The very top of his profession, thinking that what he gave us back was so much more than we had ever given him."

We had taken coffee out into the yard and were sitting on deck chairs there when my father drove up. His hair still glinted red in the sunlight as he walked toward us, but I noticed with a pang that he took the walk instead of coming, his arms swaying happy arcs of balance, across the sloping, rolling lawn. He waved, though, and we waved back. I was just about to call to him to bring himself a chair when I remembered and went to get him one myself from the stack in the garage. From the distance I saw him lean over and kiss Corinne, but by the time I got back he was sitting on my chair, leaning forward, his fingers pressed together.

"Tom's been on the phone, and Edward Sciarrha's dead in Pasadena." I knew right away that he had already told Corinne, because they both looked at me as if there were some understanding between the two of them.

"We were just this minute talking about him. What was it?"

"Stroke, Tom said. Magda Feuer was with him." Magda Feuer had always sung *Lohengrin* with him in this country, and it was because of her that he had left Mexico City a few years back and gone to live in Pasadena, where they rented from my Uncle Harry's estate the beautiful, towered Italian villa with its spectacular view of the thickly lighted canyons and hills. "Fiesole, bébé. Montmartre. The third act of *Louise*," Edward had said the year before when we were there and were sitting on the huge, arcaded porch that was the top of the tower. There was a big colony of singers and musicians around, people you would have thought dead years ago, and while we were there Edward and Magda had had a big party for them after the performance of *Rosenkavalier* in the Shrine Auditorium the night the *Staatsoper* had been reopened in Vienna. Magda, who had done the coaching on the opera, had been asked to read the congratulatory telegram to the audience from the stage during the little ceremony between the second and third acts. Edward was worried that she might not be able to negotiate the long walk from the wings to the center of the enormous stage; she was badly crippled with arthritis, and in a short skirt her legs were now monstrous. There was some business with microphones and a movie "personality" who did the introduction, but the moment she appeared, far at the left, the stage was hers. You knew what was really

meant by *personality*. This woman whose half Jewish grandmother
had kept her from Hitler's Reich for all of her greatest years read
the telegram, which was gracefully phrased in English, and then,
although it had not been planned, spoke it quietly in German with
the tears of the world in her voice and with all the vast forgiveness
of her artist's heart. Even my daughters, to whom it meant little
that Madga had first sung at Vienna under Mahler and to whom the
rubbled horror of the war was only something on the Late Show,
recognized it as purest poetry and to my great joy said so. To me
it was more than "when the lights go on again all over the world,"
because I had seen the desolation of Germany twice — once with
terror in my own eyes and again a few years later when Magda, before I knew her, had transformed the intense and beautifully realized but essentially nineteenth-century and personal lyricism of the
Winterreise to general heartbreak with the last song, *"Der Leier-
mann."* She sang it with a numbed perfection beyond sadness, as
if the flames of loving hopelessly had gutted it even of sorrow. Hide-
ously, only form was left in a formless world to give, as the angry,
the beat have not realized, the final turn of the screw: Edward and
my grandmother hearing together Alta in the madhouse and his
"Your grandmother had it too, for soon after that we were lovers."
I had a poem, "Antiphon," which I hope does this, but here I am
going to give you the Müller poem that Schubert used. The song is
about the poet, the composer, who sees the insane organ grinder,
barefoot on the ice, poor, with an empty cup. No one hears him,
no one sees him, and dogs dog his heels. Meanwhile, the hurdy-
gurdy plays mechanically under his numbed fingers, and the old
man is asked if he will use the organ for the songs the questioner
has written from his heart. Well, in 1946 I looked out on the leveled
desolation of Hamburg and somehow, somewhere, impossibly with
spring, a barrel organ was playing *"Der Lindenbaum."* When
Magda sang, I saw it, smelled it, felt it grit between my fingers,
tasted the eddying dust. Ten lines, fifty bars of music *etwas langsam.*
Here it is. Even if you can't read German, even if you don't remember the music, I think you ought to try it:

> *Drüben hinterm dorfe steht ein Leiermann*
> *Und mit starren Fingern dreht er, was er kann.*
> *Barfuss auf dem Eise wankt er hin und her,*
> *Und sein kleiner Teller bleibt ihm immer leer.*

Keiner mag ihn hören, keiner sieht ihn an,
Und die Hunde knurren um den alten Mann.
Und er lässt es gehen alles, wie es will,
Dreht, und seine Leier steht ihm nimmer still.

Wunderlicher Alter, soll ich mit dir gehn?
Willst zu meinen Liedern deine Leier drehn?

This was a personal memory, of course, but, except for the young, every memory there must have flooded with the old griefs of those terrible years and at the same time been brought to peace by the gorgeous faith in Magda's spoken voice. The Jewish producer, who was sitting on the other side of Edward, lifted his Viennese wife's hand to his lips and kissed it. The cast lined up behind Magda were in tears of shining hope, and the movie personality with his "beloved Madame Feuer," unused to such thorough up-staging, had completely disappeared. Magda, laughing about it on our way home, said, "It wasn't fair. Even though it was Los Angeles, I was on my home grounds and he didn't know it. Apart from a dozen or so starlets, everyone knew much more precisely who I was than knew him."

After Magda had finished, there were the national anthems with us all standing, but, before the applause could break, Magda moved backward to the line of the cast and, ignoring the place the Marschallin and Octavian naturally made for her, slipped in on the far side of Baron Ochs, leaving the center of the stage picture for the actual performers. The courtesy of this was so exquisite, so exactly the sort of thing that would have sent my grandmother into ecstasies, that a tiny thrill of aesthetic pleasure crept up my spine. There was no humility in the action. The gesture was one of sim-ple, comprehending justice, eloquent with the belief of seventy-odd and wise years that the rights of man were the high concern of art. The party Edward and Magda gave after the performance was a larger if less poignant indication of the same spirit, for even though Edward warned us that it would be "the fifth act of *Götter-dämmerung*, bébé, your Victor ad in shrouds," the party was given out of the goodness of their hearts. The producer had invited them both to the party he was giving for the actual cast, but they had gathered together all the strays and would not hear to any of the young performers neglecting the movie producer in their favor. I heard Magda on the phone: "A mistaken kindness. Without you we will seem brilliant to ourselves. I intend to be Madame Verdurin become the Princess de Guermantes. Armand, like Charlus, can call the sonorous roll of the sonorous dead, and no one will mind. Indeed, we will congratulate each other on having remained alive."

Oh, it was good that Edward had Magda at the last, for the Magdas of the musical world are few. Prima donnas in their prime, however sumptuous their voices, are not generally women of intellect or even articulate musical understanding. What they do, they are more apt to do intuitively, and when their voices are gone and they have become the final wives of their final, businessmen husbands, even their raffish ebullience disappears in what Edward called "the last throes of refinement." There is nothing left of them except the evening gowns of their concertizing days and the diamond brooch the boxholders gave them upon their retirement. In addition to the brooch, a one-time famous Carmen was wearing her Yale '08 chairman-of-the-board husband's fraternity pin, and the possessor of one of the most gorgeous voices I have ever heard, who once had to be forcibly restrained by a frantic stage manager from appearing from the depths of the well in Resphigi's *Sunken Bell* loaded with the five dozen gardenias that her banana merchant sweetie had sent her before the performance, spent all her time showing me the gold charm-bracelet discs that clattered with the names and birthdates of her husband's great-grandchildren. With Magda it was different, and even my older daughter saw this, for she said, "Magda Feuer means Magda Fire, doesn't it, Daddy?" I said, "It sure does, honey." I was glad they had one another, and I was enormously touched when I noticed that Edward and she spoke her soft Austrian German together. I could remember how Edward had hated learning it when we were kids and how he could send us into giggling fits so fierce that we had to clutch ourselves to keep from wetting our pants by exaggerating the northern gutturals, gathering them in the back of his throat and spitting them out as if they were I-thought-it-was-an-oyster-but-I-guess-it's-snot.

I have told you all this partly because it raced through my mind when Papa said that Magda was with him when he died, and partly because it explains what I said next. The day we left, Edward and Magda came to the car in the drive, and after we were all packed and in, the engine already running, he looked at me quizzically, his head tilted to one side as if to avoid the sun that glanced from the tower. I saw his lungs fill with a singer's breath, the eyes become brighter, and then he put his head and shoulders through my window to leave a stubbled kiss on my cheek.

"Ah, Housman, that was stupid stuff, that dying while the laurel's green" were the last words I heard him speak, and I spoke them again to Papa, who was himself to die that year, and to Corinne, my fingertips against the left cheek his happy mouth had kissed that day. We sat there, the three of us, after I spoke, in quietness. The day was incomparably beautiful — "Oh what is so rare as a day in June," as Papa was always quoting — and the white, northern climbing roses and the blaze of red moved along my brick wall with little breezes that didn't touch us in the hollow where we sat with the bluish shadows of the dark chestnut rising above us, the still leaving maples limp with thin green tatters of springtime silk. Papa was the first to speak, and he cleared his throat as if apologizing for breaking the stillness, for intruding on our private memories of Edward.

"*Im fernem Land.* I suppose it will be Forest Lawn, or Hills, or whatever. That place with the Wee Kirk o' the Heather and the replica of David."

"You know, there it's nude and disgusting, not naked and real like it is in Florence with people sprawled about it, reading newspapers, carrying briefcases," he had said years ago when he had first seen it, and now for some reason I heard the rest of it. "When I was a kid — the first time I was in Florence, it must have been — I remember my father boosting me up and putting my whole foot on his toenail. It wasn't any bigger, so I must have been very small. I remember looking up, too, to those" — he remembered Corinne and changed what he would have said to me — "that marble nakedness. I'm told that what I said was, 'He's very big even for a big boy.' I remember the guide showing us the blue vein in the marble at the back of his wrist, and looking at the blue vein in the back of my wrist for the rest of the day. Anything anatomical always fascinated me. I was thinking though of Edward in that place where even David looks vulgar. He came a long way. A long way from the Tuscan hills."

Corinne gave no indication of having heard what Papa said, but just lay back in the deck chair, her head tilted toward the sky. Her arms lay along the sides of the chair, and the thumb of her left hand kept turning around her wedding ring. When she did speak there was an odd timbre to her voice that at first I could not identify. It had nothing to do with what she said; indeed it was wildly inappropriate, because I soon placed it as the flat, toneless chipper of the society voice of the '20s. It was a voice she hadn't used for thirty years, and I'm sure she didn't use it consciously now. It was the voice of her mother that had somehow come back to her.

"The olives rot on the brown hills of California, too. Black purple. Black purple bruised. Disgusting rot. And they have to be shoveled up and carted away in bleeding bushel baskets. With my mother once — oh, I was ten — I ate one. A great believer in the empirical method, she. Not an olive at all. Nothing like. Soap and death. Greasy death."

Bertolt Brecht, you see, not *No, No Nanette,* but the '20s just the same. Zelda Fitzgerald in the sanitarium. The violation of love. My every nerve, every nerve of me — it would be better if I could use the Elizabethan "every my nerve" — was laid open and quick as if Papa with a scalpel had folded back the flesh and flooding wads of gauze dammed the blood. I had never heard Corinne talk like that. None of us ever talked like that at all. Had I constructed an interior monologue for her — and that's what this surely was, for she kept looking toward the sky, fiddling with the ring as if we weren't there — I could never have caught the rhythm, the syntax, the observation, the puritan horror. I started toward her, but my father stopped me with the peremptory gesture of authority that I remembered from his youth — the hand jerked out, the fingers spread at the end of the slanting forearm while the upper arm was held stiffly to the suddenly rigid body. When he spoke it was softly, his voice full of love.

"It's all right, Corinne. It's all right. I'd tell you if it weren't. You've known that, you've always known that, haven't you?" She rolled her head slowly back and forth against the fabric of the deck chair. "It's a long time ago. A long time."

Of course I thought they were talking about Grandmama, and yet I knew they couldn't be. Corinne and I had spoken of it so often that it couldn't be that. She let her head fall forward, and not looking at either of us said, "Tell him, Uncle Doc. We were

just talking about being twenty. Tell the goddamned noticer."
There was a tiny giggle. Pure ex-Aunt Louise. I looked to my father and knew before he spoke.

"What Corinne means is that Edward was once her lover. It was
a very short time. But it was." My father's voice was deep with embarrassment.

"Tell him when. I want to get this over and I don't want any of
his" — she snorted—"indirect questions. I just don't want to cope."

"It was that time in Milan."

"But how could — "

"It was about a month. Corinne was supposed to go to Louise
at Cannes when we left for Greece the next day."

I remembered that this was right. "But we took her to the train."
The whistle now shrilling to pierce my ear, I couldn't be mistaken.
"The brown seal coat. The porters with straps shoving bags
through the carriage window. The steam rolling along the floor of
the train shed to be turned back by the walls. All of us waving and
you waving. Mother saying, 'I don't like letting her go off like that
alone.' "

"You could remember that all right. I had a brown seal coat.
The porters always had straps and shoved bags through the carriage
windows. And steam has rolled along the floors of sheds ever since
Monet, ever since *Anna Karenina*." Corinne looked from me to
Papa and went on. "You see. It's the detail he wants. The goddamned detail. Right this very minute, he's writing, you know.
It's what I can't stand. It's one thing to come to terms with it
myself, but to watch him struggle you'd have to have the eyes of
Edward's cat." She turned back to me. "It wasn't like that. Your
train left an hour before the one I was supposed to take. I never
took it. Edward and I saw you off, snooper, and we went to the
station hotel. For a description of that sylvan glade, see E. Heming-
way, *A Farewell to Arms*. Talk about the shock of recognition when
I read that two, three years later."

"Really?"

"Really." Corinne put the coffee cup on the lawn with elaborate
care, but, as she straightened up, her eyes caught mine which I had
cast down — I suppose to hide the surmise I could feel burning
there.

"There I was deflowered. You want the bloody sheets? I give

them to you with all my heart. And valets, not chambermaids, made up those rooms, in case you want to know. There I stayed for three weeks. Telegrams to my mother signed 'Doc.' " She looked to him tenderly. For all his fascination with the anatomical, the sheets would have hurt him.

"That part of it, honey, I always forgave." He looked at her as if she were still twenty.

"I'd keep telling myself that it was romantic and" — she hesitated — "free, for that was the word then. But it wasn't much fun. I found out what I wanted to find out, but when I went to hear him sing it wasn't in my white coat and your mother's diamonds in a box, but in my brown seal, way on the side of the orchestra. Even Christmas day, we didn't dare one of the big restaurants, and God how I wanted you all and laughing. All my presents had been sent to Cannes for me, and all I had was the little gold cupid with tiny sapphire eyes that he was so proud of giving me and which I ought to have loved but didn't. Remind me, I ought to give it to one of your girls, if you don't mind the wages of sin. I don't think I ever had any thought that we'd keep it up, and if I'm going to be fair I have to say that there was always 'the exact consideration for those who . . .' " She couldn't speak the words, "were dependent on me," but indicated them with a wave of the hand in a gesture once common with her but which I hadn't seen in years. Tenors were tenors, no matter how distinguished, and Corinne could not have learned in what was left of December that the descendants of robber barons were inferior by every rule of life and art except the one rule in which they were bred. For the first time since my father had brought the news, I felt sad for Edward. Not the Edward who had died old, but the Edward in Milan where he must have arrived at the "Maybe that's why she's fond of him. Because he doesn't need her."

My father half rose as if to stop Corinne from going any further, but she kept on. "No, Edward's dead now. He's got the right to whatever life you can give him. That was good, that Ah, Housman bit. That was me, of course, and his remembering me." There was a sharp quiver of her hand, but she went on. "Edward and Magda. The greatest Marschallin of them all because she didn't have to bother about being real."

She looked to my father, who said, "After the first, I never minded. When the first war was over, it was just one of the things I came back to. I never put it into words before, but I'm pretty sure she loved Papa — my papa — while he was alive, and she was good to him when he was blind. Afterward — well, if you're not young when you're young, I think you've got a right to be young sometime. At least that's the way I hope, I still keep hoping, it was." The two of us put out our hands to him at the same time, and he pressed them together between his own. "Mama never knew about Corinne. Your mother doesn't know, either. No one except me and now you."

He was still holding our hands, leaning forward to do so, when Corinne said quietly, "He'll want to know how I got caught, Uncle Doc."

"Same way everybody gets caught." He snorted. It was the sort of thing he loved about life, but he spread his hands, letting ours fall, and lay back in the chair.

It was Corinne who spoke. "I was pregnant, and I knew it soon after we got back to Paris. I tried to get money out of you. You had sixty bucks of Christmas loot, but you were hoarding it to spend at the Folies."

My father began to laugh. "Never knew that. Wonder we didn't run into each other, bud."

"Don't begin that. I want to get this over with. No loose ends. No questions ever. Understand?"

"Sure, Corinne, sure."

"I did get Gordie's money, and I had a couple of hundred of my own. But it wasn't money. It never really was money. I just got scared and lonely, and I went to your dad. He wasn't even shocked."

"I was. I was shocked to hell. But what good would that do? I just thought, 'if she trusts me so much, I'd better be worth the trusting.' "

"Oh, Doc. You were always worth the trusting, and you didn't act shocked." Corinne was quiet a minute and Papa knew and I knew just how much she had said. But then she turned to me and went on, "He set it up for a friend of his in Metz. A doctor he had known during the war."

"But I always intended to do it myself. I just had to have a place. The next time I was supposed to go to London, Corinne went with

me, and we went to Metz instead. I must say, I haven't been back
since. I'm sure no one there believed us and that they all thought
me damned lucky." He was grunting these things out, keeping, I
could see, a close watch on Corinne. "You sent me a postcard from
there once. House Rimbaud lived in or something. Wondered if
you knew, could have known, from Edward. Still have the card
under the glass on top of the desk in my office. Never heard of
Rimbaud in 1928–29; '29, by then. Certainly no plaque on a house.
Flower clock in the park."

"Edward never said anything." I thought they both should
know, and, although I wished he had told me, I was proud of him
in a way.

"You know, I think that was the trouble." Corinne was serious.
"He tried so hard to be a gent." My heart gave a thump. I loved
Corinne, and I didn't want her to say anything. I thought, "I can
keep her if she'll let me write the words for her, but, once she's
spoken, it'll be too late." Somewhere in *Tender Is the Night*, Baby
Warren says of Dick Diver something like this, "Let him do it. Why
shouldn't he? That's what we educated him for." After that I put
her permanently in the lowest circle of hell, and I knew — I suppose for the first time — what the lowest circle was for. Baby Warren's sin is a sin of the heart, not just a sin of manner, and I didn't
want Corinne to be guilty because with her guilt I would myself
be somehow involved. I didn't at all like the sound of "He tried so
hard to be a gent." It had the glitter of high cruelty about it, and
only when I put it against what she had said of Magda — "The
greatest Marschallin of them all because she didn't have to bother
about being real" — could I begin to forgive her. A great wave of
sorrow came over me then, and for the moment I lived the deep
loneliness of the svelte Corinne in the station hotel.

She must have been looking at me or have sensed in some way
what was going through my mind, for again in her '20s voice she
said, "I never told you this — not, I think, from modesty or shame,
but because I couldn't be sure. Couldn't be sure you wouldn't turn
it into some John O'Hara or Tennessee Williams crap." She looked
at me, the appraising eyes. "Or old Hank James. Keep your
damned omniscience to yourself. What I've said, I've said, and
that's all right. What happened, happened. Okay. But none of
your odorously imagined scenes. I am what I am, and I don't want
to be created. I don't — "

"Here are the kids," my father interrupted, and waved over his head to Bob, who had a girl by each hand and began to race down the slope to where we were. His legs were longer than theirs and the giant strides he took were too much for them, but they were laughing, jerked by one arm, the free arm flying high behind them. The girls stumbled just before they reached us, but he dragged them the rest of the way and pulled them together in a heap in front of us, saying, "Any ol' white slaves for sayul. Any ol' white slaves for say-ul?" He stood above them in laughter, his faded-blue polo shirt — we had called them necking shirts — moving with his breath, the jersey band tight and high around the surprising muscles of his upper arms. My eyes went to his feet — he was barefooted and in madras Bermudas — and I thought of my father and David's toenail. The girls had extricated themselves from their tumble and stood beside him, each with a negligent arm hooked to his shoulder in angular grace, their hair so shiny, their eyes alive with light, their perfectly cut lips moist and parted with the gladness of being alive. They too were in Bermudas, but with shirts of mine, the tails looped loose beneath their waists that Bob's enormous David's hands had risen to define. It was a handsome sight, a beautiful sight really in the sun of June, and it crossed my mind that it would be the new century nearly before they, like us, sat in deck chairs in the hollow to look upon the flesh of their now beautiful flesh, the bone of their deep-marrowed bone. A hundred years would separate them from Edward, who once burned a shepherd's fire against the chill of Tuscan dawns from twisted forks of olive wood. The flowers of spring that Edward had not seen when he had sung his boysweet song were gone forever now from all but palace walls, for the hills themselves were lighted day and night with the fantastic, gassy blooms of factory fires.

My father, I think, noticed how Bob's spread thumb caught the oxford cloth of Amy's shirt to outline her breast, because he said, "Isn't the old man going to get a kiss?" — and both the girls slipped away to make over him with exaggerated embraces.

"Poor old Papa" — they called him *Papa,* which left only *Daddy* for me, and often I felt a pang about it — "doesn't he know we have this thing for older men?"

"Not old. Mature."

"Devastating maturity. So sexy."

"Positively Chinese, the veneration."

"So it's not good for us to have you encourage what we fight all the time."

I could see Papa becoming restive under the barrage, and I was thinking of some way to stop it, but they themselves were sensitive to how far they could go. Amy slipped to his feet and sat there, leaning against his knees. "Little" Corinne, my older daughter, came over to me and sprawled upon the grass, looking up to Bob who stood now, feet apart, hands on his hip bones. Was it Tom Buchanan's "cruel" body? Was there such a thing as a cruel body? That bodies became cruel, I knew. And that they were cruel to you, too, I also knew. Was there something beyond the arrogance of beautiful twenty there on the green lawn? Did the three million next year and the rest when he was thirty inform his blood? He had become rich early, the only son of an only son who lay beneath the Coral Sea. It wasn't the mere appurtenances of money that he would have — we all had these — but the golden power itself. His grandfather, old Mr. Patterson, had literally shriveled away, but hadn't that been because he had never realized the aesthetic possibilities of power? There was a little click in my head as I phrased this. I thought, "Aha, Edward's error has trapped me." There are no "aesthetic possibilities" to power. He had supposed there were, and outside, looking in, it seemed as if there should be. I couldn't be poor, he had told me, because I could not imagine myself poor and would always cling to the idea that there were aesthetic possibilities in poverty. Well, even on my Uncle Harry's tower porch of arcaded marble, he had never once felt the loneliness of possession. He didn't, as Corinne said of Magda, have to bother with being real. The reality was outside of himself. Look at the way he denied his son, who called himself George Shearer. "George Shearer Associates," the sign said on the real estate office in Los Angeles and on signboards — TO LET, FOR SALE — all over Southern California. Edward was perfectly capable of quoting *"Mignonslied"*:

> *Kennst du das Land wo die Citronen blühn*
> *In dunkeln Laub die gold' Orangen glühn*

to me on the dusk of the porch with the half-dozen orange trees of the garden rich beneath us, while not two miles away the bulldozers were uprooting a grove once fair with blossoms, heavy with scent, globed with fruit, glossy leaved. It would never have occurred to

Edward to feel even an ironic responsibility for the billboard which said SHANGRI-LA, A NEW SHEARER DEVELOPMENT. Live Modern. Live Shearer. He had never felt within himself the scalding need to imagine his own son.

My own hand went then, compulsively I suppose, to my daughter's, my darling Corey's, hair, and I pulled the scalp together with my feeling fingers that remembered so well the soft spot and how they would touch it with a fuzzy sense of miracle just after she was born. In and out my fingers moved now, flexing, relaxing, pulling, releasing. She looked to me with thankfulness and said, "I'm utterly purring," but then her gaze went back to the Bermuda'd David.

"There be none of Beauty's daughters" began within my mind, and the fingers reflexively took up the beat in much the same way as when we were children Corinne would play the soundless pianos of our skinny spines, demanding that we tell her — from the fingering, the trills, the thump of the bass — which of her pieces it was.

" 'Turkish March'?"

"Nope, dope."

"Beethoven? Mozart? At least that much?"

"That's Beethoven." There'd be a wild arpeggio running up a back. A spate of triplets might be Mozart. "But it's not the 'Turkish March.' "

The kneading, needing fingers hardly seemed a part of me at all, but I was heavily conscious of a constriction in my heart and another rhythm alive there, beating in my chest, throbbing in my arm, beneath my wrist, quivering in the moisting palm of my hand. I felt it clot with tiny pain in my elbow as if protesting the physical return to the heart of the rhythm the fingers had denied. In a minute, I'd know, but I couldn't know yet. I let my fingers go limp in the sun-warm tangles of hair.

"More, Daddy, more."

Slowly, with silky insistence, the fingers coiled and then began "Sen-t-imen-t-al Journey." Oh, neoned navy town in war when jukebox trio whined the song through beaverboard of sad motel with slimy shower floor! Not even "motel," then, my elegant elder daughter. El Dixie Cabins Bar and Grill. It was there your mother and I went hot to your begetting. Our veins poured sweat in noisy heat of Florida that mid-July beneath the dusty rattle of a land-blown wind in parching palms. Terror-sweet those nights when each might be the last of all the nights forever in a world my bride made bright with arms, soft-curious hands, eyes, smiles, and slumberous depths of newly wakened voice.

Sen*t*-imen*t*-al Journey. With the increase of tempo in my fingers, the secondary syncopation disappeared, and I was back at El Dixie the night the drunken tires shrieked in skid on gravel. Neon expired with the dawn and on the chance that the high winds among the palms might now be blowing crouched along the ground toward the sea, I took the long, naked step toward the window to raise the shade and let the dewed air in. I stood there while it had its soft way with me — the *triste* of "Dover Beach," I suppose — but I was young and it wasn't very long. On my way to the window, I had had to shrink back from the chair that held my navy white dress jacket on its low back, but, to return, I rose on the ball of my left foot, raised my right thigh, and swung my muscled leg in an arc over the back of the chair. Whether it was this unremembered attitude of body, the rippling play of fresh-found muscles, the freeing amplitude of stretch in arc, or the fact that I was touched — stroked — from beneath by the braided shoulder mark of the coat in the descent of my leg, I don't suppose matters. I was as far on my way as if I had been continent a month by the time I reached the still moist heaven of the bed.

It was then the tires shrieked, the gravel ground, and headlights swept the room and bed from darkness. There was a wild, woman's drunken whoop from the car.

"Ride her, caowboy."

I dared not move. My own nakedness was the only possible shield for the bride who lay beneath me.

"Honk the horn. Gyoddamn it I wiul honk it." He evidently kept her from it because she began a tattoo on the echoing side of the car with a bottle. There was a brief struggle and the bottle broke. For a second he got the headlights out, and before she could get them on again I, pendulous, was able to get the sheet from the wad at our feet to cover us. Even our heads we covered.

"Come on, Darlene. The show's over. We'll get our own show on the road." The headlights were gone.

Both of the car doors lurched open, and she scooped up some gravel and threw it at our screen before he got hold of her. As he pulled her along her nails clawed the rusty wire mesh, and she bawled in ghastly Southern, "Hah hoe the day-re-oh, the farmer's in the dale."

My fingers were released from "Sentimental Journey," and Corey gave a contented shake of her head as I withdrew my hand. They had begun talking about Edward, and Papa was telling them, but I still had the last of the memory to deal with. Over the years the part I've told you so far became curiously tender and uniting to us. We'd laugh and grimace "Our Song" when the orchestra'd play "Sentimental Journey" at a dance, and once we had gone upstairs for a while in the middle of a children's party — say the girls were five and six and I had got home early to see it — so ironically sweet was the sight of "Farmer in the Dell." The part I tell you now I have never managed to mention, even to Mary. It is the last modesty between us, and it never really became a part of the shared memories of El Dixie. If I had mentioned it, I suppose it would have, or if she had picked it up I know I would have gone along. But neither of us ever did, and this in itself is significant. It only takes a moment to tell, although it has lasted all these years.

Twenty minutes, a half hour later we were lying there, the cracked shade pulled again, the heavy sheet thrown back. She had wept for a time with rage, and then it had been just weeping, but now she was quiet, although the sleep of exhaustion had not come. I had comforted her and become weak with love when I realized that in letting me comfort her she had sought to comfort me, but I don't think either of us had made any attempt in our minds to think about what had happened. What had happened, had happened. That was all. I have never been even tempted to construct interior monologues for us. The fumes of Citronella, the Mark Cross honeymoon luggage, the sand-worn Congoleum rug, the Betty Grable decal along the edge of the dresser mirror — I have the period props for all this, but somehow they make no difference. They aren't a part of it. If they had been I would have planted them a while back without knowing it really, and they would be here now. But all there was, all there is, is a voice and the words it spoke.

The voice was the voice of the man from the car who had dragged the screaming Southern bitch from our window. He had returned to the car for something, but on his way back to their cabin he stopped, a shadow on the shade, for the sudden sun had risen behind him with morning. In the moment he stood there, he spoke, spoke with such resonance that the high absurdity of the situation became something more than comic. For all our never having spoken of him, I know Mary heard him too. Her little, rich-girl's hand, cupped loose in mine, trembled in reverberation. We were lesser mortals than he if afterward all we could bear to remember aloud had to wear the mask of comedy, for "How hairy thighed, the gold-braid lies" was what the voice said — clearly, distinctly, incredibly in the accents of verse. Slowly, silently, for all these years, we have let it lick away at our lollypop hearts.

It is not easy for me to write because writing, Edward taught me, meant turning myself out of house, home, skin. Having written, I trembled naked waiting for the reader to breathe — Edward's lungs, I need — my words for me. That mirror-up-to-nature business won't do, and although I have experimented with nut-house mirrors wildly skewed, the most they achieve is a single point. Henry James's figure-in-the-carpet might serve, except that in examining the figure or any one of the figures, or even the happiest conjunction of one with another, the shimmer of life, continuing life that gives the carpet sheen, is gone. Narration, like history, cannot be imprisoned except conventionally within an arbitrary beginning, middle, and end. When it is, it is no longer felt, warmed by the curious heart's blood, but merely perceived by a single, Cyclops eye. I was thankful as I sat there that day in June that I heard Amy say when they were talking of Edward's death, "Rudolph Bing will send an orchid wreath. And Magda, I think, sad-foolish flower swan. White rosebuds. Greenish. Wired stiff."

It might have been I who spoke, but just as clear to me was the counterpoint of Edward's treble voice soaring in a Tuscany I knew was gone. A third voice entered then, the voice of the man in the car. It came back now under the chestnut blue with shadows — a bass, if I were telling the story to Edward, as indeed I am — the voice of the ghost of the Commendatore, the Statue come to dine with the unrepentant Don.

DANIEL CURLEY

A Story of Love, Etc.

(FROM EPOCH)

I WAS thinking about the Depression and discovered things had
gone so far that even I could scarcely believe there had ever been
such a time. I found myself wondering if maybe I hadn't read it
all in something by Chekhov or Gogol or Dostoyevsky.

I was thinking about the story of How Father Lost the Store,
which is a story everybody knows, and about How I Lost All My
Teeth at the Age of Twenty-five, which isn't really a story at all but
a kind of blackout tableau, a quick dark hole in the face. Did you
ever notice, by the way, how Chekhov's peasants always seemed to
have plenty of teeth for whatever black bread they got? That's
remarkable, isn't it?

But I was thinking about these things only as a warm-up for
thinking about Bill and Ellie Martin, which is something I take
on from time to time when I feel particularly strong.

Now, what I know is this. Bill Martin was a master carpenter,
and if there was work he got it. He was sent for from all over —
when there was work. Mostly there was no work. He was the only
man for counties around who could hang a spiral staircase the way
they did in the old New England houses. Things like that. He
learned his trade from Ellie's father, old Charlie Grant, who before he went totally blind used to be the man who was sent for.

Old Charlie went blind over a number of years, and he would
grope his way to the ten-cent store from time to time to find a pair
of glasses he could see with, but that may be another story, and we
see him here only as a neat old man sitting in his daughter's
kitchen, listening to the ball game on the radio and god-damning

just about everyone he ever worked for, all those bastards who got
rich while he wore out his sight and cut off his fingers and laid
down in his bones a reserve of aches to last him to the grave. So there
he sits, a noise in the background, but a man of sweet disposition —
except on one or two subjects — a man who would be indignant if
he suspected anyone had ever found in him the least resemblance to
any of those stinking Reds.

Still, he crept in by way of the hanging staircase, which was no
longer of any practical use to him nor for that matter was Bill Martin making much on it either in those days, as you can well imagine.
Bill was lucky if he got a few days' work patching a roof for somebody who had been too poor in the beginning to have his chimney
fixed so it wouldn't fall through his roof. Bill would fix the chimney while he was at it, and if any wiring had been carried away in
the avalanche, he'd set that right too — that is, if the power was still
on in the house, for everything comes back to the fact that it was
then the Depression.

They all lived together in a house they themselves had built. It
was a very good house. If God had been heard muttering in the
night, "My wrath be upon the town so that one house and one only
shall remain standing," we would all have crowded into Bill Martin's house because everyone knew that Bill Martin's house would
be the house to withstand floods, earthquakes, and tornadoes of
divine wrath. Those men built like that.

Old Charlie, who was no more a dirty atheist than he was a stinking Red, had often been heard to say after a few beers, "Heaven and
earth shall pass away but my work shall not pass away." A learned
man might call that blasphemy but he would be wrong. Charlie
had no desire to usurp the powers of God. He had powers of his
own and he knew his powers and he found them good.

And Bill learned carpentry from him. And Bill also knew his
own worth and the worth of his work, but he was in no way given to
rhetoric. Perhaps if he had been given to rhetoric this story would
have been different, not the meaning, I should say, but the events.

Bill was a good man and he saved money when he was working.
Charlie had saved too in his day, and when he had to come to live
with Bill and Ellie he made them take him to the bank, and he
drew out all his savings. He put the money in their hands and said,
"When this is gone, I guess you'll have to shoot me."

"First thing I'll do with the money is buy a gun," Bill said. Charlie knew exactly what he meant, and Ellie knew exactly what he meant, and even the bank teller — that was Roger Ames, by the way, the same that is now president of the bank — even the teller knew what he meant, but Bill himself didn't know. The words frightened him. He was a very serious man. First thing in the morning he took the money to the bank and put it back in Charlie's account. Charlie never learned about that — and a good thing too, because he wouldn't have stood for it. He was a serious man himself and only the rhetoric made it look otherwise. This is something Bill never quite understood.

Charlie wouldn't have stood for it because he would literally rather have died than consider himself beholden to anyone. Bill ought to have known this because he was the same way himself. On the other hand perhaps this is exactly what he did know and mean to make manifest (darkly) by putting the money back in the bank just in case something should happen to him and Ellie.

Bill's savings lasted a long time. A man who is prudent about saving is also likely to be prudent about spending his savings. Nobody was hungry but everything was careful. Bill and Ellie planted a big garden, and Ellie canned everything she could get her hands on. They ate a lot of dandelion greens and wild berries. Bill fished day after day, and while he fished he invented details of jobs to tell Charlie about, because Charlie thought he was working pretty regularly. When he told Charlie about these jobs Charlie would nod and say, "That's right, you did exactly right." There was nothing else he could say, because, of course, Bill had learned everything he knew from Charlie. And it was good.

What is easy to suppose is that there came a time when prudence was no longer enough. At least I've never met anybody who claimed he got through the Depression on his savings. Berries, greens, and fish are all very well, but they don't heat the house or put shoes on anybody's feet, and in these parts furs from muskrats, skunks, and rabbits don't make much of a money crop either. They barely kept Charlie in pipe tobacco. Bill gave up smoking. Doctor's orders, he said, the same explanation he gave for the way they were eating, although actually they were still eating pretty well. They even had meat on the table a lot of the time, because the garden really outdid itself and produced a rabbit almost every week and pheasants when the tomatoes were ripe and once in a very great while a deer. But there was no way the garden could grow any cash because everyone else had a garden too. So it is quite clear that the savings must have given out.

About now somebody is sure to bring up the matter of Charlie's savings although I don't quite see why. It seemed to me that I had made it clear that Bill was a serious man.

There is also the matter of relief. Everyone was on relief, so what's the harm? That's the way the logic runs. But you can't have been listening very carefully if you haven't heard old Charlie say, "I will not be beholden to any man," and "When this is gone, I guess you'll have to shoot me." And of course you haven't heard tell, as I have many a time, how Bill Martin walked off the schoolhouse job, saying to the assembled School Board and the Selectmen and the General Contractor, "I don't kiss anybody's ass." In the evening Charlie said, "You did exactly right," although that was a job that would have seen them through a hard winter.

In the end what's so hard to believe, perhaps, is the fact that deep into the twentieth century there were two men who fundamentally lived by such incredible slogans as All men are created equal and A man's house is his castle and Death before dishonor — at least that's how I translate the remarks of both men. This is what makes the story difficult — that there were two such men. And a woman.

It must have been pretty obvious that I wasn't saying much about the woman. There was good reason for it, believe me, very good reason. What I was talking about before was what I knew and what I could suppose without much trouble. If thinking about how Father lost the store and how I lost my teeth is a warm-up for thinking about Charlie and Bill, then thinking about Charlie and Bill is no more than a warm-up for thinking about Ellie, because there is a good chance that she turned out to be the most serious of the lot.

She didn't have Charlie's rhetoric and she didn't have Bill's silence. She sang in the house and she sang in the garden. There were those who said her house was no cleaner than it ought to be, but no woman in town ever got out of sickbed or childbed to find her house the worse for Ellie's having stepped in for a few days or a few weeks. The children weren't even spoiled although it was commonly agreed that Ellie liked to be in a house where there were children. Those were innocent old times so nobody found anything nasty in Ellie's loving the children she couldn't have, and they were quite right. Probably if Charlie and Bill and Ellie had known about *Honi soit qui mal y pense,* they would have believed in that too.

As for Ellie's gardening, it must be said that whatever she planted came up. It prospered and multiplied. She scattered seeds about and sang. She pulled a weed and sat in the sun on a little stool and sang, and whatever she planted came up. This is not in the least to be considered proof of anything at all, because whatever Bill planted came up too, and he had been known, when it came planting time, to go to his toolbox and get a piece of string and a piece of chalk and then chalk the string and solemnly snap a line on the ground as if he were getting ready to put up a partition or lay a course of shingles.

They must have seen the moment coming for a long time, but Ellie went on singing — at least in the house — and Bill went on fishing and telling Charlie about the cabinet work he was doing in the high school principal's house. That was work that had actually been talked of at one time, although nothing ever came of it, which is a great pity, because Bill wasn't under pressure of any other work and made a very fine thing of it, a thing the principal could have sold the next day to any solvent museum in the country. Charlie, of course, saw it and felt it and smelt it and said, "That's right, Bill, that's just right."

Probably the moment was put off more than once by a day's work here and there. For instance, I can remember about then seeing Bill at work on a simple set of steps for Roger Ames when his big old porch fell off and left his side door six feet in the air. You can be as sure as you can ever be of anything you haven't seen with your own eyes that was one job Bill got paid for.

But the moment must have come at last when there not only wasn't any money in the house but there wasn't any gas in Bill's Model A pickup truck so that even if he did get a chance to work he wouldn't have been able to get to wherever the work was. Yes, there must have been that moment. Both knowledge and imagination insist there must have been that moment.

The trouble is, however, that the moment has no scene. Obviously it must have had a scene. Perhaps in bed late at night or down at the end of the garden. Perhaps in the truck with the rain drumming on the garage roof.

The trouble is that the scene has no dialogue. Bill never did have much to say, and this must have been one time Ellie wasn't singing. Still, there must have been dialogue. Ellie must have said something and she must have found some way of making Bill agree, because another fact begins to loom up ahead, a fact to be approached by way of the imagination, which at least gives us the last bit of dialogue in the hidden scene, a line to be said by either of them or both, together or alone: "It's not right, it's just not right."

The fact we have arrived at has plenty of scene, and it tells us that in the town there lived — or had lived — a boy fortunate beyond the men of his time. He had a job. From seven in the evening to seven in the morning he worked in a restaurant in a nearby city, every night without fail. He washed and polished and scrubbed and cleaned and cooked a little too and had every night a belly full of broken meats. He had a place to sleep back by the storeroom, a clean uniform every night, and even a few dollars every week to put in his pocket. There was no reason why he should be singled out for prosperity. His prosperity was simply a fact, but it isn't that fact we are getting to.

The boy himself isn't the fact either. He is simply a part of the scene like a tree on a stage when there must be apples or a park bench when there must be love or a murder. The rest of the scene includes the usual cheap restaurant sort of thing: a counter with stools, some tables and chairs, some slogans like WATCH YOUR COAT AND HAT and IN GOD WE TRUST ALL OTHERS PAY CASH. There is also a big window that looks out on a shabby street, the kind of street that runs parallel to Main Street in towns just big enough for one big street.

One night just as the boy was settling into his routine, he looked out the window and saw pulling up to the curb a Model A pickup truck he'd have known in a million. His heart suddenly burned within him because it had been a long time since he had gone home for a visit, short as the distance was. He was about to run into the street when he observed that as Ellie climbed down from the truck she was crying. He hesitated.

Then he did run into the street although there were surely a thousand men within range of a shout who would have been quite willing to work from seven to seven every night without fail, eat broken meats, share a place near the storeroom with rats, and never once run into the street. This is not to say he felt himself ill-used.

At the time he was as aware as any of the other thousand of his good fortune. Later he came to believe that his good fortune had kept him from discovering a lot that gradually loomed up as desirable knowledge. Things like what he would have done if he hadn't had that job. Would he have gone on relief? If so, what would have happened to his character? How, finally, would he have been able to come in the end to say, "That's right, that's just right, I was never beholden to any man"? He seems to have been another serious one. Perhaps everybody was serious in those days.

When he ran into the street, however, he wasn't thinking of discovery or anything like that. He ran because he had to, and then he did what he had to do next, thinking only years later how it might have looked if he had been caught. He stalked Bill and Ellie like a birdwatcher, like a boy birdwatcher.

He wasn't close enough to hear if they spoke, but they didn't seem to be speaking. They walked close together without touching, but there was nothing to suggest there had been a quarrel. Quite the contrary. Under a street light Ellie made Bill stop while she wiped something off his face. Just the way they stood together suggested she was wiping off lipstick.

He followed them until they stopped in front of a movie theater. Bill stepped up to the ticket window. Ellie waited to one side, and the boy waited at a distance. He was ready to go back to the restaurant. He was baffled but by no means as baffled yet as he was going to be, for when he expected them to go into the theater together they exchanged a look and parted. Bill went into the theater and Ellie continued along the street.

In his mind he gave up his job and followed her. It turned out that he didn't lose his job because he had friends in the restaurant who covered for him. He hadn't thought of that. He had done favors for them in the past but had never been repaid because he had never before thought of anything he wanted.

He hadn't followed her a block when a man stopped her and began to talk. Soon the man was wiping her face gently with his handkerchief, and they went on together. They went around a corner and into the Hotel Bazaar, a shabby building whose hidden splendor used to torment the boy as he lay listening to the secrets of rats in the wall. He peeped through the lobby window until Ellie and the man disappeared into the elevator. Then he ran back to work.

Each night for a week he followed. Each night it was exactly the

same: tears, silence, movies, the Hotel Bazaar. Each night the Model
A truck disappeared at some moment when he was engaged in a
frenzy of washing and scrubbing and polishing and cleaning. He
would look out and it would be gone.

So he began counting his money by day. At last, disguising his
voice, he called the Hotel Bazaar and inquired the price of a room,
double. At work he cleverly led conversations into channels where
he picked up invaluable concepts of value: two-dollar job, five buck
deluxe. He counted his money and asked for a night off.

To his own amazement, however, he found himself buying a
movie ticket and following Bill into the theater. All night he
watched from the dark how a red exit light dimly illumined one
side of Bill's face and made a thin red shine that remained constant
through both the tear jerker and the comedy. When Ellie came and
found Bill and they went out together, the boy did not follow.

But there was still one thing he had to know, so he traded shifts
with a man who had some desperation of his own, and he went
home for a day. He cleverly listened and led, and he found that
Ellie still came in for a few days or a few weeks when there was trouble and children were still loved but not spoiled, that Bill still fished,
that Charlie still smoked his pipe and listened to the ball game.
Although it meant a two-mile walk in each direction, he passed the
house and heard with his own ears that Ellie still sang in the kitchen.
When he went back to work, he left all his spare cash for his parents.

Shortly after this there began to be more work, and the Model A
stopped coming into the city. The boy went on to other things and
with the passage of time became, I suppose, a man, but there was no
passage of time that could save him from a memory. Let him only
come across a Model A, an exit lamp, a certain song, a woman's
name, and once again he felt the anguish of a thing he had only
thought and never done, that no other person had ever known, fresh
and sharp as the moment when he had first seen himself for what he
was, neither better nor worse, probably, than most people, who certainly, when you come to think of it, do far less evil than they might.

As for Ellie, very likely all this makes her a whore except, as I said
at the beginning, it all seems like a Russian novel; and everybody
knows that in the Russian Novel Sonia Marmeladov, who is a whore,
is also Jesus Christ crucified and saving the world. And if there are
springs of Grace in the Russian Novel great enough to accomplish

this mystery, I, for one, can't see why I shouldn't hope that our life, too, springs eternal with power to save Ellie — who also saves — and I think I can even hope there will be Grace for Bill, or what's the point of it all anyway? And finally for the boy, who found himself not to be so serious as he had hoped, I can at least pray although surely it must be that our trespasses are not forgivable except in the perpetual blood of a lamb.

MAY DIKEMAN

The Woman Across the Street

(FROM THE ATLANTIC MONTHLY)

"SOMEBODY IS TRYING to get me" sounded too wild for Rachel to say even to herself, much less tell anyone, least of all write home to her panicky, all-female family who lived on the outskirts of Boston.

But this was the third night it had happened. Someone was standing in the hall outside the door to her apartment. She knew he was there by the slight creak on the tile as he shifted his weight, a swallowed cough, and the blotting of the crack of light that showed along the side of her door. Three times now since she had come to New York he had stood there, with just enough time lapse in between for her almost to put it out of her mind.

She looked at the clock. It was twenty minutes to eleven. She had just washed her hair, which she did every other night for her job as a college-shop floor model. She had been sitting rubbing it with a towel. Now a drop ran down her spine inside her terry robe, but she caught the shiver it gave her in order to hold herself motionless, as if she could defeat the purpose of the man outside by getting rid of herself.

She always felt less vulnerable close to the door, even with the man on the other side of it, and she drew herself together to get up and slip barefoot into the foyer. But just as she put her foot to the floor, she saw the doorknob slowly turn. It was an old, oval brass knob outlined with a wreath of hammered protuberances like beads, and its normal position was horizontal. As Rachel watched, without moving, the blade of light on the knob turned clockwise till nearly vertical, as if aimed. For the first time, the man was trying her door.

The turning knob made no sound, but the quiet became pulsatile like a metronome. The thought of the things that other people, strident, righteously deadpan New York people, would do — call the police, demand through the door, "Who's there?" — seemed as jeeringly remote as the drone of the bus down on Third Avenue, only sealing her isolation. She looked at the telephone, she imagined her voice calling "Who's there?" But what good would it do? She could not get a man locked up for life on her charge that he had tried her door. Once challenged, he would be her enemy. She felt safer as long as he didn't know she knew, as long as he stayed unidentified. "I'm afraid of vengeance!" her elderly mother always said of any neighborhood trouble, as she might have said she was afraid of infection, and this phobia about vengeance seemed to thicken the air with another element, more noxious because it was unspecified and humanly motivated.

At a quarter to eleven, the man went away. His step was so easy that Rachel could not be certain whether he went down or up the stairs.

She felt it had to be the superintendent. Rachel was contentiously tolerant, and her letters home suggested that all her New York acquaintances were Puerto Ricans with Ph.D.'s. But actually she was afraid of opaque skin, tapered, high-instepped male feet in counterless shoes, and the risqué music of Spanish. Once, as he brought her up in the tarnished-gilt manual elevator, which, like the rest of the building, had been ornate and showed stages of decline through paint parings and detached egg and dart, the superintendent touched her elbow, shrugged invitingly, and said, "My wife says she wants a divorce." And in her fright, Rachel almost said, "But I'm terribly pro Puerto Rican!"

Still, just because the case against the superintendent seemed strong, Rachel knew it might be someone else. Growing up seemed to her to have been chiefly learning that inevitability meant the loopholes in it — mystery gifts never came from the right person, and betrayals came not from the suspect but from the friend.

She thought of the other men tenants in the building, about whom she had written home very literarily funny letters. She thought of Good Joe, so-called, although he was a lawyer named Maurice Fischer, because he liked to be called Joe and because of his continual petty good works in the neighborhood. If it suddenly rained, Joe was seen helping the newsstand man hoist his tarpaulin. When a driver parked, Joe stood in the street shouting, "Cut your wheel! You're OK. Cut your wheel!"

She thought of bald Mr. Einstein, upstairs, who composed scores for juvenile productions. Banging on his piano, he would sing in a hoarse, terrible bass, "I don't want to play today, I don't want to play; I take my dolls and go away," or "Raumschlager, raumschlager, scared to come out!"

Only by improbability itself could it be one of these people. But the possibility now blighted Rachel's jokes about them in her letters home, and peopling letters with mad characters was the only real company she had.

As for the store where she modeled, there was Bill, the photographer, a sullen clown in a Tyrolean hat, who seldom uttered anything but onomatopoeic comments like "Whoosh!" when she or another model swept past him. And there were the two window dressers, Harold and Schuyler, who were queer.

It seemed to leave only the superintendent. But by its contraction, the shadow of a doubt saturated to a pall over each of the others. The embarrassment, if it were one of the unlikely ones, seemed more terrible than real danger. What if it were Good Joe? "Good evening, how do you do, I was trying to fix your doorknob for you, it's a fire violation." Or Mr. Einstein? Would he sing, "Raumschlager, raumschlager, scared to come out"? In reaction from the fright, Rachel felt light-headedly gay and started to giggle to herself. Then the very fact that, like many lonely people, she often made up things to laugh at reminded her that when she was a gangling, solidly red-haired child, everyone had let her alone for a waif. Now that undulations in her height and hair color had transformed her into a flintily delicate beauty, photographing as shell chips of cheekbones and shoulder blades, they still let her alone for a snob, except when they did worse. Even her name had not been the result of the modern caprice by which girls were named Rebecca, Melissa, and Jennifer. She was named Rachel in naïve good faith, for her grandmother and the Bible. You're a *real* Rachel, she thought, not a piquant Rachel, and it would be easier if everybody still thought so and thought you were too weird instead of too "stunning."

She started to cry to herself in outrage as she brushed her hair in front of the mirror, and the electricity of the hair and the tears in her gray eyes reminded her of how Harold the window dresser had hugged his chest, shuddering, as he exclaimed, "But, darling, only the *absurdity* of such beauty saves one from its *terror*." She thought, only queers dare to say things to me. She threw down her brush and went over to the window.

Brought very close by the stereoptican effect, the lit-up window across the street showed the young couple whom Rachel often saw this way. Week nights, they were sloppy. Husband-and-wife jeans, thought Rachel. The boy was lounging on the bed, with one ankle crossed on his knee. He was in sock feet. By the precision of surmise with which one divines details in a stained-glass picture, Rachel knew the socks were Argyles. His wife would have knitted them. She was sitting upright, fondling his foot as they talked. Give his foot one more twist, thought Rachel, and it'll come unscrewed. Then you can unscrew his head. They would be discussing what to name their planned, spaced children when they had them: Rebecca, Melissa, and, of course, Rachel.

Both of them had a lot of black hair. This made the boy seem a poet. On the woman, the fluffed effect looked as if a beautician had told her it would shorten her nose. Rachel saw her as a little thick in the middle, with too-tapering legs, a girl who would sign "Save Bleecker Street" petitions, cook with basil, study folk dancing at the New School, and have read an editorial apropos of anything said to her.

Why should you have an Argyle ankle to hold? thought Rachel. Why should it be candles on the table for you, and somebody always breathing next to you?

Jealousy restored Rachel. Her hands were warm and steady as she set her clock and laid out her things for the morning. She checked the lock and chain on her door again, set a chair under the knob as an extra precaution, and screwed the bolt on her fire-escape window a little deeper into the sash. Actually, she was perfectly safe. Nobody could get in as long as she was all locked up, and of course she would always be sure she was.

When she lay back in her bed, the lit-up window of the young couple was out of her sight. But she still thought about them. Tomorrow night would be Friday, so the woman would suddenly be in black and pearls, holding a glass and pressing the flat of her hand to her scoop neck in protesting social hilarity ("Oh, *no!*"), and there would be too many people to distinguish the husband at all. The next night, Saturday, the window would stay dark. Saturdays they went out themselves. On Sunday they would give a party again, a cocktail party. Monday, and through the work week, they would be back in jeans, talking. I suppose it's my New England conscience, Rachel said to the imaginary husband she conjured up to talk about other people to, but where does this lead? Her imaginary husband agreed that it seemed a meaningless life.

And having made their happiness seem their delusion, Rachel forgave them and got to sleep.

A few weeks later, Rachel went to a movie by herself and got home later than she expected. It was a paint-water pink night, threatening rain, with tree shapes of mist cowering in the street. Rachel's building had a porte-cochere effect in front, casting a pit of darkness of which every gradation was a lurking man. The entrance looked like a trap no one could get through. Then Rachel saw the superintendent, with his back to her, rolling the cans into their formation at the area railing. He went down the steps into the basement. This was her chance. She dashed into the house and ran up the stairs, taking out her apartment key as she went.

On her own landing, just as she started to put her key into her door, she became aware that someone was waiting on the landing above her. She turned to run back down the stairs. But before she could take a step, the lights in the hall were blotted out momentarily by something like a flying monster bird. She screamed wildly. The man had jumped down the whole flight of stairs onto her. Pain shot through her like electric shock as her kneecap hit the tile floor. She thought he had stabbed her, and she felt hot and oozing in the middle as if she were bleeding. She screamed the name of a woman neighbor whom she hardly knew. "Mrs. Hoffman!" she screamed. "Mrs. Hoffman, Mrs. Hoffman!"

Doors crashed and echoing voices filled the stairwell. Terrible apparitions like gigantic mechanical baby dolls or bunnies, with big springs come loose from their heads, the women tenants in nightclothes and hair rollers, armed with pop bottles, all lunged for the man.

Rachel caught one flash of his face before he escaped. He was young. He had a lot of black hair, like a poet. As he dived for the stairs, she looked down and saw, as she knew she would, the Argyle socks of the husband across the street.

"Stop him!" yelled the women, thundering down the stairs after the man. Rachel was put on someone's red-painted kitchen chair underneath an ivy-planter wall clock. A woman wet her forehead and started braiding her hair tightly. More to avoid having her hair braided than anything else, Rachel said she wanted to join the chase. "I'll need to identify him," she said. "I'm all right, I'm all right."

The tenants, all eager to go, were easy to persuade. The hall was full of broken bottles. On every third step, Rachel saw a big drop of blood.

The superintendent came out of his apartment with no shirt on, his tragic eye-whites suppliant for any news he could deplore. Why, he's a sweet little man, thought Rachel. He has a crucifix on.

The evening had come to life in a drizzle that ignited the streets, with Christmas balls and stars shining in the macadam. Rachel was swept along by two sturdy women in toggle coats over their flannel pajamas, who told her repeatedly, "Just so he didn't *harm* you." Sirens rose like a serenade, and the rain fused the lights of Second Avenue to a beacon. Rachel had never seen New York so beautiful.

Three women neighbors came out of the big hospital at the corner, hauling Rachel's attacker, the young husband who lived in the apartment across the street. They had caught up with him as he tried to hide in a phone booth of the hospital lobby.

Standing at a safe distance on the far side of the Avenue, Good Joe, neatly dressed, with his checked wool scarf and fedora on, called, "Have you got him, girls?" The officers getting out of the police cars and the women howled with laughter.

Just before the police put him in the car, the man turned to Rachel. Thickened blood like paint was coming out of his black hair where the bottles had cracked his head. "I didn't do anything to you, did I?" he said to her, in an entreating, boyish voice.

An hour after she had signed at the hospital that she refused treatment, Rachel's body started to throb all over. Besides the bruises that showed, she had a pain in one breast and she found that when she flexed her knees or lowered her head, a sharp pain paralyzed her spine. The neighbors had stayed with her, vying with each other in offerings of tea, sherry, and soup, laughing at Good Joe, who had gone promptly to the prisoner's wife to offer his legal services and returned home to report to them, "I can't make out why that fellow should want to do it. He's got a wife who's a good-looking girl. Not strikingly gorgeous like yourself, but she's not bad!" "He's sick!" Mrs. Hoffman explained to the lawyer.

The neighbors now insisted on taking Rachel back to the hospital. "Anything with the breast I don't like," said one. They went and got a cab, and two of the women, still in pajamas and toggle coats, rode with her. Mrs. Hoffman promised to call the store for Rachel in the morning.

In the emergency ward, a doctor fingered Rachel's breast and spine at great length, then said, "I can't tell anything by manual examination." Rachel said, "Well, Doctor, it was a terribly good try." She had never said anything like that before, and never heard such applauding laughter.

Rachel was admitted to the hospital for observation and had the best time she had ever had in her life. When she was in bed, nobody could tell how tall she was, five-ten. They could only see her face. Everybody said over and over that it was good he hadn't "harmed" her, and she realized that having just escaped "harm" made her more desirable than anything else that could possibly have happened to her. The doctors grouped around her bed and said to each other, "You know, I don't blame that guy!" Rachel giggled chidingly in a way she never had before and told them to wait till she was back on her feet and they found out she was six-foot-three. The house doctor said if she were his girl, he'd never let her get on her feet. One doctor added musingly, "I love the name Rachel."

The store sent flowers. A buyer, wearing what appeared to be a fresh pineapple in her hat, came and told her, "Usually they only do it for a death!" Her floorwalker and her section manager came with gifts from the store, expressing thankfulness that she hadn't been "harmed," and Snookie, the junior-sizes model, brought her a black velvet halter hostess gown she had admired, bought with the 40 percent discount, but still expensive. "I knew you liked it," Snookie repeated, contentedly. "So I figured, what the hell."

Bill the photographer came in, saying "Wheee!", with his wife, Billie, who brought a mason jar of her bean and barley soup, which she said was "binding," and a kit packed with a week's supply of every possible cosmetic, including dry shampoo.

Best of all, Harold and Schuyler, the queer window dressers, came bearing a replica of the store, complete with awning and customers going in (one recognizable as an eccentric rich old lady who wore sneakers and prodded the models in the stomach with her umbrella), made entirely of flowers. While the patients on the floor flashed their lights frantically, the whole hospital staff congregated in Ra-

chel's room to admire Harold and Schuyler's flower department
store. "Schuy never stopped wiring mums all *night*," Harold boasted
fondly, hiccuping with pride. "I spoon-fed him vodka till dawn."

The neighbors also visited and reported that Rachel's attacker had
been committed to someplace upstate, while Good Joe remained
nonplussed that the attacker had had a wife who was "not bad" right
in his own home.

Rachel's X-rays didn't show anything, and she was discharged.
But even when she was back on her feet, taller in heels than many
of the men, nobody seemed afraid of her and she was not afraid of
them. She joked with Good Joe, and when she heard Mr. Einstein
howling his children's songs, she laughed and laughed. The superintendent still told her, shrugging seductively, that his wife wanted a
divorce, but she told him firmly that he must preserve his marriage
for the sake of the children, and he subsided with a disappointed air.

But in the apartment across the street, everything was changed.
The first night Rachel glanced from her window, she thought the
wife was getting ready to move, which seemed natural enough.
Everything seemed dumped out over everything. A heap of clothes
or bedding or curtains was over the big chair, with a big green thing,
possibly a cotton shag rug, draped on top. The ironing board, with
another mountain of things on it, stayed up in the middle of the
room. What had been walnut cantilever bookshelves had become
catchalls for boxes and laundry, with stockings hanging.

But as time passed, the woman never packed. The heaps of things
only rose higher. The bed was never made. Apparently it was never
even changed. It seemed that the woman was going to go on living
there, by herself, but had stopped doing anything at all. The kitch-
enette of the one-room studio, also visible through the window, was
a stack of pots, dishes, and rags. The whole place was like a giant
laundry hamper. The woman lay most of the time on the unmade
bed. She always had on a speckly black thing that looked as if it
were made of quilting, stiffened by soil. When the woman occasionally sat in the chair holding a magazine, all Rachel could see of her
was one hand flicking a cigarette and a bare foot jerking a loose
mule.

Rachel decided to give a party, her first party, a small one, and
asked Snookie, Bill and Billie, and Harold and Schuyler.

She had been in New York long enough now to know her way

around with sour cream, chervil, artichoke hearts, and vodka. The night of the party, after she had her casserole sprinkled with Parmesan and ready to run under the broiler, the avocados mashed for the dip, and the spray of eucalyptus poised to cast an Oriental shadow on her single dramatic vermilion wall, and had put on her black halter hostess gown, she was so happy that tears came into her throat. She knew that her life was not factually changed and might never be, but she felt that she could stand for years posed ready to run casseroles under the broiler in a perpetual glossy print of purest hospitality, even if nobody came for the rest of her life.

But everybody came, and everybody gave themselves completely to the party. Snookie praised the yummy dip and the yummy vermilion wall. Bill sat on the rug saying "Swoosh!" when Rachel's skirt accidentally swept his head, and Billie attributed long stories to him while everybody stared at him, trying to picture him telling these stories. Harold and Schuyler had apparently had a minor tiff due to one of them accusing the other of Trotskyist tendencies, but when Schuyler took off his loafers and skipped softly around the room singing, from *Greensleeves,* "Alas, my love, you do me wrong, to treat me thus discourt'ously, when I have lov-ed you so long — ", it was evident that Harold had melted. ("They're kind of cute," Snookie said, and Billie said, "They are cute. I mean, they are darlings. I feel, who are we to judge?") Billie told freakish narrow-escape stories, such as that of a man nearly catching a woman's ice skate in his cornea on the subway. Schuyler leaped to the radiator-cover top and sang, "I did but see her passing by, and yet her ice skate gouged my eye," and Billie was not offended.

Even the neighbors cooperated unconsciously in the party spirit. Good Joe came up to ask Rachel if her water pressure was troubling her, and Mr. Einstein sang ferociously that he would take his dolls and go away, and challenged his raumschlager to come out. Schuyler said, "How neo-Humperdinck!"

The neighbor business led to their talking about the woman across the street. They all went over to the window and looked.

"Housekeepingwise, she is in mighty bad shape," said Billie.

"What I can't figure out is what is that big green thing on the chair?" said Rachel. She felt guilty, but the woman didn't know. The woman had not been able to keep her own husband away from Rachel, and now she was a conversation piece at Rachel's party, but she couldn't know, and it couldn't hurt her. And they had all had enough vodka so that anything they did seemed cauterized of malice.

"Oof!" said Bill.

"She should pull herself *together!*" said Snookie.

"Psychologywise, she should take herself in hand," said Billie.

"The green thing is a sleeping bag!" said Schuyler. "She's camping in."

"The voyeur looks into the mirror, merely," said Harold. "What is that big green thing? What, what is that big green thing at the vortex of my being?"

"She sure has let herself go," said Snookie.

"*Floom!*" said Bill.

"She should take up something," said Billie.

"She could pluck chenilles with tweezers!" said Schuyler. "Chenille by chenille she could pluck, in patterns! Wait. I have a marvelous idea. Billie, may I borrow your brooch? Rachel, may I pierce your coasters?"

"Schuy is opthalmologically sound," said Harold, belching. "A pinhole reduces virtually to the optic axis, forming a telescopic lens!"

Stabbing the coasters through the centers with Billie's pin, Schuyler passed them out for everyone to look through.

"Oh, Schuy, we shouldn't," protested Rachel. "This is so deliberate. The poor creature!"

"We must identify the big green thing!" said Schuyler. "I was wrong. It's not a sleeping bag. It's a bolt of Easter-basket grass. She's very beforehand, actually. It isn't Easter for months!"

"Rachel, aren't others' windows our looking glass, ultimately?" said Harold. "In every view, every visitation, don't we seek to fracture our own image?"

"*She* needs *help*," said Billie.

"Can't *we* do something?" said Schuyler. "We could take her a kitten! We could serenade her. 'Dradle, dradle, dradle, I made it out of clay, and when it's dry and ready, then dradle I shall play!' "

"We could take her some *Brillo*," said Snookie.

"Oh, nothing abrasive, Snookie," said Schuyler. "A flowering plant. An azalea with a bow. A sea horse with guaranteed live delivery. Oh, if we had some fireworks. We could shoot them for her on the fire escape."

Harold cried with laughter and sat down, spilling his vodka. "Lose your self-respect, and it's the end," said Billie. "I have a cleaning woman in twice a week," said Snookie. "You cannot go to pot," said Billie. "There's such a thing as a fire hazard," said Snookie.

"Volunteers are always needed," said Billie. "The hospitals are always yelling." "Even a pay job is better than nothing," said Snookie. "Better than *nothing*, Snookie?" said Harold. "Better than nothing whatsoever, *truly* better?"

"We could take her a mason jar of bean and barley soup," said Schuyler. "It's binding, it's very binding. We could all do a play reading. I see her in *The Inca of Perusalem*."

"Nothing's wrong with bridge to kill an evening," said Snookie. "But *nothing*, darling!" cried Harold, choking. "Nothing's wrong with bridge to kill an evening!" He and Schuyler collapsed, chorusing, "Nothing's wrong with bridge to kill an evening!"

Snookie said, "What I'd like to know is, where does she get her dough?"

After everybody had gone home and Rachel had set the dishes and glasses in the sink, she was too tired to feel anything. But the calculations of zeros and figure eights of glass imprints on all the furniture tops left autographs of life in the room, and the echo of the talk and laughs of her company made her hum as she got out of her clothes. When she went to raise her window, she saw the woman lying asleep on her bed with the lights on, as she often slept. Her position made Rachel quickly look away. The woman was lying on her face with her legs spread and feet toed in, a position of abjectness embarrassing even when that of a young child or a big, fallen doll. "Oh, *dear*," murmured Rachel, as she fell asleep.

She got up late, fixed her breakfast, and cleaned up from the party. It was nearly three when she looked out the window. She thought instantly how they had stuck pinholes in the coasters and aimed their focus at the woman. Oh, no, she thought. What did we do? Oh, what did we do to you?

The woman was lying in the exact position she had been in fourteen hours before. She couldn't be, thought Rachel, but she stared till her eyes stung, trying to see some change from last night that showed that the woman had moved. But nothing was changed. The woman still lay in the position that did not look any longer like sleep.

But she could have moved around a lot in between and just be lying like that again, thought Rachel.

Rachel had to go out to the delicatessen for cigarettes and something for her supper, and she decided to go now and then see if the woman had moved by the time she came back. She deliberately prolonged her errand, as if to give the woman an added chance. She bought the papers and hunted for a drugstore open Sundays, where she might buy stamps.

When she got back, the woman was lying unchanged. Rachel's heart felt as if it had just started to beat. She thought of all the possible things to do. The police? The woman superintendent of the building across the street? The nicety of her own concern that the woman not be found by the police in the position in which she was lying made Rachel feel close to her. Then it struck Rachel that she could call the woman and see if the phone roused her. But she had put the name out of her mind after the attempted attack. She went down to Good Joe's apartment to ask him the name. But Good Joe wasn't home. Rachel went back up. The woman hadn't moved.

Rachel decided that the thing to do was to go and look at the nameplates in the house across the street. Then she could look up the number, and phone — unless, of course, it was unlisted.

Rachel was very excited when she worked out this simple plan, but she didn't act upon it. Agitation gave her the sense that the right name was flashing around the edges of her thoughts and would light up clearly at any moment, and for a while she walked around, trying different names to herself.

She was doing this when she passed the window and saw that the disheveled bed was empty.

There was the woman, standing up, then moving slowly through the mess of the room. The late Sunday afternoon light turned the very color of disappointment, the flaunting flat blue of survival when all had been guaranteed lost, of crisis ended with nobody's services needed, and all the watchers thrown back on their routine. This was the feeling Rachel had when she saw that the woman was not dead.

Held by fright at her feeling, Rachel watched the woman attentively, as if required to do so. She watched the woman grope through the debris toward the first thing all lost people crawl toward, water. She turned the faucet and filled a kettle. Certainty colored in every detail for Rachel. The woman struck a match, lighting the cigarette between her lips, then the gas range, and spooned instant coffee into a cup.

Rachel shut her blinds. What she could not look at was the will, the will that got up at 5 P.M. from a dead-doll sprawl, that crawled through the wreckage of its life to reinstall itself with all the little waking-up supports, to meet an absent poet's face that pleaded, "I didn't do anything to you, did I?"

WILLIAM EASTLAKE

A Long Day's Dying

(FROM THE VIRGINIA QUARTERLY REVIEW)

THE summer solstice was another implacable, fierce, pure blue New Mexican day, another wide panorama of empty, impossible void without faint sign or distant signal for the very young man dying at the bottom of a vast and lonely canyon called the La Jara Arroyo. Quicksand. The young man tried to remove the word from his thoughts. Quicksand, a viscid, unsubstantial whorl — phantom. Neither is quicksand fluid nor solid; neither can you stand nor swim. Quicksand, the stuff a nightmare and the rest of my life is made of. But try to think of something else, try to think of something pleasant to pass this short time. Think of your Indian friend and the day you said to Rabbit Stockings: "How many chiefs are there in that summer wickiup?"

"It's not that wickiup, it's my home."

"How many chiefs are there?"

"Plenty. You know, Santo, you've got to stop thinking like a white person."

"That's going to be difficult."

"You've got to try. You know, the whites are going to be extincted."

"What's that?"

"Blown up. Isn't that what you're trying to do?"

"Are we?"

"Sure. And when you're all gone and then you try to come back again we Indians are not going to be so nice next time."

"You Indians are not going to let the next Columbus land?"

"That's right, Santo."

The boy Sant thought about this odd, unimportant conversation. He had a great deal of time to think now so he let his mind wander over all of his short, rich past, because he had tried everything to keep from sinking, but nothing worked. The thing that seemed to work best was to lie backward and try to float on the cool boiling sand. That seemed to work best, but each long alone hour that passed he was getting in deeper. It's a grave. That's it. It's as though the earth wanted you, decided to take you now, could not wait for you to become a man. So Sant did not whine or complain, he did not cry, because he wanted to behave now like a man. When you have tried absolutely everything else and there is no way out, then you try resignation and courage. Quicksand is heavy water in which swimming is impossible and it's as if the drain below were open and you were being sucked down into the earth. Sant had been struggling alone down at the bottom of the lonely arroyo for six hours now.

Six hours before he had begun to cross on his great black horse and the animal had refused. Sant got off and tried to pull the horse, but Luto stood rooted on the edge. Sant did not notice that he himself was going down, he did not realize it was impossible to move until the rein broke and the horse moved back to firmer ground. "All right," Sant called to the horse, "when I get out of here — !" But the young man was already descending like a slow elevator. It was not until the quicksand reached his chest that he realized the horse might go forever unpunished. What had the horse done? Behaved sensibly, that's all. But they had crossed at this point at the bottom of this arroyo many times. "Yes, but I know — " Sant tried to go more on his back. "I know," he said to the sky, "that quicksand moves. It needs water to percolate from below the sand like a spring, and at this exact spot of the percolation it will keep the sand in suspension and trap anything that enters. But this spot changes." Why had he entered? To get on the other side. That horse, Luto, continues to brood there in the shadow of the arroyo, continues to wait for me to finish whatever I am up to. I wonder if he knows I'm drowning. Maybe he suspects there's something wrong. Then why doesn't he go back to the corral with his empty saddle so they will know that something happened to me? Because I did not train him. That's the last time I'll neglect a horse. Yes, it's the last time you'll neglect anything. It's the last time you'll even think about it. Sant splashed the water with his arm as it flowed around him on its way to the Rio Grande.

If I was four hundred yards up the arroyo I would be on the other side of the Continental Divide and die into the Pacific. Now I am dying into the Rio Grande and the Atlantic. It's the last time you'll die into anything. It's the first and last time. Wait. They will find me. How? They will miss me and track me here. How are they going to track you over all those hard sand rock formations between here and the house? Well then, Rabbit Stockings will know where I am. How would any Indian know where you are? Particularly one as brainless as Rabbit Stockings. Because Indians have got a lot of intuition. The less brains the more intuition? Something like that.

Sant said abruptly, "Oh God!" aloud up into the sky and then resumed his dialogue with himself. He was swimming gently and softly in fluid earth to keep taking air and he was talking to himself to beat the death that tugged on him from somewhere there below. What about the time you tamed the thunder? It will be the last time for that too. I don't think the thunder will be tamed any more. The time all of the Indians convinced you — Afraid Of His Own Horses, and Rabbit Stockings was in on it too — the time they convinced you that if you could climb a high enough ridge and shoot enough arrows, throw enough rocks into the air and shout horrible shouts, the thunder would go away and never come back. It worked. That's right. As we flew along the high pine-crested ridge hollering and shooting, the thunder paid us back. Remember it sent a bolt of lightning that nearly killed Rabbit Stockings when it shattered a tree that Rabbit Stockings was shouting under. It all proves that there is something in the Indian religion of worshiping things, and it proves that things don't like us very much. I must ask Rabbit Stockings if they worship quicksand. I will never get the chance.

The sun was fire-hot on the young man's face but he had to lie back in this position to present as much body surface as he could to the fluid sand. At times he could relieve his burning face with his wet hands but very quickly because he had to use them as flippers, swinging them gently to stay alive.

On the great haunch of the Sangre de Cristo Mountains that rose like another planet above the flat arroyo-cut land there were two riders appearing like centaurs at a distance.

"Rabbit Stockings," Big Sant said, "it's a superstition or something you dreamed up, I don't know which." The man called Big Sant, who didn't know which, was the father of the boy at the bottom of the arroyo. He had a very wide open face and a sharp, red, alive scar on his left jaw.

"I just have this feeling that Santo did not go to the mountains."

"But feeling is not enough, Rabbit Stockings."

"I have this feeling that he went the other way. Something happened to him."

"What happened?"

"He drowned."

"In the small stream from the spring in the arroyo? It would be quite a trick."

"Well, I've got this feeling." The young Indian who had this feeling was a Navajo Indian, about the same age as his partner at the bottom of the arroyo. He dressed like all the other Indians in this part of New Mexico, that is he dressed like a cowboy except the way his bun of hair was tied in the back. Cowboys didn't do that. It saves on barber's bills, Big Sant thought. But he couldn't take this Indian seriously about his son at the bottom of the arroyo. The Indian religion was part of their way of life that the white man had not been able to make a dent in. The Indians still insisted on getting their inspiration from their guardian spirit. Sometimes it was a bear, an elk, or even a certain pine tree isolated and clinging to a ledge on the mesa which they would watch from below each day. Sometimes it was only a rock, a large yellow concretion about to tumble from a ledge, threatening and high.

"Where did you get your information, Rabbit Stockings?"

"From a snake."

"I thought so. We will continue up the mountain." And he touched his horse to increase their pace to a trot, the Indian keeping up on his matching Appaloosa that had to work hard to maintain the pace. They had been traveling for about an hour now, ever since Big Sant decided that Little Sant must have gotten into some kind of difficulty. Not serious. Probably a lame horse. Indians are alarmists. Little Sant was overdue about six hours on his trip up the mountain to gather the horses, and one hour ago the remuda had come in by themselves without the boy. A strange stallion had gathered up their mares and taken them to the mountain, but it must still be too cold on the Sangre de Cristos at ten thousand feet this time in June so their mares must have turned tail and fled back down to the ranch as soon as the stallion dropped his vigilance. The stallion was not bad, but the warm weather down here must be better. But what happened to the boy? What happened to Little Sant? Probably his horse went lame. Don't ask Rabbit Stockings; Indians are alarmists. "You are, you know, Rabbit Stockings."

"What's that?"

"You want to make a big thing out of nothing. Does the peace pipe go from right to left or from left to right?"

"What's a peace pipe?"

"You see, you have gotten over many of your superstitions. Why don't you get over the rest?"

"If an Indian believes something it's called superstition; when a white man believes something it's called progress."

"How did you figure that, Rabbit Stockings?"

"Why it's everywhere around you," Rabbit Stockings said carefully. "It's everywhere around you. Aren't they going to the moon now? Well, the white man doesn't even know the earth. What do they know about quicksand?"

"Little Sant didn't go that way, Rabbit Stockings." Big Sant was annoyed at this pecking away at the ridiculous. Indians will never let a thing go, particularly if it's a prejudice. This Indian has no evidence for his belief.

"You still didn't tell me what is quicksand," Rabbit Stockings queried.

"It's caused by water rising from below a table of sand. This causes a turbid — "

"What's that mean?"

"Something that is neither water nor sand, Rabbit Stockings. You can't swim in it, neither can you get any purchase on it to get out. You founder and die."

"There's nothing down there pulling you below? Nothing that wants you? Something that says, now is the time?"

"No, Rabbit Stockings. It's like your snake again. There is nothing to it."

"Nothing to it," Rabbit Stockings repeated, bouncing on his

smaller horse. "Nothing to it. Another Indian superstition. Well, maybe you're right," Rabbit Stockings announced suddenly. "After all, we didn't chase away the thunder."

"Try to remember that, Rabbit Stockings," Big Sant said.

The young man sinking into eternity at the bottom of the arroyo was looking up at the soft gray-green slopes that led away to the world and thinking small thoughts to fight the insidious and larger thoughts as he lay dying.

Another thing about Indians, Little Sant thought, another thing about Indians is they don't plan for the future. Their future is now. Why plan for something that's happening? You notice this in the Navajo language, the past becomes the future and the present dissolves into their language mist of the day before yesterday. Navajos don't communicate, they confuse. No wonder they don't believe in progress. They couldn't tell you if they did, so it's more comfortable for the Navajos not to believe in the future. I bet they would pass a law against the future if they could — if they believed in laws. I remember Rabbit Stockings touching his head and saying, the future is here. In other words, the future isn't. It's another idea. That true? Yes, I guess it is. So why should we waste time with the future if it doesn't exist? Progress is part of the future, so that's a waste of time too. Right? Words, words, words. Now your snakes. Snakes exist, don't they? Bears, deer, elk, coyotes — they're real, really real. Right?

Really real. Right. Anything you say, Rabbit Stockings. And then the boy with the red hair, in the quicksand at the bottom of the long, deep, lonely arroyo cried suddenly up into the big, empty space. "But get me out! Find me, if your magic works." It was a quiet cry with no attempt to reach anyone, a cry to himself and the quiescent spirit of the rocks and sage, yucca and gray sad tamarisk that wept toward the Rio Grande. But there is no one, the young man thought. There is no spirit, no life, no death — no death outside this one right here. It's only a word until it happens to you. Where is the horse, Luto? I can see him there in the half shadows. Luto seems waiting for me to get it over with so he can carry me away. Was he in on this too? Was this exact time and place absolutely and perfectly arranged to the second? Luto is all black, a pure black horse. I never did like that horse waiting there in the checkered shade of the funeral tamarisk. But there was an understanding, there was always an understanding that he was the best horse in the country, the fastest, the quickest, and the best cow horse in the country. We were never friendly. We never spoke. I should have sold him, but when I had a customer Luto disappeared as though he knew. And I never bought him; that day he just showed up, unbranded, little more than a colt, but he knew everything, wasn't even green broke but he behaved like a ten-year-old. I wonder where he came from and where he will go back to now.

Little Sant felt himself sink a little more into the heavy fluid sand. He waved his slim arms, fluttered them like a wounded bird, but he could feel himself being pulled down deeper. No, no, no, he told himself. You are behaving like an Indian, thinking like a Navajo. You've been around them too long, like father, like Big Sant says, you should associate more with white boys. But where did the funeral-black horse come from? Why does Luto wait there in the solemn dappled shadows, and where is he going soon?

Sant ceased all movement and Luto emerged out of the shadow tentatively, the black horse bringing the shade, the darkness with him. Death is a cessation of movement, but more, the young man thought, life is the idea of movement. Death is a coffin-black horse, a shadow interlaced among the shadows in the tamarisk. And it wasn't my idea to cross this arroyo at this point, it was Luto who pushed down and across in that steady, stately stride, refusing only at the last second, and it was again Luto that flew, almost airborne, down Blind Wolf Canyon to bring us around in back of the ranch so that even Rabbit Stockings in his infinite stupidity would not select this arroyo as a place to search.

But it was Luto with terrific, almost deathless delicacy, who had been able to cut out a calf from its mother, a colt from a stallion, and charge from cover, then whip a mule deer to the mesa and in the snow gambol like a hoyden with a jack until the rabbit, wraithlike in the matching frost, would founder in abject capitulation to the dark mountain that moved like a cougar. The sudden darkness of Luto ascending, then descending the pine-feathered slopes of the Sangre de Cristos like a writhing storm, somber and wild. Yes, the young man thought, Luto, yes, Luto is alive. Luto is the best horse, queer, yes, but Luto is the best damn horse.

Now watch. Luto, the shadow, has moved out of the tamarisk

shadows, moving catlike, moving over here, the young man thought. Because I have been silent, ceased to struggle for seconds, now Luto is moving in. I will wait and when his tail passes by I will grab it and hold on. I will foil the horse. I will make it out of here. The young man did not believe this, he had been settling in the quicksand for too long now to have grand hope. Little Sant's helplessness had long since turned to hopelessness, but against utter despair he told to himself, I will make it out, I will make it out, as the horse nuzzled forward, fretting its monster nose towards the young man in long sweeping casts, but treading delicately in the beginning soft sand, trailing the broken reins like a shroud. Then Luto jerked up his head in discovery and wheeled to escape as Little Sant's arms rose to catch the flying, gossamer tail. He had it in his hands. It was like threads of ice, new-forming, fragile ice that exploded in his grip and Luto was gone. Now Luto came slowly back, then stopped ten feet away — Luto staring out of the beginning darkness, merging again into the shadows, spectral and huge.

"Luto!" Sant called weakly. "Luto!" Little Sant felt himself settling more into the quicksand. "Luto boy, what's happening?"

The pair of horsemen moving fast up the precipitous slope merged with mountain mahogany, then fled between brakes of aspen, trampling columbine, mariposa lilies, found a trail strewn red with gilias that led straight to the peaks, then entered a lowering and ominous cloud.

"Do you know what day it is, Rabbit Stockings?" Big Sant asked.

"Shrove Tuesday? The day after tomorrow? The day before yesterday? Ash Wednesday? What other days have you invented?"

"Invent one yourself."

"Can I?"

"It's may I, Rabbit Stockings."

"Sure you can," Rabbit Stockings said. "You whites are always doing it."

"Today is the day, three years to the day, we got Luto. I remember because it's the summer solstice."

"What's that?"

"The twenty-first of June."

"I mean, what's the summer solstice."

"It's the longest day and the shortest night of the year."

Rabbit Stockings thought about this as they cantered through bowers of ponderosa, then debouched into a quiet explosion of orange Cowboy's Delight on the old Circle B, ringed with high wavering Indian Paintbrush midst the gaunt and verdigrised collapse of a homestead, a monument to unhardihood and puerile myth; but some eastern hollyhocks rose in towering, weedlike formidability from out New England ruins in the yellow New Mexican sky. Rabbit Stockings plucked one as he passed and placed the garish Boston flower in his black Indian head knot.

"You see," Rabbit Stockings said, in sham Indian solemnity, "I've been thinking about your summer solstice. It could be the twenty-first but it could be the twenty-second because it seems to my thick Indian head that both days share that shortest night."

"Yes." Big Sant touched his head and blew out a forced breath, annoyed, and the Appaloosa horse started in sympathy. "Yes, but it was the twenty-first we got Luto." Then he said, flat and peremptory, "Rabbit Stockings, you should be a scientist."

"Yes," Rabbit Stockings said.

"They tell me, Rabbit Stockings," Big Sant said, "that an Indian can tell, that is, his religion gives him some secret insight into animals."

"That's not true," Rabbit Stockings said.

"That, for example, a horse like Luto, do you suppose — ? What do you suppose? I've always felt that Luto was too damn cooperative, that it had some ulterior purpose."

"Ulterior?"

"That there is something wrong with Luto, I mean."

"What do you mean?" the Indian asked.

"If Indians believe that each person has a guardian spirit like a rock, a stone, a snake, could it be a horse?"

"I guess it could."

"Would the guardian spirit take care of everything?"

"Except dig the grave," the Indian said. "And sometimes that."

"What do you mean?"

"Well, if it were quicksand," Rabbit Stockings said.

"Why have you got this obsession with quicksand, Rabbit Stockings?"

"Because it's the only way a horse could kill Santo."

"Oh?"

"Yes. Santo is too smart for horses with the usual tricks."

"And why would Luto want to kill Sant?"

"I don't know. I'm only a poor Indian. I only work here."

"Do you have a guardian spirit, Rabbit Stockings?"

"No, I don't," Rabbit Stockings said. "Or maybe I do, but it doesn't count because I don't believe in it, not all the time. It's difficult to believe in anything all the time. You see, if you don't believe in your guardian spirit he can't help you."

"Or hurt you?"

"That's right. In other words, if Santo doesn't believe in the horse it can't hurt him or help him. In other words, if Santo's time had come and he didn't believe the horse was anything but a horse, then the horse would have no power."

"Well, I think there is something wrong with Luto. As I said, he's too perfect for a horse. What can we do?"

"It's probably too late now," Rabbit Stockings said. "All we can do is continue up the mountain. I guess your direction is as good as mine."

"I'm sure it is, Rabbit Stockings. A horse is a horse, no matter how perfect a horse."

"My guardian spirit is a snake."

"When we get back," Big Sant said, "we'll have a drink to the snakes."

"You don't believe it? The trouble with this country is — what is it? The trouble with this country is, we are overdeveloped."

"That's a profound thought, Rabbit Stockings, but we will leave all the profound Indian thoughts for later. Right now — "

"Look! Right now there's a snake!"

The horses plunged back, rising to enormous height on their hinder feet in blurred Appaloosa furious fright and comic dance, in high awkward prance before the dice, the hard clean rattle in the sage ahead.

"I don't see. I hear, but I don't see. Can you see the diamond-back?"

"There!" Rabbit Stockings hollered and the diamond-back rattler exploded toward the plunging and furious motions of the horses, some grenade, anti-personnel or anti-horse weapon planted in the innocent sage, lashing out with shrapnel speed and sidewind perfect accuracy to the falling mark and missing the falling-away Appaloosa, but recoiling, rearming itself in fluid automation before the rapt and cold stricken-eyed terror of the horse, as Big Sant slid off and seized himself a great, vari-colored trunk of petrified wood and hefted it in a vast surging motion above his head to crush the snake.

"Wait!"

"Why?"

"He's trying to tell us something."

"Yes, that's true, Rabbit Stockings. I got the message."

"You don't understand."

"Oh, I do. I understand rattlesnakes perfectly, and they understand me. Get out of the way before the snake kills you."

Rabbit Stockings stepped deftly and quickly in a timed ballet cadence as the snake exploded again and then quickly again and then again, the snake in surly, dusty diamonds, flinging itself at the mad Indian before the Indian gained a high boulder in an unfrantic, graceful leap, resting and looking down from there at the snake, his arms akimbo.

"Well done, Rabbit Stockings. Now can I kill the other half of the act?"

"Why do you, even in your overdeveloped country, why do you have to kill things?"

"Rattlesnakes."

"Still?"

"Rattlesnakes. Oh yes." From his safe distance Big Sant let down his trunk of petrified wood and sat on it. "Or is this one a friend of yours?"

"No."

"Your guardian spirit maybe, telling you to go back?"

"I don't know."

"Some Indian nonsense like that," Big Sant said. "Still, if you want to check the arroyo instead of the mountain we will check the arroyo instead of the mountain. Anything you say. Anything your snake says, any opinion a rattler holds. If you don't kill 'em, join 'em. What do you think?"

"We will check the arroyo," Rabbit Stockings said.

"Not that I hold with snakes," Big Sant said as they quickly mounted the trembling, subdued Appaloosas, "but in an overdeveloped country I'll always go along with a legend, a good Navajo myth. Look, Rabbit Stockings, your snake has called it quits."

They scattered down the mountain, their horses tumbling in mad pursuit of home, wild and uncontrolled, the riders allowing their horses to plunge downward in furious gyrations, careening and bouncing with awful abrupt speed like some kind of huge bright chunks of ore hurtling downward from a blast above on the high, still snow-coifed in June, scintillant, far peaks of the Sangre de Cristos, flashing down, down, down in twisting horse rapture to the sage avenues of the flat earth.

"The La Jara Arroyo," Rabbit Stockings hollered to Big Sant, and beginning now to direct the horse. "That's where Little Sant must be. That's where the quicksand is. The La Jara Arroyo."

"Yes," Big Sant said quietly to himself and the horse. "Yes. Yes, at my age I'm taking orders from a fool Navajo Indian and a snake, a guardian spirit Rabbit Stockings called it, but you and I," he told the still raging horse, "you and I saw a rattler. Wait! This way," and Big Sant went the way of Rabbit Stockings, both fleeing now between yellow plumes of yucca and among a bright festooned desert carpet of the twenty-first of June.

At the bottom of the arroyo nothing moved where the young man had been struggling. The water ran serene now, limpid and innocent. Where they watched from their horses atop the great canyon their searching eyes could see all the way to where the La Jara joined the Puerco but no sign, no clue of Little Sant, only the dusky, burnished copper fire sky above the arroyo heralding the slow end of a long day.

"The summer solstice you called it?"

"Yes, Rabbit Stockings."

"It was a long day all right."

"Rabbit Stockings, we should have continued to the mountain."

"No, I'm afraid we came in the right direction," Rabbit Stockings said. "But I don't understand. I don't understand why we weren't told sooner."

"We should have continued to the mountain," Big Sant insisted. "I don't know why I had to listen to a Navajo Indian and a rattlesnake."

Rabbit Stockings slid off down the sleek sweat of his speckled horse and stared from the ground with incredulous and uncomprehending disbelief at the vast empty cut one hundred feet deep, bottomed with a thin thread of water feeding the Rio Grande and becoming bronze now as it refracted in quick shimmers the maddening and molten sky. Rabbit Stockings crawled forward on the hard earth up to the sage-sprinkled lip of the arroyo, then he thumped the earth with the palm of his small rough red hand. "Yes."

"Yes, what?"

"Yes, they crossed here, Little Sant and Luto. Look, this is Luto's hoofprint. See how it goes like a heart in front?"

"Yes, almost cloven. Yes, that's Luto. But where did they go?"

"Down," Rabbit Stockings said, capping his vision and staring across. "But I don't see where they went up." Rabbit Stockings continued to search all along the arroyo while Big Sant sat frozen. "But there's something moving down there in the tamarisk," Rabbit Stockings said finally.

"Hello!" Big Sant shouted. "Who's there?"

"It's me!"

"It sounds like Little Sant," Rabbit Stockings said. "A little weak but what can you expect. That you, Santo? Okay?"

"Yes," the voice of Little Sant called up. "But don't come down. Please don't come down."

But Big Sant had already started his Appaloosa in a steep dive down the awful slope. Rabbit Stockings tried to arrest him with an upraised hand but Big Sant was already hurtling halfway to the bottom, horse and rider commingled in a vortex of riotous earth spinning down to the sliver of bronzed stream that lazied to the big river, guiltless.

"Me too," Rabbit Stockings shouted as he gained his horse and catapulted it in one great leap out and down, the horse sprawling as it hit and never quite recovering; foundering like a novice skier on busted skis it cavorted crazy to the bottom where it righted on all four scattered legs and stood amazed and triumphant.

"Don't come!" Little Sant shouted toward them both. "Don't come over here!"

"Why not?"

"Because I'm telling you why not."

"Go ahead."

There was a long silence from the tamarisks.

"Because there's a snake here, a dangerous rattler. He killed a horse. The snake killed Luto."

"Where's the snake?" Rabbit Stockings dropped off his horse and moved into the thick interlacing tamarisk. "Where's the snake, Santo?"

"He's gone. The snake was coiled there, where you're standing now. He's gone."

"What snake?" The heavy voice of Big Sant moved into the tamarisk. "What snake? Where's the horse? Where's Luto?"

"Luto's dead. Luto went down in the quicksand." Sant stood up, a small tower of mud. "I was stuck in the quicksand and Luto just stood here and watched. Then Luto was struck by this big snake. I could see the snake strike at Luto, then Luto panicked into the quicksand, got stuck, but I was able to get out using Luto to crawl up, but Luto got stuck worse and began to go under and there was nothing I could do. Luto's dead."

"No," Rabbit Stockings announced, "Luto's not dead."

"I saw Luto die."

"No, you saw Luto sink in the sand, that's all. Luto will be back."

"Oh, you bet I'll never buy a horse that looks like that again."

"Luto won't look like that again," Rabbit Stockings said. "The next time Luto could appear as a beautiful woman, for example."

"Well, I'll never buy a beautiful woman for example."

"Get up in back," Big Sant said down from his horse.

Little Sant squished up and clasped his mudded arms around Big Sant.

"And another thing," Rabbit Stockings advised in his advising tone, "Never do anything on Shrove Tuesday."

"It's not Shrove Tuesday, it's the summer solstice," Big Sant said.

"All right, be careful of that too," Rabbit Stockings advised. "Now that we don't have any medicine bundles — "

"What?"

"So now we've got to be careful all the time," Rabbit Stockings finished.

As they passed the stream in muddy file Little Sant pointed at the spot. "That's where it almost happened."

Rabbit Stockings turned in his saddle. "That's where it did happen."

"I mean to me."

"You're not the center of the world."

"I suppose the Indians are."

"That's nice of you, Santo. I've always supposed they were too."

The horses pounded now in wild scurry up out of the fast darkening arroyo and they gained the long flat country gilded in light, all of them in the gaudy sunset.

"Well, I'll tell you," Little Sant said, "it was terrible, my almost, then Luto's death down there, but outside of that — " He stared from behind his huge father with muddied eyes at the Indian. "Outside of that I don't believe any of it."

The Indian, Rabbit Stockings, trotted forward in a wild rhythm on his dazzling pony and pointed his luminous arm up at the faltering fire going out. "Don't you believe this was the day of the white man's summer solstice?"

"Yes," Little Sant said, grabbing his hard father with stiffening arms and looking towards the darkness back at the arroyo. "Yes, Rabbit Stockings, today was very long, today was the most long, the longest day there ever was." Now Little Sant looked straight ahead into the end of a Midsummer Day. "Yes, we've all got to pray we never have a summer solstice again."

WILLIAM GOYEN

Figure Over the Town

(FROM THE SATURDAY EVENING POST)

IN THE TOWN of my beginning I saw this masked figure sitting aloft. It was never explained to me by my elders, who were thrilled and disturbed by the figure too, who it was, except that he was called Flagpole Moody. The days and nights he sat aloft were counted on calendars in the kitchens of small houses and in troubled minds, for Flagpole Moody fed the fancy of an isolated small town of practical folk whose day's work was hard and real.

Since the night he was pointed out to me from the roof of the little shed where my father sheltered grain and plowing and planting implements, his shape has never left me; in many critical experiences of my life it has suddenly appeared before me, so that I have come to see that it is a dominating emblem of my life, as often a lost lover is, or the figure of a parent, or the symbol of a faith, as the scallop shell was for so many at one time, or the Cross.

It was in the time of a war I could not understand, being so very young, that my father came to me at darkening, in the beginning wintertime, and said, "Come with me to the Patch, Son, for I want to show you something."

The Patch, which I often dream about, was a mysterious fenced-in plot of ground, about half an acre, where I never intruded. I often stood at the gate or fence and looked in through the hexagonal lenses of the chicken wire and saw how strange this little territory was, and wondered what it was for. There was the shed in it where implements and grain were stored, but nothing was ever planted nor any animal pastured here; nothing, not even grass or weed, grew here; it was just plain common ground.

This late afternoon my father took me into the Patch and led me
to the shed and hoisted me up to the roof. He waited a moment
while I looked around at all the world we lived in and had forgotten was so wide and housed so many in dwellings quite like ours.
(Later, when my grandfather, my father's father, took me across
the road and railroad tracks into a large pasture — so great I had
thought it, from a window of our house, the whole world — where
a little circus had been set up as if by magic the night before, and
raised me to the broad back of a sleepy elephant, I saw the same
sight and recalled not only the night I stood on the roof of the shed,
but also what I had seen from there, that haunting image, and
thought I saw it again, this time on the lightning rod of our house
. . . but no, it was, as always, the crowing cock that stood there,
eternally strutting out his breast and at the break of crowing.)

My father waited, and when he saw that I had steadied myself, he
said, "Well, Son, what is that you see over there, by the Methodist
church?"

I was speechless and could only gaze; and then I finally said to
him, not moving, "Something is sitting on the flagpole on top of a
building."

"It is just a man," my father said, "and his name is Flagpole
Moody. He is going to sit up there for as long as he can stand it."

When we came into the house, I heard my father say to my
mother, lightly, "I showed Son Flagpole Moody and I think it scared
him a little." And I heard my mother say, "It seems a foolish stunt,
and I think maybe children shouldn't see it."

All that night Flagpole Moody was on my mind. When it began
raining, in the very deepest night, I worried about him in the rain,
and I went to my window and looked out to see if I could see him.
When it lightninged, I saw that he was safe and dry under a little
tent he had raised over himself. Later I had a terrible dream about
him, that he was falling, falling, and when I called out in my nightmare, my parents came to me and patted me back to sleep, never
knowing that I would dream of him again.

He stayed and stayed up there, the flagpole sitter, hooded (why
would he not show his face?), and when we were in town and walked
under him, I would not look up as they told me to; but once, when
we stood across the street from the building where he was perched,
I looked up and saw how high he was in the air, and he waved down
at me with his cap in his hand.

Everywhere there was the talk of the war, but where it was or what it was I did not know. It seemed only some huge appetite that craved all our sugar and begged from the town its goods, so that people seemed paled and impoverished by it, and it made life gloomy — that was the word. One night we went into the town to watch them burn Old Man Gloom, a monstrous straw man with a sour, turned-down look on his face and dressed even to the point of having a hat — it was the Ku Klux Klan who lit him afire — and above, in the light of the flames, we saw Flagpole Moody waving his cap to us. He had been up eighteen days.

He kept staying up there. More and more the talk was about him, with the feeling of the war beneath all the talk. People began to get restless about Flagpole Moody and to want him to come on down. "It seems morbid," I remember my mother saying. What at first had been a thrill and an excitement — the whole town was there every other day when the provisions basket was raised up to him, and the contributions were extravagant: fresh pies and cakes, milk, little presents, and so forth — became an everyday sight; then he seemed ignored and forgotten by the town except for me, who kept a constant, secret watch on him; then, finally, the town became disturbed by him, for he seemed to be going on and on; he seemed an intruder now. Who could feel unlooked at or unhovered over in his house with this figure over everything? (It was discovered that Flagpole was spying on the town through binoculars.) There was an agitation to bring him down, and the city council met to this end.

There had been some irregularity in the town which had been laid to the general lawlessness and demoralizing effect of the war: robberies; the disappearance of a beautiful young girl, Sarah Nichols (but it was said she ran away to find someone in the war); and one Negro shot in the woods, which could have been the work of the Ku Klux Klan. The question at the city-council meeting was, "Who gave Flagpole Moody permission to go up there?" No one seemed to know; the merchants said it was not for advertising, or at least no one of them had arranged it, though after he was up, many of them tried to use him to advertise their products — Egg Lay or Red Goose shoes or Have a Coke at Robbins Pharmacy — and why not? The Chamber of Commerce had not brought him, nor the Women's Club; maybe the Ku Klux had, to warn and tame the Negroes, who were especially in awe of Flagpole Moody; but the Klan was as innocent as all the others, it said. The pastor was reminded of the time

a bird had built a nest on the church steeple, a huge foreign bird
that had delighted all the congregation as well as given him subject
matter for several sermons; he told how the congregation came out
on the grounds to adore the bird, which in time became suddenly
savage and swooped to pluck the feathers from women's Sunday
hats and was finally brought down by the fire department, which
found the nest full of rats and mice, half devoured, and no eggs at
all — this last fact the subject of another series of sermons by the
pastor, drawing as he did his topics from real life.

As the flagpole sitter had come to be regarded as a defacement of
the landscape, an unsightly object, a tramp, it was suggested that the
Ku Klux Klan build a fire in the square and ride round it on their
horses and in their sheets, firing their guns into the air, as they did
in their public demonstrations against immorality, to force Flagpole
down. If this failed, it was suggested someone should be sent up on
a fireman's ladder to reason with Flagpole. He was regarded now as
a *danger* to the town, and more, as a kind of criminal. (At first he
had been admired and respected for his courage, and desired, even:
many women had been intoxicated by him, sending up, in the provisions basket, love notes and photographs of themselves, which
Flagpole had read and then sailed down for anyone to pick up and
read, to the embarrassment of this woman and that. There had
been a number of local exposures.)

The town was ready for any kind of miracle or sensation, obviously. A fanatical religious group took Flagpole Moody for the Second Coming. The old man called Old Man Nay, who lived on the
edge of the town in a boarded-up house and sat at the one open window with his shotgun in his lap, watching for the Devil, unnailed his
door and appeared in the square to announce that he had seen a
light playing around Flagpole at night and that Flagpole was some
phantom representative of the Devil and should be banished by a
raising of the Cross; but others explained that what Old Man
Nay saw was St. Elmo's fire, a natural phenomenon. Whatever was
given a fantastical meaning by some was explained away by others
as of natural cause. What was right? Who was to believe what?

An evangelist who called himself "The Christian Jew" had, at the
beginning, requested of Flagpole Moody, by a letter in the basket,
the dropping of leaflets. A sample was pinned to the letter. The
leaflet, printed in red ink, said in huge letters across the top: WARN-

ING! You Are in Great Danger! Below was a long message to sinners. If Flagpole would drop these messages upon the town, he
would be aiding in the salvation of the wicked. "The Judgments of
God are soon to be poured upon the Earth! Prepare to meet God
before it is too late! Where will you spend Eternity? What can you
do to be saved? How shall we escape if we neglect so great salvation!
(Heb. 2:3)."

But there was no reply from Flagpole, which was evidence
enough for the Christian Jew to know that Flagpole was on the
Devil's side. He held meetings at night in the square, with his little
group of followers passing out the leaflets.

"Lower Cain!" he bellowed. "You sinners standing on the street
corner running a long tongue about your neighbors; you show-go-
ing, card-playing, jazz-dancing brothers — God love your soul —
you are a tribe of sinners and you know it and God knows it, but
He loves you and wants you to come into His tabernacle and give
up your hearts that are laden with wickedness. If you look in the
Bible, if you will turn to the chapter of Isaiah, you will find there
about the fallen angel, Lucifer was his name, and how his clothing
was sewn of emeralds and sapphires, for he was very beautiful; but
friends, my sin-loving friends, that didn't make any difference. 'How
art thou fallen from Heaven, O Lucifer, son of the morning!' the
Bible reads. And it says there that the Devil will walk amongst us
and that the Devil will sit on the rooftops; and I tell you we must
unite together to drive Satan from the top of the world. Listen to
me and read my message, for I was the rottenest man in this world
until I heard the voice of God. I drank, I ran with women, I sought
after the thrills of the flesh . . . and I admonish you that the past
scenes of earth *shall be remembered in Hell.*"

The old maid, Miss Hazel Bright, who had had one lover long
ago, a cowboy named Rolfe Sanderson who had gone away and
never returned, told that Flagpole was Rolfe come back, and she
wrote notes of poetic longing to put in the provisions basket. Everybody used Flagpole Moody for his own purpose, and so he, sitting
away from it all, apparently serene in his own dream and idea of
himself, became the lost lover to the lovelorn, the saint to the seek-
ers of salvation, the scapegoat of the guilty, the damned to those
who were lost.

The town went on tormenting him; they could not let him

alone. They wished him to be their own dream or hope or lost illusion, or they wished him to be what destroyed hope and illusion.
They wanted something they could get their hands on; they wanted
someone to ease the dark misgiving in themselves, to take to their
deepest bosom, into the farthest cave of themselves where they
would take no other if he would come and be for them alone.
They plagued him with love letters, and when he would not ac-
knowledge these professions of love, they wrote him messages of hate.
They told him their secrets, and when he would not show himself
to be overwhelmed, they accused him of keeping secrets of his own.
They professed to be willing to follow him, leaving everything behind, but when he would not answer "Come," they told him how
they wished he would fall and knock his brains out. They could
not make up their minds and they tried to destroy him because he
had made up his, whatever it was he had made his mind up to.

Merchants tormented him with proposals and offers — would he
wear a Stetson hat all one day, tip and wave it to the people below?
Would he hold, just for fifteen minutes every hour, a streamer with
words on it proclaiming the goodness of their bread, or allow bal-
loons, spelling out the name of something that ought to be bought,
to be floated from the flagpole? Would he throw down Life Savers?
Many a man, and most, would have done it, would have supplied
an understandable reason for his behavior, pacifying the general
observer, and in the general observer's own terms (or the general
observer would not have it), and so send him away undisturbed,
with the feeling that all the world was really just as he was, cheating a little here, disguising a little there. (Everybody was, after all,
alike, so where the pain, and why?)

But Flagpole Moody gave no answer. Apparently he had nothing
to sell, wanted to make no fortune, to play no jokes or tricks; apparently he wanted just to be let alone to do his job. But because
he was so different, they would not let him alone until they could,
by whatever means, make him quite like themselves, or cause him,
at least, to recognize them and pay *them* some attention. Was he
camping up there for the fun of it? If so, why would he not let
them all share in it? Maybe he was there for the pure devilment of
it, like a cat calm on a chimney top. Or for some very crazy and
not-to-be-tolerated reason of his own (which everyone tried to make
out, hating secrets as people do who want everything in the clear,
where they can attack it and feel moral dudgeon against it).

Was it Cray McCreery up there? Had somebody made him another bet? One time Cray had walked barefooted to the next town, eighteen miles, because of a lost bet. But no, Cray McCreery was found, as usual, in the Domino Parlor. Had any crazy people escaped from the asylum? They were counted and found to be all in. The mind reader, Madame Fritzie, was importuned: There seemed, she said, to be a dark woman in the picture; that was all she contributed: "I see a dark woman . . ." And as she had admonished so many in the town with her recurring vision of a dark woman, there was either an army of dark women tormenting the minds of men and women in the world, or only one, which was Madame Fritzie herself. She could have made a fortune out of the whole affair if she had had her wits about her. More than one Ouija board was put questions to, but the answers were either indistinguishable or not to the point.

Dogs howled and bayed at night and sometimes in the afternoons; hens crowed; the sudden death of children was laid to the evil power of Flagpole Moody over the town.

A masked buffoon came to a party dressed as Flagpole Moody and caused increasing uneasiness among the guests until three of the men at the party, deciding to take subtle action rather than force the stranger to unmask, reported to the police by telephone. The police told them to unmask him by force and they were coming. When the police arrived they found the stranger was Marcus Peters, a past president of the Lions Club and a practical joker with the biggest belly laugh in town, and everybody would have known all along who the impostor was if he had only laughed.

A new language evolved in the town: "You're crazy as Moody," "cold as a flagpole sitter's —— ", "go sit on a flagpole" and other phrases of that sort.

In that day and time there flourished, even in that little town, a group of sensitive and intellectual people, poets and artists and whatnot, who thought themselves quite mad and gay — and quite lost, too, though they would turn their lostness to a good thing. These advanced people needed an object upon which to hinge their loose and floating cause, and they chose Flagpole Moody to draw attention, which they so craved, to themselves. They exalted him with some high, esoteric meaning that they alone understood, and they developed a whole style of poetry, music and painting, the echoes of which are still heard, around the symbol of Flagpole Moody.

They wrote, and read aloud to meetings, critical explanations of the Theory of Aloftness.

Only Mrs. T. Trevor Sanderson was bored with it all, shambling restlessly about the hospital in her Japanese kimono, her spotted hands (liver trouble, the doctors said) spread like fat lizards on the knolls of her hips. She was there again for one of her rest cures, because her oil-money worries were wearing her to death, and now the Catholic Church was pursuing her with zeal to convert her — for her money, so she said. Still, there was something to the Catholic Church; you couldn't get around that, she said, turning her spotted hands to show them yellow underneath, like a lizard's belly; and she gave a golden windowpane illustrating *The Temptation of St. Anthony* to St. Mary's Church, but would do no more than that.

There were many little felonies and even big offenses of undetermined origin in the police records of the town, and Flagpole was a stimulus to the fresh inspection of unsolved crimes. He drew suspicions up to him and absorbed them like a filter, as though he might purify the town of wickedness. If only he would send down some response to what had gone up to him. But he would not budge; and now he no longer even waved to the people below as he had during the first good days. Flagpole Moody had utterly withdrawn from everybody. What the town finally decided was to put a searchlight on him at night, to keep watch on him.

With the searchlight on the flagpole sitter, the whole thing took a turn, became an excuse for a ribald attitude. When a little wartime carnival came to the town, it was invited to install itself in the square, and a bazaar was added to it by the town. The spirit of Flagpole had to be admired, it was admitted; for after a day and night of shunning the gaiety and the mockery of it all, he showed his good nature and good sportsmanship — even his daring — by participating! He began to do what looked like acrobatic stunts, as though he were an attraction of the carnival.

And what did the people do, after a while, but turn against him again and say he was, as they had said at first, a sensationalist? Still, I loved it that he had become active; that it was not a static, fastidious, precious and Olympian show, that Flagpole did not take on a self-righteous or pompous or persecuted air, although my secret conception of him was still a tragic one. I was proud that my idea fought back — otherwise he was like Old Man Gloom, a shape of

straw and sawdust in man's clothing, and let them burn him, if only
gloom stood among the executioners, watching its own effigy and
blowing on the flames. I know now that what I saw was the conflict
of an idea with a society; and I am sure that the idea was bred by
the society — raised up there, even, by the society — in short, society was in the flagpole sitter and he was in the society of the town.

There was, at the little carnival, one concession called "Ring
Flagpole's Bell." It invited customers to try to strike a bell at the
top of a tall pole resembling his — and with a replica of him on top
— by hitting a little platform with a rubber-headed sledgehammer;
this would drive a metal disk up toward the bell. There was another concession where people could throw darts at a target resembling a figure on a pole. The Ferris wheel was put so close to Flagpole that when its passengers reached the top they could almost,
for a magical instant, reach over and touch his body. Going round
and round, it was as if one were soaring up to him only to fall away,
down, from him; to have him and to lose him; and it was all felt
in a marvelous whirling sensation in the stomach that made this experience the most vaunted of the show.

This must have tantalized Flagpole, and perhaps it seemed to
him that all the beautiful and desirable people in the world rose
and fell around him, offering themselves to him only to withdraw
untaken and ungiven, a flashing wheel of faces, eyes, lips and sometimes tongues stuck out at him and sometimes a thigh shown, offering sex, and then burning away. His sky at night was filled with
voluptuous images, and often he must have imagined the faces of
those he had once loved and possessed, turning round and round
his head to torment him. But there were men on the wheel who
made profane signs to him, and women who thumbed their noses.

Soon Flagpole raised his tent again and hid himself from his tor-
mentors. What specifically caused his withdrawal was the attempt
of a drunken young man to shoot him. This young man, named
Maury, rode a motorcycle around the town at all hours and loved
the meaner streets and the women who gave him ease, especially the
fat ones, his mania. One night he stood at the hotel window and
watched the figure on the pole, who seemed to flash on and off,
real and then unreal, with the light of the electric sign beneath the
window. He took deep drags of his cigarette and blew the smoke out
toward Flagpole; then he blew smoke rings as if to lasso Flagpole

with them, or as if his figure were a pin he could hoop with the rings of smoke. "You silly bastard, do you like what you see?" he had muttered, and, "Where have I seen you before?" between his half-clenched teeth, and then he had fired the pistol. Flagpole turned away then, once and for all.

But he had not turned away from me. I, the silent observer, watching from my window or from any high place I could secretly climb to, witnessed all this conflict and the tumult of the town. One night in my dreaming of Flagpole Moody — it happened every night, this dream, and in the afternoons when I took my nap, and the dreaming had gone on so long that it seemed, finally, as if he and I were friends, that he came down secretly to a rendezvous with me in the little pasture, and it was only years later that I would know what all our conversations had been about — that night in my dream the people of the town came to me and said, "Son, we have chosen you to go up the flagpole to Flagpole Moody and tell him to come down."

In my dream they led me, with cheers and honors, to the top of the building and stood below while I shinnied up the pole. A great black bird was circling over Flagpole's tent. As I went up the pole I noticed crowded avenues of ants coming and going along the pole. And when I went into the tent, I found Flagpole gone. The tent was as if a tornado had swept through the whole inside of it. There were piles of rotten food; shreds of letters torn and retorn, as small as flakes of snow; photographs pinned to the walls of the tent were marked and scrawled over so that they looked like photographs of fiends and monsters; corpses and drifts of feathers of dead birds that had flown at night into the tent and gone so wild with fright that they had beaten themselves to death against the sides. And over it all was the vicious traffic of insects that had found the remains, in the way insects sense what human beings have left, and come from miles away.

What would I tell them below, those who were now crying up to me, "What does he say, what does Flagpole Moody say?" And there were whistles and an increasingly thunderous chant of "Bring him down! Bring him down! Bring him down!" What would I tell them? I was glad he had gone; but I would not tell them that — yet. In the tent I found one little thing that had not been touched or changed by Flagpole; a piece of paper with printed words, and

across the top the huge red words: WARNING! YOU ARE IN GREAT
DANGER!

Then, in my dream, I went to the flap of the tent and stuck out
my head. There was a searchlight upon me through which fell a
delicate curtain of light rain; and through the lighted curtain of
rain that made the people seem far, far below, under shimmering
and jeweled veils, I shouted down to the multitude, which was dead
quiet now, "He is not here! Flagpole Moody is not here!"

There was no sound from the crowd, which had not, at first,
heard what I said. They waited; then one voice bellowed up, "Tell
him to come down!" And others joined this voice until, again, the
crowd was roaring, "Tell him that we will not harm him; only tell
him he has to come down!" Then I waved down at them to be
quiet, in Flagpole Moody's gesture of salute, as he had waved down
at people on the sidewalks and streets. Again they hushed to hear
me. Again I said, this time in a voice that was not mine, but large
and round and resounding, "Flagpole Moody is not here. His place
is empty."

And then, in my magnificent dream, I closed the flap of the tent
and settled down to make Flagpole Moody's place my own, to drive
out the insects, to erase the marks on the photographs, and to piece
together, with infinite and patient care, the fragments of the letters
to see what they told. It would take me a very long time, this putting together again what had been torn into pieces, but I would
have a very long time to give to it, and I was at the source of the
mystery, removed and secure from the chaos of the world below that
could not make up its mind and tried to keep me from making
up my own.

My dream ended here, or was broken, by the hand of my mother
shaking me to morning; and when I went to eat breakfast I heard
them saying in the kitchen that Flagpole Moody had signaled
early, at dawn, around six o'clock, that he wanted to come down;
that he had come down in his own time, and that he had come down
very, very tired, after forty days and nights, the length of the Flood.
I did not tell my dream, for I had no power of telling then, but I
knew that I had a story to one day shape around the marvel and
mystery that ended in a dream and began in the world that was to
be mine.

PAUL HORGAN

Black Snowflakes

(FROM THE SATURDAY EVENING POST)

"RICHARD, Richard," they said to me often in my childhood, "when will you begin to see things as they are?"

But I always learned from one thing what another was, and it was that way when we all went from Dorchester to New York to see my grandfather off for Europe, the year before the First World War broke out.

He was German — my mother's father — and it was his habit, all during the long time he lived in Dorchester, New York, to return to Germany for a visit every year or two. I was fearful of him, for he was large, splendidly formal in his dress and majestic in his manner, and yet I loved him for he made me know that he believed me someone worthwhile. I was ten years old, and I could imagine being like him myself someday, with glossy white hair swept back from a broad, pale brow, and white eyebrows above China-blue eyes, and rosy cheeks, a fine sweeping mustache and a well-trimmed white beard that came to a point. He sometimes wore eyeglasses with thin gold rims, and I used to put them on and take them off in secret. I suppose I had no real idea of what he was like.

There was something in the air about going to New York to see him off that troubled me. I did not want to go.

"Why not, my darling?" my mother asked as I was going to bed the night before we were to leave home. Before going down to dinner, she always came in to see me, to kiss me good night, to glance about my room with her air of giving charm to all that she saw, and to whisper a prayer with me that God would keep us.

"I don't want to leave Anna."

"What a silly boy. Anna will be here when we get back, doing the laundry in the basement or making *Apfelkuchen,* just as she always does. And while we are gone, she will have a little vacation. Won't that be nice for her? You must not be selfish."

"I don't want to leave Mr. Schmitt and Ted." Mr. Schmitt was the iceman, and Ted was his horse.

My mother made a little breath of comic exasperation, looking upward for a second. "You really are killing," she said in the racy slang of the time. "Why should you mind leaving them for a few days? What is so precious about Mr. Schmitt and Ted? They only come down our street twice a week."

"They're friends of mine."

"Ah. Then I understand. We all hate to leave our friends. Well, my darling, they will be here when we get back. Don't you want to see Grosspa take the great ship? You can even go on board to say goodbye. You have no idea how huge those ships are, and how fine."

"Why can't I go the next time he sails for Germany?"

At this my mother's eyes began to shine with a new light, and I thought she might be about to cry, but she was also smiling. She gave me a hug. "This time we must all go, Richard. If we love him, we must go. Now people are coming for dinner, and your father is waiting downstairs. Now sleep. You will love the train, as you always do. And in New York you can buy a little present for each one of your friends."

It was a lustrous thought to leave with me as she went, making a silky rustle with her long dress. I lay awake thinking of each of my friends, planning my gifts.

Anna, our servant, was a large, gray, Bohemian woman who came to us four days a week. I spent much time in the kitchen or the basement laundry listening to her rambling stories of life on the "East Side" of town. She had a coarse face with deep pockmarks. I asked her about them one day, and she replied with the dread word, "Smallpox."

"They thought I was going to die," she said. "They thought I was dead."

"What is it like to be dead, Anna?"

"Oh, dear saints, who can tell that who is alive?"

It was all I could find out, but the question was often with me. Sometimes in the afternoon, when I was supposed to be taking my nap, I would hear Anna singing, way below in the laundry, and her voice was like something hooting up the chimney. What should I buy for Anna in New York?

And for Mr. Schmitt, the iceman. He was a heavy-waisted German-American with a face wider at the bottom than at the top, and when he walked he had to swing his huge belly from side to side to make room for his steps. He had a big, hard voice, and we could hear him coming blocks away, calling "Ice!" in a long cry. Other icemen used a bell, but not Mr. Schmitt. I waited for him to come, and we would talk while he stabbed at the great cakes of ice in his hooded wagon, chipping off the pieces we always took — two chunks of fifty pounds each. His skill with the tongs was magnificent, and he would swing a chunk up on his shoulder, over which he wore a sort of rubber chasuble, and move with heavy grace up the walk along the side of our house to the kitchen porch.

"Do you want to ride today?" he would ask, meaning that I was welcome to ride to the end of the block on the high seat above Ted's rump, where the shiny, rubbed reins lay in a loose knot, because Ted needed no guidance and could be trusted to stop at all the right houses and start up again whenever he felt Mr. Schmitt's heavy, vaulting rise to the seat. I often rode to the end of the block, and Ted, in the moments when he was still, would look around at me, first from one side, and then the other, and stamp a leg, and shudder his harness against flies, and in general treat me as a member of the ice company, for which I was grateful.

What could I buy for Ted? Perhaps in New York they had horse stores. My father would give me what money I would need, when I told him what I wanted to buy. I resolved to ask him, provided I could stay awake until the dinner party was over, and my father, as he always did, would come in to see if all was well. How much love there was all about me, and how greedy I was for even more of it.

The next day we assembled at the station to take the train. It was a heavy, gray, cold day, and everybody wore fur except me and my Great-aunt Barbara — Tante Bep. She was going to Germany with my grandfather, her brother.

This was an amazing thing in itself, for, first of all, he usually

went everywhere alone, and second, Tante Bep was so different
from her magnificent brother that she was generally kept out of
sight. She lived across town on the East Side in a convent of German
nuns, who received money for her board and room from Grosspa.
She resembled an ornamental cork that my grandfather often used to
stopper a wine bottle. Carved out of soft wood and painted in bright
colors, the cap of the cork represented a Bavarian peasant woman
with a blue shawl over painted gray hair. The eyes were tiny dots
of bright blue lost in wooden crinkles, and the nose was a long
wooden lump hanging over a toothless mouth sunk deep in a poor
smile.

Now, wearing her jet-spangled black bonnet with chin ribbons,
and her black shawl and heavy skirts that smelled like dog hair, she
was returning to Germany with her brother. I did not know why.

But her going was part of the strangeness I felt in all the circumstances of our journey. On the train my grandfather retired at once
to a drawing room at the end of our car. My mother went with
him. Tante Bep and I sat in swivel chairs in the open part of the
parlor car, and my father came and went between us and the private room up ahead.

In the afternoon I fell asleep after the splendors of lunch in the
dining car. Grosspa's lunch went into his room on a tray, and my
mother shared it with him. I hardly saw her all day, but when we
drew into New York, she came to wake me. "Now, Richard, all the
lovely exciting things begin! Tonight the hotel, tomorrow the ship!
Come, let me wash your face and comb your hair."

"And the shopping?" I said.

"Shopping?"

"For my presents."

"What presents?"

"Mother, Mother, you've forgotten."

"I'm afraid I have, but we'll speak of it later."

It was true that people did forget at times, and I knew how they
tried then to make unimportant what they should have remembered. Would this happen to me, and my plans for Anna, and Mr.
Schmitt, and Ted? My concern was great — but, as my mother had
said, there were excitements waiting, and even I forgot, for a
while, what it had seemed treachery in her to forget.

We drove from the station in two limousine taxis, like high glass
cages on small wheels. My father rode with me and Tante Bep. It

was snowing lightly, and the street lamps were rubbed out of shape by the snow, as if I had painted them with water colors. We went to the Waldorf-Astoria Hotel on Fifth Avenue, and soon after I had been put into the room I was to share with Tante Bep, my father came in to make an announcement. He lifted me up so that my face was level with his. His beautifully brushed hair shone under the chandelier, and his voice sounded the way his smile looked.

"Well," he said, "we re going to have a dinner party downstairs in the main dining room."

I did not know what a main dining room was, but it sounded superb, and I knew enough of dinner parties to know that they always occured after my nightly banishment to bed.

"It won't be like at home, will it?" I said. "It will be too far away for me to listen."

"Listen? You're coming with us. And do you know why you're coming with us?"

"Why?"

"Grosspa specially wants you there."

"*Ach Gott*," Tante Bep said in the shadows, and my father gave her a frowning look.

We went downstairs together a few minutes later. I was dazed by the grand rooms of the hotel, the thick textures and velvety lights, the distances of golden air, and most of all by the sound of music coming sweetly and sharply from some hidden place. In a corner of the famous main dining room was a round table sparkling with silver, glass, ice, china and flowers, and in a high-backed arm-chair sat my grandfather. He leaned forward to greet us, and seated us about him. My mother was at his right, in one of her prettiest gowns. I was on his left.

"Hup-hup!" my grandfather said, clapping his hands to summon waiters. "Tonight nothing but a happy family party, and Richard shall drink wine with us, for I want him to remember that his first glass of wine was handed to him by his *alter Münchner Freund, der Grossvater*."

At this, Tante Bep began to make a wet sound, but a look from my father quelled it, and my mother, blinking both eyes rapidly, put her hand on her father's and leaned over and kissed his cheek.

"Listen to the music," Grosspa commanded, "and be quiet, if every word I say is to be a signal for emotion!"

Everybody straightened up and looked consciously pleasant. For

me, it was no effort. The music came from within a bower of gold
lattice screens and potted palms — two violins, a cello and a harp.
I could see the players now, for they were in the corner just across
from us. The leading violinist was alive with his music, bending
to it, marking the beat with his glossy head, on which his sparse
black hair was combed flat. The dining room was full of people, and
their talk made a thick hum; to rise over this the orchestra had to
work with extra effort.

The rosy lampshades on the tables, the silver vases full of flowers,
the slow sparkling movements of the ladies and gentlemen at the
tables, and the swallow-like dartings of the waiters transported me.
I felt a lump of excitement in my throat. My eyes kept returning to
the orchestra leader, who conducted with jerks of his nearly bald
head, for what he played and what he did seemed to emphasize the
astonishing fact that I was at a dinner party in public.

"What are they playing?" I asked. "What is that music?"

"It is called 'Il Bacio,' " Grosspa said.

"What does that mean?"

"It means 'The Kiss.' "

What an odd name for a piece of music, I thought. All through
dinner — which did not last as long as it might have — I inquired
about pieces played by the orchestra, and in addition to the Arditi
waltz, I remember one called "Simple Aveu," and the Boccherini
"Minuet." The violins had a sweetish, mosquitolike sound, and the
harp was breathless, and the cello mooed like a distant cow, and
it was all entrancing. Watching the orchestra, I ate absently, chewing hardly at all, until my father, time and again, turned me back to
my plate. And then a waiter came with a silver tub on legs, which
he put at my grandfather's left, and took the wine bottle from its
nest of sparkling ice and showed it to him. The label was approved,
and a sip was poured for my grandfather to taste. He held it to the
light and twirled his glass slowly; he sniffed it, and then he tasted it.

"Yes," he declared, "it will do."

My mother watched this ritual, and over her lovely heart-shaped
face, with its rolled crown of silky hair, I saw memories pass like
shadows, as if she were thinking of all the times she had watched
this business of ordering and serving wine. She blinked her eyes
again and, opening a little jeweled *lorgnon* she wore on a fine chain,
bent forward to read the menu that stood in a little silver frame be-

side her plate. But I could see that she was not reading, and I wondered what was the matter with everybody.

"For my grandson," Grosspa said, taking a wineglass and filling it half with water, and then to the top with wine. The yellow wine turned even paler in my glass, but there was too much ceremony for me not to be impressed. When he raised his glass, I raised mine, and while the others watched, we drank together. And then he recited a proverb in German which meant something like:

> *When comrades drink red wine or white,*
> *They stand as one for what is right,*

and a flourish of intimate applause went around the table in acknowledgment of this stage of my growing up.

I was suddenly embarrassed, for the music had stopped, and I thought all the other diners were looking at me; many were, in fact, smiling at a boy of ten, ruddy with excitement and confusion, drinking a solemn pledge of some sort with an old gentleman with a pink face and very white hair and whiskers.

Mercifully, the music began again, and we were released from our pose. My grandfather drew his great gold watch from his vest pocket and unhooked from a vest button the fob that held the heavy gold chain in place. Repeating an old game we had played when I was a baby, he held the watch toward my lips, and I knew what was expected of me. I blew upon it, and — though long ago I had penetrated the secret of the magic — the gold lid of the watch flew open. My grandfather laughed softly in a deep, wheezing breath, and then shut the watch.

"Do children ever know that what we do to please them pleases us more than it does them?" he said.

"*Ach Gott,*" whispered Tante Bep, but nobody reproved her.

"Richard, I give you this watch and chain to keep all your life, and by it you will remember me," my grandfather said.

"Oh, no!" exclaimed my mother.

He looked gravely at her and said, "Yes. Now, rather than later," and put the heavy, wonderful golden objects in my hand. I regarded them in stunned silence. Mine! I could hear the wiry ticking of the watch, and I knew that now and forever I myself could make the gold lid fly open.

"Well, Richard, what do you say?" my father urged gently.

"Yes, thank you, Grosspa, thank you."

I half rose from my chair and put my arm around his great head and kissed his cheek. Up close, I could see tiny blue and scarlet veins under his skin.

"That will do, my boy," he said. Then he took the watch from me and handed it to my father. "I hand it to your father to keep for you until you are twenty-one. But remember that it is yours and you must ask to see it any time you wish."

My disappointment was huge, but even I knew how sensible it was for the treasure to be held for me instead of given into my care.

"Any time you wish. You wish. Any time," repeated my grandfather, but in a changed voice, a hollow, windy sound that was terrible to hear. He was gripping the arms of his chair and now he shut his eyes behind his gold-framed lenses, and sweat broke out on his forehead. "Any time," he tried to say through his suffering, to preserve a social air. But, seized by pain too merciless to hide, he lost his pretenses and staggered to his feet. Quickly my mother and father helped him from the table, while other diners stared with neither curiosity nor pity. I thought the musicians played harder all of a sudden to distract people from the sight of an old man in trouble being led out of the main dining room of the Waldorf-Astoria.

"What is the matter?" I asked Tante Bep, who had been ordered, with a glance, to remain behind with me.

"Grosspa is not feeling well."

"Should we go with him?"

"But your ice cream."

"Yes, the ice cream."

So we waited for the ice cream, and in a moment or two the flow and rustle of rosy-shaded life was once again in the room.

My parents did not return from upstairs, though we waited. Finally, hot with wine and excitement, I was led by Tante Bep to the elevator and to my room and put to bed. Nobody came to see me, or if anyone did, I did not know it.

More snow fell during the night. When I woke up and ran to my window, the world was covered and the air was thick with snow still falling. Word came to dress quickly, for we were going to the ship. Suddenly I was consumed with eagerness to see the great ship that would cross the ocean.

Again we went in two taxicabs, I with my father. The others had gone ahead of us. My father pulled me near him to look out the window of the cab at the falling snow. We went through narrow, dark streets to the piers on the west side of Manhattan, where we boarded the ferryboat that would take us to Hoboken.

"We are going to the docks of the North German Lloyd," my father said.

"What is that?"

"The steamship company where Grosspa's ship is docked. The *Kronprinzessin Cecilie*."

"Can I go inside her?"

"Certainly. Grosspa wants to see you in his cabin."

"Is he there now?"

"Probably. The doctor wanted him to go right to bed."

"Is he sick?"

"Yes."

"Did he eat something —" (It was a family explanation often used to account for my various illnesses at their onset.)

"Not exactly. It is something else."

"Will he get well soon?"

"We hope so."

He looked out the window as he said this, instead of at me, and I thought, *He does not sound like my father*. But we had reached the New Jersey side now, and the cab was moving past the docks. Above the gray, snowy sheds I saw the funnels and masts of ocean liners. The streets were furious with noise, horses, cars, porters running, and suddenly a white tower of steam rose from the front of one of the funnels, to be followed in a second by a deep, roaring hoot.

"There she is," my father said. "That's her first signal for departure."

It was our ship. I could see her masts with their pennons being pulled about by the blowing snow, and her four tall ocher funnels.

We went from the taxi into the freezing air of the long pier. All I could see of the *Kronprinzessin Cecilie* were glimpses, through the pier shed, of white cabins, rows of portholes, and an occasional door of polished mahogany. A confused, hollow roar filled the long shed. We went up a canvas-covered gangway and then we were on board. There was an elegant creaking from the shining woodwork. I felt that ships must be built for boys, because the ceilings were so low and made me feel so tall.

My father held my hand to keep me by him on the thronged

decks, and then we entered a narrow corridor that seemed to have no end. The walls were of dark, shining wood, and there were weak yellow lights overhead. The floor sloped down and then up again, telling of the ship's construction. Cabin doors were open on either side. There was a curious odor in the air, something like the smell of soda crackers dipped in milk, and faraway — or was it right here, all about us in the ship — there was a soft throbbing sound. It seemed impossible that anything so immense as this ship would presently detach itself from the land.

"Here we are," my father said, at a half-open cabin door.

We entered my grandfather's room, which was not like a room in a house, for none of its lines squared with the others but met only to reflect the curvature of the ship. Across the room, under two portholes whose silk curtains were drawn, my grandfather lay in a narrow brass bed. He lay at a slight slope, with his arms outside the covers, and he wore a white nightgown. I had never before seen him in anything but his formal day and evening clothes. He looked white — there was hardly a difference of color between his beard and his cheeks and his brow. He did not turn his head, only his eyes. He seemed suddenly dreadfully small, and fearfully cautious, where before he had gone his way magnificently, ignoring whatever threatened him with inconvenience, rudeness or disadvantage. My mother stood by his side, and Tante Bep was at the foot of the bed, wearing her black shawl and peasant skirts.

"Yes, come, Richard," Grosspa said in a faint, wheezy voice, looking for me without turning his head.

I went to his side, and he moved his hand an inch or two toward me — not enough to risk such a pain as had thrown him down the night before, but enough to call for a response. I gave him my hand and he tightened his fingers over mine.

"Will you come to see me?" he said.

"Where?" I asked in a loud, clear voice. My parents looked at each other, as if to inquire how in the world the chasms which divide age from youth, and pain from health, and sorrow from innocence could ever be bridged.

"In Germany," he whispered. He shut his eyes and held my hand, and I had a vision of Germany which may have been sweetly near his own; for what I saw were the pieces of brilliantly colored cardboard scenery that belonged to the toy theater he had once brought me from Germany.

"Yes, Grosspa," I replied, "in Germany."

"Yes," he whispered, opening his eyes and making the Sign of the Cross on my hand with his thumb. Then he looked at my mother, who understood at once.

"You go now with Daddy," she said, "and wait for me on deck. We must leave the ship soon. *Schnell*, now, skip!"

My father took me along the corridor and down the grand stairway. The ship's orchestra was playing somewhere — it sounded like the Waldorf. We went out to the deck just as the ship's whistle let go again, and now it shook me gloriously and terribly. I covered my ears, but still I was held by that immense, deep voice. For a moment, when it stopped, the ordinary sounds around us did not come close. It was still snowing — heavy, slow, thick flakes, each like several flakes stuck together.

A cabin boy came along beating a brass cymbal, calling out for all visitors to leave the ship.

I began to fear that my mother might be taken away to sea after my father and I were forced ashore. I saw her at last. She came toward us with a rapid, light step and, saying nothing, turned us to the gangway, and we went down. She was wearing a little spotted veil, and with one hand she lifted it and put her handkerchief to her mouth. She was weeping and I was abashed by her grief.

We hurried to the dock street, and there we lingered to watch the *Kronprinzessin Cecilie* sail.

We did not talk. It was bitter cold. Wind came strongly from the west, and then, after a third great whistle blast the ship slowly began to change — she moved like water itself as she left the dock, guided by three tugboats that made heavy black smoke in the thick air. At last I could see all of the ship at one time.

I was amazed how tall and narrow she was. Her four funnels rose like a city's chimneys against the blowy sky. Stern first, she moved out into the river. I squinted at her with my head on one side and knew exactly how I would make a small model of her when I got home. In midstream she turned slowly to head toward the Lower Bay. She looked gaunt and proud and topheavy as she ceased backing and turning and began to steam down the river and away.

"Oh, Dan!" my mother cried in a broken sob, and put her face against my father's shoulder. He folded his arm around her. Their faces were white.

Just then a break in the sky across the river lightened the snowy day, and I stared in wonder at the change. My father, watching after the liner, said to my mother: "Like some wounded old lion crawling home to die."

"Oh, Dan," she sobbed, "don't, don't!"

I could not imagine what they were talking about. I tugged at my mother's arm and said with excitement, pointing to the thick flakes everywhere about us, and against the light beyond, "Look, look, the snowflakes are all black!"

My mother suddenly could bear no more. She leaned down and shook me, and her voice was strong with anger: "Richard, why do you say black! What nonsense. Stop it. Snowflakes are white, Richard. White! White! When will you ever see things as they are! Oh!"

"Come, everybody," my father said. "I have the taxi waiting."

"But they *are* black!" I cried.

"Quiet!" my father commanded.

We were to return to Dorchester on the night train. All day I was too proud to mention what I alone seemed to remember, but after my nap, during which I refused to sleep, my mother came to me.

"You think I have forgotten," she said. "Well, I remember. We will go and arrange for your presents."

My world was full of joy again. The first two presents were easy to find — there was a little shop full of novelties a block from the hotel, and there I bought for Anna a folding package of views of New York and for Mr. Schmitt a cast-iron savings bank, made in the shape of the Statue of Liberty, to receive dimes. It was harder to think of something Ted would like. My mother let me consider many possibilities among the variety available in the novelty shop, but the one thing I wanted for Ted I did not see. Finally I asked the shopkeeper: "Do you have any straw hats for horses?"

"What?"

"Straw hats for horses, with holes for their ears to come through. They wear them in summer."

"Oh. I know what you mean. No, we don't."

My mother took charge. "Then, Richard, I don't think this gentleman has what we need for Ted. Let's go back to the hotel. I think we will find it there."

"What will it be?"

"You'll see."

When tea had been served in her room, she asked, "What do horses love?"

"Hay. Oats."

"Yes. What else?"

Her eyes sparkled playfully. I followed her glance, and knew the answer.

"I know! Sugar!"

"Exactly" — and she made a little packet of sugar cubes in a Waldorf envelope from the desk in the corner, and my main concern about the trip to New York was satisfied.

At home I could not wait to present my gifts. Would they like them? Whether Anna and Mr. Schmitt did or not, I never really knew. Anna accepted her folder of views and opened it up to let the pleated pages fall in one sweep, and said, "When we came to New York from the old country I was a baby and I do not remember one thing about it." Mr. Schmitt took his Statue of Liberty savings bank, turned it over carefully, and said, "Well . . ."

But Ted — Ted very clearly loved my gift, for he nibbled the sugar cubes off my outstretched palm until there were none left, and then he bumped at me with his hard, itchy head, making me laugh and hurt at the same time.

"He likes sugar," I said to Mr. Schmitt.

"*Ja*. Do you want to ride?"

Life, then, was much as before until the day, a few weeks later, that we received a cablegram telling us that my grandfather had died in Munich. My father came home from the office to comfort my mother. They told me the news in our long living room, with the curtains drawn. I listened, a lump of pity came into my throat for the look on my mother's face, but I did not feel anything else.

"He dearly loved you," they said.

"May I go now?" I asked.

They were shocked. What an unfeeling child. Did he have no heart? How could the loss of so great and dear a figure in the family not move him?

But I had never seen anything dead; I had no idea of what death was like; Grosspa had gone away before and I had soon ceased to miss him. What if they did say now that I would never see him again? They shook their heads and sent me off.

Anna was more offhand than my parents. "You know," she said, letting me watch her work at the deep zinc laundry tubs in the dark, steamy basement, "that your Grosspa went home to Germany to die, don't you?"

"Is that the reason he went?" I asked.

"That's the reason."

"Did he know it?"

"Oh, yes, sure he knew it."

"Why couldn't he die right here?"

"Well, when our time comes, maybe we all want to go back where we came from."

Her voice contained a doleful pleasure, but the greatest mystery in the world was still closed to me. When I left her, she raised her old tune under the furnace pipes, and I wished I was as happy and full of knowledge as she was.

My time soon came.

On the following Saturday, I was watching for Mr. Schmitt and Ted when I heard heavy footsteps running up the front porch and someone shaking the doorknob, as if he had forgotten there was a bell. I went to see. It was Mr. Schmitt. He was panting and he looked wild. When I opened the door, he ran past me, calling out, "Telephone! Let me have the telephone!"

I pointed to it in the front hall, where it stood on a gilded wicker taboret. He began frantically to click the receiver hook. I was amazed to see tears roll down his cheeks.

"What's the matter, Mr. Schmitt?"

I heard my mother coming along the upstairs hallway from her sitting room.

Mr. Schmitt put the phone down suddenly and pulled off his hat, and shook his head. "What's the use?" he said. "I know it is too late. I was calling the ice plant to send someone."

"Good morning, Mr. Schmitt," my mother said, coming downstairs. "What on earth is the matter?"

"My poor old Ted," he said, waving his hat toward the street. "He just fell down and died up the street in front of the Weiners' house."

I ran out of the house and up the sidewalk to the Weiners' house, and sure enough, there was the ice wagon, and still in the shafts, lying heavy and gone on his side, was Ted.

There lay death on the asphalt pavement. I confronted the mystery at last. The one eye that I could see was open. Ted's teeth gaped apart, and his long tongue touched the street. His body seemed twice as big and heavy as before. His front legs were crossed, and the great horn cup of the upper hoof was slightly tipped, the way he used to rest it in ease. In his fall he had twisted the shafts that he had pulled for so many years. His harness was awry. Water dripped from the back of the hooded wagon. Its wheels looked as if they had never turned. What would ever turn them?

"Never," I said, half aloud. I knew the meaning of this word now.

In another moment my mother came and took me back to our house, and Mr. Schmitt settled down on the curbstone to wait for people to arrive and take away the leavings of his changed world.

"Richard," my mother said, "don't go out again until I tell you."

I went and told Anna what I knew. She listened with her head to one side, her eyes half closed, and she nodded at my news and sighed.

"Poor old Ted," she said, "he couldn't even crawl home to die."

This made my mouth fall open, for it reminded me of something I had heard before, and all day I was subdued and private. Late that night I woke in a storm of grief so noisy that my parents heard the wild gusts of weeping and came to ask what the trouble was.

I could not speak at first, for their tender, warm, bed-sweet presences doubled my emotion, and I sobbed against them as they held me. But at last, when they said again, "What's this all about, Richard? Richard?" I was able to say brokenly, "It's all about Ted."

It was true, if not all the truth, for I was thinking also of Grosspa crawling home to die, and I knew what that meant now, and what death was like. I imagined Grosspa's heavy death, with one eye open, and his sameness and his difference all mingled, and I wept for him at last, and for myself if I should die, and for my ardent mother and my sovereign father, and for the iceman's old horse, and for everyone.

"Hush, dear, hush, Richard," they said.

A pain in my head began to throb remotely as my outburst diminished, and another thought entered. I said bitterly: "But they were black! Really they were!"

They looked at each other and then at me, but I was too spent to continue, and I fell back on my pillow. Even if they insisted that snowflakes were white, I knew that when seen against the light, falling out of the sky into the dark water all about the *Kronprinzessin Cecilie*, they were black. Black snowflakes against the sky. Black.

WILLIAM HUMPHREY

The Pump

(FROM ESQUIRE)

FOR WEEKS Jordan Terry has been down on his knees promising God to drink the first barrelful if only they would go on drilling and not give up; but they were about ready to haul out the rig and call it another dry hole when they brought in a gusher at fifty-nine hundred feet. Jordan was digging turnips in a field that he was being paid by the government not to grow anything on when he got the news, and though he went out and drank a barrelful all right, it wasn't oil.

A day or so later old Jordan was rocking on his front porch and smoking a White Owl when he saw a couple of men of the rigging crew up on top of his derrick with hammers and crowbars taking it apart. Barefoot as he was he jumped out of his rocker and tore down to see what the hell was going on. They told him they were fixing to cap his well.

"Cap it?" cried Jordan with a white face. "Put ere a cap on it? Why? For God's sake, misters, let her come! Don't go a-putting ere a cap on it!"

They explained that the derrick was just for the drilling. Like a pile driver. There was no further need of it now. They were fixing to install a pump.

"Pump! What do we need ere a pump for?" asked Jordan, remembering how it had shot up in the air, like Old Faithful. "The way it spurted out."

"It's like opening a bottle of beer, ol' hoss," said the chief engineer. "That first little bit that foams over comes by itself. The rest you have to work for."

Work! Hah! Set on your ass in a rocking chair and knock down two bits on every barrelful! That kind of work suited old Jordan to a T.

So the derrick was dismantled and taken away and in its stead the pump was set up. It was like an off-balance seesaw, a beam the size of a crosstie set off-center in the notch of an upright post. To either end of the beam was attached a rod which disappeared into the ground. Up and down it went, up and down, bowing in frenzied, untiring obeisance. Yes, sir! Listening with your ear to the ground you could hear, or could fancy that you did, a sound like a seashell makes, of endless vast waves lapping the shore of a vast underground sea. And in the pipe you could hear the mighty surge, like the pulse of a great artery drawing up a steady stream of rich, black blood. Day and night the pump went, night and day, working for him: rocket-a-bump, rocket-a-bump, rocket-a-bump . . . In the daytime it went at about the same trot that Jordan went at in his rocking chair, at night as he lay awake grinning in the dark each stroke of the cycle matched a beat of his heart: rocket-a-bump, rocket-a-bump, rocket-a-bump . . .

"How much you reckon she draws every time she goes up and down?" he asked the engineers.

They told him how many barrels it pumped per day. Jordan worked it out from there. He wanted to know just how much he was worth by the minute, how much richer he had grown with each rock of his rocker, each beat of his heart. He got twenty-five cents a barrel. A barrel held fifty-five gallons. It averaged twenty-five strokes a minute. Call it half a cent a stroke. Rocket-a-bump: half a cent. Rocket-a-bump: that makes a penny. Rocket-a-bump, rocket-a-bump — the last thing he heard at night, and the first thing he heard in the morning. Sixty times twenty-five was fifteen hundred. And twenty-four times fifteen hundred times three hundred and sixty-five . . .

Jordan — though he was far from being its first owner — had for some years been driving a 1921 Durant, driving it, that is to say, whenever it felt like going. And only now did he possess somewhere about the amount of oil it demanded. Naturally a man in his position couldn't be seen around in that old wreck any more. As even the hungriest car dealer was not going to allow him anything for it on a trade-in, it occurred to Jordan that he would be doing a mighty fine deed by making a present of it to his next-door neighbor, Clarence Bywaters. Poor son of a bitch. It must be hard on a man to have oil struck right next door to you. Like a canary bird in a cage hung out of a window, and having to watch a fat sassy old bluejay hopping about in the trees and plucking juicy worms out of the ground. They had begun drilling on poor old Clarence's land even before Jordan's, and they were still at it, but only because they had poured so much money down that dry hole that they just hated to call it quits. They were talking about pulling out any day now. Jordan remembered what he had gone through. He didn't think Bywaters would take exception to his offer. Poor son of a bitch, with all that raft of kids he wasn't in any position to despise a little charity.

Delivery on a new Duesenberg, especially one with as many custom accessories as Jordan had put in for, took some time. Meanwhile he still went about in the old Durant. He hadn't got around to giving it to Clarence Bywaters when the news broke one morning that they had brought in a gusher on his neighbor's holdings.

Jordan Terry was not the sort to begrudge another his good fortune. Christ, he had his! He went over and took Clarence Bywaters by the hand and congratulated him. He could not help mentioning his intention to have given him the Durant; but, rather to his irritation, Bywaters thought it was an even better joke than he did. He got fifty dollars allowance on it (not that he needed the damn fifty dollars, but them that had it never got it by throwing any away) by threatening to cancel the order on his new Duesenberg.

The Duesenberg looked like a Pullman car. And it turned out to use a bit more gas and oil than the Durant. But what the hell! If there was one thing he had plenty of that was it. While he was out burning it up in those thirsty big-bore cylinders, back home that little old pump, going steady as the heart in his breast, was bringing up more. And at night while the car rested, and after he himself had been lulled to sleep by that sweet cradlelike rhythm, the pump worked on, rocket-a-bump, rocket-a-bump, rocket-a-bump . . .

One day the man who maintained the pump, on one of his periodical visits, happened to let drop something which suggested that both Jordan's and his neighbor's wells were drawing upon the same subterranean pool.

"You mean," said Jordan with a white face, "you mean that son of a bitch is tapping onto my oil?"

What could he do about it? Nothing! Couldn't he go to law? He had got there first. Didn't a man have no rights? Couldn't they do something? Install a second pump? Replace this one with a bigger, stronger, faster one? Sink a thicker pipe? Christ, wasn't there nothing could be done to stop him, keep ahead of him, get it before he took it all?

But they didn't care, the oilmen. The same company (a Yankee outfit) had drilled both wells, his and his neighbor's. They were getting theirs on both sides of the fence, the sons of bitches. What the hell did they care which of them got more on his royalty check? It was all one and the same to them.

Jordan tried to visualize the lake of oil deep underground. It seemed to have shrunk. It had seemed bigger before, when he had thought of it as lying just under his own thirty acres, than it did now that he must think of it as extending also under his neighbor's forty-odd. Twelve acres more of it that damned Bywaters had than he had! To think there was a time when he could have bought him out at fifteen dollars an acre! A piddling six hundred dollars! Christalmighty, he spent more than that a week now. To be sure, at the time he didn't have six dollars cash money, much less six hundred, and wouldn't have spent it on Clarence Bywaters' forty acres of dust and erosion if he had had. It was enough to bring on heart failure now when Jordan recalled that he had countered Bywaters' price by offering to sell out to him at ten an acre.

They had had to drill deeper on his neighbor's land. Did that mean that it was shallower on his side, that his oil was draining downhill into Bywaters' deeper pool? Was he just on the edge of it and Bywaters sitting in the middle? Since they had had to drill deeper that meant that his neighbor had a longer pipe. Jordan pictured the two of them underground, both sucking away, and the level of the pool dropping lower and lower, and suddenly his pipe made a sound like a soda straw makes at the bottom of the glass when the ice-cream soda is all gone. But his neighbor's pipe went on sucking greedily away.

The sound of his neighbor's pump, now that he knew it was

pumping *his* oil, was like the steady drip of a leaky faucet: Jordan couldn't not hear it. Rocket-a-bump, rocket-a-bump, rocket-a-bump, all day long and into the night, growing louder and louder, drowning out nearer sounds, including that of his own pump.

Once Jordan's pump stopped. He was lying in bed one night, sweating, tossing, the pounding of his neighbor's pump like a migraine headache, hating his wife for her deep untroubled sleep at his side, when suddenly his pump stopped. That was his own damned heart he heard, his pump had stopped. He leapt out of bed, ignoring his wife's sleepy questioning whine, and dashed outdoors in his B.V.D.'s. It was going. Thank God, it was going. The relief was almost more than Jordan could stand. But wasn't it going slower, weaker? It seemed to be going slower. Had it reached bottom and was it having to strain to draw up the last little bit? Or was it only that his heart was beating so fast?

From that time on the rocket-a-bump, rocket-a-bump, instead of lulling Jordan to sleep at night, kept him awake, listening, afraid it was going to stop, uncertain whether it was his own he was hearing or his neighbor's. He had to give up rocking in his rocking chair: the noise it made interfered with his listening. He sat very still, listening. He was afraid to go off for a ride in his car for fear his pump might stop while he was gone. Sometimes at night when at last out of exhaustion he dropped off and momentarily ceased to hear the fevered rhythm of his own pulse drumming in his ear against his twisted and sweaty pillow, he awoke with a jerk, sure that his pump had stopped, that it was the other that he heard, and at such times as he bolted up in the darkness his heart gasped and gurgled as if it had drawn up the very last drop.

The bills for his new style of living began pouring in, bills of a size to take your breath away, in numbers like germs. Debts Jordan had always had, money to pay them with never before. The one was real, the other just paper, something in a bank. He lectured his wife and daughters on their extravagance. He reminded them how well they had always got by before without jewels and permanent waves. How much money a rich man needed!

Meanwhile that s.o.b. next door was really living high. Burning up the road in a Graham roadster. A blowout every weekend. Delivery vans from Ardmore and Oklahoma City pulling up to the door all day long. And his womenfolks going around bundled up in furs when it was 110° in the shade, looking like an escaped zoo. He was not economizing. Whenever they met, Bywaters gave him such a glad hand and such a big fat grin that the conviction grew on Jordan's mind that his neighbor was laughing at him. If Bywaters knew — and how could he not know? — that they were both pumping out of the same pool, it never fazed him. Which could only mean that he somehow knew he was getting the lion's share.

Jordan was not the only one to notice those fur coats, those delivery vans. Complaining that they were tackier now than when they were poor, his wife and daughters whined at him from morn till night. Clarence Bywaters now, his wife and daughters were dressed as women in their position ought to be. Were the Bywaters any better off than they were? And they would catalogue the finery which Mrs. Bywaters and each of the Bywaters girls had worn to church that morning. As if Jordan hadn't seen! As if it wasn't him who was paying for every stitch of all those glad rags! How could he afford to deck out his own women when it was him who was outfitting Bywaters' like four grand duchesses?

Often poor Jordan chewed the bitter cud of that moment when his neighbor had offered to sell out to him. The scene was vivid in his mind. He saw Bywaters' furrowed brow, saw him stroke his stubby chin, saw his head shake, heard him say, "It's a dog's life. Crops burning up. Soil all blown away. Cotton selling for nothing. If I could just raise the money I'd leave tomorrow. You know anybody that'll give me fifteen an acre?" Jordan had laughed. Oh, how he wished now he had it to do over again! Surely he could have raised six hundred dollars if he had only tried. He could have borrowed that on his own place. It already had a first lien on it, but he could have got a second. Oh, why had he let that golden opportunity slip? Then all seventy-two acres of that lake of oil would have been his. Both those pumps his alone. These days to lay his hands on six hundred dollars all he had to do was reach in his pocket. He saw himself doing so. He saw Bywaters' face break into a grateful smile, felt the grateful pressure of his hand. His heart melted with pity for his neighbor, poor son of a bitch, and with the warmth of its own generosity. "California, here I come!" said Bywaters, hope shining like a rainbow through the tears brimming in his eyes. "Best of luck, ol' hoss," Jordan said. "I'll miss you." From this dream he was awakened by the throb of his neighbor's pump.

To wash the bitter taste from his mouth Jordan would take a pull at the bottle, drinking red whisky now instead of white, his sole extravagance. Presently, despite himself, he would slip into another reverie. Rocking faster and faster as the figures mounted, he would calculate how much ahead he would be if his neighbor's pump was to break down, be out of commission for a week, ten days, two weeks. A month. Two months! Three! By then he was rocking so fast that when he caught himself and slowed down he was out of breath and panting, in a sweat. All he had succeeded in doing was in figuring how much his neighbor was making every minute. Then he would feel the hairs on the nape of his neck rise up and tingle as if someone was watching him.

Then Jordan knew he was in for it, and his heart seized with dread. For any misfortune wished upon another is a boomerang, it circles back and hits you. A man can't think one mean thought, not even in a whisper, not even alone in a dark room at night nor down in a cave deep in the earth without Him hearing it and visiting it right back on you. Once a thought has been thought there is no calling it back. It goes out on the air like the radio waves, with the thinker's name all over it. He gets a whiff of it and says, "Who made that bad smell?" He looks down, right at you, and grabs you by the scruff of the neck and rubs your nose in your own mess.

So it was bound to happen. Try as he might to unwish the wish that his neighbor's pump might fail, Jordan went right on wishing it. So it was only a matter of time until his own broke down. Really. Not just a false alarm. And who knew for how long? Two weeks? Not likely! He had wished three months against Bywaters.

As is so often the case in such matters, for all his anxiety, Jordan was unaware of it when it befell. He had lain awake that night listening so intently to the hateful sound of his neighbor's pump that he didn't hear his. Or maybe he fondly imagined that it was Bywaters' which had stopped, permitting him to fall asleep at last. The silence awoke him early next morning: steady, throbbing silence, and, in the background, Bywaters' pump going double time. He went out on the porch and looked. The beam hung down as if pole-axed.

Jordan called the Company, his wife called the doctor. Keep him in bed and away from drink, the doctor advised; but he was no sooner gone than Jordan was out on the front porch rocking nerv-

ously and drinking steadily as he awaited the repairmen. It was
midmorning before they showed up.

"Have her going for you again in no time now, Colonel," they
said.

But they fiddled and laid down their tools to talk and roll and
smoke cigarettes and dawdled in the shade over their lunch and
started looking at their watches half an hour before quitting time,
and by then Bywaters' pump was going in jig time. So was Jordan
in his rocker, until all of a sudden he came to a dead stop. He was
still warm when they got to him but it was as if rigor mortis had set
in while he was still alive. They had to pry him loose from that
chair, and getting him into his coffin was like straightening a bent
nail.

There is nothing on earth as dry as a handful of red Oklahoma
dirt, though deeper down may lie an ocean of black gold. They
crumbled their handfuls over Jordan Terry and shook their heads.
A crying shame, said Jordan's longtime friend and neighbor Clarence Bywaters, a crying shame the poor son of a bitch had only lived
to enjoy his wealth such a little while.

SHIRLEY JACKSON

Birthday Party

(FROM VOGUE)

IT WAS planned by Jannie herself. Jannie even went so far as to say that if she could have a pajama party she would keep her room picked up for one solid month, a promise so far beyond the realms of possibility that I could only believe that she wanted the pajama party more than anything else in the world. My husband thought it was a mistake. "You are making a terrible, an awful mistake," he said to me. "And don't try to say I didn't tell you so." My older son Laurie told me it was a mistake. "Mommy-O," he said, "*this* you will regret. For the rest of your life you will be saying to yourself 'Why did I let that dopey girl ever, *ever* have a pajama party that night?' For the rest of your life. When you're an old lady you will be saying . . ."

"What can I do?" I said. "I promised." We were all at the breakfast table, and it was seven-thirty on the morning of Jannie's eleventh birthday. Jannie sat unhearing, her spoon poised blissfully over her cereal, her eyes dreamy with speculation over what was going to turn up in the packages to be presented that evening after dinner. Her list of wanted birthday presents had included a live pony, a pare of roller scates, high-heeled shoes of her very own, a make-up kit with reel lipstick, a record player and records, and a dear little monkey to play with, and any or all of these things might be in the offing.

"You know of course," Laurie said to me, "I have the room right next to her? I'm going to be sleeping in there like I do every night? You know I'm going to be in my bed trying to sleep?" He shuddered.

"Giggle," he said. "Giggle, giggle, giggle, giggle, giggle, giggle. Two, three o'clock in the morning — giggle, giggle, giggle. A human being can't bear it."

Jannie focused her eyes on him. "Why don't we burn up this boy's birth certificate?" she asked.

"Giggle giggle," Laurie said.

Barry spoke, waving his toast. "When Jannie gets her birthday presents can I play with it?" he asked. "If I am very careful can I play with just the . . ."

Everyone began to talk at once to drown him out. "Giggle giggle," Laurie shouted. "Don't say I didn't warn you," my husband said loudly. "Anyway I promised," I said. "Happy birthday dear sister," Sally sang. Jannie giggled.

"There," Laurie said. "You hear her? All night long — five of them." Shaking his head as one who has been telling them and telling them and *telling* them not to bring that wooden horse through the gates of Troy, he stamped off to get his schoolbooks and his trumpet. Jannie sighed happily. Barry opened his mouth to speak and his father and Sally and I all said "Shhh."

Jannie had to be excused from her cereal, because she was too excited to eat. It was a cold frosty morning, and I forced the girls into their winter coats. Laurie, who believes that he is impervious to cold, came downstairs, said, "Mad, I tell you, mad," sympathetically to me, "Bye, cat," to his father, and went out the back door toward his bike, ignoring my insistence that he put on at least a sweater.

I told the girls to hold Barry's hand crossing the street, told Barry to hold the girls' hands crossing the street, put Barry's midmorning cookies into his jacket pocket, reminded Jannie for the third time about her spelling book, held the dogs so they could not get out when the door was opened, told everyone goodbye and happy birthday again to Jannie, and watched from the kitchen window while they made their haphazard way down the driveway, lingering, chatting. I opened the door once more to call to them to move along, they would be late for school, and they disregarded me. I called to hurry *up,* and for a minute they moved more quickly, hopping, and then came to the end of the driveway and onto the sidewalk where they merged at once into the general traffic going to school. I came back to the table and sat down wearily, reaching for the coffeepot. "Five of them are too many," my husband explained. "One would have been quite enough."

"You can't have a pajama party with just one guest," I said sullenly. "And anyway no matter who she invited the other three would have been offended."

By lunchtime I had set up four cots, two of them borrowed from a neighbour who was flatly taken aback when she heard what I wanted them for. "I think you must be crazy," she said. Jannie's bedroom is actually two rooms, one small and one, which she calls her library because her bookcase is in there, much larger. I put one cot in her bedroom next to her bed, which left almost no room in there to move around. The other three cots I lined up in her library, making a kind of dormitory effect. Beyond Jannie's library is the guest room, and all the other bedrooms except Laurie's are on the other side of the guest room. Laurie's room is separated by only the thinnest wall from Jannie's library.

When Jannie came home from school I told her to lie down and rest, pointing out in one of the most poignant understatements of my life that she would probably be up late that night. In fifteen minutes she was downstairs asking if she could get dressed for her party. I said her party was not going to start until eight o'clock and to take an apple and go lie down again. In another ten minutes she was down to explain that she would probably be too excited to dress later and it would really be only common sense to put her party dress on now. I said if she came downstairs again before dinner was on the table I would personally call her four guests and cancel the pajama party. She finally rested for half an hour or so in the chair by the upstairs phone, talking to her friend Carole.

She was, of course, unable to eat her dinner, although she had chosen the menu. She nibbled at a piece of lamb, rearranged her mashed potatoes, and told her father and me that she could not understand how we had endured as many birthdays as we had. Her father said that he personally had gotten kind of used to them, and that as a matter of fact a certain quality of excitement did seem to go out of them after — say — thirty, and Jannie sighed unbelievingly.

"One more birthday like this would *kill* her," Laurie said. He groaned. "Carole," he said, as one telling over a fearful list. "Kate. Laura. Linda. Jannie. You must be *crazy*," he said to me.

"I suppose your friends are so much?" Jannie said. "I suppose Joey didn't get sent down to Miss Corcoran's office six times today for throwing paper wads? I suppose Billy . . ."

"You didn't seem to think Billy was so terrible, walking home from school," Laurie said. "I guess that wasn't *you* walking with . . ."

Jannie turned pink. "Does my own brother have any right to insult me on my own birthday?" she asked her father.

In honor of Jannie's birthday Sally helped me clear the table, and Jannie sat in state with her hands folded, waiting. When the table was cleared we left Jannie there alone, and assembled in the study. While my husband lighted the candles on the pink and white cake, Sally and Barry took from the back of the hall closet the gifts they had chosen themselves and lovingly wrapped. Barry's gift was clearly a leathercraft set, since his most careful wrapping had been unable to make the paper go right around the box, and the name showed clearly. Sally had three books. Laurie had an album of records he had chosen himself. ("This is for my *sister*," he had told the clerk in the music store, most earnestly, with an Elvis Presley record in each hand, "for my sister — not *me*, my *sister*.")

Laurie also had to carry the little blue record player which my husband and I had decided was a more suitable gift for our elder daughter than a dear little monkey or even a pair of high-heeled shoes. I carried the boxes from the two sets of grandparents, one holding a flowered quilted skirt and a fancy blouse, and the other holding a stiff, lacy, beribboned crinoline petticoat. With the cake leading, we filed into the dining room where Jannie sat. "Happy birthday to you," we sang, and Jannie looked once and then leaped past us to the phone. "Be there in a minute," she said, and then "Carole? Carole, listen, I *got* it, the record player. Bye."

By a quarter to eight Jannie was dressed in the new blouse and skirt over the petticoat, Barry was happily taking apart the leathercraft set, the record player had been plugged in and we had heard, more or less involuntarily, four sides of Elvis Presley. Laurie had shut himself in his room, dissociating himself utterly from the festivities. "I was willing to *buy* them," he explained, "I even spent good money out of my bank, but no one can make me *listen*."

I took a card table up to Jannie's room and squeezed it in among the beds; on it I put a pretty cloth and a bowl of apples, a small dish of candy, a plate of decorated cupcakes, and an ice bucket in which were five bottles of grape soda embedded in ice. Jannie brought her record player upstairs and put it on the table and Laurie plugged it

in for her on condition that she would not turn it on until he was
safely back in his room. With what Laurie felt indignantly was a
complete and absolute disregard for the peace of mind and healthy
sleep of a cherished older son I put a deck of fortunetelling cards
on the table, and a book on the meaning of dreams.

Everything was ready, and Jannie and her father and I were sitting apprehensively in the living room when the first guest came. It
was Laura. She was dressed in a blue party dress, and she brought
Jannie a small package containing a charm bracelet which Jannie
put on. Then Carole and Linda arrived together, one wearing a
green party dress and the other a fancy blouse and skirt, like Jannie.
They all admired Jannie's new blouse and skirt, and one of them
had brought her a book and the other had brought a dress and hat
for her doll. Kate came almost immediately afterward. She was
wearing a wide skirt like Jannie's, and she had a crinoline, too. She
and Jannie compared crinolines, and each of them insisted that the
other's was much, *much* prettier. Kate had brought Jannie a pocketbook with a penny inside for luck. All the girls carried overnight
bags but Kate, who had a small suitcase. "You'll think I'm going to
stay for a *month*, the stuff I brought," she said, and I felt my husband shudder.

Each of the girls complimented, individually, each item of apparel
on each of the others. It was conceded that Jannie's skirt, which
came from California, was of a much more advanced style than skirts
obtainable in Vermont. The pocketbook was a most fortunate
choice, they agreed, because it perfectly matched the little red flowers in Jannie's skirt. Laura's shoes were the prettiest anyone had
ever seen. Linda's party dress was of Orlon, which all of them
simply *adored*. Linda said if she *did* say it herself, the ruffles never
got limp. Carole was wearing a necklace which no one could *possibly* tell was not made of real pearls. Linda said we had the *nicest*
house, she was always telling her mother and father that she wished
they had one just like it. My husband said he would consider any
reasonable offer. Kate said our dogs were just *darling*, and Laura
said she *loved* that green chair. I said somewhat ungraciously that
they had all of them spent a matter of thousands of hours in our
house and the green chair was no newer or prettier than it had been
the last time Laura was here, when she was bouncing up and down
on the seat. Jannie said hastily that there were cupcakes and Elvis

Presley records up in her room, and they were gone. They went up the back stairs like a troop of horses, saying "Cupcakes, cupcakes."

Sally and Barry were in bed, but permitted to stay awake because it was Friday night and Jannie's birthday. Barry had taken Jannie's leathercraft set up to his room, planning to make his dear sister a pair of moccasins. Because Sally and Barry were not invited to the party I took them each a tray with one cupcake, a glass of fruit juice, and three candies. Sally asked if she could play *her* phonograph while she read fairy tales and ate her cupcake and I said certainly, since I did not think that in the general air of excitement even Barry would fall asleep for a while yet. As I started downstairs Barry called after me to ask if *he* could play *his* phonograph, and of course I could hardly say no.

When I got downstairs my husband had settled down to reading freshman themes in the living room. "Everything seems . . ." he said; I believe he was going to finish "quiet," but Elvis Presley started then from Jannie's room. There was a howl of fury from Laurie's room, and then *his* phonograph started; to answer Elvis Presley he had chosen an old Louis Armstrong record, and he was holding his own. From the front of the house upstairs drifted down the opening announcement of "Peter and the Wolf," from Sally, and then, distantly, from Barry's room, the crashing chords which heralded (blast off!) "Space Men on the Moon."

"What did you say?" I asked my husband.

"Oh, when the saints come marching in . . ."

"I said it seemed quiet," my husband yelled.

"The cat, by a clarinet in a loooow register . . ."

"I want you, I need you . . ."

"Prepare for blast: five — four — three — two — "

"The golden trumpets will begin . . ."

"It sure does," I yelled back.

"BOOM." Barry's rocket was in space.

Jannie had switched to "Hound Dog," and Laurie called on his reserves and took out his trumpet. He played without a mute, which is ordinarily forbidden in the house, so for a few minutes he was definitely ascendant, even though a certain undeniable guitar beat intruded from Jannie's room, but then Jannie and her guests began to sing and Laurie faltered, lost "the Saints," fell irresistibly into "Hound Dog," cursed, picked up "the Saints," and finally conceded in time for four — three — two — one — BOOM. Peter's gay strain came through clearly for a minute and then Jannie finished changing records and our house rocked to its foundations with "Heartbreak Hotel."

Laurie's door slammed and he came pounding down the back stairs and into the living room. "Dad," he said pathetically.

His father nodded bleakly. "I'll stop them," I said, and went to the back stairs; in the kitchen I could only hear a kind of steady combined beat which shivered the window frames and got the pots and pans crashing together softly where they hung on the wall. I waited till the record was finished and then called up to Jannie that it was time for Sally and Barry to go to sleep and she must turn off the record player for the night.

She agreed amiably, saying that they had played every record three times anyway, and the phonograph stopped. Since it was close to nine-thirty I went up to Sally's room, and found that Sally had turned off *her* phonograph because she was getting sleepy. I went on to Barry's room, where Barry had fallen asleep in his space suit somewhere on the dim craters of the moon, fragments of leather all over his bed. I came back to the living room to find my husband back at his freshman themes and Laurie sprawled all over the couch reading *Downbeat*.

"See?" I said. "They were very nice about quieting down."

"Yeah," Laurie said. *"Suuuure."*

I took up my book and sat down. It was so quiet I could almost hear the kitten purring on Sally's bed.

"I hope you notice," I said to my husband, "that — *just* as I said — it is perfectly possible for a group of five girls to have a quiet, almost grown-up party overnight. I used to do it all the time when I was a girl, and I can't remember that we ever made much of a disturbance."

"The trouble with girls," Laurie said in a tone of dire foreboding, "is that as soon as you don't know what they're doing, it's probably something no one in their right minds would ever think of."

"That's not the *only* trouble with girls," his father said.

We read peacefully in a silence broken only by Laurie's whistling between his teeth and an occasional remark from my husband or myself to the effect that if Laurie was unable to control that infuriating racket he could take himself off to bed. After a while Laurie went into the kitchen and consumed three cold cube steaks, a quart of milk, and two cupcakes. When he came back to the living room I said I hoped he was already regretting his unkind words about his sister and her friends, because —

Laurie lifted his head. "Now it starts," he said.

He was right.

After about half an hour I went to the foot of the back stairs and tried to call up to the girls to be quiet, but they could not hear me. They were apparently using the fortunetelling cards, because I could hear someone calling on a tall, dark man and someone else remarking bitterly upon jealousy from a friend. I went halfway up the stairs and shouted, but they still could not hear me. I went to the top and pounded on the door and I could have been banging my head against a stone wall. I could hear the name of a young gentleman of Laurie's acquaintance being bandied about lightly by the ladies inside, coupled with Laura's name and references to a certain cake-sharing incident at recess, and insane shrieks, presumably from the maligned Laura. I banged both fists on the door, and there was silence for a second until someone said, "Maybe it's your *brother*," and then there was a great screaming of "Go away! Stay out! Don't come in!"

"Joanne," I said, and there was absolute silence.

"Yes, Mother?" said Jannie at last.

"May I come in?" I asked gently.

"Oh, yes," said all the little girls.

I opened the door and went in. They were all sitting on the two beds in Jannie's room. The needle arm had been taken off the record but I could see Elvis Presley going around and around. All the cupcakes and soda were gone, and so was the candy. The fortunetelling cards were scattered over the two beds. Jannie was wearing her pink shortie pajamas, which were certainly too light for that cold night. Linda was wearing blue shortie pajamas. Kate was wearing a college-girl-type ski pajama. Laura was wearing a lace-trimmed nightgown, white with pink roses. Carole was wearing yellow shortie pajamas. Their hair was mussed, their cheeks were pink, they were crammed uncomfortably together onto the two beds, and they were clearly awake long after their several bedtimes.

"Don't you think," I said, "that you had better get some sleep?"

"Oh, noooo," they all said, and Jannie added, "The party's just *beginning.*" They looked incredibly pretty and happy, and so I said, with a deplorable lack of firmness, that they could stay up for just five minutes more, if they were very, very quiet.

"Dickie," Kate whispered, clearly referring to some private joke and the little girls dissolved into helpless giggles, all except Carole, who cried out indignantly, "I did *not,* I never *did,* I *don't.*"

Downstairs again, I said nostalgically to my husband and Laurie, "I can remember, when *I* used to have pajama parties . . ."

"Mommy," Jannie said urgently from the darkness of the dining room. Startled, I hurried in.

"Listen," she said, "something's gone *terribly* wrong."

"What's the matter?"

"Shhh," Jannie said. "It's Kate and Linda. I thought they would both sleep in my library but now Kate isn't talking to Linda because Linda took her lunch box today in school and said she didn't and wouldn't give it back so now Kate won't sleep with Linda."

"Well then, why not put Linda . . ."

"Well, you see, I was going to have Carole in with me because really only don't tell the others, but really she's my *best* friend of all of them only now I can't put Kate and Linda together and . . ."

"Why not put one of them with you?"

"Well, I *can't* put Carole in with Laura."

"Why not?" I was getting tired of whispering.

"Well, because they *both* like Jimmie *Watson.*"

"Oh," I said.

"And anyway Carole's wearing a shortie and Kate and Laura *aren't.*"

"Look," I said, "how about my sneaking up right now through the front hall and making up the guest-room bed? Then you can put someone in there. Jimmie Watson, maybe."

"*Mother.*" Jannie turned bright red.

"Sorry," I said. "Take a pillow from one of the beds in your library. Put someone in the guest room. Keep them busy for a few minutes and I'll have it ready. I just hope I have two more sheets."

"Oh, *thank* you." Jannie turned, and then stopped. "Mother?" she said. "Don't think from what I said that *I* like Jimmie Watson."

"The thought never crossed my mind," I said.

I raced upstairs and found two sheets; they were smallish, and not colored, which meant that they were the very bottom of the pile, but as I closed the guest-room door behind me I thought optimistically that at least Jannie's problems were solved, if I excepted Jimmie Watson and the dangerous rivalry of Carole, who is a natural platinum blonde.

Jannie came down to the dining room again in about fifteen minutes. "Shhh," she whispered when I came in to talk to her. "Kate and Linda want to sleep together in the guest room."

"But I thought you just said that Kate and Linda . . ."

"But they made up and Linda apologized for taking Kate's lunch box and Kate apologized for thinking she did, and they're all friends now, except Laura is kind of mad because now Kate says she likes Harry Benson better."

"Better than Laura?" I asked stupidly.

"Oh, *Mother*. Better than Jimmie Watson, of course. Except *I* think Harry Benson is goony."

"If he was the one on patrol who let your brother Barry go across the street by himself he certainly *is* goony. As a matter of fact, if there is one word I would automatically and instinctively apply to young Harry Benson it would surely be . . ."

"Oh, *Mother*. He is *not*."

I had been kept up slightly past my own bedtime. "All right," I said. "Harry Benson is not goony and it is fine with me if Kate and Carole sleep in the guest room if they will only . . ."

"Kate and *Linda*."

"Kate and Linda. If they will only *only* go to *sleep*."

"*Thank* you. And may I sleep in the guest room too?"

"What?"

"It's a big bed. And we wanted to talk very quietly about . . ."

"Never mind," I said. "Sleep anywhere, but *sleep*."

In about ten minutes Jannie was back downstairs again. "Listen," she said, when I came wearily into the dining room, "can Kate sleep in the guest room, too?"

"I don't care where Kate sleeps," I said. "I don't care where *any* of you sleep."

"Anyway, Kate and I are sleeping in the guest room, because now everyone else is mad at Kate. And Carole is mad at Linda so Carole is sleeping in my room and Linda and Laura are sleeping in my library. Except I just really don't know *what* will happen," she sighed, "if anyone tells Laura what Linda said about Jerry. Jerry Harper."

"Why can't Carole change with Linda and sleep with Laura?"

"Oh, *Mother*. You *know* about Carole and Laura and Jimmie Watson."

"I guess I just forgot for a minute," I said.

"Well," Jannie said, "I only wanted to let you know where everyone was."

It was perhaps twenty minutes later when Laurie held up his hand and said "Listen." I had been trying to identify the sensation, and thought it was like the sudden lull in a heavy wind which has been beating against the house for hours.

I went up the back stairs in my stocking feet, not making a sound, and opened the door to Jannie's room, easing it to avoid even the slightest squeak.

Jannie was peacefully asleep in her own bed. The other bed in her room and the three beds in her library were empty. Reflecting upon the sorcery of Jimmie Watson's name, I found the other four girls all asleep on the guest-room bed. None of them were covered, but there was no way of putting a blanket over them without smothering somebody. I closed the window, and tiptoed away, called softly downstairs to let my husband and Laurie know that all was quiet, and got myself to my own bed and fell into it. I slept soundly until seventeen minutes past three by the bedroom clock, when I was awakened by Jannie.

"Kate feels sick," she said. "You've got to get up right away and take her home."

EDITH KONECKY

The Power

(FROM THE MASSACHUSETTS REVIEW)

PRUDENCE DEWHURST was fourteen years old when she became absolutely certain of The Power. It was growing in her breast just inside the rib cage and she could feel it opening like a flower, or like a fist uncurling. She had discovered during the past year that she was in direct contact with God, but only lately had she understood that this contact conferred a special power, real and palpable as a physical fact.

It made all the difference. It lit her pale face with small, secret smiles during French class and at night in her narrow corner of the dormitory she hugged herself to sleep feeling warm and snug and special. She no longer awaited the mail with anything like the old eagerness; it was, in fact, a matter of complete indifference to her whether her mother wrote at all. Packages, too, had lost their charm, for with the coming of The Power her needs had altered completely. She had entirely lost her sweet tooth and there were times when she would have forgotten even meals if the bell had not summoned so imperatively.

No, she was different, special. Not like the others at all. There was no question of it. She had The Power. The problem, though, was that she did not yet know what to do with it. If only she'd been born a Catholic! If only this were a convent! She would go, humbly, to the Mother Superior and confess the whole thing. At first they might suspect her of the sin of pride, but in time her humility and her sincerity would convince them. They would know that she had A Calling. They would hover over her, watchful and loving. They would pray with her, comfort her, they would bring her, at last, to fullness.

But, alas, Abigail Carruther's school was not a Catholic institution. Dr. Abigail was an agnostic and her school was run along more or less ethical culture lines. There was high purpose, there were lofty character goals, there were frequent expressions of a morality to which they all subscribed, there was a good deal of music and art, but of spiritual guidance and religious fervor there were none.

No, Dr. Abigail's school was definitely not a cradle for saints; and incipient sainthood, Prudence felt sure, was the nature of her infection. The fantastic thing, though, was that no one seemed to have noticed anything, no one at all, not the girls, not Miss Burney who taught mathematics and social graces, not Madame Delacroix, not Auntie Flo or Nurse James or even Miss Elfrieda whose sharp eyes could see through walls. Not even Dr. Abigail with all her prying, with her endless "Tell me your dreams, dear." It was past all understanding that something of such shattering magnitude, something that Prudence was so full of that she felt herself bursting at the seams with it, should escape all notice.

Who could blame her, then, for not being able to hold it inside herself? It had been a difficult week and she was too tired, now, to resist the temptation to share her new importance. Besides, God had spoken to her during the night and she was worried. She had not understood Him. Austerity's face is clear but it speaks in distances. She could hear the voice, but the words came blurred enough through the echoing tunnel and the thick, curly beard.

In time, of course, she would understand. Why else be singled out thus? She was almost sure that The Power was there because she was going to do a miracle, but it seemed to her that if she was going to do a miracle she ought first to predict it. She was waiting for God to tell her the miracle and she was cranky and nervous and tired, and here was Marjorie Harkavy, who was not her best friend (Prudence had never been able to manage a best friend) but who, since their beds adjoined, might be said to be her closest friend. Prudence, too tired for volleyball, had begged to be excused and she sat, now, watching the game from the sidelines but not really seeing it, for the excitement of volleyball as a spectator sport is limited. And here came Marjorie Harkavy, ejected fom the game because of the violent redness of her face and the unchecked fury of her play. Marjorie flopped on the ground beside Prudence and lay there like a drowning fish strangling on air.

"You give too much of yourself," Prudence said. "You really do."

Slowly, Marjorie's breathing regulated itself. Air, Prudence thought. How we use it and use it without even thinking about it. Like God. Die without it. Maybe air is God.

"I can't help it," Marjorie whined. "I play to win. I can't stand losing and I always play to win."

"Yes. But you *over*do."

"I hate to lose. I'm a real competitor."

Ridiculous! How could air be God? Then God would have to be air.

"Anyhow, it's just my complexion," Marjorie said. "I can't help it if I have this kind of high complexion."

The air today was delicious. Though it came down snow-washed over the mountains, it held, this early April day, the soft promise of spring. Spring was not actually due for another month, for it came late to Dr. Abigail's little valley, which was tucked high in a corner of a mountain near Lugano, facing south toward Italy. Sitting as she was now, with the mountain behind her, Prudence looked across the playing field that sloped gently down to the line of somber firs, and knew that only the horizon and the limits of her vision prevented her seeing her mother, who was in Palermo some six hundred miles due south and who was perhaps at this very moment standing at the edge of the blue Tyrrhenian Sea, looking north above the fishing nets and thinking with love, *Prudence, Prudence*. Fat chance!

Marjorie rolled over onto her back and looked up at the sky.

"How soft the ground is," she said. "Did you go for your X-ray this morning? Wasn't she a character?"

"Who?"

"The X-ray lady. Frau Stettenheimer."

But Prudence had not gone for her X-ray. She must have missed the announcement. Regular physical examinations were an important part of the school's curriculum, for some of the girls were delicate. But it was Prudence's private opinion that the school's concern with their physical welfare was not only excessive but a calculated sop to the guilt of their parents who, free of their daughters, could not be accused of neglecting either their education or their

health. There were the checkups and the therapy and the endless,
idiotic injections and, if that were not enough, Nurse James was an
expert in matters of diet, a great believer in wheat germ and berries
and nuts. Furthermore, the school was expensive.

"Are you going home for the spring holidays?" Marjorie asked.
Prudence paused before answering, waiting for a mental image to
correspond with the word "home." She tried to review, chronologi-
cally, the long succession of pensions and hotel rooms and boarding
schools that had been home. Once, a long time ago and dimly remembered, there had really been a home.

"My mother's in Palermo," she said. "I'm going there to be with
her for the holidays."

Marjorie sighed.

"You're so lucky," she said. "I'm going to have to stay."

Please, God, *let* me be lucky, Prudence thought. Let nothing happen to spoil Palermo. For something was always happening. Something had happened at Christmas and before that at Thanksgiving.
She hadn't seen her mother since the summer. But then, of course,
she was forgetting. It no longer mattered. Not now.

"Listen, Marjorie," she said. "I have to tell you something."

"What?"

"It's a secret."

Marjorie composed a face that assured Prudence that she was
good at secrets.

"It's . . . it's not easy to tell."

"You've started to menstruate!"

"Oh, Marjorie! You know I've been for over a year!"

"You've got a crush on Miss Elfrieda!"

"Please, Marjorie, it's nothing like that. And you don't have to
guess because I'm going to tell you."

"Well, then, tell!"

"It's . . . you see . . . something's been happening to me.
I've been having . . . well, visions!"

"Visions?"

"God. Marjorie, God's been talking to me. And something else.
There's going to be a miracle."

Marjorie's face registered her total dismay.

"Oh, Prudence," she wailed. "You're such an oddball! You can't
really believe the things you say!"

Stung, Prudence said, "May God strike me dead on this spot if every word isn't the absolute truth!"

Marjorie shook her head. "This religion kick," she said. "I don't know how you can be so serious about it. I mean, it's not as though you were a Catholic, or anything."

"Faith," Prudence murmured. "It's a question of faith. Either you've got it or you haven't. It's as simple as that."

Faith, faith. Once you closed your eyes and jumped, took that incredible plunge into faith's arms, then everything once again became possible. You could live there, in those arms.

"Well, anyway," Prudence said, "you'll see. Because there's going to be a miracle."

"What kind of miracle?" Marjorie said, her voice impatient with scorn. "I know! Dr. Abigail's going to get married. There's going to be a *man* on the premises. A whole, real man."

"That's all you ever think of," Prudence said. "Sex. Sex and games."

"Come on, Prudence," Marjorie said. "Tell me what kind of miracle. I want to spread the word. Maybe I can drum up some diciples for you among those kooks on the volleyball court."

Prudence closed her eyes. She had made a terrible mistake. She had wanted only to share her joy and instead she was being made to share Marjorie's scorn.

"Honestly, Pru!" Marjorie said. "Sometimes I think you're just plain crazy."

"Naturally," Prudence murmured. "Naturally you would think that."

Marjorie got up. "The ground is cold," she said. "I'm going to see if they'll let me get back into the game."

Prudence did not open her eyes. Still, she could feel Marjorie withdraw, could feel herself alone again. From the playing field came the sudden, sharp sound of violent dispute and, without looking, Prudence knew that it was probably little Sally Manning who had been thrown to the ground and whose anguish now cut the air like a scythe. They were strange girls, ordinarily so well-mannered and quiet, sometimes even too quiet, yet from time to time they erupted in such unexpected, bestial ways. Sally Manning was terrible at games; she could not keep her mind on them. Once, holding on to the ball, she had simply strolled off the field like a sleepwalker.

Everything Sally Manning did enraged the other girls, and especially Marjorie Harkavy. It was probably she who had thrown Sally down.

It was all so revolting! Girls ought not to engage in any kind of physical activity that called for teams. It made them monstrous and hateful. Prudence could not bring herself to open her eyes, even when Miss Elfrieda's whistle shrilled and order had been restored. Through her closed eyelids, the sunlight wove shifting patterns. Light and dark, light and dark. Whatever could she have been thinking to have chosen Marjorie Harkavy for a confidante? Stupid! She would have to be even more careful. She was different. She must learn to withdraw even further from the society of those around her. She must learn better to live within herself. Deep in her eyes, the sunlight danced, dark and light, light and dark. Fatigue shrouded her like a mist and wound thus, she drifted for a while in the limbo between waking and sleep. Was the mountain coming down? It seemed to her that perhaps it was. And where the mountain had been a man stood, his cruel and handsome face lined with sorrow. Stood and softly called her name. Who was he? Was he after all her father? But her father was dead and she had never seen him. *Tell me,* she called to the man, *tell me the secret.* But the man only stood and softly called her name. *Prudence,* he said, and she saw that there were tears in his eyes. *Prudence, Prudence.*

She opened her eyes. Between her and the sun, Miss Elfrieda towered, laughing down at her.

"Prudence?" Miss Elfrieda said. "Are you awake?"

Prudence blinked. From this angle, Miss Elfrieda's legs in the black slacks she always wore, seemed impossibly long.

"What a funny girl!" Miss Elfrieda said. "Sitting so straight . . . and fast asleep." She held the volleyball in one hand, the furled net in the other. Behind her, Prudence saw, the field was empty. The game was over and the girls had gone. She looked up at Miss Elfrieda and blinked again. How handsome Miss Elfrieda was, her teeth so white in the healthy sunburned face, her short fair hair blown across her clear brow. She looked so physical, so vital, so overwhelmingly alive. Prudence wondered if it could be true, what Marjorie was always hinting about her.

Miss Elfrieda shifted the volleyball into the crook of her other arm and reached her freed hand down to Prudence. The whistle hanging round her neck swayed and caught the sun, a charm against evil.

"Come," she said. "Time to go back. You will catch your death sitting on the damp ground."

Prudence avoided the offered hand and got quickly to her feet. "I guess I was asleep," she said. "I didn't hear the girls go."

"You are a strange child," Miss Elfrieda said as they walked across the field. She turned on Prudence her grave, penetrating eyes and Prudence, meeting them, felt a slight chill and thought, *perhaps she knows.* "You are so quiet, so thoughtful. What deep sorrows you seem to be hiding. Is it so?"

"No," Prudence said and, turning to look over her shoulder, saw that the mountain was still there.

"How you have grown this year!" Miss Elfrieda said. "You know, I think you are going to be, very soon, a beautiful woman. Yes, I think so. Like your mother, eh?"

Beautiful? She, Prudence, beautiful? The idea was so preposterous that she was for an instant stunned by it.

"But too thin. And too pale. You must come more in the open air. I will teach you how to breathe."

"How to breathe?" Prudence said, aware that Miss Elfrieda was waiting for her to say something. She looked at the woman walking beside her and her spirits, so damaged by the encounter with Marjorie, began to rise. Yes, perhaps if she learned how to breathe.

They had reached the west terrace and as they crossed the flagstone the warm smells of lunch reached out to them. An inside smell, Prudence thought. Inside smells, outside smells, air, and Miss Elfrieda to teach one to breathe it. She smiled at Miss Elfrieda. But beautiful? Surely not, no, not like her mother a beautiful woman, no. Not she.

Inside, she watched Miss Elfrieda's straight back disappear into the shadows at the end of the hall and listened to the girls, already assembled in the dining room, singing one of the invocations they had learned to make them worthy of the impending meal.

> *Faith, truth and lo-ove,*
> *Knowledge, health and beauty,*
> *To higher service*
> *Now we dedicate . . .*

Prudence slipped into the dining room and, taking her place, joined her voice to the others.

Till our ideals
Shall reign o'er all victorious
And light of knowledge
Guide us on our way.

She was seated, this month, next to one of the younger girls, an American named Harriet Melody. Harriet was newly arrived at the school. She was given to shrill nightmares and all day she talked gloomily and everlastingly about The Bomb.

"In America they have grown quite accustomed to The Bomb," was her unvarying prefatory remark. "You see, once you make the first compromise, you are doomed."

First, she explained, had come the sirens. "Did you know that every Saturday at noon, the voice of the sirens is heard in the land?"

Then there were the little children huddled beneath the desks. Next, white sheets and an organization called, familiarly, CD. It sounded like a disease and, of course, it was, an insidious and virulent one that warned of its coming with lying little stickers pasted everywhere, saying "CD may save YOUR life."

Yes, in the beginning a few people had balked. Mothers, mostly. But then mothers were notorious cranks, always against anything that is against life.

Harriet had a scrapbook in which she kept all the newsclippings she could find relating to The Bomb. On the cover of the scrapbook, she had elaborately lettered in red india ink, "LEARNING TO ACCEPT THE DEATH OF THE WORLD, A CHRONICLE."

"They have developed a survival cracker," Harriet was saying as Prudence tore off a corner of her roll and spread it with butter. "There are I forget how many tons of them in this shelter in Albany, New York, where five hundred state employees, including the governor, are going to survive. And then after they have survived they will come out again and go on govering the state of New York."

Prudence nodded, agreeing that it sounded grim.

"The governor of New York State is an extremely wealthy man," Harriet said. "He is going to have shelters with crackers in them at all his homes. He has homes in the country and homes at the seashore and homes in the city and he plans to survive in all of them. He is a stubborn man. He is determined to survive. He is determined to be absolutely the *fittest*."

Prudence tried not to listen. Although she knew that, unlike some of the wildly improbable fears so many of the girls indulged in, it was correct to be disturbed by The Bomb, Harriet Melody carried it too far. She was a bright girl, Harriet Melody. Too bright, Prudence had heard them say, too bright for her own good. Most of them here at the school were too bright, too sophisticated, too something for their own good. Why else had they been sent so far from home, to a place so isolated?

". . . once you accept any part of it, the first, the smallest part of it," Harriet was saying, "then you have opened the door to all of it. The whole thing. Total destruction. It's like jumping off a cliff. You can't just jump a little bit."

"All right, Harriet, knock it off," Marjorie Harkavy said from across the table. "It seems to me we already had this sermon once today."

"And at least three times yesterday."

"I'd like you to see my scrapbook, Prudence," Harriet said, ignoring the others and the fact that Prudence had already seen it more than once. "I think you would appreciate it."

But Prudence had discovered a note at her place and she pretended total absorption in it, though it said only that she was to report without fail to Nurse James directly after classes at three o'clock. But by three o'clock she had forgotten. She went, instead, as was her habit, to the study hall to prepare her lessons for the next day. Many of the girls were gathered there, quietly studying. Prudence found an empty desk and, sitting at it, was annoyed to discover that she had neglected to bring her books. No matter; she would borrow one. She looked around at her schoolmates and was alarmed to see that none of them had books. They sat, dreamlike, staring into their laps, at their hands, into space.

"But where are your books?" Prudence cried. A few of the girls looked up, startled, and off in a corner someone sniggered, as though Prudence had said something wildly stupid. Confused, Prudence took paper and pen from the desk drawer and began a letter to her mother.

"Dear Mother," she wrote, "I have been meaning to write all week but I have been, as usual, terribly busy. I don't know where the days go."

Where *do* the days go, she thought, biting the end of her pen. It seemed to her that she had spent a million days in this place and that they had all, after all, been only one day, *this* day. She stared at the sheet of paper, wondering what she could say to the distant blurred outlines of her mother. Today Miss Elfrieda said that I am going to be beautiful. *That* happened. And if she did not lie, what will I do with beauty? Will I spend it like the days? Miss Elfrieda says she will teach me to breathe. Perhaps if I learn to breathe. In and out. Oh, Mother, I have such a wonderful secret. I can't tell it, even to you. Especially not to you. In and out. There is a girl here who worries about atom bombs. She says that when they made the very first bomb they killed the world. She says you don't have to jump off the cliff; you can walk away. But once you jump, by God, you have *jumped!*

It was hopeless. There was nothing in her life that she could say to her mother, nothing that would have any meaning to her mother. She put her head on her arm and closed her eyes. In and out. And if I learn to breathe, she thought, what then? What will change? She fell asleep.

She had no idea how long she slept. Someone tugged at her arm.

"Get up P-Prudence. P-please." It was Sally Manning and she looked frightened.

"What's the matter?"

"I've b-been trying and trying to w-wake you."

"Why? What?"

"They want you in the library."

"The library?"

"I think you have a v-visitor."

A visitor? She could not remember if she had ever had a visitor. There was some mistake, surely. She walked quickly towards the library but the corridor seemed endless; the double baize doors seemed to recede as she drew near.

She pushed the doors ajar and peered nervously inside. The library was a long room. At its far end, through tall mullioned windows, the north light slanted obliquely in, diffuse and mote-flecked, making the high book-lined walls shadowy and unreal. Half in and half out of the shadows a woman stood looking out at the mountain. She seemed lost in thought, or perhaps it was only that she did not hear Prudence. She stood motionless for what seemed a very long time while Prudence watched her from the door, listening to the beating of her own heart. She knew at once that the woman was her mother; she had caught the scent from the moment she had pushed against the door, but she stood, nonetheless, immobilized by a premonition of fear. It was so long since she had seen her mother. Still, with the holidays so near there was no reason for her to be here now, visiting this remote corner of a Swiss mountain. No reason, of course, unless . . . *Think of God,* she told herself and shut the door behind her.

Her mother turned from the window and, peering through the long shadows, tilted her head a little to one side, like a dog, listening.

"Prudence? Is that you?"

Prudence stepped inside the room.

"Hello, Mother," she said.

They met in the center of the room and her mother leaned to kiss her. They were very nearly the same size.

"How you've grown!" her mother said, sounding nervous. "Come, let me look at you. Why is it so dark in here?"

"They don't turn on the lights until five," Prudence said. Her mother took her arm and, surprised, Prudence felt that her mother was trembling. They walked together out of the shadows to the far end of the room.

"Yes," her mother said, studying Purdence's face in the cold light under the window. "You're changing. You're not a little girl any longer." She spoke wistfully, as though she were going to miss the little girl she had scarcely known. And Prudence, looking into her mother's face, saw changes, too. Her mother's beauty had edges that she'd never noticed before (perhaps they had not been there?) — something around the mouth that was a little too fixed, too rigid. Something in the gray eyes that was both cold and pleading. For the first time, Prudence wondered what her mother was really like.

"Are you happy, darling?" her mother asked, fitting a cigarette into a long jade holder. Prudence, who did not know what happiness was, stared at her mother. Was she happy? Well, then, was she not happy? And then, as her mother lit her cigarette and puffed extravagantly at it, Prudence realized that the question was rhetorical.

"Yes," she said dully. "I suppose I am happy."

Her mother, holding the burnt match, looked about for a place to drop it.

"No ashtrays, I'm afraid," Prudence said. "They don't encourage us to smoke."

"That's all right," her mother said, dropping the match at the base of a potted rubber tree plant, of which the room held several. "I'll use one of these ghastly trees. I'm sure they're entirely indestructible." Prudence smiled, remembering the long list of her mother's dislikes: potted plants, parakeets, things crocheted, mousy little girls in pinafores, pink gold, vanilla ice cream, military bands, umbrellas, sachet, Tschaikovsky, hairpins.

"It's a good place, though, isn't it, darling?" her mother asked. "They do treat you well?"

"Of course."

"And you're getting enough to eat? You don't look as though you're getting enough to eat."

"The meals are very generous," she assured her mother. "They serve far more than I can eat."

"Then you must eat more."

Prudence sighed. She knew that her mother was playing at her notion of motherhood, but she wished she would show a little more imagination. God. Think of God.

"Tell me," her mother said. "What did you have for lunch today?"

"Lunch? Today?"

"Yes. For instance."

Prudence hadn't the vaguest recollection what lunch had been. She thought very hard but she could remember only that, after Harriet Melody had been silenced, she had become aware that one of the Beethoven Quartets had been on the hi-fi, and that she had strained to hear it above the clatter of cutlery. She looked at the eagerness shining in her mother's beautiful eyes, the eagerness to be told the luncheon menu. Prudence's mind was a total blank.

"Peaches!" she cried, at last, inspired by a sudden vision of row on row of golden canned peaches.

"Peaches?" her mother said, clearly disappointed.

"Yes, peach halves with raspberries and ice cream," she invented, carefully watching her success in her mother's face. "For dessert, of course. And let me see . . . what was the entrée? Yes, chicken livers and mushrooms. They do that awfully well here." She felt terribly sly, rewarded by the relief that gradually softened the worried lines on her mother's face. "And hot biscuits," she added, "with scads of butter." Her mother was very nearly beaming. "And cocoa, too. We have cocoa with every meal, you know."

"Good!" her mother said. "Oh, very good."

"You're not hungry, are you, Mother?"

Her mother laughed. "Of course I'm not hungry, darling," she said. "I only wanted to know . . . to feel . . . a little more closely . . . how it is with you. How it is here."

She stared at her mother across the small space that separated them.

"Yes," she said. "I see. How is Palermo, Mother?"

"Palermo was charming," her mother said with sudden enthusiasm. "Dirty and ancient and there's the most marvelous cathedral! But we've left Palermo, you know."

Left Palermo? We?

"Oh?"

"That's why I'm here, darling. Peter has to be back in London next week and so we drove up to do a little skiing first. And, of course, to see you. The drive across the mountains was fantastic, darling. I can still taste my heart in my mouth."

"Peter?" Prudence searched her mind, but Peter was nowhere in it. "Who is Peter?"

"Oh, Prudence!" her mother said and laughed her small, delightful laugh. "Surely I wrote you! Of course I did. Don't you ever read my letters?"

Prudence shifted her feet, sorry she had asked. She wanted to spare her mother the need to tell her that Peter was her father's second cousin or Uncle John's baby brother, you remember Aunt Sophie, don't you, well . . . It didn't matter at all who Peter was. Only, she was mildly curious about what had happened to Alan. It had been Alan only last summer, hadn't it? Or had it been the summer before? Or ten summers ago? Was it possible that she was really only fourteen years old?

"Let's sit down," she said, pulling her mother away from the window to one of the dark corners where a huge leather sofa brooded. "I'm tired. We had volleyball this morning."

"Volleyball?" her mother said, trying to make her voice gay. The scarred, badly cracked leather creaked beneath them. "And how will volleyball prepare you for . . . for the future?"

"It sharpens the eye and strengthens the wrist," Prudence said, glad to be out of the light where she needn't feel so transparent. "A strong wrist is so important, don't you think?"

They both laughed and then her mother sighed and said, "Peter did so want to meet you." Prudence allowed herself to know, finally, that the holidays were off. She would not be going anywhere. She would be staying right here until the summer holidays. "Well, it can't be helped!" her mother said stoically. "It will just have to wait until June."

"You're going to London, too?"

"Yes, darling, I must. I'm so sorry. I can't tell you how disappointed I am."

Prudence closed her eyes and remembered God. It was nice to know that she did not even have to hate her mother.

"That's all right," she said, and her voice sounded perfectly normal. "It's only three months." Consoling her mother; how mature she felt! "Time goes so quickly here," she lied. "There's so much to do."

"Oh, I nearly forgot," her mother said, her voice tinkling with relief. "I brought you something. Now, where did I put it?" She got up and moved about in the shadows. "Damn!" she said, bumping against something. "Turn a light on, for God's sake, Pru. There's no reason to be stumbling about in the dark."

Prudence leaned across the sofa to where she knew there was a table with a lamp. She found the switch and pressed it. The small glow lighted the scarred surface of the table and little else, but it seemed to mollify her mother. "There it is!" she said, spying the small package that lay beside her gloves and purse. She snatched it up and brought it to Prudence. "I hope you'll like it, darling."

"Of course I'll like it," she said, knowing that it would be expensive and beautiful, whatever it was, but that it would not be anything that she could care about. "Do you mind if I don't open it now? I'd like to save it."

"No, of course not, angel." Her mother looked quickly at her watch. "I've got to run, sweet. It gets dark so early in the mountains and I don't want to be caught. Not on these frightening roads."

She leaned to kiss Prudence, holding her close for a moment.

"And do try to write more often, Pru. I look forward so much to your letters."

"Yes, Mother," she said, surprised that there should be tears in her mother's eyes. "I was just beginning a letter when you came."

"And eat more. Try, darling."

"Yes, Mother."

Her mother moved towards the door.

"You needn't see me out," she said. "It's turned quite chilly."

"All right. Anyhow, it's against the rules . . ."

"Goodbye, darling."

"Goodbye."

"And Pru?"

"Yes?"

"You do forgive me, don't you?"

"Forgive you?"

"I mean about the holidays? You do understand, don't you?"

"Yes, Mother. It's all right."

"Goodbye, darling."

She stood at the window and looked out at the gathering dusk. In a little while a car . . . what was it, a Land Rover? . . . wound past on the road below. There were two of them in the car. Peter, she supposed, who was so eager to meet her. She felt infinitely sad and depressed and at the same time unreal, as if the encounter with her mother had not really happened, though the smell of her mother's perfume was strong on the air. She looked up at the mountain, wanting suddenly to shout something at it. It stood there so solid, so smug, so eternal, so white and pure and lofty. She saw the lights of the Land Rover recede in an arc toward the edge of the mountain. In about five minutes more it would reach the pass and vanish from her view. Slowly, she counted, feeling The Power pulsing inside her, pounding, swelling, like a muscle screaming to be used. When she had counted to three hundred, she closed her eyes and clenched her teeth and whispered through them, "Now, now, *now!*"

NOW!

She heard it, then, softly at first, a distant rumbling that gradually grew in volume. She opened her eyes and saw (surely she saw it?) the great blocks of snow tumbling down the side of the mountain, roaring as they grew into an avalanche. And then, quite suddenly, the thunder ceased. The mountain shuddered and grew still. It was over.

"Naughty girl!"

Prudence started and wheeled at the voice that was right behind her. Miss Elfrieda was standing there, shaking her head. "Naughty,

naughty child," she said. "I have been looking for you everywhere."

Had she been there all along?

"I . . . I was here. I had a visitor."

"A visitor?"

"My mother."

Miss Elfrieda's eyes, catching the last of the light, glinted. "Ah," she said sadly. "Then that explains it."

"Explains it?"

"Why you did not come again this afternoon for your X-ray. Nurse James is beside herself. She asked me to come for you and to bring you back. By the scruff of the neck, if necessary."

The tightness in Prudence's chest eased; Miss Elfrieda had obviously neither seen nor heard. Perhaps no one had. And if no one knew, Prudence thought, it might be days, even weeks, before they were discovered.

"Did you hear something just now, Miss Elfrieda?" she asked. "Something like . . . thunder, I thought."

"Nonsense, my dear. Too early for thunder. Come along, now, we mustn't keep Nurse James waiting any longer."

"I . . . one minute, please, Miss Elfrieda." Prudence felt, all at once, too weak to move. She was both exhausted and elated. The Power was real. The Power was hers. God had taken her hand and moved it with wonderful justice.

"You're trembling, Prudence!" Miss Elfrieda said and caught one of the girl's hands between her own. "And how cold your hand is! Are you all right?"

Prudence fought the impulse to snatch her hand away. The woman's touch, physical contact of any sort with another human being, seemed at this moment particularly vile.

"It's nothing," she said, drawing back from Miss Elfrieda. "Just a chill."

They began to walk towards the door. Miss Elfrieda looked at her sideways, appraisingly. "And your mother?" she said. "Is she well?"

Dead, Prudence thought. Crushed, smothered beneath tons of pure white snow, washed clean and virginal and innocent. This, her bridal night. Sleep well, sleep well.

"Yes, well," she said.

When they reached the corridor, she saw that the lights had been lit. But I don't want to be X-rayed, she thought wildly. I need to be private.

"No," she said to Miss Elfrieda. "I won't go."

"Won't go?" Miss Elfrieda said, turning the searchlight of her dark brilliant stare on Prudence. "What's the matter with you, child? You know Nurse James won't hurt you. Has she ever yet hurt you?"

"I don't need an X-ray," Prudence cried. "I won't!" She must run, she knew, looking desperately about for a direction. But there was none. There was nowhere. There was only out into the cold, falling night. She could not run out. Not out there. "I don't need an X-ray," she said, controlling her voice, trying to sound reasonable. "I'm perfectly all right."

Miss Elfrieda's hand tightened around her arm.

"Of course you are, my dear," she said softly. "And in any case, it's too late for an X-ray. Frau Stettenheimer has already gone with her machine. She could not wait for you forever, you know."

Slowly, they moved down the corridor towards the infirmary. It was all right, then, if there wasn't going to be an X-ray, if they weren't going to peer inside her.

"But all the same, we'll just go along and see Nurse James," Miss Elfrieda said firmly, her hand strong as a chain round Prudence's upper arm. "Just to please her."

Docile as a lamb, Prudence walked alongside Miss Elfrieda, remembering that she had left her mother's present in the library and wondering vaguely if it was another wristwatch. How many would that make? Six? Seven? And she never wore a watch. She was afraid of time.

Inside the infirmary, the sudden glare of the white walls was, as always, startling. Too sterile, Prudence thought, too glacial. The glare hurt her eyes. The door shut behind them and Miss Elfrieda let go her grip on Prudence's arm. Nurse James looked up from her desk and glowered at Prudence from beneath her heavy straight brows.

"Well! At last we have the pleasure of your company," Nurse James said. "So glad you could finally make it, Prudence Dewhurst."

"She has an excuse," Miss Elfrieda said. "Her mother came unexpectedly to see her this afternoon. So, of course, in all the excitement, she forgot."

Prudence saw the two women exchange glances, saw Miss Elfrieda shrug and grimace as though she were in some pain. In the next room, she heard someone moan. The baths were in there. Through the half-open door, she caught a glimpse of Marjorie Harkavy swathed in white like a winding sheet, floating in the warm bath with her eyes shut. She saw with shock that Marjorie Harkavy's hair was shot with gray. She was not a girl at all!

Too light, too bright, she thought, watching Nurse James rise from her desk and go to the sterilizer. The needles, she thought. Too bright, too white. One sees too much. Her heart began to knock with terror and she knew that she was about to have a moment of perfect lucidity, and that in that moment she would see through her blind eyes what was real and what was fancied, for there was a place where there were differences like that and in that place those differences mattered.

Oh hurry, she thought, oh hurry hurry hurry!

"Take your clothes off, dear."

Faith. With faith everything once again became possible. There was order and system there within those arms and you could live with that. The logic and sense of a world where you could, conceivably, accept even annihilation in preference to other things, the logic and order of religion and God and The Power and, yes, the sanity, even the sanity, within . . .

You had only to close your eyes and, at last, finally, to leap. She had leaped! She had long ago leaped. It was not fair to be called back. She would not let them call her back to their chaos and their terror.

"Take off your clothes," Nurse James said sharply, and Miss Elfrieda advanced to help her but Prudence struck away her hands and cried out as though she were wounded for in that instant she understood where she was and why she was there.

She watched Nurse James approach with the needle and she closed her eyes and began, without words, to pray. She prayed, not to God who was absent, but to something, to herself, and, praying, she waited for the moment to pass.

KIMON LOLOS

Mule No. 095

(FROM THE CARLETON MISCELLANY)

THE ITALIANS broke through the border at five o'clock in the morning. The Greeks mobilized anybody and anything that could fight, walk, carry, supply. And the Italians were pushed back into Albania. And the war settled. And it was three weeks before the rains.

G. A. Mula No. 095 was drafted while she was grazing by the olive oil mill at Koropi. The regimental farrier made his brands ready. Her driver-to-be spooled her halter around his hand. The Corporal lifted, curled and held her front right leg. But when the hoof brand — G.A. — placed its burning kiss on the horn wall of the left hoof, and a thin cord of smoke rose, the mule gave the holding team such a mighty yank that the Corporal was forced to release her leg; and the blacksmith backed up.

The muleteer did his best to hang on to the halter. But she kicked high, leaped and gyrated like a maenad. And the muleteer let the halter go and blew on his rope-rasped palm while he watched her hoof away, free and beautifully wild. She stopped only when she reached the silver-gray grove of olive trees.

The Major, who was in charge of the commandeering for the reserve regiment, lost his temper:

— I . . . on your head, he said with clenched teeth.

— Please, Mr. Major, don't swear at me, protested the muleteer tending his palm.

— Oh, go and . . . on yourself. Get her!

— Mr. Major, I said —

There was a slap, and for a moment they thought the muleteer

was going to slap back. But he kept his head, and he only spat on the
ground sideways, significantly. And now they knew he was not going to get the beast even if the Major pulled out his pistol. He detached himself with dignity. And the Major was sorry and was
angry that he was sorry.

The owner of the mule moved towards the grove.

This time the farrier and the Corporal and another soldier dou-
ble-roped the animal. Even so she gave them a rough time, and the
indignant muleteer was glad she did; he hoped she would kick the
Major in the groin as he was supervising the operation at close range.
But she was already shaking from effort and frustration. When the
blacksmith began to burn in the serial number on the hoof wall —
a digit at a time — she opened her quivering haunches, and short
squirts of water shot out in the rhythm of her clonic spasms.

— I'll tell you something, Mr. Major, said the owner. It isn't for
nothing we call her Cat. I give you my word she will give the Army
trouble by the kilo. She obeys nobody but me. And then again I
must pay attention to her moods.

But the Major was too pressed to sift draftees. He gave the man
his official receipt, and the man said, "Good victory, Mr. Major,"
patted the Cat's neck, kind of sniffled, rubbed his nose, and
departed.

They attempted to break in the Cat many times all through the
trial period — when they tested the army packsaddles for fitness, or
rehearsed packing, or loaded the beasts just to work the new starchy-
like ropes and render them pliable. She finally accepted the saddle
but no burden, and the Corporal called her names and threatened
a left hook on her tender restless nostrils, for he was an amateur
boxer.

After that they let her be — they were frantic with a heap of
chores. They tied her on an outside pole as she was a constant menace when stabled with others. The Athenian November sun lit her
glossy russet coat and she was in flames. And her smallness and her
shape were unmulelike, because all angularities were modulated
into a gentle and yet tough roundness. And her compact head with
the slanty distrusting eyes and the clever ears, and her attractive and
alert hips that triggered flashes of kicks spoke of the unconquered,
the stubborn and the self-dependent who live and die alone.

Her driver did not even try to come to terms with her. He could not forgive her that he had been slapped because of her. He just condemned her as noncombatant material, and spat at her shapely legs, and missed.

— I know what you need, he mumbled. You need a he-mule first and a ton of beating after.

When the regiment moved he pulled her halter with contempt. He was now concerned with his personal comfort only, his knapsack, haversack and canteen. These she accepted as long as they did not touch her skin.

When they reached Skaramanga and the cranes hoisted mules and officers' horses onto the ships, she put up such a fight it was a big show. Somehow they managed to pass the bands under her panting belly and lock the slings. But, unlike all other beasts, she did not become paralyzed when she was lifted. She kicked the air, made the ropes sway and twirl, the whole affair tilted, she slid through the slings, just like a cat, and plunged.

The troops on the decks leaned on the rails and shouted as at a soccer game, the muleteers ran to the edge of the jetty, and everybody watched her swim alongside, her dainty head above the water. At the shallows she came out sparkling and drippy in the sunset light, sea-born animal Venus. Her wet coat showed her elastic contours in relief.

— She is beautiful, the bitch, said the Corporal.

Her driver spat.

During the trip she kicked badly and bit both her neighbors, two resigned peaceful giants. In the end she made the crowd so nervous and restless they had to take her away and tie her behind a divider of the hold, alone.

At Volos the Army left the ships. They were hurried across Thessaly, then rushed across Macedonia, through wind and rain. When about to cross the border and pass into Albania, the sick list of mules with swollen or saddle-wounded backs was a page long. On the last march in Greek territory the Major trotted his horse up and down the marching column for a running inspection of "the beasts-of-burden situation." He yelled his instructions which would have been very sensible in peace time. Then he saw the Cat fresh and unruffled and unused.

— Who is the princess? he demanded. Then he recognized her

and remembered the slapping and how he had lost in points of dignity to her moody driver — Are you by any chance reserving her for the conveyance of your mastership, soldier?

The Corporal intervened and explained. The Major exploded:

— Corporal, you make the driver break that cat first thing tomorrow morning! *Before* we cross the border!

— I'll kill her! said the muleteer to the Corporal after the Major trotted away. She's cost me a slapping, and now the Major suspects I ride her whenever we march in the dark. I only wish I did. I'll kill her, Mr. Corporal, I'm telling you, when we touch the front line.

— Yeah? The Army will be only too happy to charge you for her cost.

— If you'll be able to prove, Mr. Corporal, it was my bullet and not the enemy's, he said, and performed his side spitting.

In the morning they brought two village carts close side by side and trapped the Cat in between. The Corporal gripped her nose. The heel of his hand then knew the tenderness of her nostrils. With the other hand he clamped one of her ears. Her driver held the halter tight with hate. Another muleteer caught her tail fast, brought it around her rump, held it these. Two loaders were ready with giant sacks of potatoes on their shoulders, and they thudded them on her sides, and a third loader threw a third sack right on the very top of the packsaddle, which was against regulations. The convulsion of revolt activated her hips; but the kick did not materialize; it was too late: the conspirators had looped and locked the ropes with magic speed, and the weight was crushing her to the ground.

They managed to make her move for some fifty meters, pushing or pulling with all their might. But then she nailed her hooves on the village path that led to the highroad and it was final. By now the men were panting and cursing and puffs of steam from their mouths hit the morning air.

The platoons had already reached the highroad, and the mule train had fallen behind, and there was very little time left. The cortege tried once more to give the Cat momentum, but it was no use. So they recalled three mules from the column's tail. As the men unloaded the Cat and distributed the sacks onto the three mules, the Corporal suffered a crisis. He swore at her like a Piraeus pimp and began to punch her on the nose; he let her have a couple of scraping hooks; he was getting warm; next thing he was boxing her in earnest, and her driver was holding her head low by the halter to make sure no punch was wasted.

— Didn't I tell you she was no good? the driver kept saying. Didn't I?

Then they saw blood and it was hers, but it was also the Corporal's — her nostrils and his knuckles were cut, and they didn't know whose blood was on whom, a communion.

Later on they crossed the border, marched into Albanian territory, and the Corporal felt bad. He remembered how she had looked when she came out of the water at Skaramanga, shiny and elastic and defiant like a brand-new untouched woman. But then his anger returned after they marched through the plains of Biglista and Korytsa and the long list of sick mules became even longer. And they were now at the end of the highroad. And the new rain was two days old and still persisting and soaking men, beasts, burdens, and slushing the mountain trail to Varvara.

It was a steep climb. Most of the time the platoons and the muleteers walked on the edgy banks of the carved-in trail: recurring pools of liquid mud forced them to tie the halters on the pommels, prick or strike the mules and urge them to negotiate the treacherous spots alone. They themselves inchwormed on the skimpy ledges over the gaping canyons below, like acrobats. Their only connection then with their beasts was vocal, *hai, aha, dee!*

There were mud pools that reached as high as the bellies of the mules. The beasts fought their way, cutting the mud seas without protest. But now and then they lost their footing on the bottoms and made to sink and their big sad slave eyes were frantic and their nostrils shuddered. Each time they came out of those potential traps, they wore a fresh yellow-brown coat.

Five hundred meters before the rapids a big mule collapsed. He was carrying four boxes, fifteen hundred 6.5-mm cartridges a box. While they were removing the cases off his back, the rain densed and they said, "Of course." The water ran down their faces as they kneaded the mud with their boots, as they helped the mule up. He had the chills and if they wanted him to make Varvara at all they would have to let him march without burden.

Wordless and murderous, they jumped at the Cat. Strangely, she offered no resistance. As though the bitterness in their foul breaths, their hate for everybody and everything that escapes war overcame

her. They loaded her in a flash, like automatic loaders, tap-tap —
tap-tap. The four lead-heavy cases were too much for her size and
they knew it. Yet she followed the train, first tentatively, then steadily. Yes, this time, yes.

— It's about time! yelled the Corporal to the men, wanting to be
very pleased.

He saw the effort in her hooves trampling the slippery ground,
the excessive tension in her tendons. If she pressed now, he thought,
with all she had she would have no reserves left for the big climbing.
He could see the rainy upright menace of the opposite slope across
the rapids.

They crossed, and the primitive wooden bridge shook. Two wind-
ings of the trail farther up they met with a dead mule glued to the
slanty bank like a clay fossil, like a macabre collage. The eyes were
wide open, asking but not questioning. The upper lip, withdrawn
in a frozen spasm of pain, revealed the teeth. Who knows, thought
the Corporal, what urgent matériel he had been carrying in the rush
of the counterattack, and the weight, the mud and the climb had
shattered his heart.

The Corporal turned and saw the Cat on her way up an abrupt
hump of the trail. Her burden swayed and made to topple. She
quickly sidestepped and stopped short like a good seasoned mule;
and she was panting — What made her accept the burden today?
the Corporal asked himself. What?

A hundred meters higher they saw another cadaver. The Slope
of the Dead Mules, said the Corporal to himself. The Cat was now
panting heavily. Now and then a tremor would run down her
thighs. But she is young, she is young and strong, the Corporal reassured himself. Yet he wished he could take two or even one box off
her. He scanned the climbing train, saw the sick mules who carried trifles — a knapsack, a haversack, a couple of blankets, a pup-
tent. And he saw the ones with the swollen or bleeding or pus-fes-
tered backs who carried nothing, not even their own packsaddles.
Then he inspected the others who carried their own plus the burdens of the sick and the wounded. He knew that if only one mule
collapsed now it would mean abandoning his burden, whether food
or ammunition or stretchers. For he had exhausted all possible re-
distribution of loads. And still he wished two boxes taken off the
Cat.

Then the whole single file column, troops and beasts, was delayed

by a wide and long pool of mud. The drivers swore and spoke the
old platitude that there was nothing worse than stopping the uphill
momentum of a laden human, animal or machine. And for the nth
time they said, outraged: "Could you ever, ever expect any mountains to be muddy like flooded Thessaly fields?" And they praised
the stoniness of the Greek mountains and they cursed the mountains of Albania.

It took the troops at the head of the column a long time to file like
khaki ants on the one and only passable bank — the other gave
warnings of landslide when an officer tested it. And the beasts were
restless, shifting the center of gravity from shoulders to rump, from
left to right, constantly. And the Cat was the shiftiest of all.

At last the platoons passed the spot and the drivers said, "To the
devil with the old platoons," and they tied the halters on the saddle
pegs and urged the mules to brave the sea of mud. There was a shallower zone near the passable bank. Here the level was mule-chest
high, not too bad. The beasts bore to this side keeping as far as possible from the deeps. It was not easy, because of the bottom that
slanted from left to right and threw them off balance at every step.
But instinct and deliberation did the trick.

When the Cat's turn came she was already much unnerved by the
prolonged stop. She acted hastily, as though she couldn't wait to
cross the pool, climb the next grade, and the next, and the next,
reach Varvara on the cloud-capped top in one breath, and drop her
burden. The Corporal and her driver went up the bank and tried to
slow her down, *seii, seii!* But she would not listen.

And then it happened: for one thing, the mud level was up to
her neckline as she was smaller than the others. And she did not
first test the bottom with every step then proceed, as the others did.
She just went ahead boldly, and she created a rubbery wave that hit
the bank and kicked back at her, and she was pushed off the shallows
towards the deeps. And she was under now, burden and all, except
for her upper neck.

The Corporal and the driver shouted encouragements. Her eyes
panicked, her nostrils dilated to burst, her ears batted the air for
leverage. They could tell her effort to swim from the jerky ups and
downs of her head. But the mud monster was sucking her down. She
sank more. And the mud licked her jawbones. Then she and the
element were still.

— She is in her depth! cried the Corporal with relief.

He ran ahead, dangerously, and to the path beyond, and caught up with the tail of the mule train. He flashed his jackknife and cut all the extra lengths he could from loading ropes and he joined them into one piece and it was long enough and he came back and made the loop.

He, then the driver cast it some dozen times as fishermen do with nets, missing every time. Then the Corporal tried once more and was lucky.

— We might choke her, have you thought of that, Mr. Corporal?

— Just to start her towards the shallows, said the Corporal. Then we'll just guide her. Besides this is not a slipknot, see?

They gave the rope a catercorner tentative pull, but there was no response, so they pulled harder. No result. Either she was too frightened to leave her spot or she was very weak now.

They waited a little, then they pulled hard, then they pulled with all they had. They began to perspire. Suddenly the loop slipped over her head, crushing her ears, snapped off and fell midpool with a wet slap. The team listed backwards like dancers and they barely had the time to pivot, throw their flanks on the bank and cling, or else they would be rolling down the slope.

They collected themselves and considered other angles. They rejected the other bank, although it was closer to the Cat, because it would mean pulling her perhaps through even deeper spots. And then there was the landslide possibility. They also rejected both front and rear approaches to the pool from the path because the rope was too short and even if it was long it wouldn't do; because distance would defeat the effort.

Right then and there the rain stopped and there was failure and death in the comment of silence. The driver glanced beyond the end of the pool, up the slope, and saw the mule train at the next grade where maybe there was another mud trap, and he wished there *was* one to delay troops and mules, otherwise it would cost him and the Corporal some breath-cutting pace to catch up with the column. He spat and said:

— Let's go.

The Corporal looked him in the eye, inscrutable.

— Am I wrong again, Mr. Corporal?

— We'll come back and get her, said the Corporal and he sounded as though he threatened the driver.

— Yeah, yeah.

— With more help and rope.

The driver did not speak. When they took to the path the Corporal turned and looked back. She was a lonely russet head floating in a muddy limbo.

A wind rose and chased the clouds and dried the slopes. When the Army reached Varvara the sun came out just before dipping gloriously behind the mountain peak. And the men said: "Of course. It shines when we are sheltered, it pours frogs when we march. Naturally."

The Corporal did not have the strength, the heart or the nerve to order any man or mule to the rescue of the Cat. He reported to his Captain.

— I don't expect us to move before tomorrow noon, said the Captain. The Major said before *sunset,* if the weather stays clear — for once we scale the mountain, we are under the enemy's sight and fire. Only, do you really think she'll be able to stand on her feet till you get there?

— She is young and strong.

— Four cases of ammunition, Corporal . . .

— Beasts have a way.

— All right. Do as you think best.

At ten o'clock the Corporal was awakened by a sentry. He said, "Thanks," and the sentry went out to his post. The Corporal thought to himself: I'm getting up now. And he fell asleep.

At midnight he started up. He heard the wind rattle the tin awning of the billet's door. He ached all over as if he had lain under a pile of stones. He longed for more sleep. He peeled off his blanket, sat up and shook his head violently. His eyes were dry and itchy.

He woke the Cat's driver and two more muleteers. They were altogether four men, two coils of good rope, and two rested mules to take over the Cat's boxes.

They reached the spot at the crack of dawn. Her head was still floating.

They decided to operate from both sides at the same time, to make her sail towards the exit of the pool like a ship pulled from both banks of a river. The Corporal went to test the dangerous bank.

— It holds! he yelled back. The wind's hardened the dirt.

— And thickened the mud, think of this! retorted the Cat's driver from across.

— We'll manage, said the Corporal.

They made a loop with one rope and they tied the second rope on the opposite side of the loop. They split into two teams and, holding the ends of the ropes, climbed up the banks. The loop traveled in the air over the pool and descended on the Cat's head like a crown or a hangman's noose.

Suddenly the tip of the sun came up from behind the heights across the rapids and it was full morning, and they saw the eyes of the Cat. A film of sickly mist clouded them. The wind must have punished them all night. It must have made them smart; and tears came out; and the tears were now a whitish, yellowish stuff on the eyelids. She looked ugly, sick, maybe dying of acute pneumonia.

They began twisting the ropes to narrow the loop and prevent slippage. They twisted more, tightened the loop, but not too much. Then they yanked the ropes a few times, gently, to let her know what they meant to do and in what direction they were going. Then the Corporal spoke to her, the ropes became taut, trembled and:

— Ready? Go! yelled the Corporal.

They pulled and their palms felt all the tonnage of her own weight and of her burden and of the cubic meters of mortar on her and around her. And the pulling only punished her nape.

They took a breath and then started all over again. One muleteer picked up a couple of flakes of schist stone from the crumbling slope and threw them into the pool to arouse the Cat. The disks slapped the mud and they did not sink and the Corporal now knew the real thickness of the mud.

But they kept pulling, now in a hurry as if to beat the cementing mud, and after two or three more tries the pulling became wild and the two teams lost their coordination.

— It can't be done, said the Cat's driver out of breath.

— If she'd only just budge a little.

— She can't, Mr. Corporal, she can't. She is trapped for keeps.

— Well? inquired the team from the other bank.

— We try once more! yelled the Corporal.

They did and failed.

— Once more!

— Christ! retorted the other bank. D'you think we're capstans or tractors, Mr. Corporal?

— Once more! bellowed the Corporal and he was wild.

They did, and the pulling was cruel, and the Cat's neck was so stretched it could very well be part of the rope. Right then she turned her sick eyes towards the Corporal. No use, the sick eyes said, or so the Corporal felt. And they stopped pulling. There was a long pause while the teams caught their breath. Then without a word they untwisted the ropes slowly, avoiding each other's look. The loop loosened, rose in the air and waited to travel back the way it came. But there was no motion from the Corporal's side. So the two muleteers on the other bank began to gather rope. It left the Corporal's hands, fell, and slipped on the surface, spelling sibilant whispers of sorrow.

The team across walked to the path where the two mules were waiting.

The Corporal wished he could use the mules to pull out the Cat. But how, how in the world? And from where?

— Come on, said the Cat's driver softly. Let's finish her.

The Corporal said nothing. The driver walked slowly on the bank, down the bank and onto the path, picked up his rifle from one of the mules, came back. He palmed the bolt: *Krock Kraack — Kraack Krock.* Then a dead pause. Then the driver said:

— It's legal now, Mr. Corporal? All right?

The Corporal said nothing.

— Is it?

— Yeah, mumbled the Corporal.

— Don't feel so bad, Mr. Corporal, about the creature. This is a mercy killing.

— Yeah.

The driver raised the rifle, aimed and fired, and the sound soared in the crisp morning air, went above the rapids below, hit the slope on the other side of the canyon. The echo returned accusingly.

The Corporal saw the black-red selfsealing-like puncture. A thin rivulet of blood, slow and hesitant, wormed down her temple. It was drained before it reached the flat of the neck. The slanty eyes were still open, neither sad, nor relieved, just estranged. Then they began to fall asleep and the dainty head with the intelligent ears to sink. Slowly.

The Corporal started along the bank.

The Cat's driver spat in the pool. This time it was not at the Cat . . .

BERNARD MALAMUD

The German Refugee

(FROM THE SATURDAY EVENING POST)

OSKAR GASSNER sits in his cotton-mesh undershirt and summer bath-robe at the window of his stuffy, hot, dark hotel room on West Tenth Street while I cautiously knock. Outside, across the sky, a late-June green twilight fades in darkness. The refugee fumbles for the light and stares at me, hiding despair but not pain.

I was in those days a poor student and would brashly attempt to teach anybody anything for a buck an hour, although I have since learned better. Mostly I gave English lessons to recently arrived refugees. The college sent me; I had acquired a little experience. Already a few of my students were trying their broken English, theirs and mine, in the American marketplace. I was then just twenty, on my way into my senior year in college, a skinny, life-hungry kid, eating himself waiting for the next world war to start. It was a goddamn cheat. Here I was palpitating to get going, and across the ocean Adolf Hitler, in black boots and a square mustache, was tearing up all the flowers. Will I ever forget what went on with Danzig that summer?

Times were still hard from the depression but anyway I made a little living from the poor refugees. They were all over uptown Broadway in 1939. I had four I tutored — Karl Otto Alp, the former film star; Wolfgang Novak, once a brilliant economist; Friedrich Wilhelm Wolff, who had taught medieval history at Heidelberg; and, after that night I met him in his disordered cheap hotel room, Oskar Gassner, the Berlin critic and journalist, at one time on the *Acht Uhr Abendblatt*. They were accomplished men.

I had my nerve associating with them, but that's what a world crisis does for people — they get educated.

Oskar was maybe fifty, his thick hair turning gray. He had a big face and heavy hands. His shoulders sagged. His eyes, too, were heavy, a clouded blue; and as he stared at me after I had identified myself, doubt spread in them like underwater currents. It was as if, on seeing me, he had again been defeated. I stayed at the door in silence. In such cases I would rather be elsewhere, but I had to make a living. Finally he opened the door and I entered. Rather he released it and I was in. *"Bitte . . ."* He offered me a seat and didn't know where to sit himself. He would attempt to say something and then stop, as though it could not possibly be said. The room was cluttered with clothing, boxes of books he had managed to get out of Germany and some paintings. Oskar sat on a box and attempted to fan himself with his meaty hand. "Zis heat," he muttered, forcing his mind to the deed. "Impozzible. I do not know such heat." It was bad enough for me but terrible for him. He had difficulty breathing. He tried again to speak, lifted a hand and let it drop like a dead duck. He breathed as though he were fighting a battle; and maybe he won because after ten minutes we sat and slowly talked.

Like most educated Germans Oskar had at one time studied English. Although he was certain he couldn't say a word, he managed sometimes to put together a fairly decent, if rather comical, English sentence. He misplaced consonants, mixed up nouns and verbs and mangled idioms, yet we were able at once to communicate. We conversed mostly in English, with an occasional assist by me in pidgin-German or Yiddish, what he called "Jiddish." He had been to America before — last year for a short visit. He had come a month before *Kristallnacht,* when the Nazis shattered the Jewish store windows and burned all the synagogues, to see if he could find a job for himself; he had no relatives in America, and getting a job would permit him quickly to enter the country. He had been promised something, not in journalism but with the help of a foundation, as a lecturer. Then he had returned to Berlin, and after a frightening delay of six months was permitted to emigrate. He had sold whatever he could, managed to get some paintings, gifts of Bauhaus friends, and some boxes of books out by bribing two Nazi border guards; he had said goodbye to his wife and left the accursed

country. He gazed at me with cloudy eyes. "We parted amicably,"
he said in German. "My wife was gentile. Her mother was an ap-
palling anti-Semite. They returned to live in Stettin." I asked no
questions. Gentile is gentile, Germany is Germany.

His new job was in the Institute for Public Studies here in New
York. He was to give a lecture a week in the fall term, and during
next spring, a course, in English translation, on "The Literature of
the Weimar Republic." He had never taught before and was afraid
to. He was in that way to be introduced to the public, but the
thought of giving the lecture in English just about paralyzed him.
He didn't see how he could do it. "How is it pozzible? I cannot say
two words. I cannot pronounziate. I will make a fool of myself."
His melancholy deepened. Already in the two months since his
arrival, and after a round of diminishingly expensive hotel rooms,
he had had two English tutors, and I was the third. The others had
given him up, he said, because his progress was so poor, and he
thought also that he depressed them. He asked me whether I felt
I could do something for him, or should he go to a speech specialist
— someone, say, who charged five dollars an hour — and beg his
assistance? "You could try him," I said, "and then come back to
me." In those days I figured what I knew, I knew. At that he managed a smile. Still I wanted him to make up his mind, or it would
be no confidence down the line. He said, after a while, that he
would stay with me. If he went to the five-dollar professor it might
help his tongue but not his stomach. He would have no money left
to eat with. The institute had paid him in advance for the summer,
but it was only three hundred dollars and all he had.

He looked at me dully. *"Ich weiss nicht wie ich weiter machen
soll."*

I figured it was time to move past the first step. Either we did
that quickly or it would be like drilling rock for a long time.
"Let's stand at the mirror," I said.

He rose with a sigh and stood there beside me: I thin, elongated,
redheaded, praying for success, his and mine; Oskar uneasy, fearful, finding it hard to face either of us in the faded round glass
above his dresser.

"Please," I said to him, "could you say 'right'?"

"Ghight," he gargled.

"No. 'Right.' You put your tongue here." I showed him where.

As he tensely watched the mirror, I tensely watched him. "The tip of it curls behind the ridge on top, like this."

He placed his tongue where I showed him.

"Please," I said, "now say 'right.' "

Oskar's tongue fluttered, "Rright."

"That's good. Now say 'treasure' — that's harder."

"Tgheasure."

"The tongue goes up in front, not in the back of the mouth. Look."

He tried, his brow wet, eyes straining. "Trreasure."

"That's it."

"A miracle," Oskar murmured.

I said if he had done that he could do the rest.

We went for a bus ride up Fifth Avenue and then walked for a while around Central Park Lake. He had put on his German hat, with its hatband bow at the back, a broad-lapeled wool suit, a necktie twice as wide as the one I was wearing, and walked with a small-footed waddle. The night wasn't bad; it had got a bit cooler. There were a few large stars in the sky and they made me sad.

"Do you sink I will succezz?"

"Why not?" I asked.

Later he bought me a bottle of beer.

To many of these people, articulate as they were, the great loss was the loss of language — that they could no longer say what was in them to say. They could, of course, manage to communicate, but just to communicate was frustrating. As Karl Otto Alp, the ex-film star who became a buyer for Macy's, put it years later, "I felt like a child, or worse, often like a moron. I am left with myself unexpressed. What I knew, indeed, what I am, becomes to me a burden. My tongue hangs useless." The same with Oskar it figures. There was a terrible sense of useless tongue, and I think the reason for his trouble with his other tutors was that to keep from drowning in things unsaid he wanted to swallow the ocean in a gulp: Today he would learn English and tomorrow wow them with an impeccable Fourth of July speech, followed by a successful lecture at the Institute for Public Studies.

We performed our lessons slowly, step by step, everything in its place. After Oskar moved to a two-room apartment in a house on

West Eighty-fifth Street, near the Drive, we met three times a week at four-thirty, worked an hour and a half; then, since it was too hot to cook, had supper at the Seventy-second Street automat and conversed on my time. The lessons we divided into three parts: diction exercises and reading aloud, then grammar, because Oskar felt the necessity of it, and composition correction; with conversation, as I said, thrown in at supper. So far as I could see, he was coming along. None of these exercises was giving him as much trouble as they apparently had in the past. He seemed to be learning and his mood lightened. There were moments of elation as he heard his accent flying off. For instance, when "sink" became "think." He stopped calling himself "hopelezz."

Neither of us said much about the lecture he had to give early in October, and I kept my fingers crossed. It was somehow to come out of what we were doing daily, I think I felt, but exactly *how*, I had no idea; and to tell the truth, although I didn't say so to Oskar, the lecture frightened me. That and the ten more to follow during the fall term. Later when I learned that he had been attempting, with the help of the dictionary, to write in English, and had produced "a complete disahster," I suggested maybe he ought to stick to German and we could afterward both try to put it into passable English. I was cheating when I said that, because my German is meager. Anyway the idea was to get Oskar into production and worry about translating later. He sweated, from enervating morning to exhausted night, but no matter what language he tried, though he had been a professional writer for most of his life and knew his subject cold, the lecture refused to move past page one.

It was a sticky, hot July and the heat didn't help at all.

I had met Oskar at the end of June, and by the seventeenth of July we were no longer doing lessons. They had foundered on the "impozzible" lecture. He had worked on it each day in frenzy and growing despair. After writing more than a hundred opening pages, he furiously flung his pen against the wall, shouting he could no longer write in that filthy tongue. He cursed the German language. He hated the damned country and the damned people. After that, what was bad became worse. When he gave up attempting to write the lecture, he stopped making progress in English. He seemed to forget what he already knew. His tongue thickened and the accent returned in all its fruitiness. The little he had to say was in hand-cuffed and tortured English. The only German I heard him speak was in a whisper to himself. I doubt he knew he was talking it. That ended our formal work together, though I did drop in every other day or so to sit with him. For hours he sat motionless in a large green velours armchair, hot enough to broil in, and through the tall windows stared at the colorless sky above Eighty-fifth Street, with a wet depressed eye.

Then once he said to me, "If I do not this legture prepare, I will take my life."

"Let's begin again, Oskar," I said. "You dictate and I'll write. The ideas count, not the spelling."

He didn't answer so I stopped talking.

He had plunged into an involved melancholy. We sat for hours, often in profound silence. This was alarming to me, though I had already had some experience with such depression. Wolfgang Novak, the economist, though English came more easily to him, was another. His problems arose mainly, I think, from physical illness. And he felt a greater sense of the lost country than Oskar. Sometimes in the early evening I persuaded Oskar to come with me for a short walk on the Drive. The tail end of sunsets over the Palisades seemed to appeal to him. At least he looked. He would put on full regalia — hat, suit coat, tie, no matter how hot — and we went slowly down the stairs, I wondering whether he would ever make it to the bottom. He seemed to me always suspended between two floors.

We walked slowly uptown, stopping to sit on a bench and watch night rise above the Hudson. When we returned to his room, if I sensed he had loosened up a bit, we listened to music on the radio; but if I tried to sneak in a news broadcast, he said to me, "Please I can not more stand of world misery." I shut off the radio. He was right, it was a time of no good news. I squeezed my brain. What could I tell him? Was it good news to be alive? Who could argue the point? Sometimes I read aloud to him — I remember he liked the first part of *Life on the Mississippi*. We still went to the Automat once or twice a week; he perhaps out of habit, because he didn't feel like going anywhere, and I to get him out of his room. Oskar ate little, he toyed with a spoon. His dull eyes looked as though they had been squirted with a dark dye.

Once after a momentary cooling rainstorm we sat on newspapers on a wet bench overlooking the river, and Oskar at last began to talk. In tormented English he conveyed his intense and everlasting hatred of the Nazis for destroying his career, uprooting his life after half a century and flinging him like a piece of bleeding meat to hawks. He cursed them thickly, the German nation, as an inhuman, conscienceless, merciless people. "They are pigs mazquerading as peacogs," he said. "I feel certain that my wife, in her heart, was a Jew hater." It was a terrible bitterness, an eloquence almost without vocabulary. He became silent again. I hoped to hear more about his wife but decided not to ask.

Afterwards, in the dark Oskar confessed that he had attempted suicide during his first week in America. He was living, at the end of May, in a small hotel, and had filled himself with barbiturates one night, but his phone had fallen off the table and the hotel operator had sent up the elevator boy, who found him unconscious and called the police. He was revived in the hospital.

"I did not mean to do it," he said. "It was a mistage."

"Don't ever think of it again," I said. "It's total defeat."

"I don't," he said wearily, "because it is so arduouz to come back to life."

"Please, for any reason whatever."

Later, when we were walking, he surprised me by saying, "Maybe we ought to try now the legture onze more."

We trudged back to the house and he sat at his hot desk, I trying to read as he slowly began to reconstruct the first page of his lecture. He wrote, of course, in German.

He got nowhere. We were back to nothing, to sitting in silence in the heat. Sometimes after a few minutes I had to take off before his mood overcame mine. One afternoon I came unwillingly up the stairs — there were times I felt momentary surges of irritation with him — and was frightened to find Oskar's door ajar. When I knocked, no one answered. As I stood there, chilled down the spine, I realized I was thinking about the possibility of his attempting suicide again. "Oskar?" I went into the apartment, looked into both rooms and the bathroom, but he wasn't there. I thought he might have drifted out to get something from a store, and took the opportunity to look quickly around. There was nothing startling in the medicine chest, no pills but aspirin, no iodine. Thinking, for some reason, of a gun, I searched his desk drawer. In it I found a thin-paper airmail letter from Germany. Even if I had wanted to, I couldn't have read the handwriting, but as I held the thin paper in my hand I did make out one sentence: *"Ich bin dir siebenundzwanzig Jahre treu gewesen."* Twenty-seven years is a long time, I thought. There was no gun in the drawer. I shut it and stopped looking. It had occurred to me that if you want to kill yourself, all you need is a straight pin. When Oskar returned he said he had been sitting in the public library, unable to read.

Now we are once more enacting the changeless scene, curtain rising on two speechless characters in a furnished apartment, I in a straight-back chair, Oskar in the velours armchair that smothered rather than supported him, his flesh gray, the big gray face, unfocused, sagging. I reached over to switch on the radio, but he looked at me in a way that begged no. I then got up to leave, but Oskar, clearing his throat, thickly asked me to stay. I stayed, thinking, was there more to this than I could see into? His problems, God knows, were real enough, but could there be something more than a refugee's displacement, alienation, financial insecurity, being in a strange land without friends or a speakable tongue? My speculation was the old one: Not all drown in this ocean, why does he? After a while I shaped the thought and asked him was there something below the surface, invisible? I was full of this thing from college, and wondered if there mightn't be some unknown quantity in his depression that a psychiatrist maybe might help him with, enough to get him started on his lecture.

He meditated on this, and after a few minutes haltingly said he had been psychoanalyzed in Vienna as a young man. "Just the jusual *drek,*" he said, "fears and fantazies that afterwaards no longer bothered me."

"They don't now?"

"Not."

"You've written many articles and lectures before," I said. "What I can't understand, though I know how hard the situation is, is why you can never get past page one."

He half lifted his hand. "It is a paralyzis of my will. The whole legture is clear in my mind, but the minute I write down a single word — or in English or in German — I have a terrible fear I will not be able to write the negst. As though someone has thrown a stone at a window and the whole house — the whole idea — zmashes. This repeats until I am dezperate."

He said the fear grew as he worked that he would die before he completed the lecture, or if not that, that he would write it so disgracefully he would wish for death. The fear immobilized him.

"I have lozt faith. I do not — not longer possezz my former value of myself. In my life there has been too much illusion."

I tried to believe what I was saying: "Have confidence, the feeling will pass."

"Confidenze I have not. For this, and alzo whatever elze I have lozt, I thank the Nazis."

It was by then mid-August and things were growing steadily worse wherever one looked. The Poles were mobilizing for war. Oskar hardly moved. I was full of worries though I pretended calm weather.

He sat in his massive armchair with sick eyes, breathing like a wounded animal.

"Who can write about Walt Whitman in such terrible times?"

"Why don't you change the subject?"

"It mages no differenze what is the subject. It is all uzelezz."

I came every day to see him, neglecting my other students and therefore my livelihood. I had a panicky feeling that if things went on as they were going, they would end in Oskar's suicide; and I felt a frenzied desire to prevent that. What's more, I was sometimes afraid I was myself becoming melancholy, a new talent, call it, of taking less pleasure in my little pleasures. And the heat continued, oppressive, relentless. We thought of escape into the country, but neither of us had the money. One day I bought Oskar a secondhand fan — wondering why we hadn't thought of that before — and he sat in the breeze for hours each day until after a week, shortly after the Soviet-Nazi nonaggression pact was signed, the motor gave out. He could not sleep at night and sat at his desk with a wet towel on his head, still attempting to write his lecture. He wrote reams on a treadmill; it came out nothing. When he did sleep, out of exhaustion, he had fantastic frightening dreams of the Nazis inflicting tortures on him, sometimes forcing him to look upon the corpses of those they had slain. In one dream he told me about, he had gone back to Germany to visit his wife. She wasn't home and he had been directed to a cemetery. There, though the tombstone read another name, her blood seeped out of the earth above her shallow grave. He groaned at the memory of the dream.

Afterwards, he told me something about her. They had met as students, lived together, and were married at twenty-three. It wasn't a very happy marriage. She had turned into a sickly woman, physically unable to have children. "Something was wrong with her interior strugture."

Though I asked no questions, Oskar said, "I offered her to come with me here but she refused this."

"For what reason?"

"She did not think I wished her to come."

"Did you?" I asked.

"Not," he said.

He explained he had lived with her for almost twenty-seven years under difficult circumstances. She had been ambivalent about their Jewish friends and his relatives, though outwardly she seemed not a prejudiced person. But her mother was always a violent anti-Semite.

"I have nothing to blame myself," Oskar said.

He took to his bed. I took to the New York Public Library. I read some of the German poets he was trying to write about, in English translation. Then I read *Leaves of Grass* and wrote down what I thought one or two of them had got from Whitman. One day toward the end of August I brought Oskar what I had written. It was in good part guessing, but my idea wasn't to write the lecture for him. He lay on his back, motionless, and listened utterly sadly to what I had written. Then he said, no, it wasn't the love of death they had got from Whitman — that ran through German poetry — but it was most of all his feeling for *Brudermensch*, his humanity.

"But this does not grow long on German earth," he said, "and is soon deztroyed."

I said I was sorry I had got it wrong, but he thanked me anyway.

I left defeated, and as I was going down the stairs, heard someone sobbing. I will quit this, I thought. It has gotten to be too much for me. I can't drown with him.

I stayed home the next day, tasting a new kind of private misery too old for somebody my age, but that same night Oskar called me on the phone, blessing me wildly for having read those notes to him. He had got up to write me a letter to say what I had missed, and it ended by his having written half the lecture. He had slept all day and tonight intended to finish it up.

"I thank you," he said, "for much, alzo including your faith in me."

"Thank God," I said, not telling him I had just about lost it.

Oskar completed his lecture — wrote and rewrote it — during the first week in September. The Nazis had invaded Poland, and though we were greatly troubled, there was some sense of release; maybe the brave Poles would beat them. It took another week to translate the lecture, but here we had the assistance of Friedrich Wilhelm Wolff, the historian, a gentle, erudite man, who liked translating and promised his help with future lectures. We then had about two weeks to work on Oskar's delivery. The weather had changed, and so, slowly, had he. He had awakened from defeat, battered, after a wearying battle. He had lost close to twenty pounds. His complexion was still gray; when I looked at his face I expected to see scars, but it had lost its flabby unfocused quality. His blue eyes had returned to life and he walked with quick steps, as though to pick up a few for all the steps he hadn't taken during those long, hot days he had lain torpid in his room.

We went back to our former routine, meeting three late afternoons a week for diction, grammar and the other exercises. I taught him the phonetic alphabet and transcribed long lists of words he was mispronouncing. He worked many hours trying to fit each sound into place, holding half a matchstick between his teeth to keep his jaws apart as he exercised his tongue. All this can be a dreadfully boring business unless you think you have a future. Looking at him I realized what's meant when somebody is called "another man."

The lecture, which I now knew by heart, went off well. The director of the institute had invited a number of prominent people. Oskar was the first refugee they had employed, and there was a move to make the public cognizant of what was then a new ingredient in American life. Two reporters had come with a lady photographer. The auditorium was crowded. I sat in the last row, promising to put up my hand if he couldn't be heard, but it wasn't necessary. Oskar, in a blue suit, his hair cut, was of course nervous, but you couldn't see it unless you studied him. When he stepped up to the

lectern, spread out his manuscript and spoke his first English sentence in public, my heart hesitated; only he and I, of all the people
there, had any idea of the anguish he had been through. His enun-
ciation wasn't at all bad — a few *s*'s for *th*'s, and he once said "bag"
for "back," but otherwise he did all right. He read poetry well — in
both languages — and though Walt Whitman, in his mouth,
sounded a little as though he had come to the shores of Long Island
as a German immigrant, still the poetry read as poetry:

And I know that the spirit of God is the brother of my own,
And that all the men ever born are also my brothers, and the women
    my sisters and lovers,
And that a kelson of creation is love . . .

Oskar read it as though he believed it. Warsaw had fallen but
the verses were somehow protective. I sat back, conscious of two
things: how easy it is to hide the deepest wounds; and the pride
I felt in the job I had done.

Two days later I came up the stairs into Oskar's apartment to
find a crowd there. The refugee, his face beet red, lips bluish, a
trace of froth in the corners of his mouth, lay on the floor in his
limp pajamas, two firemen on their knees, working over him with
an inhalator. The windows were open and the air stank of gas.

A policeman asked me who I was and I could only answer, "No,
oh no."

I said no, but it was unchangeably yes. He had taken his life —
gas — I hadn't even thought of the stove in the kitchen.

"Why?" I asked myself. "Why did he do it?" Maybe it was the fate
of Poland on top of everything else, but the only answer anyone
could come up with was Oskar's scribbled note that he was not
well, and that he left Martin Goldberg all his possessions. I am
Martin Goldberg.

I was sick for a week, had no desire either to inherit or investigate,
but I thought I ought to look through his things before the court
impounded them, so I spent a morning sitting in the depths of Oskar's velours armchair, trying to read his correspondence. I had
found in the top drawer of his desk a thin packet of letters from his
wife and an airmail letter of recent date from his anti-Semitic
mother-in-law.

She writes, in a tight script it takes me hours to decipher, that her daughter, after Oskar abandons her, against her own mother's fervent pleas and anguish, is converted to Judaism by a vengeful rabbi. One night the Brown Shirts appear, and though the mother wildly waves her bronze crucifix in their faces, they drag Frau Gassner, together with the other Jews, out of the apartment house, and transport them in lorries to a small border town in conquered Poland. There, it is rumored, she is shot in the head and topples into an open tank ditch, with the naked Jewish men, their wives and children, some Polish soldiers and a handful of gypsies.

CARSON McCULLERS

Sucker

(FROM THE SATURDAY EVENING POST)

IT WAS always like I had a room to myself. Sucker slept in my bed with me but that didn't interfere with anything. The room was mine and I used it as I wanted to. Once I remember sawing a trap door in the floor. Last year when I was a sophomore in high school I tacked on my wall some pictures of girls from magazines and one of them was just in her underwear. My mother never bothered me because she had the younger kids to look after. And Sucker thought anything I did was always swell.

Whenever I would bring any of my friends back to my room all I had to do was just glance once at Sucker and he would get up from whatever he was busy with and maybe half smile at me, and leave without saying a word. He never brought kids back there. He's twelve, four years younger than I am, and he always knew without me even telling him that I didn't want kids that age meddling with my things.

Half the time I used to forget that Sucker isn't my brother. He's my first cousin but practically ever since I remember he's been in our family. You see his folks were killed in a wreck when he was a baby. To me and my kid sisters he was like our brother.

Sucker used to always remember and believe every word I said. That's how he got his nick-name. Once a couple of years ago I told him that if he'd jump off our garage with an umbrella it would act as a parachute and he wouldn't fall hard. He did it and busted his knee. That's just one instance. And the funny thing was that no matter how many times he got fooled he would still believe me.

Not that he was dumb in other ways — it was just the way he acted with me. He would look at everything I did and quietly take it in.

There is one thing I have learned, but it makes me feel guilty and is hard to figure out. If a person admires you a lot you despise him and don't care — and it is the person who doesn't notice you that you are apt to admire. This is not easy to realize. Maybelle Watts, this senior at school, acted like she was the Queen of Sheba and even humiliated me. Yet at this same time I would have done anything in the world to get her attentions. All I could think about day and night was Maybelle until I was nearly crazy. When Sucker was a little kid and on up until the time he was twelve I guess I treated him as bad as Maybelle did me.

Now that Sucker has changed so much it is a little hard to remember him as he used to be. I never imagined anything would suddenly happen that would make us both very different. I never knew that in order to get what has happened straight in my mind I would want to think back on him as he used to be and compare and try to get things settled. If I could have seen ahead maybe I would have acted different.

I never noticed him much or thought about him and when you consider how long we have had the same room together it is funny the few things I remember. He used to talk to himself a lot when he'd think he was alone — all about him fighting gangsters and being on ranches and that sort of kids' stuff. He'd get in the bathroom and stay as long as an hour and sometimes his voice would go up high and excited and you could hear him all over the house. Usually, though, he was very quiet. He didn't have many boys in the neighborhood to buddy with and his face had the look of a kid who is watching a game and waiting to be asked to play. He didn't mind wearing the sweaters and coats that I outgrew, even if the sleeves did flop down too big and make his wrists look as thin and white as a little girl's. That is how I remember him — getting a little bigger every year but still being the same. That was Sucker up until a few months ago when all this trouble began.

Maybelle was somehow mixed up in what happened so I guess I ought to start with her. Until I knew her I hadn't given much time to girls. Last fall she sat next to me in General Science class and that was when I first began to notice her. Her hair is the brightest yellow I ever saw and occasionally she will wear it set into curls with some sort of gluey stuff. Her fingernails are pointed and manicured and painted a shiny red. All during class I used to watch Maybelle, nearly all the time except when I thought she was going to look my way or when the teacher called on me. I couldn't keep my eyes off her hands, for one thing. They are very little and white except for that red stuff, and when she would turn the pages of her book she always licked her thumb and held out her little finger and turned very slowly. It is impossible to describe Maybelle. All the boys are crazy about her but she didn't even notice me. For one thing she's almost two years older than I am. Between periods I used to try and pass very close to her in the halls but she would hardly ever smile at me. All I could do was sit and look at her in class — and sometimes it was like the whole room could hear my heart beating and I wanted to holler or light out and run for Hell.

At night, in bed, I would imagine about Maybelle. Often this would keep me from sleeping until as late as one or two o'clock. Sometimes Sucker would wake up and ask me why I couldn't get settled and I'd tell him to hush his mouth. I suppose I was mean to him lots of times. I guess I wanted to ignore somebody like Maybelle did me. You could always tell by Sucker's face when his feelings were hurt. I don't remember all the ugly remarks I must have made because even when I was saying them my mind was on Maybelle.

That went on for nearly three months and then somehow she began to change. In the halls she would speak to me and every morning she copied my homework. At lunch time once I danced with her in the gym. One afternoon I got up nerve and went around to her house with a carton of cigarettes. I knew she smoked in the girls' basement and sometimes outside of school — and I didn't want to take her candy because I think that's been run into the ground. She was very nice and it seemed to me everything was going to change.

It was that night when this trouble really started. I had come into my room late and Sucker was already asleep. I felt too happy and keyed up to get in a comfortable position and I was awake thinking about Maybelle a long time. Then I dreamed about her and it seemed I kissed her. It was a surprise to wake up and see the dark. I lay still and a little while passed before I could come to and understand where I was. The house was quiet and it was a very dark night.

Sucker's voice was a shock to me. "Pete? . . ."

I didn't answer anything or even move.

"You do like me as much as if I was your own brother, don't you Pete?"

I couldn't get over the surprise of everything and it was like this was the real dream instead of the other.

"You have liked me all the time like I was your own brother, haven't you?"

"Sure," I said.

Then I got up for a few minutes. It was cold and I was glad to come back to bed. Sucker hung on to my back. He felt little and warm and I could feel his warm breathing on my shoulder.

"No matter what you did I always knew you liked me."

I was wide awake and my mind seemed mixed up in a strange way. There was this happiness about Maybelle and all that — but at the same time something about Sucker and his voice when he said these things made me take notice. Anyway I guess you understand people better when you are happy than when something is worrying you. It was like I had never really thought about Sucker until then. I felt I had always been mean to him. One night a few weeks before I had heard him crying in the dark. He said he had lost a boy's beebee gun and was scared to let anybody know. He wanted me to tell him what to do. I was sleepy and tried to make him hush and when he wouldn't I kicked at him. That was just one of the things I remembered. It seemed to me he had always been a lonesome kid. I felt bad.

There is something about a dark cold night that makes you feel close to someone you're sleeping with. When you talk together it is like you are the only people awake in the town.

"You're a swell kid, Sucker," I said.

It seemed to me suddenly that I did like him more than anybody else I knew — more than any other boy, more than my sisters, more in a certain way even than Maybelle. I felt good all over and it was like when they play sad music in the movies. I wanted to show Sucker how much I really thought of him and make up for the way I had always treated him.

We talked for a good while that night. His voice was fast and it was like he had been saving up these things to tell me for a long time. He mentioned that he was going to try to build a canoe and that the kids down the block wouldn't let him in on their football team and I don't know what all. I talked some too and it was a good feeling to think of him taking in everything I said so seriously. I even spoke of Maybelle a little, only I made out like it was her who had been running after me all this time. He asked questions about high school and so forth. His voice was excited and he kept on talking fast like he could never get the words out in time. When I went to sleep he was still talking and I could still feel his breathing on my shoulder, warm and close.

During the next couple of weeks I saw a lot of Maybelle. She acted as though she really cared for me a little. Half the time I felt so good I hardly knew what to do with myself.

But I didn't forget about Sucker. There were a lot of old things in my bureau drawer I'd been saving — boxing gloves and Tom Swift books and second rate fishing tackle. All this I turned over to him. We had some more talks together and it was really like I was knowing him for the first time. When there was a long cut on his cheek I knew he had been monkeying around with this new first razor set of mine, but I didn't say anything. His face seemed different now. He used to look timid and sort of like he was afraid of a whack over the head. That expression was gone. His face, with those wide-open eyes and his ears sticking out and his mouth never quite shut, had the look of a person who is surprised and expecting something swell.

Once I started to point him out to Maybelle and tell her he was my kid brother. It was an afternoon when a murder mystery was on at the movie. I had earned a dollar working for my Dad and I gave Sucker a quarter to go and get candy and so forth. With the rest I took Maybelle. We were sitting near the back and I saw Sucker come in. He began to stare at the screen the minute he stepped past the ticket man and he stumbled down the aisle without noticing where he was going. I started to punch Maybelle but couldn't quite make up my mind. Sucker looked a little silly — walking like a drunk with his eyes glued to the movie. He was wiping his reading glasses on his shirt tail and his knickers flopped down. He went on until he got to the first few rows where the kids usually sit. I never did punch Maybelle. But I got to thinking it was good to have both of them at the movie with the money I earned.

I guess things went on like this for about a month or six weeks. I felt so good I couldn't settle down to study or put my mind on

anything. I wanted to be friendly with everybody. There were
times when I just had to talk to some person. And usually that
would be Sucker. He felt as good as I did. Once he said: "Pete, I
am gladder that you are like my brother than anything else in the
world."

Then something happened between Maybelle and me. I never
have figured out just what it was. Girls like her are hard to understand. She began to act different toward me. At first I wouldn't let
myself believe this and tried to think it was just my imagination.
She didn't act glad to see me any more. Often she went out riding
with this fellow on the football team who owns this yellow roadster.
The car was the color of her hair and after school she would ride
off with him, laughing and looking into his face. I couldn't think
of anything to do about it and she was on my mind all day and
night. When I did get a chance to go out with her she was snippy
and didn't seem to notice me. This made me feel like something
was the matter — I would worry about my shoes clopping too loud
on the floor, or the fly of my pants, or the bumps on my chin. Sometimes when Maybelle was around, a devil would get into me and I'd
hold my face stiff and call grown men by their last names without
the Mister and say rough things. In the night I would wonder
what made me do all this until I was too tired for sleep.

At first I was so worried I just forgot about Sucker. Then later he
began to get on my nerves. He was always hanging around until I
would get back from high school, always looking like he had something to say to me or wanted me to tell him. He made me a magazine rack in his Manual Training class and one week he saved his
lunch money and bought me three packs of cigarettes. He couldn't
seem to take it in that I had things on my mind and didn't want to
fool with him. Every afternoon it would be the same — him in my
room with this waiting expression on his face. Then I wouldn't
say anything or I'd maybe answer him rough-like and he would
finally go on out.

I can't divide that time up and say this happened one day and
that the next. For one thing I was so mixed up the weeks just
slid along into each other and I felt like Hell and didn't care. Nothing definite was said or done. Maybelle still rode around with this
fellow in his yellow roadster and sometimes she would smile at me
and sometimes not. Every afternoon I went from one place to another where I thought she would be. Either she would act almost

nice and I would begin thinking how things would finally clear up and she would care for me — or else she'd behave so that if she hadn't been a girl I'd have wanted to grab her by that white little neck and choke her. The more ashamed I felt for making a fool of myself the more I ran after her.

Sucker kept getting on my nerves more and more. He would look at me as though he sort of blamed me for something, but at the same time knew that it wouldn't last long. He was growing fast and for some reason began to stutter when he talked. Sometimes he had nightmares or would throw up his breakfast. Mom got him a bottle of cod liver oil.

Then the finish came between Maybelle and me. I met her going to the drug store and asked for a date. When she said no I remarked something sarcastic. She told me she was sick and tired of my being around and that she had never cared a rap about me. She said all that. I just stood there and didn't answer anything. I walked home very slowly.

For several afternoons I stayed in my room by myself. I didn't want to go anywhere or talk to anyone. When Sucker would come in and look at me sort of funny I'd yell at him to get out. I didn't want to think of Maybelle and I sat at my desk reading *Popular Mechanics* or whittling at a toothbrush rack I was making. It seemed to me I was putting that girl out of my mind pretty well.

But you can't help what happens to you at night. That is what made things how they are now.

You see a few nights after Maybelle said those words to me I dreamed about her again. It was like that first time and I was squeezing Sucker's arm so tight I woke him up. He reached for my hand.

"Pete, what's the matter with you?"

All of a sudden I felt so mad my throat choked — at myself and the dream and Maybelle and Sucker and every single person I knew. I remembered all the times Maybelle had humiliated me and everything bad that had ever happened. It seemed to me for a second that nobody would ever like me but a sap like Sucker.

"Why is it we aren't buddies like we were before? Why — ?"

"Shut your damn trap!" I threw off the cover and got up and turned on the light. He sat in the middle of the bed, his eyes blinking and scared.

There was something in me and I couldn't help myself. I don't

think anybody ever gets that mad but once. Words came without
me knowing what they would be. It was only afterward that I
could remember each thing I said and see it all in a clear way.

"Why aren't we buddies? Because you're the dumbest slob I ever
saw! Nobody cares anything about you! And just because I felt
sorry for you sometimes and tried to act decent don't think I give a
damn about a dumb-bunny like you!"

If I talked loud or hit him it wouldn't have been so bad. But
my voice was slow and like I was very calm. Sucker's mouth was part
way open and he looked as though he'd knocked his funny bone.
His face was white and sweat came out on his forehead. He wiped
it away with the back of his hand and for a minute his arm stayed
raised that way as though he was holding something away from him.

"Don't you know a single thing? Haven't you ever been around
at all? Why don't you get a girl friend instead of me? What kind of
a sissy do you want to grow up to be anyway?"

I didn't know what was coming next. I couldn't help myself or
think.

Sucker didn't move. He had on one of my pajama jackets and his
neck stuck out skinny and small. His hair was damp on his forehead.

"Why do you always hang around me? Don't you know when
you're not wanted?"

Afterward I could remember the change in Sucker's face.
Slowly that blank look went way and he closed his mouth. His
eyes got narrow and his fists shut. There had never been such a look
on him before. It was like every second he was getting older. There
was a hard look to his eyes you don't see usually in a kid. A drop
of sweat rolled down his chin and he didn't notice. He just sat there
with those eyes on me and he didn't speak and his face was hard
and didn't move.

"No you don't know when you're not wanted. You're too dumb.
Just like your name — a dumb Sucker."

It was like something had busted inside me. I turned off the light
and sat down in the chair by the window. My legs were shaking
and I was so tired I could have bawled. The room was cold and
dark. I sat there for a long time and smoked a squashed cigarette
I had saved. Outside the yard was black and quiet. After a while
I heard Sucker lie down.

I wasn't mad any more, only tired. It seemed awful to me that I had talked like that to a kid only twelve. I couldn't take it all in. I told myself I would go over to him and try to make it up. But I just sat there in the cold until a long time had passed. I planned how I could straighten it out in the morning. Then, trying not to squeak the springs, I got back in bed.

Sucker was gone when I woke up the next day. And later when I wanted to apologize as I had planned he looked at me in this new hard way so that I couldn't say a word.

All of that was two or three months ago. Since then Sucker has grown faster than any boy I ever saw. He's almost as tall as I am and his bones have gotten heavier and bigger. He won't wear any of my old clothes any more and has bought his first pair of long pants — with some leather suspenders to hold them up. Those are just the changes that are easy to see and put into words.

Our room isn't mine at all any more. He's gotten up this gang of kids and they have a club. When they aren't digging trenches in some vacant lot and fighting they are always in my room. On the door there is some foolishness written in Mercurochrome saying "Woe to the Outsider who Enters" and signed with crossed bones and their secret initials. They have rigged up a radio and every afternoon it blares out music. Once as I was coming in I heard a boy telling something in a low voice about what he saw in the back of his big brother's automobile. I could guess what I didn't hear. *That's what her and my brother do. It's the truth — parked in the car.* For a minute Sucker looked surprised and his face was almost like it used to be. Then he got hard and tough again. "Sure, dumbell. We know all that." They didn't notice me. Sucker began telling them how in two years he was planning to be a trapper in Alaska.

But most of the time Sucker stays by himself. It is worse when we are alone together in the room. He sprawls across the bed in those long corduroy pants with the suspenders and just stares at me with that hard, half sneering look. I fiddle around my desk and can't get settled because of those eyes of his. And the thing is I just have to study because I've gotten three bad cards this term already. If I flunk English I can't graduate next year. I don't want to be a bum and I just have to get my mind on it. I don't care a flip for Maybelle or any particular girl any more and it's only this thing between

Sucker and me that is the trouble now. We never speak except when we have to before the family. I don't even want to call him Sucker any more and unless I forget I call him by his real name, Richard. At night I can't study with him in the room and I have to hang around the drug store, smoking and doing nothing, with the fellows who loaf there.

More than anything I want to be easy in my mind again. And I miss the way Sucker and I were for a while in a funny, sad way that before this I never would have believed. But everything is so different that there seems to be nothing I can do to get it right. I've sometimes thought if we could have it out in a big fight that would help. But I can't fight him because he's four years younger. And another thing — sometimes this look in his eyes makes me almost believe that if Sucker could he would kill me.

VIRGINIA MORICONI

Simple Arithmetic

(FROM THE TRANSATLANTIC REVIEW)

Geneva, January 15

Dear Father:

Well, I am back in School, as you can see, and the place is just as miserable as ever. My only friend, the one I talked to you about, Ronald Fletcher, is not coming back any more because someone persuaded his mother that she was letting him go to waste, since he was extremely photogenic, so now he is going to become a child actor. I was very surprised to hear this, as the one thing Ronnie liked to do was play basketball. He was very shy.

The flight wasn't too bad. I mean nobody had to be carried off the plane. The only thing was, we were six hours late and they forgot to give us anything to eat, so for fourteen hours we had a chance to get quite hungry but, as you say, for the money you save going tourist class, you should be prepared to make a few little sacrifices.

I did what you told me, and when we got to Idlewild I paid the taxi driver his fare and gave him a fifty-cent tip. He was very dissatisfied. In fact he wouldn't give me my suitcase. In fact I don't know what would have happened if a man hadn't come up just while the argument was going on and when he heard what it was all about he gave the taxi driver a dollar and I took my suitcase and got to the plane on time.

During the trip I thought the whole thing over. I did not come to any conclusion. I know I have been very extravagant and unreasonable about money and you have done the best you can to explain this to me. Still, while I was thinking about it, it seemed to me that there were only three possibilities. I could just have given up and let the taxi driver have the suitcase, but when you realize that if we had to buy everything over again that was in the suit-case we would probably have had to spend at least five hundred dol-lars, it does not seem very economical. Or I could have gone on arguing with him and missed the plane, but then we would have had to pay something like three hundred dollars for another ticket. Or else I could have given him an extra twenty-five cents which, as you say, is just throwing money around to create an impression. What would you have done?

Anyway I got here, with the suitcase, which was the main thing. They took two week-end privileges away from me because I was late for the opening of School. I tried to explain to M. Frisch that it had nothing to do with me if the weather was so bad that the plane was delayed for six hours, but he said that prudent persons allow for continjensies of this kind and make earlier reservations. I don't care about this because the next two week-ends are skiing week-ends and I have never seen any point in waking up at six o'clock in the morning just to get frozen stiff and endure terrible pain even if sports are a part of growing up, as you say. Besides, we will save twenty-seven dollars by having me stay in my room.

In closing I want to say that I had a very nice Christmas and I apreciate everything you tried to do for me and I hope I wasn't too much of a bother. (Martha explained to me that you had had to take time off from your honeymoon in order to make Christmas for me and I am very sorry even though I do not think I am to blame if Christmas falls on the twenty-fifth of December, especially since everybody knows that it does. What I mean is, if you had wanted to have a long honeymoon you and Martha could have gotten married earlier, or you could have waited until Christmas was over, or you could just have told me not to come and I would have un-derstood.)

I will try not to spend so much money in the future and I will keep accounts and send them to you. I will also try to remember to do the eye exercises and the exercises for fallen arches that the doctors in New York prescribed.

Love,
STEPHEN

New York, January 19

Dear Stephen:

Thank you very much for the long letter of January fifteenth. I was very glad to know that you had gotten back safely, even though the flight was late. (I do not agree with M. Frisch that prudent persons allow for "continjensies" of this kind, now that air travel is as standard as it is, and the service usually so good, but we must remember that Swiss people are, by and large, the most meticulous in the world and nothing offends them more than other people who are not punctual.)

In the affair of the suitcase, I'm afraid that we were both at fault. I had forgotten that there would be an extra charge for luggage when I suggested that you should tip the driver fifty cents. You, on the other hand, might have inferred from his argument that he was simply asking that the tariff — i.e. the fare, plus the overcharge for the suitcase — should be paid in full, and regulated yourself accordingly. In any event you arrived, and I am only sorry that obviously you had no time to learn the name and address of your benefactor so that we might have paid him back for his kindness.

I will look forward to going over your accounting and I am sure you will find that in keeping a clear record of what you spend you will be able to cut your cloth according to the bolt and that, in turn, will help you to develop a real regard for yourself. It is a common failing, as I told you, to spend too much money in order to compensate oneself for a lack of inner security, but you can easily see that a foolish purchase does not insure stability, and if you are chronically insolvent you can hardly hope for peace of mind. Your allowance is more than adequate and when you learn to make both ends meet you will have taken a decisive step ahead. I have great faith in you and I know you will find your anchor to windward in your studies, in your sports, and in your companions.

As to what you say about Christmas, you are not obliged to "apreciate" what we did for you. The important thing was that you should have had a good time, and I think we had some wonderful fun together, the three of us, don't you? Until your mother decides where she wants to live and settles down, this is your *home* and you must always think of it that way. Even though I have remarried, I am still your father, first and last, and Martha is very fond of you too, and very understanding about your problems. You may not be aware of it but in fact she is one of the best friends you have. New ideas and new stepmothers take a little getting used to, of course.

Please write me as regularly as you can, since your letters mean a great deal to me. Please try too, at all times, to keep your marks up to scratch, as college entrance is getting harder and harder in this country, and there are thousands of candidates each year for the good universities. Concentrate particularly on spelling. "Contingency" is difficult, I know, but there is no excuse for only one "p" in "appreciate"! And *do* the exercises.

Love,
FATHER

Geneva, January 22

Dear Mummy:

Last Sunday I had to write to Father to thank him for my Christmas vacation and to tell him that I got back all right. This Sunday I thought I would write to you even though you are on a cruze so perhaps you will never get my letter. I must say that if they didn't make us write home once a week I don't believe that I would ever write any letters at all. What I mean is that once you get to a point like this, in a place like this, you see that you are supposed to have your life and your parents are supposed to have their lives, and you have lost the connection.

Anyway I have to tell you that Father was wonderful to me and Martha was very nice too. They had thought it all out, what a child of my age might like to do in his vacation, and sometimes it was pretty strenuous, as you can imagine. At the end the School sent the bill for the first term, where they charge you for the extras which they let you have here and it seems that I had gone way over my allowance and besides I had signed for a whole lot of things I did not deserve. So there was a terrible scene and Father was very angry and Martha cried and said that if Father always made such an effort to consider me as a person I should make an effort to consider him as a person too and wake up to the fact that he was not Rockefeller and that even if he was sacrificing himself so that I could go to one of the most expensive schools in the world it did not mean that I should drag everybody down in the mud by my reckless spending. So now I have to turn over a new leaf and keep accounts of every penny and not buy anything which is out of proportion to our scale of living.

Except for that one time they were very affectionate to me and did everything they could for my happiness. Of course it was awful without you. It was the first time we hadn't been together and I couldn't really believe it was Christmas.

I hope you are having a wonderful time and getting the rest you need and please write me when you can.

ALL MY LOVE,
STEPHEN

Geneva, January 29

Dear Father:

Well it is your turn for a letter this week because I wrote to Mummy last Sunday. (I am sure I can say this to you without hurting your feelings because you always said that the one thing you and Mummy wanted was a civilized divorce so we could all be friends.) Anyway Mummy hasn't answered my letter so probably she doesn't aprove of my spelling any more than you do. I am beginning to wonder if maybe it wouldn't be much simpler and much cheaper too if I didn't go to college after all. I really don't know what this education is for in the first place.

There is a terrible scandal here at School which has been very interesting for the rest of us. One of the girls, who is only sixteen, has gotten pregnant and everyone knows that it is all on account of the science instructer, who is a drip. We are waiting to see if he will marry her, but in the meantime she is terrifically upset and she has been expelled from the School. She is going away on Friday.

I always liked her very much and I had a long talk with her last night. I wanted to tell her that maybe it was not the end of the world, that my stepmother was going to have a baby in May, although she never got married until December, and the sky didn't fall in or anything. I thought it might have comforted her to think that grownups make the same mistakes that children do (if you can call her a child) but then I was afraid that it might be disloyal to drag you and Martha into the conversation, so I just let it go.

I'm fine and things are just the same.

Love,
STEPHEN

New York, February 2

Dear Stephen:

It would be a great relief to think that your mother did not "a-prove" of your spelling either, but I'm sure that it's not for that rea-son that you haven't heard from her. She was never any good as a correspondent, and now it is probably more difficult for her than ever. We did indeed try for what you call a "civilized divorce" for all our sakes, but divorce is not any easy thing for any of the persons in-volved, as you well know, and if you try to put yourself in your mother's place for a moment, you will see that she is in need of time and solitude to work things out for herself. She will certainly write to you as soon as she has found herself again, and meanwhile you must continue to believe in her affection for you and not let im-patience get the better of you.

Again, in case you are really in doubt about it, the purpose of your education is to enable you to stand on your own feet when you are a man and make something of yourself. Inaccuracies in spelling will not *simplify* anything.

I can easily see how you might have made a parallel between your friend who has gotten into trouble, and Martha who is expecting the baby in May, but there is only a superficial similarity in the two cases.

Your friend is, or was, still a child, and would have done better to have accepted the limitations of the world of childhood — as you can clearly see for yourself, now that she is in this predicament. Martha, on the other hand, was hardly a child. She was a mature human being, responsible for her own actions and prepared to be responsible for the baby when it came. Moreover I, unlike the science "instructer," am not a drip, I too am responsible for *my* actions, and so Martha and I are married and I will do my best to live up to her and the baby.

Speaking of which, we have just found a new apartment because this one will be too small for us in May. It is right across the street from your old school and we have a kitchen, a dining alcove, a liv-ing room, two bedrooms — one for me and Martha, and one for the new baby — and another room which will be for you. Martha felt that it was very important for you to feel that you had a place of your own when you came home to us, and so it is largely thanks to her that we have taken such a big place. The room will double as a study for me when you are not with us, but we will move all my books and papers and paraphernalia whenever you come, and Martha is planning to hang the Japanese silk screen you liked at the foot of the bed.

Please keep in touch, and *please* don't forget the exercises.

Love,

FATHER

Geneva, February 5

Dear Father:

There is one thing which I would like to say to you which is that if it hadn't been for you *I* would never have heard of a "civilized divorce," but that is the way you explained it to me. I always thought it was crazy. What I mean is, wouldn't it have been better if you had said, "I don't like your mother any more and I would rather live with Martha," instead of insisting that you and Mummy were always going to be the greatest friends? Because the way things are now Mummy probably thinks that you still like her very much, and it must be hard for Martha to believe that she was chosen, and I'm pretty much confused myself, although it is really none of my business.

You will be sorry to hear that I am not able to do any of the exercises any longer. I cannot do the eye exercises because my roommate got so fassinated by the stereo gadget that he broke it. (But the School Nurse says she thinks it may be just as well to let the whole thing go since in her opinion there was a good chance that I might have gotten more cross-eyed than ever, fidgeting with the viewer.) And I can not do the exercises for fallen arches, at least for one foot, because when I was decorating the Assembly Hall for the dance last Saturday, I fell off the stepladder and broke my ankle. So now I am in the Infirmary and the School wants to know whether to send the doctor's bill to you or to Mummy, because they had to call in a specialist from outside, since the regular School Doctor only knows how to do a very limited number of things. So I have cost a lot of money again and I am very very sorry, but if they were halfway decent in this School they would pay to have proper equipment and not let the students risk their lives on broken stepladders, which is something you could write to the Bookkeeping Department, if you felt like it, because I can't, but you could, and it might do some good in the end.

The girl who got into so much trouble took too many sleeping pills and died. I felt terrible about it, in fact I cried when I heard it. Life is very crewel, isn't it?

I agree with what you said, that she was a child, but I think she knew that, from her point of view. I think she did what she did because she thought of the science instructer as a grownup, so she imagined that she was perfectly safe with him. You may think she was just bad, because she was a child and should have known better, but I think that it was not entirely her fault since here at School we are all encouraged to take the teachers seriously.

I am very glad you have found a new apartment and I hope you won't move all your books and papers when I come home, because that would only make me feel that I was more of a nuisance than ever.

Love,
STEPHEN

New York, February 8

Dear Stephen:

This will have to be a very short letter because we are to move into the new apartment tomorrow and Martha needs my help with the packing.

We were exceedingly shocked by the tragic death of your friend and very sorry that you should have had such a sad experience. Life can be "crewel" indeed to the people who do not learn how to live it.

When I was exactly your age I broke my ankle too — I wasn't on a defective stepladder, I was playing hockey — and it hurt like the devil. I still remember it and you have all my sympathy. (I have written to the School Physician to ask how long you will have to be immobilized, and to urge him to get you back into the athletic program as fast as possible. The specialist's bill should be sent to me.)

I have also ordered another stereo viewer because, in spite of the opinion of the School Nurse, the exercises are most important and you are to do them *religiously*. Please be more careful with this one no matter how much it may "fassinate" your roommate.

Martha sends love and wants to know what you would like for your birthday. Let us know how the ankle is mending.

Love,
FATHER

Geneva, February 12

Dear Father:

I was very surprised by your letter. I was surprised that you said you were helping Martha to pack because when you and Mummy were married I do not ever remember you packing or anything like that so I guess Martha is reforming your charactor. I was also surprised by what you said about the girl who died. What I mean is, if anyone had told me a story like that I think I would have just let myself get a little worked up about the science instructer because it seems to me that he was a villan too. Of course you are much more riserved than I am.

I am out of the Infirmary and they have given me a pair of crutches, but I'm afraid it will be a long time before I can do sports again.

I hope the new apartment is nice and I do not want anything for my birthday because it will seem very funny having a birthday in School so I would rather not be reminded of it.

Love,
STEPHEN

New York, February 15

Dear Stephen:

This is not an answer to your letter of February twelfth, but an attempt to have a serious discussion with you, as if we were face to face.

You are almost fifteen years old. Shortly you will be up against the stiffest competition of your life when you apply for college entrance. No examiner is going to find himself favorably impressed by "charactor" or "instructer" or "villan" or "riserved" or similar errors. You will have to face the fact that in this world we succeed on our merits, and if we are unsuccessful, on account of sloppy habits of mind, we suffer for it. You are still too young to understand me entirely, but you are not too young to recognize the importance of effort. People who do not make the grade are desperately unhappy all their lives because they have no place in society. If you do not pass the college entrance examinations simply because you are unable to spell, it will be nobody's fault but your own, and you will be gravely handicapped for the rest of your life.

Every time you are in doubt about a word you are to look it up in the dictionary and *memorize* the spelling. This is the least you can do to help yourself.

We are still at sixes and sevens in the new apartment but when Martha accomplishes all she has planned it should be very nice indeed and I think you will like it.

Love,
Father

Geneva, February 19

Dear Father:

I guess we do not understand each other at all. If you immagine for one minute that just by making a little effort I could imaggine how to spell immaggine without looking it up and finding that actually it is "imagine," then you are all wrong. In other words, if you get a letter from me and there are only two or three mistakes well you just have to take my word for it that I have had to look up practically every single word in the dictionary and that is one reason I hate having to write you these letters because they take so long and in the end they are not at all spontainious, no, just wait a second, here it is, "spontaneous," and believe me only two or three mistakes in a letter from me is one of the seven wonders of the world. What I'm saying is that I am doing the best I can as you would aggree if you could see my dictionary which is falling apart and when you say I should *memmorize* the spelling I can't because it doesn't make any sence to me and never did.

Love,
Stephen

New York, February 23

Dear Stephen:

It is probably just as well that you have gotten everything off your chest. We all need to blow up once in a while. It clears the air.

Please don't ever forget that I am aware that spelling is difficult for you. I know you are making a great effort and I am very proud of you. I just want to be sure that you *keep trying.*

I am enclosing a small check for your birthday because even if you do not want to be reminded of it I wouldn't want to forget it and you must know that we are thinking of you.

Love,
Father

Geneva, February 26

Dear Father:

We are not allowed to cash personal checks here in the School, but thank you anyway for the money.

I am not able to write any more because we are going to have the exams and I have to study.

Love,
STEPHEN

New York, March 2

NIGHT LETTER

BEST OF LUCK STOP KEEP ME POSTED EXAM RESULTS LOVE

FATHER.

Geneva, March 12

Dear Father:

Well, the exams are over. I got a C in English because aparently I do not know how to spell, which should not come as too much of a surprise to you. In Science, Mathematics, and Latin I got A, and in French and History I got a B plus. This makes me first in the class, which doesn't mean very much since none of the children here have any life of the mind, as you would say. I mean they are all jerks, more or less. What am I supposed to do in the Easter vacation? Do you want me to come to New York, or shall I just stay here and get a rest, which I could use?

Love,
STEPHEN

New York, March 16

Dear Stephen:

I am *immensely* pleased with the examination results. Congratulations. Pull up the spelling and our worries are over.

Just yesterday I had a letter from your mother. She has taken a little house in Majorca, which is an island off the Spanish coast, as you probably know, and she suggests that you should come to her for the Easter holidays. Of course you are always welcome here — and you could rest as much as you wanted — but Majorca is very beautiful and would certainly appeal to the artistic side of your nature. I have written to your mother, urging her to write to you immediately, and I enclose her address in case you should want to write yourself. Let me know what you would like to do.

Love,
FATHER

Geneva, March 19

Dear Mummy:

Father says that you have invited me to come to you in Majorca for the Easter vacation. Is that true? I would be very very happy if it were. It has been very hard to be away from you for all this time and if you wanted to see me it would mean a great deal to me. I mean if you are feeling well enough. I could do a lot of things for you so you would not get too tired.

I wonder if you will think that I have changed when you see me. As a matter of fact I have changed a lot because I have become quite bitter. I have become bitter on account of this School.

I know that you and Father wanted me to have some expearience of what the world was like outside of America but what you didn't know is that Geneva is not the world at all. I mean, if you were born here, then perhaps you would have a real life, but I do not know anyone who was born here so all the people I see are just like myself, we are just waiting not to be lost any more. I think it would have been better to have left me in some place where I belonged even if Americans are getting very loud and money conscious. Because actually most of the children here are Americans, if you come right down to it, only it seems their parents didn't know what to do with them any longer.

Mummy I have written all this because I'm afraid that I have spent too much money all over again, and M. Frisch says that Father will have a crise des nerfs when he sees what I have done, and I thought that maybe you would understand that I only bought these things because there didn't seem to be anything else to do and that you could help me some how or other. Anyway, according to the School, we will have to pay for all these things.

Concert, Segovia	(Worth it)	16.00	(Swiss Francs)
School Dance		5.00	
English Drama	(What do they mean?)	10.00	
Controle de l'habitant	(?)	9.10	
Co-op purchases		65.90	

Ballets Russes	(Disappointing)	47.00
Librairie Prior		59.30
Concert piano	(For practicing)	61.00
Teinturie	(They ruined everything)	56.50
Toilet and Medicine		35.00
Escalade Ball		7.00
Pocket Money		160.00
77 Yoghurts	(Doctor's advice)	42.40
Book account		295.70
	Total	869.90 (Swiss Francs)

Now you see the trouble is that Father told me I was to spend about fifty dollars a month, because that was my allowance, and that I was not to spend anything more. Anyway, fifty dollars a month would be about two hundred and ten Swiss Francs, and then I had fifteen dollars for Christmas from Granny, and when I got back to School I found four Francs in the pocket of my leather jacket and then I had seventy-nine cents left over from New York, but that doesn't help much, and then Father sent me twenty-five dollars for my birthday but I couldn't cash the check because they do not allow that here in School, so what shall I do?

It is a serious situation as you can see, and it is going to get a lot more serious when Father sees the bill. But whatever you do, I imploar you not to write to Father because the trouble seems to be that I never had a balance foreward and I am afraid that it is impossible to keep accounts without a balance foreward, and even more afraid that by this time the accounts have gone a little bizerk.

Do you want me to take a plane when I come to Majorca? Who shall I say is going to pay for the ticket?

Please do write me as soon as you can, because the holidays begin on March 30 and if you don't tell me what to do I will be way out on a lim.

Lots and lots of love,
STEPHEN

Geneva, March 26

Dear Father:

I wrote to Mummy a week ago to say that I would like very much to spend my Easter vacation in Majorca. So far she has not answered my letter, but I guess she will pretty soon. I hope she will because the holidays begin on Thursday.

I am afraid you are going to be upset about the bill all over again, but in the Spring term I will start anew and keep you in touch with what is going on.

Love,
STEPHEN

P.S. If Mummy doesn't write what shall I do?

JOYCE CAROL OATES

Upon the Sweeping Flood

(FROM SOUTHWEST REVIEW)

NOT LONG AGO in Eden County, in the remote marsh and swamp-
lands to the south, a man named Walter Stuart was stopped in the
rain by a sheriff's deputy along a country road. Stuart was in a
hurry to get home to his family — his wife and two daughters —
after having endured a week at his father's old farm, arranging for
his father's funeral, surrounded by aging relatives who had sucked
at him for the strength of his youth. He was a stern, quiet man of
thirty-nine, beginning to lose some of the muscular hardness that
had always baffled others, masking as it did Stuart's remoteness, his
refinement, his faith in discipline and order which seemed to have
belonged, even in his youth, to a person already grown safely old.
He was a district vice-president for one of the gypsum mining plants,
a man to whom financial success and success in love had come naturally, without fuss. When only a child he had shifted his faith with
little difficulty from the unreliable God of his family's tradition to
the things and emotions of this world, which he admired in his
thoughtful, rather conservative way, and this faith had given him
access, as if by magic, to a communion with persons vastly different
from himself — with someone like the sheriff's deputy, for instance, who approached him that day in the hard, cold rain. "Is
something wrong?" Stuart said. He rolled down the window and
had nearly opened the door when the deputy, an old man with
gray eyebrows and a slack, sunburned face, began shouting against
the wind, "Just the weather, mister. You going far along here? How
far are you going?"

"Two hundred miles," Stuart said. "What about the weather? Is it a hurricane?"

"A hurricane — yes— a hurricane!" the man said, bending to shout at Stuart's face. "You better go back to town and stay put. They're evacuating up there. We're not letting anyone through."

A long line of cars and pickup trucks, tarnished and gloomy in the rain, passed them on the other side of the road. "How bad is it?" said Stuart. "Do you need help?"

"Back at town, maybe, they need help," the man said. "They're putting up folks at the schoolhouse and the churches, and different families — The eye was spost to come by here, but last word we got it's veered further south. Just the same, though — "

"Yes, it's good to evacuate them," Stuart said. At the back window of an automobile passing them two children's faces peered out at the rain, white and blurred. "The last hurricane here — "

"Ah, God, leave off of that!" the old man said, so harshly that Stuart felt, inexplicably, hurt. "You better turn around, now, and get on back to town. You got money they can put you up somewheres good — not with these folks coming along here."

This was said without contempt, but Stuart flinched at its assumptions. "I'm going in to see if anybody needs help," he said. He had the car going again before the deputy could even protest. "I know what I'm doing! I know what I'm doing!" Stuart said.

The car lunged forward into the rain, drowning out the deputy's outraged shouts. The slashing of rain against Stuart's face excited him. Faces staring out of oncoming cars were pale and startled, and Stuart felt rising in him a strange compulsion to grin, to laugh madly at their alarm . . . He passed cars for some time. Houses looked deserted, yards bare. Things had the look of haste about them, even trees — in haste to rid themselves of their leaves, to be stripped bare. Grass was twisted and wild. A ditch by the road was overflowing and at spots the churning, muddy water stretched across the red clay road. Stuart drove splashing through it. After a while his enthusiasm slowed, his foot eased up on the gas pedal. He had not passed any cars or trucks for some time.

The sky had darkened and the storm had increased. Stuart thought of turning back when he saw, a short distance ahead, someone standing in the road. A car approached from the opposite direction. Stuart slowed, bearing to the right. He came upon a farm —

a small, run-down one with just a few barns and a small pasture in which a horse stood drooping in the rain. Behind the roofs of the buildings a shifting edge of foliage from the trees beyond curled in the wind, now dark, now silver. In a neat harsh line against the bottom of the buildings the wind had driven up dust and red clay. Rain streamed off roofs, plunged into fat, tilted rainbarrels, and exploded back out of them. As Stuart watched another figure appeared, running out of the house. Both persons — they looked like children — jumped about in the road, waving their arms. A spray of leaves was driven against them and against the muddy windshield of the car that approached and passed them. They turned: a girl and a boy, waving their fists in rage, their faces white and distorted. As the car sped past Stuart water and mud splashed up in a vicious wave.

When Stuart stopped and opened the door the girl was already there, shouting, "Going the wrong way! Wrong way!" Her face was coarse, pimply about her forehead and chin. The boy pounded up behind her, straining for air. "Where the hell are you going, mister?" the girl cried. "The storm's coming from this way. Did you see that bastard, going right by us? Did you see him? If I see him when I get to town —" A wall of rain struck. The girl lunged forward and tried to push her way into the car; Stuart had to hold her back. "Where are your folks?" he shouted. "Let me in!" cried the girl savagely. "We're getting out of here!" "Your folks," said Stuart. He had to cup his mouth to make her hear. "Your folks in there!" "There ain't anybody there — Gah*dam* you!" she said, twisting about to slap her brother, who had been pushing at her from behind. She whirled upon Stuart again. "You letting us in, mister? You letting us in?" she screamed, raising her hands as if to claw him. But Stuart's size must have calmed her, for she shouted hoarsely and mechanically: "There ain't nobody in there. Our pa's been gone the last two days. LAST TWO DAYS. Gone into town BY HIMSELF. Gone drunk somewhere. He ain't here. He left us here. LEFT US HERE!" Again she rushed at Stuart, and he leaned forward against the steering wheel to let her get in back. The boy was about to follow when something caught his eye back at the farm. "Get in," said Stuart. "Get in. Please. Get in." "My horse there," the boy muttered. "You little bastard! You get in here!" his sister screamed.

But once the boy got in, once the door was closed, Stuart knew that it was too late. Rain struck the car in solid walls and the road, when he could see it, had turned to mud. "Let's go! Let's go!" cried the girl, pounding on the back of the seat. "Turn it around! Go up on our drive and turn it around!" The engine and the wind roared together. "Turn it! Get it going!" cried the girl. There was a scuffle and someone fell against Stuart. "It ain't no good," the boy said. "Let me out." He lunged for the door and Stuart grabbed him. "I'm going back to the house!" the boy cried, appealing to Stuart with his frightened eyes, and his sister, giving up suddenly, pushed him violently forward. "It's no use," Stuart said. "Gahdam fool," the girl screamed, "gahdam fool!"

The water was ankle deep as they ran to the house. The girl splashed ahead of Stuart, running with her head up and her eyes wide open in spite of the flying scud. When Stuart shouted to the boy his voice was slammed back to him as if he were being mocked. "Where are you going? Go to the house! Go to the house!" The boy had turned and was running toward the pasture. His sister took no notice but ran to the house. "Come back, kid!" Stuart cried. Wind tore at him, pushing him back. "What are you — "

The horse was undersized, skinny and brown. It ran to the boy as if it wanted to run him down but the boy, stooping through the fence, avoided the frightened hooves and grabbed the rope that dangled from the horse's halter. "That's it! That's it!" Stuart shouted as if the boy could hear. At the gate the boy stopped and looked around wildly, up to the sky — he might have been looking for someone who had just called him; then he shook the gate madly. Stuart reached the gate and opened it, pushing it back against the boy, who now turned to gape at him. "What? What are you doing here?" he said.

The thought crossed Stuart's mind that the child was insane. "Bring the horse through!" he said. "We don't have much time."

"What are you doing here?" the boy shouted. The horse's eyes rolled, its mane lifted and haloed about its head. Suddenly it lunged through the gate and jerked the boy off the ground. The boy ran in the air, his legs kicking. "Hang on and bring him around!" Stuart shouted. "Let me take hold!" He grabbed the boy instead of the rope. They stumbled together against the horse. It had stopped now and was looking intently at something just to the right of Stuart's head. The boy pulled himself along the rope, hand over hand, and Stuart held on to him by the strap of his overalls. "He's scairt of you!" the boy said. "He's scairt of you!" Stuart reached over and took hold of the rope above the boy's fingers and tugged gently at it. His face was about a foot away from the horse's. "Watch out for him," said the boy. The horse reared and broke free, throwing Stuart back against the boy. "Hey, hey!" screamed the boy, as if mad. The horse turned in midair as if whirled about by the wind, and Stuart looked up through his fingers to see its hooves and a vicious flicking of its tail, and the face of the boy being yanked past him and away with incredible speed. The boy fell heavily on his side in the mud, arms outstretched above him, hands still gripping the rope with wooden fists. But he scrambled to his feet at once and ran alongside the horse. He flung one arm up around its neck as Stuart shouted, "Let him go! Forget about him!" Horse and boy pivoted together back toward the fence, slashing wildly at the earth, feet and hooves together. The ground erupted beneath them. But the boy landed upright, still holding the rope, still with his arm about the horse's neck. "Let me help," Stuart said. "No," said the boy, "he's my horse, he knows me — " "Have you got him good?" Stuart shouted. "We got — we got each other here," the boy cried, his eyes shut tight.

Stuart went to the barn to open the door. While he struggled with it the boy led the horse forward. When the door was open far enough Stuart threw himself against it and slammed it around to the side of the barn. A cloud of hay and scud filled the air. Stuart outstretched his arms, as if pleading with the boy to hurry, and he murmured, "Come on. Please. Come on." The boy did not hear him, or even glance at him: his own lips were moving as he caressed the horse's neck and head. The horse's muddy hoof had just begun to grope about the step before the door when something like an explosion came against the back of Stuart's head, slammed his back, and sent him sprawling out at the horse.

"Damn you! Damn you!" the boy screamed. Stuart saw nothing except rain. Then something struck him, his shoulder and hand, and his fingers were driven down into the mud. Something slammed beside him in the mud and he seized it — the horse's foreleg — and tried to pull himself up, insanely, lurching to his knees. The horse threw him backward. It seemed to emerge out of the air before and above him, coming into sight as though out of a cloud. The boy he did not see at all — only the hooves — and then the boy appeared, inexplicably, under the horse, peering intently at Stuart, his face struck completely blank. "Damn you!" Stuart heard. "He's my horse! My horse! I hope he kills you!" Stuart crawled back in the water, crab fashion, watching the horse form and dissolve, hearing its vicious tattoo against the barn. The door, swinging madly back and forth, parodied the horse's rage, seemed to challenge its frenzy; then the door was all Stuart heard, and he got to his feet, gasping, to see that the horse was out of sight.

. The boy ran bent against the wind, out toward nowhere, and Stuart ran after him. "Come in the house, kid! Come on! Forget about it, kid!" He grabbed the boy's arm. The boy struck at him with his elbow. "He was my horse!" he cried.

In the kitchen of the house they pushed furniture against the door. Stuart had to stand between the boy and the girl to keep them from fighting. "Gahdam sniffling fool!" said the girl. "So your gahdam horse run off for the night!" The boy crouched down on the floor, crying steadily. He was about thirteen: small for his age, with bony wrists and face. "We're all going to be blownt to hell, let alone your horse," the girl said. She sat with one big thigh and leg outstretched on the table, watching Stuart. He thought her perhaps eighteen. "Glad you came down to get us?" she said. "Where are you from, mister?" Stuart's revulsion surprised him; he had not supposed there was room in his stunned mind for emotion of this sort. If the girl noticed it she gave no sign, but only grinned at him. "I was — I was on my way home," he said. "My wife and daughters — " It occurred to him that he had forgotten about them entirely. He had not thought of them until now and, even now, no image came to his mind: no woman's face, no little girls' faces. Could he have imagined their lives, their love for him? For an instant he doubted everything. "Wife and daughters," said the girl, as if wondering whether to believe him. "Are they in this storm too?" "No — no," Stuart said. To get away from her he went to the window. He could no longer see the road. Something struck the house and he flinched away. "Them trees!" chortled the girl. "I knew it! Pa always said how he ought to cut them down, so close to the house like they are! I knew it! I knew it! And the old bastard off safe now where they can't get him!"

"Trees?" said Stuart slowly.

"Them trees! Old oak trees!" said the girl.

The boy, struck with fear, stopped crying suddenly. He crawled on the floor to a woodbox beside the big old iron stove and got in, patting the disorderly pile of wood as if he were blind. The girl ran to him and pushed him. "What are you doing?" Stuart cried in anguish. The girl took no notice of him. "What am I doing?" he said aloud. "What the hell am I doing here?" It seemed to him that the end would come in a minute or two, that the howling outside could get no louder, that the howling inside his mind could get no more intense, no more accusing. A goddam fool! A goddam fool! he thought. The deputy's face came to mind, and Stuart pictured himself groveling before the man, clutching at his knees, asking forgiveness and for time to be turned back . . . Then he saw himself back at the old farm, the farm of his childhood, listening to tales of his father's agonizing sickness, the old peoples' heads craning around, seeing how he took it, their eyes charged with horror and delight . . . "My wife and daughters," Stuart muttered.

The wind made a hollow, drumlike sound. It seemed to be tolling. The boy, crouching back in the woodbox, shouted: "I ain't scairt! I ain't scairt!" The girl gave a shriek. "Our chicken coop, I'll be gahdammed!" she cried. Try as he could Stuart could see nothing out the window. "Come away from the window," Stuart said, pulling the girl's arm. She whirled upon him. "Watch yourself, mister," she said, "you want to go out to your gahdam bastardly worthless car?" Her body was strong and big in her men's clothing; her shoulders looked muscular beneath the filthy shirt. Cords in her young neck stood out. Her hair had been cut short and was now wet, plastered about her blemished face. She grinned at Stuart as if she were about to poke him in the stomach, for fun. "I ain't scairt of what God can do!" the boy cried behind them.

When the water began to bubble up through the floorboards they decided to climb to the attic. "There's an ax!" Stuart exclaimed, but the boy got on his hands and knees and crawled to the corner where the ax was propped before Stuart could reach it. The boy cradled it in his arms. "What do you want with that?" Stuart said, and for an instant his heart was pierced with fear. "Let me take it. I'll take it." He grabbed it out of the boy's dazed fingers.

The attic was about half as large as the kitchen and the

roof jutted down sharply on either side. Tree limbs rubbed and slammed against the roof on all sides. The three of them crouched on the middle beam, Stuart with the ax tight in his embrace, the boy pushing against him as if for warmth, and the girl kneeling with her thighs straining her overalls. She watched the little paneless window at one end of the attic without much emotion or interest, like a large, wet turkey. The house trembled beneath them. "I'm going to the window," Stuart said, and was oddly relieved when the girl did not sneer at him. He crawled forward along the dirty beam, dragging the ax along with him, and lay full length on the floor about a yard from the window. There was not much to see. At times the rain relaxed, and objects beneath in the water took shape: tree stumps, parts of buildings, junk whirling about in the water. The thumping on the roof was so loud at that end that he had to crawl backward to the middle again. "I ain't scairt, nothing God can do!" the boy cried. "Listen to the sniveling baby," said the girl, "he thinks God pays him any mind! Hah!" Stuart crouched beside them, waiting for the boy to press against him again. "As if God gives a good damn about him," the girl said. Stuart looked at her. In the near dark her face did not seem so coarse; the set of her eyes was almost attractive. "You don't think God cares about you?" Stuart said slowly. "No, not specially," the girl said, shrugging her shoulders. "The hell with it. You seen the last one of these?" She tugged at Stuart's arm. "Mister? It was something to see. Me an' Jackie was little then — him just a baby. We drove a far ways north to get out of it. When we come back the roads was so thick with sightseers from the cities! They took all the dead ones floating in the water and put them in one place, part of a swamp they cleared out. The families and things — they were mostly fruitpickers — had to come by on rafts and rowboats to look and see could they find the ones they knew. That was there for a day. The bodies would turn round and round in the wash from the boats. Then the faces all got alike and they wouldn't let anyone come anymore and put oil on them and set them afire. We stood on top of the car and watched all that day. I wasn't but nine then."

When the house began to shake, some time later, Stuart cried aloud: "This is it!" He stumbled to his feet, waving the ax. He turned around and around as if he were in a daze. "You goin' to chop somethin with that?" the boy said, pulling at him. "Hey, no, that ain't yours to — it ain't yours to chop — " They struggled for the ax. The boy sobbed, "It ain't yours! It ain't yours!" and Stuart's rage at his own helplessness, at the folly of his being here, for an instant almost made him strike the boy with the ax. But the girl slapped the boy furiously. "Get away from him! I swear I'll kill you!" she screamed.

Something exploded beneath them. "That's the windows," the girl muttered, clinging to Stuart, "and how am I to clean it again! The old bastard will want it clean, and mud over everything!" Stuart pushed her away so that he could swing the ax. Pieces of soft, rotted wood exploded back onto his face. The boy screamed insanely as the boards gave way to a deluge of wind and water, and even Stuart wondered if he had made a mistake. The three of them fell beneath the onslaught and Stuart lost the ax, felt the handle slam against his leg. "You! You!" Stuart cried, pulling at the girl — for an instant, blinded by pain, he could not think who he was, what he was doing, whether he had any life beyond this moment. The big-faced, husky girl made no effort to hide her fear and cried, "Wait, wait!" But he dragged her to the hole and tried to force her out. "My brother — " she gasped. She seized his wrists and tried to get away. "Get out there! There isn't any time!" Stuart muttered. The house seemed about to collapse at any moment. He was pushing her through the hole, against the shattered wood, when she suddenly flinched back against him and he saw that her cheek was cut and she was choking. He snatched her hands away from her mouth as if he wanted to see something secret: blood welled out between her lips. She coughed and spat blood onto him. "You're all right," he said, oddly pleased, "now get out there and I'll get the kid. I'll take care of him." This time she managed to crawl through the hole, with Stuart pushing her from behind; when he turned to seize the boy the boy clung to his neck sobbing something about God. "God loves you!" Stuart yelled. "Loves the least of you! The least of you!" The girl pulled her brother up in her great arms and Stuart was free to climb through himself.

It was actually quite a while — perhaps an hour — before the battering of the trees and the wind pushed the house in. The roof fell slowly, and the section to which they clung was washed free. "We're going somewheres!" shouted the girl. "Look at the house! That gahdam old shanty seen the last storm!"

The boy lay with his legs pushed in under Stuart's and had not spoken for some time. When the girl cried, "Look at that!" he tried to burrow in farther. Stuart wiped his eyes to see the wall of darkness dissolve. The rain took on another look — a smooth, piercing, metallic glint, like nails driving against their faces and bodies. There was no horizon. They could see nothing except the rushing water and a thickening mist that must have been rain, miles and miles of rain, slammed by the wind into one great wall that moved remorselessly upon them. "Hang on," Stuart said, gripping the girl. "Hang on to me."

Waves washed over the roof, pushing objects at them with soft, muted thuds — pieces of fence, boards, branches heavy with foliage. Stuart tried to ward them off with his feet. Water swirled around them, sucking at them, sucking the roof, until they were pushed against one of the farm buildings. Something crashed against the roof — another section of the house — and splintered, flying up against the girl. She was thrown backward, away from Stuart, who lunged after her. They fell into the water while the boy screamed. The girl's arms threshed wildly against Stuart. The water was cold and its aliveness, its sinister energy, surprised him more than the thought that he would drown — that he would never endure the night. Struggling with the girl he forced her back to the roof, pushed her up. Bare, twisted nails raked his hands. "Gahdam you, Jackie, you give a hand!" the girl said as Stuart crawled back up. He lay, exhausted, flat on his stomach and let the water and debris slush over him.

His mind was calm beneath the surface buzzing. He liked to think that his mind was a clear, sane circle of quiet carefully preserved inside the chaos of the storm — that the three of them were safe within the sanctity of this circle; this was how man always conquered nature, how he subdued things greater than himself. But whenever he spoke to the girl it was in short grunts, in her own idiom: "This ain't so bad!" or "It'll let up pretty soon!" Now the girl held him in her arms as if he were a child, and he did not have the strength to pull away. Of his own free will he had given himself to this storm, or to the strange desire to save someone in it — but now he felt grateful for the girl, even for her brother, for they had saved him as much as he had saved them. Stuart thought of his wife at home, walking through the rooms, waiting for him; he thought of his daughters in their twin beds, two glasses of water on their bureau

. . . But these people knew nothing of him: in his experience now he did not belong to them. Perhaps he had misunderstood his role, his life? Perhaps he had blundered out of his way, drawn into the wrong life, surrendered to the wrong role. What had blinded him to the possibility of many lives, many masks, many arms which might so embrace him? A word not heard one day, a gesture misinterpreted, a· leveling of someone's eyes in a certain unmistakable manner, which he had mistaken just the same! The consequences of such errors might trail on insanely into the future, across miles of land, across worlds. He only now sensed the incompleteness of his former life . . . "Look! Look!" the girl cried, jostling him out of his stupor. "Take a look at that, mister!"

He raised himself on one elbow. A streak of light broke out of the dark. Lanterns, he thought, a rescue party already . . . but the rain dissolved the light; then it reappeared with a beauty that startled him. "What is it?" the boy screamed. "How come it's here?" They watched it filter through the rain, rays knifing through and showing, now, how buildings and trees crouched ·close about them. "It's the sun, the sun going down," the girl said. "The sun!" said Stuart, who had thought it was night. "The sun!" They stared at it until it disappeared.

The waves calmed sometime before dawn. By then the roof had lost its peak and water ran unchecked over it, in generous waves and then in thin waves, alternately, as the roof bobbed up and down. The three huddled together with their backs to the wind. Water came now in slow drifts. "It's just got to spread itself out far enough so's it will be even," said the girl, "then it'll go down." She spoke without sounding tired, only a little disgusted — as if things weren't working fast enough to suit her. "Soon as it goes down we'll start toward town and see if there ain't somebody coming out to get us, in a boat," she said, chattily and comfortably, into Stuart's ear. Her manner astonished Stuart, who had been thinking all night of the humiliation and pain he had suffered. "Bet the old bastard will be glad to see us," she said, "even if he did go off like that. Well, he never knew a storm was coming. Me and him get along pretty well — he ain't so bad." She wiped her face; it was filthy with dirt and blood. "He'll buy you a drink, mister, for saving us how you did. That was something to have happen — a man just driving up to get us!" And she poked Stuart in the ribs.

The wind warmed as the sun rose. Rain turned to mist and back
to rain again, still falling heavily, and now objects were clear about
them. The roof had been shoved against the corner of the barn and
a mound of dirt, and eddied there without much trouble. Right
about them, in a kind of halo, a thick blanket of vegetation and filth
bobbed. The fence had disappeared and the house had collapsed
and been driven against a ridge of land. The barn itself had fallen
in, but the stone support looked untouched, and it was against this
they had been shoved. Stuart thought he could see his car — or
something over there where the road used to be.

"I bet it ain't deep. Hell," said the girl, sticking her foot into
the water. The boy leaned over the edge and scooped up some of
the filth in his hands. "Lookit all the spiders," he said. He wiped
his face slowly. "Leave them gahdam spiders alone," said the girl.
"You want me to shove them down your throat?" She slid to the
edge and lowered her legs. "Yah, I touched bottom. It ain't bad."
But then she began coughing and drew herself back. Her coughing
made Stuart cough: his chest and throat were ravaged, shaken. He
lay exhausted when the fit left him and realized, suddenly, that they
were all sick — that something had happened to them. They had to
get off the roof. Now, with the sun up, things did not look so bad:
there was a ridge of trees a short distance away on a long, red clay
hill. "We'll go over there," Stuart said. "Do you think you can make
it?"

The boy played in the filth, without looking up, but the girl
gnawed at her lip to show she was thinking. "I spose so," she said.
"But him — I don't know about him."

"Your brother? What's wrong?"

"Turn around. Hey, stupid. Turn around." She prodded the
boy, who jerked around, terrified, to stare at Stuart. His thin bony
face gave way to a drooping mouth. "Gone loony, it looks like,"
the girl said with a touch of regret. "Oh, he had times like this before. It might go away."

Stuart was transfixed by the boy's stare. The realization of what
had happened struck him like a blow, sickening his stomach. "We'll
get him over there," he said, making his words sound good. "We can
wait there for someone to come. Someone in a boat. He'll be better
there."

"I spose so," said the girl vaguely.

Stuart carried the boy while the girl splashed eagerly ahead. The water was sometimes up to his thighs. "Hold on another minute," he pleaded. The boy stared out at the water as if he thought he were being taken somewhere to be drowned. "Put your arms around my neck. Hold on," Stuart said. He shut his eyes and every time he looked up the girl was still a few yards ahead and the hill looked no closer. The boy breathed hollowly, coughing into Stuart's face. His own face and neck were covered with small red bites. Ahead the girl walked with her shoulders lunged forward as if to hurry her there, her great thighs straining against the water, more than a match for it. As Stuart watched her something was on the side of his face — in his ear — and with a scream he slapped at it, nearly dropping the boy. The girl whirled around. Stuart slapped at his face and must have knocked it off — probably a spider. The boy, upset by Stuart's outcry, began sucking in air faster and faster as if he were dying. "I'm all right, I'm all right," Stuart whispered, "just hold on another minute . . ."

When he finally got to the hill the girl helped pull him up. He set the boy down with a grunt, trying to put the boy's legs under him so he could stand. But the boy sank to the ground and turned over and vomited into the water; his body shook as if he were having convulsions. Again the thought that the night had poisoned them, their own breaths had sucked germs into their bodies, struck Stuart with an irresistible force. "Let him lay down and rest," the girl said, pulling tentatively at the back of her brother's belt, as if she were thinking of dragging him farther up the slope. "We sure do thank you, mister," she said.

Stuart climbed to the crest of the hill. His heart pounded madly, blood pounded in his ears. What was going to happen? Was anything going to happen? How disappointing it looked, ridges of land showing through the water, and the healthy sunlight pushing back the mist. Who would believe him when he told of the night, of the times when death seemed certain . . . ? Anger welled up in him already, as he imagined the tolerant faces of his friends, his children's faces ready to turn to other amusements, other oddities. His wife would believe him; she would shudder, holding him, burying her small face in his neck. But what could she understand of his experience, having had no part in it? — Stuart cried out; he had nearly stepped on a tangle of snakes. Were they alive? He backed away in terror. The snakes gleamed wetly in the morning light, heads together as if conspiring. Four — five of them — they too

had swum for this land, they too had survived the night, they had
as much reason to be proud of themselves as Stuart.

He gagged and turned away. Down by the water line the boy lay
flat on his stomach and the girl squatted nearby, wringing out her
denim jacket. The water behind them caught the sunlight and
gleamed mightily, putting them into silhouette. The girl's arms
moved slowly, hard with muscle. The boy lay coughing gently.
Watching them Stuart was beset by a strange desire: he wanted to
run at them, demand their gratitude, their love. Why should they
not love him, when he had saved their lives? When he had lost what
he was just the day before, turned now into a different person, a
stranger even to himself? Stuart stooped and picked up a rock. A
broad hot hand seemed to press against his chest. He threw the rock
out into the water and said, "Hey!"

The girl glanced around but the boy did not move. Stuart sat
down on the soggy ground and waited. After a while the girl looked
away; she spread the jacket out to dry. Great banked clouds rose
into the sky, reflected in the water — jagged and bent in the
waves. Stuart waited as the sun took over the sky. Mist at the horizon glowed, thinned, gave way to solid shapes. Light did not strike
cleanly across the land, but was marred by ridges of trees and parts
of buildings, and around a corner at any time Stuart expected to
see a rescuing party — in a rowboat or something.

"Hey, mister!" He woke; he must have been dozing. The girl had
called him. "Hey! Whyn't you come down here? There's all them
snakes up there."

Stuart scrambled to his feet. When he stumbled downhill, embarrassed and frightened, the girl said chattily, "The sons of bitches
are crawling all over here. He chast some away." The boy was on
his feet and looking around with an important air. His coming alive
startled Stuart — indeed, the coming alive of the day, of the world,
evoked alarm in him. All things came back to what they were. The
girl's alert eyes, the firm set of her mouth, had not changed — the
sunlight had not changed, or the land, really; only Stuart had been
changed. He wondered at it . . . and the girl must have seen something in his face that he himself did not yet know about, for her
eyes narrowed, her throat gulped a big swallow, her arms moved
slowly up to show her raw elbows. "We'll get rid of them," Stuart
said, breaking the silence. "Him and me. We'll do it."

The boy was delighted. "I got a stick," he said, waving a thin whiplike branch. "There's some over here."

"We'll get them," Stuart said. But when he started to walk a rock slipped loose and he fell back into the mud. He laughed aloud. The girl, squatting a few feet away, watched him silently. Stuart got to his feet, still laughing. "You know much about it, kid?" he said, cupping his hand on the boy's head.

"About what?" said the boy.

"Killing snakes," said Stuart.

"I spose — I spose you just kill them."

The boy hurried alongside Stuart. "I need a stick," Stuart said; they got him one from the water, about the size of an ax. "Go by that bush," Stuart said, "there might be some there."

The boy attacked the bush in a frenzy. He nearly fell into it. His enthusiasm somehow pleased Stuart, but there were no snakes in the bush. "Go down that way," Stuart ordered. He glanced back at the girl: she watched them. Stuart and the boy went on with their sticks held in midair. "God put them here to keep us awake," the boy said brightly, "see we don't forget about Him." Mud sucked at their feet. "Last year we couldn't fire the woods on account of it so dry. This year can't either on account of the water. We got to get the snakes like this."

Stuart hurried as if he had somewhere to go. The boy, matching his steps, went faster and faster, panting, waving his stick angrily in the air. The boy complained about snakes and, listening to him, fascinated by him, in that instant Stuart saw everything. He saw the conventional dawn that had mocked the night, had mocked his desire to help people in trouble; he saw, beyond that, his father's home emptied now even of ghosts. He realized that the God of these people had indeed arranged things, had breathed the order of chaos into forms, animated them, had animated even Stuart himself forty years ago. The knowledge of this fact struck him about the same way as the nest of snakes had struck him — an image leaping right to the eye, pouncing upon the mind, joining itself with the perceiver. "Hey, hey!" cried the boy, who had found a snake: the snake crawled noisily and not very quickly up the slope, a brown-speckled snake. The boy ran clumsily after it. Stuart was astonished at the boy's stupidity, at his inability to see, now, that the snake had vanished. Still he ran along the slope, waving his stick, shouting, "I'll get you! I'll get you!" This must have been the sign Stuart was waiting for. When the boy turned Stuart was right behind him. "It got away up there," the boy said. "We got to get it." When Stuart lifted his stick the boy fell back a step but went on in mechanical excitement, "It's up there, gotten hid in the weeds. It ain't me," he said, "it ain't me that — " Stuart's blow struck the boy on the side of the head, and the rotted limb shattered into soft wet pieces. The boy stumbled down toward the water. He was coughing when Stuart took hold of him and began shaking him madly, and he did nothing but cough, violently and with all his concentration, even when Stuart bent to grab a rock and brought it down on his head. Stuart let him fall into the water. He could hear him breathing and he could see, about the boy's lips, tiny flecks or bubbles of blood appearing and disappearing with his breath.

When the boy's eyes opened Stuart fell upon him. They struggled savagely in the water. Again the boy went limp; Stuart stood, panting, and waited. Nothing happened for a minute or so. But then he saw something — the boy's fingers moving up through the water, soaring to the surface! "Will you quit it!" Stuart screamed. He was about to throw himself upon the boy again when the thought of the boy's life, bubbling out between his lips, moving his fingers, filled him with such outraged disgust that he backed away. He threw the rock out into the water and ran back, stumbling, to where the girl stood.

She had nothing to say: her jaw was hard, her mouth a narrow line, her thick nose oddly white against her dirty face. Only her eyes moved, and these were black, lustrous, at once demanding and terrified. She held a board in one hand. Stuart did not have time to think, but, as he lunged toward her, he could already see himself grappling with her in the mud, forcing her down, tearing her ugly clothing from her body — "Lookit!" she cried, the way a person might speak to a horse, cautious and coaxing, and pointed behind him. Stuart turned to see a white boat moving toward them, a half mile or so away. Immediately his hands dropped, his mouth opened in awe. The girl still pointed, breathing carefully, and Stuart, his mind shattered by the broken sunshine upon the water, turned to the boat, raised his hands, cried out, "Save me! Save me!" He had waded out a short distance into the water by the time the men arrived.

REYNOLDS PRICE

The Names and Faces of Heroes

(FROM SHENANDOAH)

AFTER an hour I believe it and think, "We are people in love. We flee through hard winter night. What our enemies want is to separate us. Will we end together? Will we end alive?" And my lips part to ask him, but seeing his face in dashboard light (his gray eyes set on the road and the dark), I muffle my question and know the reason — "We have not broke silence for an hour by the clock. We must flee on silent. Maybe if we speak even close as we are, we will speak separate tongues after so long a time." I shut my eyes, press hard with the lids till my mind's eye opens, then balloon it light through roof through steel, set it high and cold in January night, staring down to see us whole. First we are one black car on a slim strip of road laid white through pines, drawn slowly west by the hoop of light we cast ahead — the one light burning for fifty miles, it being past eleven, all farms and houses crouched into sleep, all riders but us. Then my eye falls downward, hovers on the roof in the wind we make, pierces steel, sees us close — huddled on the worn mohair of a 1939 Pontiac, he slumped huge at the wheel, I the thin fork of flesh thrust out of his groin on the seat beside him, my dark head the burden in his lap his only hollow that flushes beneath me with rhythm I predict to force blood against my weight through nodes of tissue, squabs of muscle that made me ten years ago, made half anyhow, he being my father and I being nine, we heading towards home not fleeing, silent as I say, my real eyes shut, his eyes on nothing but road. So we are not lovers nor spies nor thieves and speaking for me, my foes are inward not there in the night. My mind's eye enters me calm again, and I brace to look, to say "How much further?" but he drops a hand which stalls me, testing my flannel pajamas for warmth, ringing my ankle and shin and ticklish knee (in earnest, tight not gentle), slipping between two buttons of the coat to brush one breast then out again and down to rest on my hip. His thumb and fingers ride the high saddle bone, the fat of his hand in the hollow *I* have, heavy but still on the dry knots of boyish equipment waiting for life to start. I roll back on my head to see him again, to meet his eyes. He looks on forward so I go back blind and slide my right hand to his, probing with a finger till I find his only wound — a round yellow socket beneath his thumb where he shot himself when he was eight, by surprise, showing off his father's pistol to friends (the one fool thing I know he has done). My finger rests there and we last that way maybe two or three miles while the road is straight. Then a curve begins. He says "Excuse me, Preacher" in his natural voice and takes his hand. My eyes stay blind and I think what I know, "I love you tonight more than all my life before" — think it in *my* natural voice. But I do not say it, and I do not say I excuse him though I do. I open my eyes on his face in dashboard light.

I search it for a hero. For the first time. I have searched nearly every other face since last July, the final Sunday at camp when a minister told us, "The short cut to being a man is finding your hero, somebody who is what you are not but need to be. What I mean is this. Examine yourself. When you find what your main lack is, seek that in some great man. Say your trouble is fear — you are scared of the dark, scared of that bully in your grade at school, scared of striking out when you come up to bat. Take some great brave, some warrior — Douglas MacArthur, Enos Slaughter. Say your trouble is worse. Say it's telling lies. Take George Washington — personal heroes don't need to be living just so they lived once. Read a book about him. Study his picture. (You may think he looks a little stiff. That is because his teeth were carved out of cypress. A man makes his face and making a good one is as hard a job as laying road through solid rock, and Washington made himself as fine a face as any man since Jesus — and He was not a man.) Then imitate him. Chin yourself on his example and you will be a man before you need a razor." I need to be a man hard as anybody so riding home from camp and that sermon, I sat among lanyards I plaited and whistles I

carved and searched my life for the one great lack my foe. He had
mentioned lacking courage — that minister. I lack it. I will not try
to do what I think I cannot do well such as make friends or play
games where somebody hands you a ball and bat and asks the world
of you, asks you to launch without thinking some act on the air with
natural grace easy as laughing. He had mentioned lying. I lie every
day — telling my mother for instance that the weeks at camp were
happy when what I did was by day whittle all that trashy equipment, climb through snakes in July sun with brogans grating my
heels, swim in ice water with boys that would just as soon drown
you as smile and by night pray for three large things — that I not
wet the bed, that I choke the homesickness one more day, that these
five weeks vanish and leave no sign no memory. But they were only
two on a string of lacks which unreeled behind me that Sunday riding home from camp (unseen beyond glass the hateful tan rock
turning to round pine hills where Randolph is and home), and on
the string were selfishness to Marcia my cousin who is my main
friend and gives me whatever she has, envy of my brother who is one
year old and whose arms I purposely threw out of joint three months
ago, envy of people my age who do so easily things I will not and
thus lock together in tangles of friendship, pride in the things I
can do which they cannot (but half pride at worst as the things I
can do, they do not want to do — drawing, carving, solo singing.
I am Randolph's leading boy soprano and was ashamed to be till a
Saturday night last August when I sang to a room of sweating soldiers at the U.S.O. I was asked by the hostess for something pa-
triotic, but I thought they would not need that on their weekend off
any more than they needed me in Buster Brown collar and white
short pants so I sang Brahms' "Lullaby" which you can hum if you
forget, and if it was a mistake, they never let on. I do not mean anybody cried. They kept on swallowing Coca-Colas and their boots
kept smelling, but they shut up talking and clapped at the end, and
as I left the platform and aimed for the door blistered with shame,
one long soldier gave me the blue and gold enamel shield off his
cap, saying "Here you are"), and far graver things — wishing death
nightly on two boys I know, breaking God's law about honoring parents by failing to do simple things they ask such as look at people
when I talk, by doubting they can care for me daily (when my
mother thinks of little else and Father would no more sleep without

kissing me goodnight than he would strike me), sometimes doubting I am theirs at all but just some orphan they took in kindness. I
made that list without trying seven months ago, and it has grown
since then. Whenever I speak or move these days new faults stare
out of my heart. The trouble though is I still do not know my greatest lack, my *mortal* foe. Any one if I stare back long enough seems
bound to sink me. So I seek a hero grand enough to take on all my
lacks, but for seven months now I have looked — looked hard —
and am nowhere near him. Who *is* there these days, who has there
ever been broad enough, grand enough to stand day and night and
ward off all my foes? Nobody, I begin to think. I have looked
everywhere I know to look, first in books I had or bought for the
purpose — *Little People Who Became Great* (Abraham Lincoln,
Helen Keller, Andrew Carnegie), *Minute Lives of Great Men and
Women* (a page and a picture for everybody including Stephen Fos-
ter) and a set called *Living Biographies of Great Composers, Phi-
losophers, Prophets, Poets and Statesmen.* I have not read books that
do not show faces because I study a man's face first. Then if that
calls me on, I read his deeds. I read for three months and taking
deeds and faces together, I settled on Caesar Augustus and Alexander the Great as final candidates. They were already great when
they were young, and they both wore faces like hard silver medals
awarded for lasting — I got that much from *Minute Lives* — so I
thought they were safe and that I would read further and then
choose one. But as I read they fell in before me — Alexander crushing that boy's head who brought bad news and when they were lost
in a desert and famished and his men found one drink of water and
gladly brought it to him in a helmet, him pouring it out in the sand
to waste, and Augustus leading the wives of his friends into private
rooms during public banquets, making them do what they could not
refuse. All the dead have failed me. That is why I study my father
tonight. He is the last living man I know or can think of that I
have not considered, which is no slight to him — you do not seek
heroes at home. No, when the dead played out, I turned to my autographs and started there. I have written to famous men for over a
year since the war began. I write on Boy Scout stationery (I am not
a Scout), give my age and ask for their names in ink. I have got
answers from several generals on the battlefield (MacArthur who
sent good luck from the Philippines, Mark Clark who typed a note

from secret headquarters, Eisenhower who said in his wide leaning hand, "I do not think it would be possible for me to refuse a nine-year-old American anything I could do for him"), from most of Roosevelt's cabinet (but not from him though I have three notes from Miss Grace Tully to say he does not have time and neither does his wife), from Toscanini and a picture of Johnny Weissmuller on a limb crouched with his bare knife to leap, saying "Hello from Tarzan your friend." But studying them I saw I could not know enough to decide. They are surely famous but I cannot see or watch them move, and until they die and their secrets appear, how can I know they are genuine heroes? — that they do not have yawning holes of their own which they hide? So from them I have turned to men I can watch and hear, and since I seldom travel this means the men I am kin to. I will not think against my blood, but of all my uncles and cousins (my grandfathers died before I was born), the two I love and that seem to love me — that listen when I speak — and that have dark happy faces are the ones who are liable at any time to start drinking and disappear, spending money hand over fist in Richmond or Washington until they are broke and wire for my father who drives up and finds them in a bar with a new suit on and a rosebud and some temporary friends and brings them home to their wives. My father has one brother who fought in France in the First World War and was playing cards in a hole one night when a bomb landed, and when he came to, he picked up his best friend who was quiet at his side and crawled with him half a mile before he saw that the friend lacked a head, but later he was gassed and retired from battle so that now, sitting or standing, he slumps round a hole in his chest and scrapes up blood every hour or two even summer nights visiting on our porch from Tennessee his home. My other male kin live even farther away or do not notice me or are fat which is why as I say I have come to my father tonight — my head rolled back on his lap, my ears sunk in his shifting kernels so I cannot hear only see, my eyes strained up through his arms to his face.

It is round as a watch when he does not smile which he does not now, and even in warm yellow light of speedometer, amp meter, oil-pressure gauges, it is red as if he was cold, as if there was no plate glass to hold off the wind we make rushing home. It is always red and reddest I know, though I cannot see, under his collar on the

back of his neck where the hair leaves off. There is not much hair
anywhere on his head. It has vanished two inches back on his forehead, and where it starts it is dark but seems no color or the color of
shadows in old photographs. Above his ears it is already white (he
is forty-two and the white is real, but five years ago when it was not,
I was singing in bed one night "When I Grow Too Old To Dream,"
and he heard me and went to the toilet and powdered his hair and
came and stood in the door ghostly, old with the hall light behind
him and said, "I am too old to dream, Preacher." I sang on a minute, looking, and then cried "Stop. Stop" and wept which of course
he did not intend), and each morning he wets it and brushes every
strand at least five minutes till it lies on his skull like paint and stays
all day. It is one of his things you cannot touch. His glasses are another. He treats them kindly as if they were delicate people — un-
rimmed octagons hooked to gold wires that ride the start of his firm
long nose and loop back over his large flat ears — and in return they
do not hide his eyes which are gray and wide and which even in the
dark draw light to them so he generally seems to be thinking of fun
when he may be thinking we have lost our house (we have just done
that) or his heart is failing (he thinks his heart stood still last Christmas when he was on a ladder swapping lights in our tree, and whenever I look he is taking his pulse). And with all his worries it mostly
is fun he thinks because when he opens his mouth, if people are
there they generally laugh — with him or at him, he does not mind
which. I know a string of his jokes as long as the string of my personal lacks, and he adds on new ones most days he feels well enough.
A lot of his jokes of course I do not understand but I no longer ask.
I used to ask and he would say, "Wait a little, Preacher. Your day
will come" so I hold them mysterious in my skull till the day they
burst into meaning. But most of his fun is open to view, to anybody's eyes that will look because what he mainly loves is turning
himself into other people before your eyes. Whenever in the evenings we visit our friends, everybody will talk a while including my
father, and then he may go silent and stare into space, pecking his
teeth with a fingernail till his eyes come back from where they have
been and his long lips stretch straight which is how he smiles, and
then whoever we are visiting — if he has been watching my father —
will know to say, "Mock somebody for us, Jeff." ("Mocking" is
what most people call it. My father calls it "taking people off.") He

will look sheepish a minute, then lean forward in his chair — and I sitting on the rug, my heart will rise for I know he has something to give us now — and looking at the floor say, "Remember how Dr. Tucker pulled teeth?" Everybody will grin Yes but somebody (sometimes me) will say "How?" and he will start becoming Dr. Tucker, not lying, just seriously turning himself into that old dentist — greeting his patient at the door, bowing him over to the chair (this is when he shrinks eight inches, dries, goes balder still, hikes his voice up half a scale), talking every step to soothe the patient, sneaking behind him, rinsing his rusty pullers at the tap, cooing "Open your mouth, sweet *thing*," leaping on the mouth like a boa constrictor, holding up the tooth victorious, smiling *"There* he is and you didn't even feel it, did you, darling?" Then he will be Jeff McCraw again, hitching up his trousers with the sides of his wrists, leading us into the laughter. When it starts to die somebody will say, "Jeff, you beat all. You missed your calling. You ought to be in the movies," and if he is not worried that night he may move on through one or two more transformations — Miss Georgie Ballard singing in church with her head like an owl swiveling, Mrs. V. L. Womble on her velvet pillow, President Roosevelt in a "My friends" speech, or on request little pieces of people — Mr. Jim Bender's walk, Miss Amma Godwin's hand on her stomach. But it suits me more when he stops after one. That way I can laugh and take pride in his gifts, but if he continues I may take fright at him spinning on through crowds of old people, dead people, people I do not know as if his own life — his life with us — is not enough. One such night when he was happy and everybody was egging him on I cried to him "Stop" before it was too late and ran from the room. I am not known as a problem so people notice when I cry. My mother came behind me at once and sitting in a cold stairwell, calmed me while I made up a reason for what I had done. She said, "Let your father have a little fun. He does not have much." I remembered how she often warned me against crossing my eyes at school to make children laugh, saying they might get stuck, so I told her he might stick and then we would carry him home as Dr. Tucker or Mrs. Womble or Miss Lula Fleming at the Baptist organ. That was a lie but it was all I knew, all I could offer on such short notice to justify terror, and telling it made us laugh, calmed me, stopped me thinking of reasons. And I did not worry or think of my terror again till several months later when he came in disguise. It was not the first time he had worn disguise (half the stories about him are about his disguises), but he did not wear it often, and though I was seven I had never seen him that way before. Maybe it is why he came that night, thinking I was old enough and would like the joke since I loved his other fun. Anyhow the joke was not for me but for Uncle Hawk, an old colored man who lived with us. I was just the one who answered the door. It was night of course. I had finished my supper and leaving the others, had gone to the living room and was on the floor by the radio. After a while there came a knock on the panes of the door. I said, "I will get it" to the empty room, thinking they were all in the kitchen, turned on the porch light and opened the door on a tall man heavy-set with white hair, a black derby hat, a black overcoat to his ankles, gray kid gloves, a briefcase, a long white face coiled back under pinch-nose glasses looking down. It was nobody I knew, nobody I had seen and what could he sell at this time of night? My heart seized like a fist and I thought, "He has come for me" (as I say, it is my darkest fear that I am not the blood child of Jeff and Rhew McCraw, that I was adopted at birth, that someday a strange man will come and rightfully claim me). But still looking down he said, "Does an old colored man named Hawk work here?" and I tore to the kitchen for Uncle Hawk who was scraping dishes while my mother cleared table. They were silent a moment. Then my mother said, "Who in the world could it be, Uncle Hawk?" and he said "I wonder myself." I said, "Well, hurry. It is a stranger and the screen door is not even locked." He did not hurry. My mother and I stood and watched him get ready — washing with the Castile soap he keeps for his fine long hands tough as shark hide, adjusting suspenders, the garters on his sleeves, inspecting his shoes. Towards the end I looked at my mother in anxiety. She winked at me and said, "Go on, Uncle Hawk. It certainly is not Jesus *yet*." Not smiling he said, "I wish it was" and went. Again I looked to my mother and again she winked and beckoned me behind her into the hall where we could watch the door and the meeting. Uncle Hawk said "Good evening" but did not bow, and the man said, "Are you Hawk Reid?" Then he mumbled something about life insurance — did Uncle Hawk have enough life, fire, burial insurance? Uncle Hawk said, "My life is not worth paying on every week. I do not have nothing to insure

for fire but a pocketknife and it is iron, and Mr. Jeff McCraw is
burying me." The man mumbled some more. Uncle Hawk said
"No" and the man reached for the handle to the screen that separated them. Uncle Hawk reached to lock the screen but too slow,
and there was the man on us, two feet from Hawk, fifteen from my
mother and me. Hawk said, "Nobody asked you to come in here"
and drew back his arm (nearly eighty years old) to strike. My
mother and I had not made a sound, and I had mostly watched her
not the door as she was grinning but then she laughed. Uncle
Hawk turned on her, his arm still coiled, then back to the man who
was looking up now not moving, and then Hawk laughed, doubled
over and helpless. The man walked in right past him slowly and
stopped six feet from me, holding out his hand to take — he and I
the two in the room not laughing. So I knew he had come for
me, that I was his and would have to go. His hand stayed out in
the glove towards me. There were three lines of careful black stitch-
ing down the back of the pale gray leather, the kind of gloves I
wanted that are not made for boys. Still I could not take his hand
just then, and not for terror. I was really not afraid but suddenly
sorry to leave people who had been good to me, the house which
I knew. That was what locked me there. I must have stood half a
minute that way, and I must have looked worse and worse because
my mother said, "Look at his eyes" and pointed me towards the
man's face. I looked and at once they were what they had been all
along — Jeff McCraw's eyes, the size and color of used nickels; gentle beyond disguising. I said to him then fast and high, "I thought
you were my real father and had come to get me." He took off his
derby and the old glasses and said, "I *am*, Preacher. I *have*,
Preacher," and I ran to circle his thighs with my arms, to hide my
tears in the hollow beneath the black overcoat. And I did hide
them. When I looked up, everybody thought I had loved the joke
like them. But I had not. I had loved my father found at the end
with his hand stretched out. But I hoped not to find him again
that way under glasses and powder, mumbling, so when he came
into my bedroom to kiss me that night, I asked would he do me a
favor. He said "What?" and I said, "Please warn me before you
dress up ever again." He said he would and then my mother
walked in and hearing us said, "You will not need warning. Just
stare at his eyes first thing. He cannot hide those." But he always

warns me as he promised he would — except at Christmas when he
comes in a cheap flannel suit and rayon beard that any baby could
see is false — and even though in advance that on a certain evening
he will arrive as a tramp to scare my Aunt Lola or as a tax collector
or a man from the farm office to tell my Uncle Paul he has planted
illegal tobacco and must plow it under or suffer, still I fasten on
his eyes and hold to them till somebody laughs and he finds time to
wink at me.

    As I fasten on them now heading home. He travels of course as
himself tonight in a brown vested suit and a solid green tie so I see
him plain — what is clear in dashboard light — and though I love
him, though I rest in his hollow lap now happier than any other
place, I know he cannot be my hero. And I list the reasons to myself. Heroes are generally made by war. My father was born in
1900 so the nearest he got to First World War was the National
Guard and in October 1918 an Army camp near Morehead City,
N. C. where he spent six weeks in a very wrinkled uniform (my
mother has his picture) till peace arrived, so desperately homesick
that he saved through the whole six weeks the bones of a chicken
lunch his mother gave him on leaving home. And when I woke
him a year ago from his Sunday nap to ask what was Pearl Harbor
that the radio was suddenly full of, he was well and young enough
to sign for the Draft and be nervous but too old to serve. He
does own two guns — for protection an Army .45 that his brother
brought him from France, never wanting to see it again, and for
hunting a double-barreled shotgun with cracked stock — but far
as I know he has never shot anything but himself (that time he was
a boy) and two or three dozen wharf rats, rabbits, and squirrels.
Nor is he even in his quiet life what heroes generally must be —
physically brave. Not that chances often arise for that class of brav-
ery. I had not seen him face any ordeals worse than a flat tire till a
while ago when we had our first mock air raid in Randolph. He
took an armband, helmet, blackjack and me, and we drove slowly
to the power station which was his post and sat in the cold car
thinking it would end soon, but it did not and I began to wonder
was it real, were the Germans just beyond hearing, heading towards
us? Then he opened his door and we slid out and stood on the hill
with great power batteries singing behind us and looked down at
the smothered town. I said, "What will we do if the Germans really

come?" Not waiting he pointed towards what I guessed was Sunset Avenue (his sense of direction being good) and said, "We
would high-tail it there to where your mother is liable to burn
down the house any minute with all those candles." He did not
laugh but the siren went and lights began and we headed home —
the house stinking tallow on through the night and I awake in
bed wondering should I tell him, "If you feel that way you ought
to resign as warden"? deciding "No, if Hitler comes let him have
the power. What could we do anyway, Father with a blackjack
and me with nothing? — hold off steel with our pitiful hands?" (the
hand he touches me with again now, his wounded hand but the
wrist so whole so full, under its curls so ropey I cannot ring it, trying now I cannot capture it in my hand so I trace one finger
through its curls, tracing my name into him as older boys gouge
names, gouge love into trees, into posts — gouge proudly. But with
all the love I mentioned before, I do not trace proudly. I know
him too well, know too many lacks, and my finger stops in the rut
where his pulse would be if I could ever find it (I have tried, I
cannot find it, maybe could not stand it if I did). I shut my eyes
not to see his face for fear he will smile, and continue to name his
lacks to myself. He makes people wait — meaning me and my
mother. He is a salesman and travels, and sometimes when school
is out, I travel with him, hoping each time things will go differ-
ently. They start well always (riding and looking though never
much talking) till we come to the house where he hopes to sell a
stove or refrigerator. We will stop in the yard. He will sit a minute,
looking for dangerous dogs, then reach for his briefcase, open
his door and say, "Wait here, Preacher. I will be straight back."
I will say "All right" and he will turn back to me, "You do not
mind that, do you, darling?" — "Not if you remember I am out
here and do not spend the day." He of course says he will remember and goes but before he has gone ten yards I can see that memory rise through his straw hat like steam, and by the time a
woman says, "Step in the house," I am out of his mind as if I was
part of the car that welcomed this chance to cool and rest. Nothing
cool about it (being always summer when I travel with him), and
I sit and sweat, shooting out flies and freezing if a yellowjacket
comes, and when twenty minutes has gone by the clock, I begin to
think, "If this was all the time he meant to give me, why did he

bring me along?" And that rushes on into, "Why did he get me, why did he want me at all if he meant to treat me the way he does, giving me as much time each day as it takes to kiss me goodbye when I go to school and again at night in case we die in each other's absence?" And soon I am rushing through ways he neglects me daily. He will not for instance *teach* me. Last fall I ordered an axe from Sears Roebuck with my own money, asking nobody's permission, and when it came — so beautiful — he acted as if I had ordered mustard gas and finally said I could keep it if I promised not to use it till he showed me the right way. I promised — and kept my promise — and until this day that axe has done nothing but wait on my wall, being taken down every night, having its lovely handle stroked, its dulling edge felt fearfully. And baseball. He has told me how he played baseball when he was my age, making it sound the happiest he ever was, but he cannot make me catch a fly ball. I have asked him for help, and he went so far as to buy me a glove and spend half an hour in the yard throwing at me, saying "Like this, Preacher" when I threw at him, but when I failed to stop ball after ball, he finally stopped trying and went in the house, not angry or even impatient but never again offering to teach me what he loved when he was my age, what had won him friends. Maybe he thought he was being kind. Maybe he thought he had shamed me, letting me show him my failure. He had, he had. But if he knew how furious I pray when I am the outfield at school recess (pray that flies go any way but mine), how struck, how shrunk, how abandoned I feel when prayer fails and a ball splits hot through my hopeless hand to lie daring me to take it up and throw it right while some loud boy no bigger than I, no better made, trots a free homerun — he would try again, do nothing but try. Or maybe there just come stretches when he does not care, when he does not love me or want me in his mind much less his sight — scrambling on the ground like a hungry fice for a white leather ball any third-grade girl could catch, sucking his life, his time, his fun for the food I need, the silly clothes, sucking the joy out of what few hopes he may have seen when his eyes were shut ten years ago, when he and my mother made me late in the night. — That is the stuff he makes me think when he goes and leaves me stuck in the car, stuck for an hour many times so that finally sunk in desperation I begin to know he is sick in there — that his heart has seized as he knows it will or that strange woman is wild and has killed him silent with a knife, with poison or that he has sold his stove and said goodbye and gone out the back in secret across a field into pines to leave us forever, to change his life. And I will say to myself, "You have got to move — run to the road and flag a car and go for the sheriff," but the house door will open and he will be there alive still grinning, then calming his face in the walk through the yard, wiping his forehead, smiling when he sees me again, when he recollects he has a son and I am it (am one anyhow, the one old enough to follow him places and wait). Before I can swallow what has jammed my throat, my heart in the previous hour, he will have us rolling — the cool breeze started and shortly his amends, my reward for waiting. It is always the same, his amends. It is stories about him being my age, especially about his father — Charles McCraw, "Cupe" McCraw who was clerk to the Copeland Register of Deeds, raised six children which were what he left (and a house, a wife, several dozen jokes) when he died sometime before I was born — and he needs no crutch to enter his stories such as "Have I told you this?" He knows he has told me, knows I want it again every time he can spare. He will light a cigarette with a safety match (he threw away the car's lighter long ago out the window down an embankment, thinking *it* was a match) and then say, "No sir. If I live to be ninety, I never want to swallow another cigarette." That is the first of the story about him at my age being sent outdoors by his father to shut off the water when a hard freeze threatened. The valve was sunk in the ground behind the house, and he was squatting over it cursing because it was stiff and pulling on the cigarette he had lit to warm him — when he looked in the frozen grass by his hand and there were black shoes and the ends of trousers. He did not need to look further. It was his father so while he gave one last great turn to the valve, he flipped his lower lip out and up (and here at age forty-two he imitates the flip, swift but credible) and swallowed the cigarette, fire included. Then he may say, "How is your bladder holding out, Preacher? Do you want to run yonder into those bushes?" I will say No since I cannot leak in open air, and he will say, "Father had a colored boy named Peter who worked around the house. *Peee-ter*, Peter called it. The first day we had a telephone connected, Father called home from the courthouse to test it.

I was home from school — supposed to be sick — and I answered. He did not catch my voice so he said 'Who is this?' I said *'Peee-ter,'* and he thought he would joke a little. He said 'Peter *who?'* I said 'Mr. *McCraw's* Peee-ter,' and he said, 'Hang up, fool, and don't ever answer that thing again!' I waited for him to come home that evening, and he finally came with a box of Grapenuts for me, but he did not mention Peter or the telephone so I didn't either, never mentioned it till the day he died. He died at night . . ."

But *tonight.* This hard winter night in 1942 and he is silent — my father — his eyes on darkness and road to get me safely home as if I was cherished, while I rush on behind shut eyes through all that last — his size, his lacks, his distances — still threading my finger through curls of his wrist, a grander wrist than he needs or deserves. I find his pulse. It rises sudden to my winnowing finger, waylays, appalls, *traps* it. I ride his life with the pad of flesh on my middle finger, and it heaves against me steady and calm as if it did not know I ruled its flow, that poor as I am at games and play, I could press in now, press lightly first so he would not notice, then in and in till his foot would slack on the gas, his head sink heavy to his chest, his eyes shut on me (on what I cause), the car roll still and I be left with what I have made — his permanent death. Towards that picture, that chance, my own pulse rises untouched, unwanted — grunting aloud in the damp stripes under my groins, the tender sides of my windpipe, sides of my heels, the pad of my sinking finger. My finger coils to my side, my whole hand clenches, my eyes clamp tighter, but — innocent surely — he speaks for the first time since begging my pardon. "Am I dying, Preacher?"

I look up at him. "No sir. What do you mean?"

"I mean you left my pulse like a bat out of Hell. I wondered did you feel bad news?"

"No sir, it is going fine. I just never felt it before, and it gave me chills." He smiles at the road and we slide on a mile or more till I say, "Are you *scared* of dying?"

He keeps me waiting so I look past him through glass to the sky for a distant point to anchor on — the moon, a planet, Betelgeuse. Nothing is there. All is drowned under cloud but I narrow my eyes and strain to pierce the screen. Then when I am no longer waiting, he says, "It is the main thing I am scared of."

I come back to him. "Everybody is going to die."

"So they tell me. So they tell me. But that is one crowd I would miss if I could. Gladly."

I am not really thinking. "What do people mean when they say somebody is their personal hero?"

It comes sooner than I expect. "Your hero is what you need to be."

"Then is Jesus your hero?"

"Why do you think that?"

"You say you are scared of dying. Jesus is the one that did not die."

He does not take it as funny which is right, and being no Bible scholar he does not name me the others that live on — Enoch, Elijah. I name them to myself but not to him. I have seen my chance. I am aiming now at discovery, and I strike inwards like Balboa mean and brave, not knowing where I go or will end or if I can live with what I find. But the next move is his. He must see me off. And he does. He tells me, "I think your hero has to be a man. Was Jesus a man?"

"No sir. He was God disguised."

"Well, that is it, you see. You would not stand a chance of being God — need to or not — so you pick somebody you have got half a chance of measuring up to."

In all my seeking I have not asked him. I ask him now. "Have you got a hero?"

Again he makes me wait and I *wait*. I look nowhere but at him. I do not think. Then he says, "Yes, I guess I do. But I never called it that to myself."

"What did you call it?"

"I didn't call it nothing. I was too busy trying to get through alive."

"Sir?"

" — Get through some trouble I had. I *had* some troubles and when I did there was generally a person I could visit and talk to till I eased. Then when I left him and the trouble came back, I would press down on *him* in my mind — something he told me or how he shook my hand goodbye. Sometimes that tided me over. Sometimes."

He has still not offered a name. To help him I hold out the first

one at hand. "Is it Dr. Truett?" (That is where we are coming
from now tonight — a sermon in Raleigh by George W. Truett
from Texas.)

The offer is good enough to make him think. (I know how much
he admires Dr. Truett. He has one of his books and a sermon
on records — "The Need for Encouragement" — that he plays two
or three nights a year, standing in the midst of the room, giving
what wide curved gestures seem right when Dr. Truett says for instance, " 'Yet now be strong, O Zerubbabel, saith the Lord; and be
strong O Joshua, son of Josedech, the high priest; and be strong, all
ye people of the land, saith the Lord, and work; for I am with you,
saith the Lord of hosts: according to the word that I covenanted
with you when ye came out of Egypt, so my spirit remaineth among
you: fear ye not.' " And here we have come this long way to see
him in January with snow due to fall by morning.) But he says —
my father, "No, not really. Still you are close." Then a wait —
"You are warm."

"Does that mean it is a preacher?"

"Yes."

"Mr. Barden?"

"I guess he is it."

I knew he was — or would have known if I had thought — but I
do not know why. He is nothing but the Baptist minister in Copeland, my father's home — half a head shorter than Father, twenty
years older, light and dry as kindling with flat bands of gray hair,
white skin the day shines through if he stands by windows, Chinese
eyes, bird ankles, a long voice for saying things such as "Jeff, I am
happy to slide my legs under the same table with yours" and poor
digestion (he said that last the one day he ate with us; my mother
had cooked all morning, and he ate a cup of warm milk) — but he
is one of the people my father loves, one my mother is jealous of,
and whenever we visit Copeland (we left there when I was two),
there will come a point after dinner on Sunday when my father
will stand and without speaking start for the car. If it is winter
he may get away unseen, but in summer everybody will be on the
porch and Junie will say, "Jeff is headed to save Brother Barden's
soul." My mother will laugh. My father will smile and nod but go
and be gone till evening and feel no need to explain when he returns, only grin and agree to people's jokes.

But *tonight,* has he not just offered to explain? and to me who have never asked? So I ask, "Mr. Barden is so skinny. What has he got that you need to be?"

"Before you were born he used to be a lot of things. Still is."

All this time he has not needed his hand on the wheel. It has stayed heavy on me. I slip my hand towards it. I test with my finger, tapping. He turns his palm and takes me, gives me the right to say "Name some things." I fear if he looks at me, we will go back silent (he has not looked down since we started with his pulse), and I roll my face deep into his side, not to take his eyes. But they do not come. He does not look. He does not press my hand in his, and the load of his wrist even lightens. I think it will leave but it lifts a little and settles further on like a folded shield over where I am warmest, takes up guard, and then he is talking the way he must, the best he can, to everything but me — the glass, the hood, the loop of light we push towards home.

"I have done things you would not believe — and will not believe when you get old enough to do them yourself. I have come home at night where your mother was waiting and said things to her that were worse than a beating, then gone again and left her still waiting till morning, till sometimes night again. And did them knowing I would not do them to a dog. Did them drunk and wild, knowing she loved me and would not leave me even though her sisters said, 'Leave him. He won't change now,' would not even raise her voice. O Preacher, it was Hell. We were both in Hell with the lid screwed down, not a dollar between us except what I borrowed — from Negroes sometimes when friends ran out — to buy my liquor to keep me wild. You were not born yet, were not thought of, God knows not wanted the way I was going. It was 1930. I was thirty years old and my life looked over, and I didn't know why or whether I wanted it different, but here came Mr. Barden skinny as you say, just sitting by me when I could sit still, talking when I could listen, saying 'Hold up, Jeff. Promise God something before you *die.*' But Preacher, I didn't. I drank up two more years, driving thousands of miles on mirey roads in a model-A Ford to sell little scraps of life insurance to wiped-out farmers that did not have a pot to pee in, giving your mother a dollar or so to buy liver with on a Saturday or a pound of hominy I could not swallow. And then that spring when the bottom looked close, I slipped and started you on the way. When I knew you were coming — Preacher, for days I was out of what mind I had left myself. I do not know what I did but I *did* things, and finally when I had run some sort of course, your mother sent for Mr. Barden and they got me still. He said, 'Jeff, I cherish you, mean as you are. But what can I do if you go on murdering yourself, tormenting your wife?' I told him, 'You can ask the Lord to stop that baby.' I told him that. But you came on every day *every day* like a tumor till late January and she hollered to me you were nearly here. But you were not. You held back twenty-four hours as if you knew who was waiting outside, and Dr. Haskins told me — after he had struggled with your mother all day, all night — 'Jeff, one of your family is going to die but I don't know which.' I said, 'Let it be me' and he said he wished he could. I went outdoors to Paul's woodshed and told Jesus, 'If You take Rhew or take that baby, then take me too. But if You can, save her and save that baby, and I make You this promise — I will change my life.' I asked Him, 'Change my life.' So He saved you two and I started to change my life, am trying right now God knows. Well, Mr. Barden has helped me out every once in a while — talking to me or just sitting calm, showing me his good heart. Which, Preacher, I need."

I can tell by his voice he is not through, but he stops, leaving raw quiet like a hole beneath us. I feel that because I have stayed awake, and my finger slips to the trough of his wrist where the pulse was before. It is there again awful. I take it, count it long as I can and say, "It feels all right to me, sir" (not knowing of course how right would feel). He says he is glad which frees me to see Mr. Barden again. I call up his face and pick it for anything new. At first it is very much the same — bloodless, old — but I settle on the faded stripes of his lips and strain to picture them years ago saying the things that were just now reported. They move, speak and for a moment I manage to see his face as a wedge — but aimed elsewhere, making no offer to split me clean from my lacks, *my* foes. So I let it die and I say to my father, "I still think Jesus is your real hero."

Glad for his rest, he is ready again. "Maybe so. Maybe so. But Mr. Barden was what I could *see.*"

"Who has seen Jesus?"

"Since He died, you mean?"

"Yes sir."

"Several, I guess. Dr. Truett for one."

I know the story — it is why I have come this far to hear an old man tremble for an hour — but I request it again.

"Well, as I understand it, years ago when he was young, he asked a friend to come hunting with him. He came and they went in the woods together, and after a while he shot his friend. By accident but that didn't make him feel any better. He knew some people would always say he killed the man on purpose."

"Maybe he did."

"No he didn't. Hold on."

"How do you know?"

"The same way *he* knew — because after he sweated drops of blood in misery, Jesus came to him one evening in a dream and said not to grieve any more but to live his life and do what he could."

"Does that mean he really saw Jesus? — seeing Him in his sleep?"

"How else could you see Him since He is dead so long?"

I tell him the chance that is one of my hopes, my terrors — "He could walk in your house in daylight. Then you could step around Him. You could put out your hand and He would be there. But in just a dream how would you know? What would keep Him from being a trick?"

"The way He would look. His face, His hands."

"The scars, you mean?"

"They would help. But no —" This is hard for him. He stops and thinks for fully a mile. "I mean whether or not He had the face to say things such as 'Be ye perfect as God is perfect' — not even say '*try* to be,' just '*be*' — a face that could change people's lives."

"People do not *know* what He looks like, Father. That is half the trouble." (We are now on one of our oldest subjects. We started three years ago when I first went to vacation Bible school. At the end of that two weeks after we had made our flour-paste model of a Hebrew water hole, they gave us diplomas that were folded leaflets with our name inside and a golden star but on the cover their idea of Jesus — set by a palm under light such as comes after storms (blurred, with piece of a rainbow) and huddled around Him, one each of the earth's children in native dress, two or three inside His arms but all aiming smiles at His face (jellied eyes, tan silk beard, clean silk hair, pink lips that could not call a dog to heel much less children or say to His mother, "Who is my mother?" and call her "Woman" from the bitter cross). I took the picture but at home that night I handed it to my father and asked if he thought that face was possible? He looked and said it was one man's guess, not to worry about it, but I did and later after I had studied picture Bibles and *Christ and the Fine Arts* by Cynthia Pearl Maus full of hairy Jesuses by Germans mostly — Clementz, Dietrich, Hofman, Lang, Plockhorst, Von Uhde, Wehle — I asked him if in all the guessers, there was one who knew? any Jesus to count on? He said he thought there was but in Student's Bibles, the ones they give to boys studying ministry. I said had he seen one? He had not and I asked if he could buy me one or borrow Mr. Barden's for me to trace? He said he did not think so, that Student's Bibles were confidential, secrets for good men.

So tonight I ask him, "Then how did He look in your mind when I was being born and Mother was dying?"

"He didn't look nohow *that* day. I was not seeing faces. I was doing business. If I saw anything it was rocks underfoot, those smooth little rocks Paul hauled from the creek to spread in his yard."

"I think it is awful."

"What?"

"Him not appearing. Why did Dr. Truett see Him and you could not?"

"Maybe he needed to worse than me. He had killed a man. Killed somebody else. I was just killing me, making others watch me do it."

"That is no reason."

"Preacher, if I was as good a man as George W. Truett — half the man — I would be seeing Jesus every day or so, be *fishing* with Him."

"I am not joking, Father. It is awful, I think — Him not helping you better than that."

"Preacher, I didn't mind" — which even with this night's new information is more or less where we always end. It does not worry my father that he is not privileged to see the secret. But it scalds, torments any day of mine in which I think that the face with power to change my life is hid from me and reserved for men who have won their fight (when He Himself claimed He sought the lost), will always be hid, leaving me to work dark. As my father has done, does, must do — not minding, just turning on himself his foe with nothing for hero but Mr. Barden when it could have been Jesus if He had appeared, His gouged hands, His real face, the one He deserved that changes men.

We are quiet again, so quiet I notice the sound of the engine. I have not heard it tonight before. It bores through the floor, crowds my ears, and turning my eyes I take the mileage — sixty-three thousand to round it off. My father travels in his work as I say, and this Pontiac has borne him three times around the earth — the equal of that nearly. It will get us home together, alive, and since in a heavy rush I am tired, I sleep where I am, in his heat, in his hollow. Of course I do not think I am sleeping. I dream I am awake, that I stand on the near side of sleep and yearn, but it *is* a dream and as sudden again I wake — my head laid flat on the mohair seat, blood gathered hot in my eyes that stare up at nothing. My head lifts a little (stiff on my neck), my eyes jerk round collecting terror — the motor runs gentle, the knob of the heater burns red, burns warm, but the car is still and my father is gone. Where he was the dashboard light strikes empty nothing. My head falls back and still half dreaming I think, "They have won at last. They have caught us, come between us. We have ended apart." I say that last aloud and it wakes me fully so I lie on (my head where his loaded lap should be) and think what seems nearer the truth — "He has left as I always knew he would to take up his life in secret." Then I plunge towards the heart of my fear — "He knew just now what I thought when I pressed his pulse, and he could not bear my sight any more." Then deeper towards the heart — "God has taken him from me as punishment for causing his death just now in my mind. But why did He not take me?" Still He did not. I am left. So I rise and strain to see out the glass, to know my purpose for being here, what trails lie between me and morning, what vengeance. The first is snow. The headlights shine and in their outward upward hoop there is only flat gobs of snow that saunter into frozen grass and survive. The grass of the shoulder is all but smothered, the weeds of the bank already bent, meaning I have slept long enough for my life to wreck beyond hope —

my father vanished and I sealed in a black Pontiac with stiff death
held back only long as the draining battery lasts and now too late,
no hero to turn to. My forehead presses into the dark windshield.
For all the heater's work, the cold crawls in through glass, through
flesh, through skull to my blood, my brain.

So I pray. My eyes clamped now, still pressed to the glass, knowing I have not prayed for many weeks past (with things going well),
I swallow my shame and naked in fear ask, "Send me my father.
Send me help. If you help me now, if you save my life, I will
change — be brave, be free with my gifts. Send somebody good."
My eyes click open on answered prayer — coming slow from the far
edge of light a tall man hunched, his face to the ground hid, head
wrapped in black, a black robe bound close about him, his arms
inside, bearing towards me borne on the snow as if on water leaving no tracks, his shadow crouched on the snow like a following
bird, giant, black (killing? kind?). I stay at the glass, my further
prayer locked in my throat, waiting only for the sign of my fate.
Then the robe spreads open. The man's broad hands are clasped
on his heart, turned inward, dark. It is Jesus I see, Jesus I shall
touch moments from now — shall lift His face, probe His wounds,
kiss His eyes. He is five steps away. I slip from the glass, fall back
on my haunches, turn to the driver's door where He already stands,
say silent, "If Father could not see Your face, why must I?" — say to
the opening door "Thank you, Sir," close my lips to take His unknown kiss.

He says, "Excuse me leaving you asleep," and it is my father
come back disguised. "I had to go pee — down that hill in the
snow." (He points down the road as if he had covered miles not
feet.) "I thought you were dead to the world."

I say, "I *was*" — I laugh — "and I thought you were Jesus, that
you had been taken and I was left and Jesus was coming to claim
me. I was about to *see* Him."

Standing outside, the warm air rushing towards him, he shrugs
the coat from his shoulders, lifts the scarf from his head, lays them
in back, slides onto the seat. Shrinking from cold I have crawled almost to the opposite door, but kneeling towards him. He faces me
and says, "I am sorry to disappoint you, Preacher."

I say "Yes sir" and notice he smiles very slow, very deep from his
eyes — but ahead at the road. Then he says I had better lie down.

I crawl the two steps and lie as before, and we move on so I have
no chance to return his smile, to show I share his pleasure. Still I
root my head deep in his lap and hope for a chance before sleep
returns. The chance never comes. Snow occupies his eyes, his hands.
He cannot face me again or test for warmth. Even his mind is
surely on nothing but safety. Yet his face is new. Some scraps of
the beauty I planned for Jesus hang there — on the corners of his
mouth serious now, beneath his glasses in eyes that are no longer
simply kind and gray but have darkened and burn new power far
back and steady (the power to stop in his tracks and *turn*), on his
ears still purple with cold but flared against danger like perfect
ugly shells of blind sea life, on his wrists I cannot ring with my
hand, stretched from white cuffs at peace on the wheel but shifting
with strength beyond soldier's, beyond slave's — and I think "I will
look till I know my father, till all this new disguise falls away leaving him clear as before." I look but his face shows no sign of retreat,
and still as he is and distant, it is hard to stare, painful then numbing. I feel sleep rise from my feet like blood. When it reaches my
head I shut my eyes to flush it back, but it surges again, and I know
I have lost. My own hands are free — he has not touched me, cannot — so my right hand slips to the gap in my pants, cups itself warm
on warmer trinkets long since asleep, soft with blood like new birds
nested drowsy. I follow them into darkness, thinking on the
threshold, "Now I have lost all hope of knowing my father's life,"
cupping closer, warmer this hand as I sink.

First in my dreams I am only this hand yet have eyes to see —
but only this hand and a circle of light around it. It is larger by
half than tonight, and black stubble has sprung to shade its back,
its new thick veins, its gristly cords showing plain because this hand
is cupped too, round like a mold, hiding what it makes. It lifts.
What it has molded are the kernels, the knobs of a man still twice
the size of mine I held before I slept, but cold, shrunk and shrinking as my hand lifts — their little life pouring out blue through
veins gorged like sewers that tunnel and vanish under short lank
hairs, grizzled. Then I have ears. I hear the blood rustle like silk
as it leaves, retreats, *abandons,* and my hand shuts down, clamps
on the blood to turn its race, to warm again, fill again what I hold.
But the rustle continues not muffled, and my hand presses harder,
squeezes the kernels. Through my fingers green piss streams cold,

corrosive. But my hand is locked. It cannot move. I am bound to
what I have made, have caused, and seeing only this terror, I find
a voice to say, "If I cannot leave may I see what I do?" The light
swells in a hoop from my hand filling dimly a room and in that
room my whole body standing by a bed — the body I will have as a
man — my hand at the core of a man's stripped body laid yellow on
the narrow bed. Yet with this new light my original eyes have
stayed where they started — on my crushing hand and beneath it.
I tear them left to see the rest. So I start at his feet raised parallel
now but the soles pressed flat by years of weight, the rims of the
heels and the crowded toes guarded by clear callus, the veins of the
instep branching towards shins like blades of antique war polished
deadly, marred by sparse hair, the knees like grips to the blades,
the thighs ditched inward to what I crush — his hollow, his core
that streams on thin with no native force but sure as if drained by
magnets in the earth. Then his hands at his sides clenched but
the little fingers separate, crouched, gathering ridges in the sheet.
Then his firm belly drilled deep by the navel, his chest like the hull
of a stranded boat, shaved raw, violet paps sunk and from under his
left armpit a line traced carefully down his side, curved under his
ribs, climbing to the midst of his breast — the letter J perfect, black,
cut into him hopeless to dredge out a lung, laced with gut as stiff
as wire. Then under a tent of soft wrinkled glass his face which of
course is my father's — the face he will have when I am this man —
turned from me, eyes shut, lips shut, locked in the monstrous stillness of his rest. So he does not watch me, shows no sign of the pain
I must cause. Yet I try again to lift my fingers, to set him free, but
rocking the heel of my hand, I see our skin has joined maybe past
parting. I struggle though — gentle to spare his rest. I step back
slowly, hoping this natural movement will peel us clean, but what
I have pressed comes with me as if I had given love not pain. I
speak again silent to whoever gave me light just now, say, "Set
him free. Let me leave him whole in peace." But that prayer fails
and turning my eyes I pull against him ready to wound us both
if I must. Our joint holds fast but the rustle beneath my hand
swells to scraping, to high short grunts. "Jesus," I say — I speak
aloud — "Come again. Come now. I do not ask to see Your face
but come in *some* shape now." A shudder begins beneath my hand
in his core, our core that floods through his belly, his breast to his

throat, bearing with it the noise that dims as it enters the tent. I
stare through the glass. His head rolls toward me, his yellow lips
split to release the noise, his eyes slide open on a quarter-inch of
white. The noise scrapes on but behind the tent it is not words —
it is rage or pain or wish, is it meant for me? With my free left
hand I reach for the tent to throw it back, saying, "Stop. Stop,"
but I cannot reach so "Father," I say, "I beg your pardon. Pardon me this, I will change my life — will turn in my tracks on myself my foe with you as shield." But he yields no signal. The eyes
shut again, the lips shut down on the noise, the shudder runs out
as it came, to our core. What my free hand can reach it touches —
his wrist. What pulse was there is stopped, and cold succeeds it till
with both hands I press hard ice, final as any trapped in the Pole.
I can see clearer now, my terror calmed by his grander terror, the
peace of his wounds, and facing his abandoned face I say again
(to the place, the dream), "Pardon me this, I will change my life.
I make this . . ." But pardon comes to stop my speech. My cold
hands lift from his hollow, his wrist. My own hot life pours back
to claim them. Then those hands fail, those eyes, my dream. A
shift of my headrest lifts me from sleep.

I face my live father's present body — my present eyes on his
belly but *him, tonight,* above me, around me, shifting beneath
me. My lips are still open, a trail of spit snails down my cheek, my
throat still holds the end of my dream, "I make this promise."
So my first thought is fear. Have I spoken aloud what I watched in
my dream? Have I warned my father of his waiting death? Offered my promise, my life too early? I roll away from his belt to see
— and see I am safe. He is what he has been before tonight, been
all my life, unchanged by my awful news, my knowledge, undisguised — his ears, his cheeks flushed with healthy blood that also
throbs in the broad undersides of his wrists on the wheel, in the
wounded fat of his hand, his hollow, even in his eyes which are
still ahead on the road for safety, able, unblinking but calm and
light as if through snow he watched boys playing skillful games
with natural grace.

His legs shift often under me now — braking, turning, accelerat-
ing — and we move forward slowly past regular street lamps that
soar through the rim of my sight, gold at the ends of green arms.
We are in some town. From its lamps, its wires, its hidden sky, I

cannot say which — but not home yet I trust, I hope. I am not prepared for home and my mother, the rooms that surround my swelling lacks, direct sight of my doomed father. I need silent time to
hoard my secret out of my face deep into my mind, granting my
father twelve years fearless to work at his promise, freeing myself
to gather in private the strength I will need for my own promise
the night he dies, my own first turn on what giant foes I will have
as a man. And clamping my eyes I seize my dream and thrust it
inward, watching it suck down a blackening funnel, longing to follow it. But his legs shift again, his arms swing left, our wheels strike
gravel, stop. Beyond the glass in our stationary light are bare maple
limbs accepting snow, limbs of the one tree I climb with ease. Too
sudden we are home and my father expels in a seamless shudder the
care, the attention that bound him these last three hours. His legs
tense once, gather to spring from beneath my weight, then subside,
soften. I ride that final surge, then face him — smiling as if just
startled from sleep.

He takes my smile, stores it as a gift. "Did you sleep well,
Preacher?"

I hunch my shoulders, say "Thank you, sir," and behind my lie
floods sudden need — to rise, board him, cherish with my hands,
my arms while there still is time this huge gentle body I know
like my own, which made my own (made half anyhow) and has
hurt nobody since the day I was born.

But he says, "Lift up. Look yonder at the door."

I roll to my knees. Through glass and snow, behind small panes,
white curtains, in the center of the house no longer ours stands
my mother in a flannel robe, hand raised in welcome the shape
of fire. "She waited," I say.

"She waited," he says and reaches for his scarf, his coat, beckons
me to him, drapes them around me, steps to the white ground and
turning offers me open arms. Kneeling I ask him, "What do you
mean?"

"I mean to save your life, to carry you over this snow."

"Heavy as *I* am? — you and *your* heart?"

But he says no more. His mind is made, his trip is ended. He is
nearly home, facing rest, accepting snow like the trees while I stall.
Then he claps his palms one time, and I go on my knees out of dry
car heat through momentary snow into arms that circle, enfold me,

lift me, bear me these last steps home over ice — my legs hung bare
down his cooling side, face to his heart, eyes blind again, mind folding in me for years to come his literal death and my own swelling foes, lips against rough brown wool saying to myself as we rise
to the porch, to my waiting mother (silent, in the voice I will have
as a man), "They did not separate us tonight. We finished alive,
together, whole. This one more time."

VERA RANDAL

Waiting for Jim

(FROM THE COLORADO QUARTERLY)

"Nancy, honey, would you do my back now?" Mrs. Hanna said.

Her mother's voice blended with the steady, incoming roar of the ocean, yet reached her clearly enough. In a minute, Nancy thought. In just a minute. And she stood motionless, her slim, still boyish flat back turned toward the bright splash of blanket, her feet set slightly apart, half buried in sand, and her bony, sharp-planed face uptilted on its slender stalk of neck.

The small section of beach belonging to the summer colony was empty except for the two of them. The lifeguard stand rose dead white and skeletal from the sand, but Jim, the lifeguard, had been there earlier to plant the giant stakes in the ocean floor and tie the ropes that marked off the outer limits for the children. It was, Nancy told herself, like being at a play long anticipated. The stage was set and soon the curtain would go up. The mothers and children would come, the beach chairs, the pails and shovels, the swimming tubes, the gaily colored beach balls. And Jim would climb on his stand to watch over this safe little world. For a moment, almost as if she were a thing apart, Nancy could see herself, blade lean against the flat stretch of beach, with the sun burning on her square, fleshless, winter-pale shoulders, awaiting her cue. "The fourteenth summer," she whispered. "This is my fourteenth summer."

"Nancy, honey, my back." Nancy turned slowly. "The oil's right there, honey, on the edge of the blanket, next to my books."

The beach and the ocean were gone, and there was only the

blanket now, blood red as though the earth itself were wounded, and its liquid life had trickled up through the immaculate white of the sand. "Perhaps I shall be sick." Nancy formed the words soundlessly and bent from the waist, knees straight, to pick up the bottle. "Copper Glow," she read aloud in a thin, precise voice. "Promotes even tanning without burn."

"Promotes even tanning without burn," Mrs. Hanna echoed complacently. "A good tan, and perhaps a couple of pounds off around the middle." She reached out a scarlet-tipped hand to pinch at the flesh around her waist. "Just a pound or two should do it," she said cheerfully, rolling over on her stomach and exposing the naked, blue-white expanse of her back.

Nancy knelt and cupped her hand to hold the amber oil. "I'm a little sandy." She held her hand poised. Beneath the back was the great swell of hips, fleshy like soft, overripe fruit, and then the thighs with their tiny purple lines, broken veins under skin gone slack. "I'm a little sandy," she repeated, waiting.

"You should have wiped your hands, darling." Mrs. Hanna propped herself on an elbow and half turned her head, her eyes dark circles of glass framed in gold. "We have dozens of towels. But go ahead anyhow."

The tiny purple lines on her mother's thighs interconnected like rivers on a map, lost themselves in seas of bluish discoloration. Nancy remained motionless, at once fascinated and repelled.

"Well, dear?"

Abruptly Nancy bent her head and spread the oil, her hand moving swiftly in long strokes from shoulder to waist, neck to waist. The heat of her mother's body reached her through the palm of her hand, and she jerked her hand away, rubbing it against the gray wool of her bathing suit. "It's warm," she said. "It's getting pretty warm."

Mrs. Hanna nodded. "It is warm. You're going to roast in those wool things you insisted on wearing." The green lenses moved downward from Nancy's face. "They're too tight, anyway. You've — " Mrs. Hanna paused, and the glasses moved upward. "You've grown a good deal since last summer."

Nancy raised her arms with what had become an automatic gesture, folding them across the round, hard, alien lumps on her chest. "They're not tight," she said sullenly. "And you can't swim in

ruffles and frills." She moved away from her mother and settled herself on the blanket, clutching her knees tight against herself.

"There are other things besides swimming, Nancy, honey. There
are lots of things."

There were lots of things, things like the hard lumps on her chest
and the damp matted hair under her arms. "I like to swim," she
said. "That's the only thing I like to do. Swim."

"Now, Nancy, honey. You like to read." Mrs. Hanna pushed
herself up onto hands and knees and turned clumsily to sit beside
her.

"I like to read all right." The waves were breaking against the
shore, creeping upward over the dark dampness of the sand, sliding
back. Turning her head slightly Nancy could see the deep cleft
between her mother's breasts, the loose hanging ovals of flesh under
rosebud cotton. "You gave me a book to read." The book was at
home in the city, hidden in the closet, buried under toys she no
longer played with but couldn't bear to part with: a worn, eye-
less plush elephant, a red-haired rag doll with a rent in its side
roughly sewn, a music box with scenes of Switzerland painted on
the sides, the little handle broken off, the music gone. The book
was there too, as though somehow contact with this innocence could
wipe its pages clean. "You gave me a book," Nancy said with a kind
of finality. "I read it."

"I try to talk to you. There are things. Things a girl has to know.
Things a mother — " Mrs. Hanna stopped, silent, waiting.

"I read it."

"It's a stage you're going through, honey," Mrs. Hanna said wearily. "Another year or two." Her voice drifted off, and she reached
for one of the thick books on the blanket, opened it at random,
and closed it again. "It's just a stage you're going through."

"All the world's a stage." Nancy looked at her mother contemp-
tuously. "Shakespeare said that. Did you know?"

"No. I didn't know. Your father would know."

Father would know of course. Father knew more than anyone,
even more than her English teacher, and sometimes in the evenings they would make a game of guessing quotations. And all the
time Mother would sit beneath a pink-shaded lamp, mending, or
turning the pages of those huge, thick books she never managed to
read. "One day I'm going to be as smart as you two," Mother would

say, sighing a little. Then Father would reach out a scrubbed, short-nailed hand with fine golden hairs curling along the back, curling along his hand and up on his wrist and his muscle-knotted forearm, and move his hand, slowly, slowly, over Mother's knee. And Mother would smile, a soft-eyed, contented smile.

Nancy scooped up a handful of sand, and, spreading her fingers, watched it fall in fine, swift streams. She looked over to the life-guard stand. "I wish Jim would come so I could swim."

"He'll be along. It's not eleven yet." Mrs. Hanna pulled off her sun glasses and looked at Nancy with mild, pale brown eyes. "I do believe you have a crush, honey."

"All I said was I wanted to swim." Her mother was smiling, the terrible, mocking smile of adulthood, and she could feel the heat rising to her cheeks, spreading upward over her forehead, and down to the soft hollow at the base of her throat. "I haven't even seen Jim since last summer. I don't even remember what he looks like, hardly."

"All right," Mrs. Hanna said. "All right, then."

Sand spattered as John and Timmy Royce raced past, lifting their feet high, their young boy bodies smooth and hard above brief navy shorts. "Hi," they shouted. "Hi, Mrs. Hanna. Hi, Nancy."

"Hi," Nancy said. Turning her head she could see Mrs. Royce, a circus creature in the distance, jutting pails and shovels, sinking heavily into the sand as she walked.

"Hello, Margaret." Mrs. Royce stopped beside the blanket, thick legs set apart, eyes black slits in a flat biscuit of a face. "It's a fine day."

"Fine," Mrs. Hanna said.

"Did you have a good winter?"

"Good enough. Colds and such. The usual."

"Nancy's grown so. She doesn't look like the same child." Mrs. Royce tittered, and the black slits of eyes widened slightly. Nancy raised her arms to cover her chest. "I guess she's not the same child, is she?"

"She has grown, hasn't she?" Mrs. Hanna said.

"Mummy," one of the boys shrieked. They were kneeling in the damp sand near the water, digging, their hands scoop-shaped.

"My master's call." The biscuit face split into a nicotine-stained smile, and Mrs. Royce walked on, pails clanking, narrow shoulders widening to broad hips and heavy, shapeless legs, feet plodding.

"Bridge tonight at my place," Mrs. Hanna called after her.

Mrs. Royce turned her head. "Good," she said. "That'll be fine."

The beach was filling now, splattered here and there with bits of red and yellow and orange, children's swimsuits vivid against the sand. "I'm going to dig. I'm going to dig all the way to China. Anyone wanna help me?" a little girl shouted.

That was I, Nancy thought, and the sadness rose in her, wavelike. Once that was I. Mrs. Royce's buttocks were quivering, jellylike, under violet silk as she walked. "I won't be," Nancy said softly to herself. "I just won't."

"What won't you be, honey?" Mrs. Hanna reached for a multi-colored towel to mop at the thin stream of sweat that trickled between her breasts. "What is it you won't be?"

"Like her." Nancy spat out the words, her head jerking forward on its reed neck, in line with Mrs. Royce's retreating back.

"She's a perfectly nice woman," Mrs. Hanna said. "She's a lovely woman."

Mrs. Royce was squatting near her sons, cautiously lowering her huge, quivering rear to the sand. Beyond her, way out where the ocean met the sky, a boat, tiny, a child's toy, hung against the vastness. "Lovely," Nancy said flatly. Turning her head she could see the tiny balls of moisture clinging to the oiled surface above her mother's upper lip.

"All the way to China," the little girl shouted again. "All the way. Anyone wanna help me?" She had come quite close to the blanket, and stood there, a brightly painted pail in one hand, a tiny tin shovel in the other, her elf face eager, and her compact little body golden in the sun.

Nancy turned around and flung herself face down on the blanket. "I won't be," she whispered into the fuzz. "I won't be," and nausea, like a cold damp hand, twisted in her stomach.

"Hello, baby," Mrs. Hanna said. "You go dig a nice hole. A nice deep hole."

"To China," the child said, half questioning.

Mrs. Hanna laughed. "Of course to China. Nancy, honey, you're going to burn. You'd better let me put some oil on you."

"No." Nancy's voice was muffled by the blanket.

"You'll blister, honey. It's the first day out. You know you have to be careful the first few days, or you'll blister."

"I don't care." She would blister, then. All over her back there would be pale raised bumps, with colorless liquid beneath. And she would burn. She would burn right through her skin and her flesh, right through all those unspeakable things her mother told her she had inside her, that the little book said she had inside her. And finally there would be nothing left, nothing but bones to be washed clean by the rising tide, bleached white by the summer sun. "I don't care," she cried into the sand-flecked wool of the blanket. "I don't care."

"Here's Mrs. Henderson to join us," her mother said brightly.

"I don't care."

"It's Mrs. Henderson, honey."

Hearing the annoyance in her mother's voice she sat up, out of old habit, and then rose to help Mrs. Henderson unfold her beach chair and settle herself in it. Mrs. Henderson kissed her with white, chapped lips. "You're a good girl," she said. "A sweet child. She's a sweet child, Margaret."

"Yes." Mrs. Hanna said.

The mole on the tip of Mrs. Henderson's nose was like a giant fly. If I just flick it with my little finger, Nancy thought, just ever so gently. And she giggled.

"Is something funny?" Mrs. Henderson asked, taking her knitting from the straw basket at her side.

"No," Nancy said. Mrs. Henderson was older than her mother, maybe forty-five or even fifty. Mrs. Henderson had raised blue veins on the sides of her legs, and bony, yellow knees, and her face was thin except for the cheeks that looked like they had tiny, plump cushions inserted under the skin. Mrs. Henderson was flatter in front than her mother or Mrs. Royce, but not really flat. More like the brown paper bags that Nancy used to blow up when she was little, and then punch, so that they would make a loud banging sound, and then collapse, wrinkled, empty. "No," she said. "Nothing's funny. Nothing at all."

"Nancy's bored," Mrs. Hanna said. "I'm afraid she's going to be very bored here."

Mrs. Henderson nodded over her clicking needles. "This is a good place for children," she said. "Children and old ladies like me. She needs to be with young people her own age."

"I'm not bored." Nancy sat again, arms wrapped around her knees, face turned to the ocean. "I'm not a bit bored."

Mrs. Hanna plucked idly at a corner of the blanket. "I know, Emily. Bill and I felt that way. There was a tour to the coast some of the girls in her class were going on. And there are camps. But she wanted this. She wanted to come back here."

"We've always come here," Nancy said. She tried to recapture her morning vision, the vision that had comforted her through the cold confused winter. The mothers, the children. And above it all Jim, sitting in his high chair, watching, making the world small and safe. Staring out she could see that the toy boat had moved a bit. Its smoke stacks were matched sticks in the distance, scarcely visible. Near her the little girl sat, her smooth blond head bent, her lower lip beaded with tiny pearls of teeth, her shovel moving busily in and out of the hole she was digging between her widespread legs. When Jim comes, Nancy thought. Then it will be all right, when Jim comes.

"I hardly know what to do with her," Mrs. Hanna said. "Sometimes I hardly know what I'm supposed to do with her. She's so difficult. So — different."

"They're all difficult." Mrs. Henderson reached the end of her line, swung the long brown mass of knitting about, and settled it again in her lap. "And they're all different. I've raised a couple of them."

"Boys," Mrs. Hanna said. "Boys are easier."

"I suppose so. I suppose boys are easier."

"She's growing so fast," Mrs. Hanna said. "She's sprouting like a weed."

"Give her another year or two. She'll be just like the rest of them. It's a stage." Mrs. Henderson paused, staring thoughtfully out over the sand, then bobbed her head down once and up again. "That's what it is, Margaret. The child's going through a stage."

Nancy rested her chin on her raised knees. When Jim comes, she thought. "What time is it? It must be eleven by now."

"Eleven?" Mrs. Henderson peered at her wristwatch. "It's almost eleven. What's happening at eleven?"

"She's waiting for Jim," Mrs. Hanna said. "We've been here since half past nine, waiting for Jim."

"Jim?"

"You know. The lifeguard." Her mother's voice rose teasingly, making an alliance with Mrs. Henderson, excluding her. "I think my daughter has a crush."

"Well now, Nancy. What did I tell you, Margaret?" Mrs. Henderson's voice was mock serious. Nancy sat rigidly, tense, silent. "Well, tell us all about it, Nancy." Mrs. Henderson's fingers moved swiftly, spiders in the yarn.

"She's been waiting for him since half past nine," Mrs. Hanna laughed. "Surely that must mean something."

"A beachcomber is an interesting first choice for a young girl," Mrs. Henderson said. "Mine, as far as I can recall, was a riding instructor, but that is, after all, rather more conventional. A beachcomber, now." Her knitting rested in her lap, her hands were momentarily idle, and she waited, watching the girl.

Nancy turned to them, thin-faced, thin-lipped, feeling herself shrunken to smallness. "He's not a beachcomber." She spoke quietly, spacing her words. "He's not."

"He's a knight," Mrs. Hanna said. "They're all knights, Emily, complete with shining armor. The riding instructors, the music instructors, the lifeguards on the beach."

"You don't know everything," Nancy said to her mother. "You don't know anything."

"Nancy," Mrs. Hanna turned the name into a reproach.

But Mrs. Henderson stuck out a bony hand to touch Nancy on the cheek. "Perhaps your mother has forgotten," she said. "Perhaps she never knew a riding instructor, or a music teacher, or a lifeguard. Or perhaps she's just forgotten."

Nancy pulled her head back and rubbed at her cheek, feeling the heat of her face, knowing that she was reddening. It's not like that, she wanted to scream. It's not like you think. It's not any of it like you think. "It's getting awfully hot," she said.

"It is hot." Mrs. Hanna's voice was again warm with concern. "I wish you'd let me put some oil on you, honey. I'm afraid you're going to burn."

Timmy Royce had walked back from the water's edge. He stood over Nancy, snub-nosed, frowning. "Our tunnel keeps busting. Would you help us with our tunnel? Mummy said maybe you would help us with our tunnel."

"I'm too big to make tunnels, Timmy," Nancy said. "I don't make tunnels any more."

"Mummy said you make the best tunnels. Our tunnel keeps busting."

"Maybe later she'll help you," Mrs. Hanna said. "Maybe after a bit, Timmy."

"Okay, Nancy? Later will you? Because ours keeps busting."

"Maybe. Maybe later." Too big to make tunnels any more. She was too big.

Mrs. Hanna looked across the sand. "There's your fellow," she said. "There he is now, finally."

Jim was standing near the lifeguard stand, dwarfed by its skeletal height, with his navy canvas bag in one hand, the bag that would be full of sandwiches and soda to last him through the day. He lowered the bag to the sand and raised his arms to pull off his sweat shirt. "Yes," Nancy said. "There he is."

"Well," Mrs. Henderson said. "After all this waiting about, are you just going to sit there?" The teasing tone had returned. "The poor man may have been counting the minutes until he would see you again. He may have pined all summer. He may — "

"You see what I mean, Emily," Mrs. Hanna said. "We've been here since nine-thirty this morning. She can be difficult sometimes."

"I just wanted to swim." Nancy remained where she was, arms around her knees, waiting. "All I ever said was I wanted to swim." Jim's sweat shirt was off now, and he was looking out over the water, one hand lifted to shade his eyes, his skin dark against the white of his swimming trunks.

"You see what I mean, Emily," Mrs. Hanna said. Mrs. Henderson bent over her knitting, nodding slightly. "That's the way she is, Emily. We've been here for hours waiting. And now he's come, and she sits. Just sits." Mrs. Hanna sighed lengthily. "I find her very difficult to understand."

Nancy's hands had grown cold, and she felt herself trembling slightly, despite the heat of the morning. It wasn't like they thought, not any of it. If only he would climb onto his high white seat and sit watching over the safe little summertime world of the children. Didn't they understand that this was what he was, not a man at all really, but just this? Didn't her mother understand? Alone, lost, she looked to her mother, plumpness encased in rosebud cotton, and thought briefly, fleetingly, who is she? And pushed the thought from her in panic. This was her mother. "Mother," she said softly, almost questioningly.

Mrs. Hanna jerked erect from the waist, removed her sunglasses, frowned. "What is it, Nancy, honey? Is something wrong?" And, after a pause, her voice worried, "Did you get too much sun?"

"No," Nancy said. Did you get too much sun? Did you brush your teeth? You're a bit hoarse, honey. Does your throat hurt? "No. It's nothing."

"Are you sure?"

"Yes. Yes, I'm sure."

"Then go along, honey. All this fuss about Jim and swimming." Mrs. Hanna slouched backward on the blanket. "It will be time to go back for lunch before you know it."

Nancy rose reluctantly. The ocean air seemed poisoned with words, and the small, weather-beaten summer cottage up the road from the beach was suddenly a haven to her. She was starved, for hamburgers, hot dogs, milk, coke, a sandwich — anything. Her dog Sambo would be waiting for her, eager after his long morning's confinement, leaping at the screen door when he heard her footsteps, his long black ears flopping forward, his plume tail high. She could go to her tiny cell of a room with its high old painted chest of drawers, its iron cot, its little nighttable with her books. *David Copperfield*, and *Oliver Twist*, and *Great Expectations*. She was going to read straight through Dickens this summer, just the way Father had when he was a boy. What if she said she wanted to leave? She did want to. She wanted to turn and run, to lock herself away.

"We're leaving in an hour, honey," Mrs. Hanna said.

"An hour?"

"That's right, honey. Go along now."

Nancy nodded, mute. She stooped and picked up her terry cloth robe, slipped her arms through the sleeves, belted it loosely.

Mrs. Henderson smiled slyly over her clicking needles. "If I had a fine young body like yours, I wouldn't hide myself. I'd strut."

Nancy turned away, walking slowly toward the lifeguard stand. I hate them, she thought. God, how I hate them. And then, realizing she had included her mother in her hatred, she whispered softly, experimentally, "I hate my mother." But children didn't hate their mothers. It was wrong, like stealing and telling lies. "I hate my mother," she whispered again.

"Run along, honey."

Nancy looked back, startled, and saw that she had not moved

more than half a dozen steps from the blanket. "Yes, Mother," she said.

"Have a good swim."

"Yes, Mother."

"And be careful."

"Yes, Mother. I'll be careful."

The sand was hot, fire against the bottoms of her feet, glinting gold, with here and there the sharp jut of a broken fragment of shell. She picked her way around the clusters of women, and paused to let a tiny creature in red and black plaid dart in front of her, and walked on as voices greeted her, heads lifted or twisted to look at her. But why were they looking at her like that? Did her front jiggle like Mrs. Royce and Mrs. Henderson and her mother? Surely not, she reassured herself. The robe was so loose. But she flushed, painfully self-conscious, feeling herself stripped naked by prying eyes.

The sun was almost directly overhead, pouring molten gold on the women, the heavy thighs, the loose-fleshed upper arms, the flaccid breasts, the layers of fat, broken veins, bodies stretched shapeless from child-bearing. Almost Nancy thought she could smell them, a smell heavy and sweetish with oil and stale lipstick, perspiring armpits, caked face powder, decay — a smell penetrating and overpowering the clean salt smell of the ocean. Voices reached after her, poked and pawed at her. "Nancy, you've grown so. How you've grown, dear. Peggy, lamb, come let Mummy wipe your nose. It's dripping. See, here's Nancy. Hasn't she grown? You have grown incredibly, Nancy. Almost a little woman, really."

Almost a little woman. Almost a woman. Nancy ran, arms bent, hands fisted, the loose ends of her belt flapping back between her thighs, ran feeling her small breasts quivering and the nausea twisting snakelike in her stomach. The sand was cool and damp against her feet now, and the water lapped icily at her toes. She pulled off her robe and tossed it backward, away from the ocean edge. Glancing sideward she could see Jim, standing at the foot of his high seat, idle, quiet, as if waiting. She shut her eyes. Let him climb up and sit as he always has, she willed. Let him climb up and sit and watch. Let it be as it was.

But he was walking toward her, and she knew without looking that he was coming. "Hi, Nancy," he said. "How's the girl?"

The feet next to her own were slender, with long, almost finger-

like toes and purplish-blue nails. She raised her eyes slowly, seeing the hairy legs, the heavily muscled thighs, the trunks white
against sunbrowned skin, the skin taut over the ribs, the neck, sur-
prisingly short and thick. "Hi, Jim." His eyes were greenish and
bloodshot, and his brown hair was clipped short. "I'm okay, I guess."
He was a stranger to her, lost between summer and summer. "I
guess I'm okay."

"Gonna swim the ocean this year?"

He was smiling at her. He had deep wrinkles like bloodless cuts
in his leathery cheeks, but the eyes were familiar now, laughing
somehow along with the full-lipped mouth. It was their private
joke, continued from one summer to the next for as far back as she
could remember. "Gonna swim the ocean this year?" And suddenly
it was all right. Here was the safe little world of her childhood, the
beach, the ocean, the children digging their holes and tunnels, the
pails, the shovels, the mothers stretched on their blankets. She
laughed, a high-pitched childish giggle that seemed, as she heard it,
to belong to another, earlier self. "Yep," she said, "This is the year."
She waited, a small girl again, for the swift, silly exchange of ban-
ter before he climbed on his stand to watch.

"Surprised you're back, Nancy," he said. "Mostly they stop coming when they get your size."

She was sullen, disappointed. "I just wanted to come back." She
looked down at the sand, at the feet in a row, his long and brown,
hers pale, narrow, pink-toed.

"I'm glad you did. It's nice to have someone to talk to besides
mamas and babies. And someone to look at. Someone cute."

Someone cute? Bewildered, she groped for something to say.
"Are you a beachcomber, Jim? Mrs. Henderson says you're a beachcomber."

"A beachcomber?" He touched her arm lightly.

"A person who hangs around a beach and doesn't do anything
much. They have them in South Sea stories." She stared at the
hand resting on her arm. It was a long brown hand, hot against her
skin, covered with curling, golden hairs. Like Father's, she thought.
Golden hairs like Father's. But what was Father's hand — Jim's
hand doing on her arm?

"Sure," he said. "Your folks pay me a couple of hundred to watch
their kids summers. And I maybe pick up an odd job or two during

the winter. I guess that's what I am all right. A beachcomber." He laughed, a thick throaty sound. "I never had a name for what I was before. You're a cute girl, Nancy."

She was sharply aware of the slight pressure of his hand on her arm, of the naked upper half of his body so close to her own. "Don't you work any?" Her breath was coming in hard little gasps. "I mean don't you have a regular kind of job?"

"Don't need to," he said. "Got enough to eat on. Got a little shack up there, back away. Its a good enough little place. I'll show it to you one day if you like."

"No," she said nervously. "I mean Mother wouldn't let me."

"Mother wouldn't let me," he mimicked, and his teeth glistened whitely against the brown of his skin. "What a baby you are, Nancy."

He was squeezing her arm. Glancing sideways she watched a fat pink worm of a tongue crawl from between his lips. She stood motionless an instant. Then, shaking her head frantically, she jerked away from his hand and darted forward. She lifted her feet high, running, with the water splashing against her legs, pushed forward against an oncoming breaker, half fell, and stood again, holding the thick wet rope with one hand.

Looking back, she could see the beach, the mothers on their blankets, the children playing in the sand. Off to the left was her own mother, with the tiny blond girl, very close, still digging. She watched Jim climb to the top of his stand and sit, brown and still and watchful. It was for this that she had waited, all through the winter. She turned away, and the ocean stretched vast and terrifying before her. "Mother," she said. And her lips sought and found an earlier name. "Mama, mama." She hesitated briefly, her eyes burning with unshed tears. Taking a deep breath, she ducked under the rope that marked off the outermost limit for children.

HARVEY SWADOS

A Story for Teddy

(FROM THE SATURDAY EVENING POST)

WHAT is it that drives us to consider the girls of our youth, those we enjoyed for a day or a month, those whose scruples we strained to overcome, those who scorned us, those who fled? I am not sure, since even the easy nostalgia rising from the memory of success must give way to other emotions when defeats, not victories, come to mind. In the case of Teddy, it was an accident, a typically New York accident, that brought her back to me not long ago, but it is only as a result of my own deliberate life as a writer, and a painful, endless effort to understand, that she has come back with such clarity. I can close my eyes now and see not merely as much, but *more* than I saw twenty years ago.

When I try to recall how I first came to know Teddy, I think back to a double date early in the war, arranged by an acquaintance. Teddy was his date, but my own I cannot visualize in any way — she was surely one of those girls who sit near the telephone, waiting to be fixed up by an attractive cousin. Teddy must have been that cousin. Within an hour of our having met, while the other two danced (we were in some collegiate hangout in Yorkville), I was urging her to go out with me.

Teddy colored. With her fingertips, she pushed her ginger ale glass toward my bourbon glass. "You're pretty fast."

"I have to be."

Teddy was not very strong on repartee, and I fancied that I was ruthless. She was just eighteen, went to college at night, was taking courses in child psychology, and worked by day as a stenographer for some agency that helped soldiers' families, like Travelers Aid. She lived with her little brother and their widowed mother in an apartment house in some remote fastness of the Bronx. All that mattered to me was that she was lovely.

As for me, I was twenty-three and terribly world-weary. I had worked as a copy boy on the old New York *Sun* the year between college and the merchant marine, long enough to learn my way around town. I had only three months left before I would finish boot camp at Sheepshead Bay and ship out, and I was anxious to waste as little time as possible.

Teddy was not sharp and competitive, like the girls I had known at Ohio State and around Manhattan. She was simple, unambitious and vulnerable. She made no pretense of being smart or well read, but she was gentle and modest and virginal, and utterly unsophisticated — you might have thought she was the one from Ashtabula instead of me. Her skin was clean and glowing, her blond hair tumbled over her forehead, her lavender eyes were soft and troubled.

I picked up her small, defenseless hand, ostensibly so that I could admire her charm bracelet, from which dangled a little Scottie and a windmill with revolving sails; she had gotten it from her father for her fourteenth birthday. Squeezing her still-childish fingers, I said, with a self-pity that was realer than she could imagine, "I've only got my weekends — and not too many of them — before I ship out. Won't you meet me next Saturday? In the afternoon, as early as I can get in? Say at two-thirty, under the clock at the Biltmore?"

All that week I thought about Teddy. In the clapboard barracks where, like college boys all over America, I was learning with a thrill of despair that my fellow citizens from farm and factory were foul-mouthed, ignorant and bigoted, it was difficult enough to remember that girls like Teddy still existed. Teddy, snubnosed and sincere, in awe of me because I came from out of town and had hitchhiked to California and back, and eager to help me forget that hellhole of training — such a girl took on the proportions of a prize, one I had been awarded without even being fully eligible.

When I pushed my way into the Biltmore lobby through the swirling Saturday crowds, I was struck speechless at the sight of Teddy, already waiting for me. Not only was she unaware that she had breached the code by arriving early, but she did not even seem to notice how she was being sized up by a group of nudging sailors. She was nervous, yes, but only — I could tell — because she was looking for me. The tip of her blunt little nose was pinker than her cheeks, and she dabbed at it with a handkerchief that she took from the pocket of her fur-trimmed plaid coat as she squinted this way and that, searching for me. I realized for the first time that she was near-sighted.

I hung back for just a moment, then stepped forward and called out her name.

With a glad cry she hastened toward me. "I was afraid I might have missed you, in all this crowd!"

"I was afraid you wouldn't show up at all."

"Silly." This was a word Teddy used often. But she was pleased, and as she pressed my arm, I could smell her perfume, light and girlish. "What are we going to do?"

I wanted to show her off. Outside, I led her over to Fifth Avenue, then north, and we paused now and then in the faltering late October sunlight to look in the shop windows. With Teddy at my side I felt once again a part of the life of the city, secure for the moment at least, as I had not felt wandering forlornly with my false liberty, or hanging, miserable, around the battered Ping-pong tables of the USO, waiting for nothing.

At Fifty-third Street we headed west and stopped before the Museum of Modern Art. The bulletin board announced an old Garbo movie. I turned to Teddy.

"We're just in time for the three o'clock showing."

"Don't you have to be a member or something?" Teddy looked at me uneasily.

I was still learning how provincial some of these New York girls could be. I led Teddy through the revolving glass doors and took unhesitating advantage of my uniform to get us two tickets. Skirting the crowd waiting for the elevator, we skipped down the stairs to the auditorium.

The movie was *The Story of Gösta Berling*. I remember very little about it other than the astonishingly plump whiteness of the youthful Garbo's arms, for I was burningly aware of Teddy's forearm alongside mine. After a while I took her hand and held it through the picture. As our body warmth flowed back and forth, coursing between us like some underground hot spring, I peered covertly at her. She was staring intently — too intently — at the screen; and I knew, as I knew the thud of my own pulse in my ears, that I would never be content with simply sitting at her side. I would have to possess her. Somewhere near the end of the movie, when it seemed reasonably certain that no one would be observing us, I raised her hand, palm up, to my mouth and pressed it against my lips. At that she turned her head and gazed at me tremulously.

"You mustn't," she whispered.

She meant the contrary, I was positive. Giddily, I allowed her to retrieve her hand. When the picture ended I slipped her coat over her shoulders and led her up the stairs to the main gallery.

"I'll show you my favorite picture here," I said. We stood before the big canvas that used to be everybody's favorite in those old days before everybody went totally abstract. It was by Tchelitchew, it was called "Hide and Seek." and it's too bad it didn't get burned up in the fire they had not long ago; I grew to detest it as I got older. It consisted mostly of an enormous, thickly foliated tree, like an old oak, aswarm with embryolike little figures, some partly hidden, some revealed, some forming part of the tree itself.

Teddy appraised it carefully. Finally she said, "You know what it reminds me of? Those contests I used to enter. Find the seven mystery faces hidden in the drawing and win a Pierce bicycle."

I was nettled. "Did you win?"

"Sure. But instead of giving me the girls' twenty-six-inch bike, they'd send me huge boxes of Christmas cards to sell."

By the time Teddy and I were walking south on Lexington, with the wind comfortably at our backs, we had exchanged considerable information about our childhoods, none of hers important enough for me to recall now, except that her father had dropped dead in the street during his lunch hour, in the garment center, two years earlier.

"Where are we going?" she asked, clinging to my arm.

"I thought we'd eat in an Armenian restaurant. Unless you don't care for Armenian food?"

"I never tasted it. Not that I know of."

No other girl that I knew would have admitted it. Not in that way. We hastened to Twenty-eighth Street, to a basement restaurant, with candlelit tables and a motherly proprietress.

I thought I was doing not badly at all. Over the steaming glasses of tea and the nutty *baklava* Teddy's eyes glowed, and she held my hand tightly on the crumpled linen cloth. Her face was still un-formed, but I observed, for the first time, that her cheekbones slanted, almost sharply, beneath the soft freshness of her delicate skin and, in the shadow cast by the uncertain candle, that there was the suggestion of a cleft in her chin. I couldn't wait to be alone with her, and I judged that the time had come for me to tell her about my friends in the Village who sometimes loaned me their little apart-ment for my weekend liberties, as they had this weekend.

"Phil is in 4-F with a hernia, but he's nervous about being reclassi-fied, so he's been trying to line up a Navy commission in Washing-ton. Charlene — that's his wife — just found out she can't have children. She's planning to start her own nursery school in Wash-ington if Phil gets into Navy Intelligence."

"If they're your friends," Teddy said gravely, "they must be nice."

I winced for her. Now I know a little better; don't we all flatter ourselves by thinking that way of our friends, when all too often it simply isn't true? Phil was not nice, he was a climber; his ambition, combined with his terror of death, drove him to get that commission. After the Japanese had surrendered, the Navy sent him on to Tokyo. While he was there, making connections for the postwar world, Charlene, still flabbergasted by her husband's miraculous survival, walked into the side of a Washington trolleybus and died of a fractured skull. Phil recovered from his grief not long after, in time to marry the daughter of a progressive industrialist who was in a position to be helpful. Even though our paths haven't crossed in many years I still see Phil from time to time on TV panel shows.

But to Teddy I explained, earnestly and wholeheartedly: "Phil is an anthropologist, and Charlene paints. They've been to Mexico, and their place is full of things like beaten silver masks and temple fragments."

"It sounds lovely."

"Let's go. It's not far, just down on Jane Street."

Teddy was not quick, but she was not stupid either. "Will there be anyone there?"

I knew at once that I had moved too fast. And lying could only make things worse. "They probably won't be back from Washing-ton before tomorrow."

"In that case I think I'd better not." Teddy flushed, and forced herself to look at me. "You're not angry, are you?"

"I wasn't planning on assaulting you," I said, trying hard not to sound sullen. "I mean, the place isn't an opium den."

"I know. It's just that I don't think it would be a good idea."

When we were out on the street once again, walking west into a fall rain as fine as spray from an atomizer, Teddy stopped suddenly before a darkened courtyard and looked up at me anxiously.

"I didn't mean to hurt your feelings. I guess I'm just not very sophisticated about those things."

Pressing her against the wrought-iron picket fence before which she stood trying, her head tilted, to catch some light in my eyes or across my face which would tell her what I was feeling, I folded her in my arms and kissed her for the first time.

I kissed her again, and a third time, and maybe I wouldn't have been able to stop, but Teddy passed her hand across her forehead to brush back her damp hair and said, laughing somewhat shakily, "Don't you know that it's raining?"

So we went on to the Village Vanguard, and then to Romany Marie's, where Teddy assured me, after she had had her fortune told, that this had been the loveliest evening she had ever spent. Like a dream, she said — the whole day had been like a dream.

At two o'clock in the morning I offered to see her home. She insisted, as we stood arguing by the mountain of Sunday papers at the Sheridan Square newsstand, that she wouldn't think of my riding the subway all the way up to the East Bronx for an hour and then all the way back for another hour. Not when I had to get up almost every morning at five-thirty, do calisthenics, and practice lowering lifeboats into the icy waters of Sheepshead Bay. I yielded, but not before I had gotten her promise that we would meet that afternoon at the Central Park Zoo, where she had to take her younger brother. I stood at the head of the subway stairs and watched, bemused, as she tripped down them as lightly and swiftly as if she were still a child hurrying so as not to be late for school.

At the zoo I found Teddy as easily as if we had been alone in that vast rectangle of rock and grass, instead of being surrounded as we were by thousands of Sunday strollers. She was standing before the monkey cages with her younger brother Stevie, a solemn-looking mouth breather with glasses and the big behind that many boys acquire during the final years of childhood. She whirled about at my touch, her face already alight with pleasure.

"Did you sleep well, Teddy?"

"Like a baby. Such sweet dreams!" And she introduced me to her brother.

What he wanted was to attend a War Bond rally at Columbus Circle, where they were going to display a Jap Zero and a movie star. I think the star was Victor Mature; in any case, on the way to see him and the captured airplane I pulled Teddy aside and asked if we couldn't cut out for a couple of hours and run down to Phil's apartment.

She stared at me. "Honestly, I think you have a one-track mind."

"Phil and Charlene are in from Washington," I explained hastily. "They'd like to meet you."

"But I'm hardly even dressed to meet *you!*" Dismayed, she pointed to her loafers, her sweater and skirt, her trench coat, but I succeeded in persuading her.

As we stood in line to see the airplane, Teddy asked Stevie if he'd mind if we left him alone for a while. He promised to wait for her through the Army Band concert, and we hurried off to the downtown bus. All the way down to the Village Teddy kept me busy reassuring her that we weren't going to be barging in where we weren't wanted.

Phil's place was strewn not only with various sections of the Sunday *Times,* but with a crowd of weary weekend loungers who hadn't been there when I left that morning: an unmilitary army officer and his hungover girl friend; a dancer in blue jeans, from the apartment across the hall, who was studying the want ads while she picked at her bare toes; a nursery-school teacher friend of Charlene's who was arguing heatedly with her in the kitchen about child development. The radio on the bookcase was blasting away with the New York Philharmonic.

Teddy sat primly on a corner of the studio couch with her knees pressed together and a paper napkin spread over them, sipping coffee and nibbling on a cracker, speaking only when spoken to. Phil got me off in the john at one point and said, grinning and shaking his head and winking in his nervous way, "You'll never make that girl."

I was annoyed, but I wasn't exactly sure why. "What makes you say that?"

"Aside from the fact that she's a virgin and terrified of you and your highbrow friends, she's too clean. I'll swear she uses those soaps they advertise in *The American Girl*."

"How would you know about *The American Girl?*"

"I've got a little sister."

I thought of the contests that Teddy used to enter — Find 7 Hidden Faces — and I found myself hurrying back to her side with her trench coat.

"Yes, let's go," she said. "I'm getting worried about Stevie. If my mother knew, she'd kill me."

"I wouldn't let her do that," I replied manfully.

"I'd like to see you stop her," Teddy said to me over her shoulder as we went out. "You don't know my mother."

I didn't know quite how to answer that, so I busied myself with finding a cab, no mean trick in those days, when they weren't allowed to cruise. I didn't want to know her mother, but on the other hand I wasn't about to come out and say so.

When we were settled in the cab that I had gone several blocks to find, Teddy said mournfully, "Your friends are very talented people."

That made me a little suspicious. "Most of them aren't my friends. And besides, who's talented?"

"Well, take that army lieutenant. He's an artist. He told me so."

"Rollini? He paints camouflage on the sides of airplane hangars. I don't see that that's such a big deal."

"You know what I mean. I just don't think I fit in with those people. I can't do anything special." She gestured helplessly. "Look at me."

The cab swung sharply onto Sixth Avenue, and Teddy was flung into my arms. I kissed her while her mouth was still open to say something else.

"Wait," she panted, breaking free. "I want to ask you something." She huddled up, very small, in a corner of the seat. "Do you really like me?"

"Like you?" I asked. "My God, you're the most beautiful girl I've ever known. All week in those cruddy barracks I keep telling myself —— "

She interrupted my protestations. "That's not what I mean. I wasn't fishing for compliments. I didn't ask you if you thought I was pretty; I asked you how much you liked me."

She knew as well as I how hard that was going to be for me to answer. Maybe that was why she didn't stop me when I reached for her once again, wanting to substitute caresses for words. Only when we were within a few blocks of Columbus Circle did she part from me again, her forehead wrinkled and her lower lip trembling just the slightest bit.

"I just don't understand," she said wonderingly, and not very happily. "It's all wrong."

What was I going to tell her, that I wanted to make love to her? She knew that already. Before I could say anything, we were caught up and blocked in the traffic of the Bond rally, which was on the point of breaking up. Teddy darted out of the cab door, calling over her shoulder, "I'll write you!" as she dashed off in search of Stevie. As I stood there in the eddying crowd, paying the driver, the rally band broke into "Praise the Lord and Pass the Ammunition," and I saw Stevie, the mouth breather, standing with his jaw agape, staring at the trombones through his eyeglasses.

Before the week was over I had my letter from Teddy. I am not going to try to reproduce it here. I will only say that it can best be described as a love letter, and that it was so gauche, so overwritten, so excruciatingly true ("I am simply not used to going out with boys like you") and at the same time so transparently false ("My brother Stevie thinks the world of you") that it was immediately, painfully, terribly clear to me that I would never be able to answer in kind, and that there was no sense in deluding myself into believing that I would. I hope it does not make me sound completely impossible if I add that her words not only released me from thinking seriously about her but also made it all but impossible for me to think of anything but conquering her.

What inflamed me all the more was that shortly after I found Teddy's provocative letter on my bunk, my entire platoon was restricted to the base for the weekend. Trapped in that raw, artificial place, in the womanless wooden huts thrown up hastily to house some thousands of frightened boys being converted into sailors of a sort, I spent my mornings bobbing on a whaleboat in the bay, rowing in ragged unison with my freezing mates, and my afternoons ostensibly learning knots and braiding lines, but actually lost in an erotic reverie of Teddy — of her slim arms, her tumbling hair, her pulsing lips — gone all wanton and yielding.

By the time we finally met again, I had memorized every line of
her, from her slanted cheekbones to the small feet that toed out
the least bit — and I could hardly remember what she looked like.
We were constrained then, two weeks after the Bond rally, not only
by what had passed between us but by the heedless souls shoving us
away from each other in the arcade of the Forty-second Street entrance to the Times Square subway station. It was the worst possible place for a boy and a girl to meet on a Saturday afternoon, in
that blowing surf of old newspapers and candy wrappers, with the
hot rancid smell of the nut stands assailing us. We hardly knew
what to say to each other.

She smiled at me nervously, and I was emboldened to take her by
the hand. "Let's get out of here." Willingly she mounted the stairs
with me to the street, but when we came out onto the sidewalk the
raw rain had turned to sleet; it cut at our faces like knives. I cursed
the world, the war, the weather.

"But if you were stationed at that Merchant Marine camp in St.
Petersburg," Teddy pointed out, "we would never have met."

"Oh great," I said. "Now you're going to do the Pollyanna routine."

"I didn't mean it like that," Teddy replied humbly.

"I want to kiss you, that's all. Are we supposed to stand out here
in public and freeze to death while I make love to you? Come on,
Teddy, let's go down to my friends' apartment. Like civilized people, like folks. What do you say?"

She could tell I wasn't going to push it too hard, so she laughed
and tucked her arm in mine. "Come on, Mr. One Track Mind, let's
get out of the sleet."

It was driving down hard, and we had to run into a doorway,
which turned out to be the stairway entrance to a second-floor chess-
and-checkers parlor. When Teddy laughed, still gasping a little and
shaking off wetness like a puppy, and said, "I wonder what it's like
up there," I took her by the arm and led her up the stairs. It never
ceased to amaze me, how a New York girl could know so little.

Teddy hadn't played much chess, only with her brother — their
father had taught them — so I showed her a few openings, but she
was frankly more interested in sizing up the habitués.

Later, while we were having a drink at an Eighth Avenue hotel
bar — I teased Teddy into having a pink lady instead of her usual

ginger ale — I asked her if she'd ever eaten a real Chinese dinner.
She looked a little disappointed. "We have Chink's in the Bronx
almost every Saturday. Sometimes we even take it home with us."

"I'm not talking about chop suey, Teddy. I'm talking about the
greatest cooking this side of Paris."

As if I'd ever eaten in Paris, much less in Peking! But that made
no difference. I knew a real restaurant down on Doyers Street, and
when we got there the headwaiter even remembered me. Or at least
he claimed to, which was just as good; and when he followed the
bird's-nest soup with platters of crisp glazed duck, Teddy gazed at
me in awe.

We walked off the dinner afterward through the dim, narrow
streets of Chinatown, echoing with soft slurring voices, and then
took a subway back up to midtown in order to see Noel Coward's
Blithe Spirit, with Clifton Webb and Mildred Natwick. We were
fortunate to get tickets, and made it just after the curtain had gone
up, groping our way to our seats.

Teddy poked frantically in her purse and came up at last with a
pair of shell-rimmed eyeglasses. She was seeing bright comedy on
the stage for the first time; I was seeing her in glasses for the first
time. For both of us, it was a revelation. She thought the play was
brilliant; I thought she was delicious.

When the play let out, we stopped in at Jimmy Ryan's on Fifty-
second Street, ostensibly for a drink, but actually so that Teddy
could see how casually I greeted the boys who were playing there —
Pee Wee Russell, and George Brunies, and Zutty Singleton, poker-
faced at the drums like Joe Louis, and Art Hodes, whose daily jazz
program, I told Teddy, I used to follow on WNYC. But since
Teddy's musical background was confined to André Kostelanetz and
Lily Pons, she was only impressed, not overwhelmed, by my acquaintance with the great. I took her across the street to hear Billie
Holiday.

We stood at the bar, Teddy's back against my chest, and stared
through the throat-tearing smoke at Billie, who sang "My Man," and
"Strange Fruit" and "Gloomy Sunday."

Teddy's eyes were wet and shining. She raised her head. "You're
opening a whole new world for me."

That was precisely what I was trying to do, but it bothered me to
have her put it so patly. It reinforced my conviction that she would

always be like that, forever, that there was no point in my even considering that she might ever be otherwise.

She went on, "And I don't know that it's such a good thing. For
either of us. Why should we kid ourselves? It's not going to be my
world — it never will."

It was a somewhat melancholy note on which to end the evening,
but in a way I preferred that. It struck me that it would be almost
diabolically patient to let Teddy stew overnight, torn between guilt
and gratitude. The next day was to be the climactic one. I forced
myself to kiss her more lightly in parting than I wanted to, and we
agreed to meet the next day by the lions in front of the Public Library.

For a change the weather was on my side. The wind was brisk,
and Teddy had tied a print scarf around her blond hair, babushka-
style — it accentuated the slope of her cheekbones when she laughed
— but the sun was out. We walked all the way up to the Frick Collection, and were lucky enough to get tickets to the Sunday concert.
Teddy had never even heard of the institution, but she made no attempt to conceal her ignorance.

Although she knew no more of chamber music than she did of
jazz, Schubert stirred her, and she held tight to my arm throughout
Death and the Maiden, breathing softly and shallowly while she
squinted (no glasses in the daytime) at the musicians. When the re-
cital was over, we walked on up to the Metropolitan Museum, which
Teddy hadn't visited since she was ten.

I led her directly to El Greco's "View of Toledo." "This is worth
the trip, this and the Courbets inside. Better to see just these than
to get a headache from looking at too many."

How insufferable I must have been, lecturing Teddy first on music, then on painting, about which I knew so little! But she smiled
at me gratefully and let me know by the way in which she clung to
me that I was both patient and wise.

As we left the Metropolitan and walked south through Central
Park, darkness caught up with us and the wind came up too. Our
breaths frosting, we hurried on across Central Park South against the
traffic, skipping in and out of the dimmed blurry headlights until
we had gained the rococo refuge of Rumpelmayer's.

Warm, snug, soothed, we spooned up the great blobs of whipped
cream floating on our hot chocolates and laughed over inconsequential things, and then suddenly, as if by common accord, we both

stopped. I stared into Teddy's lavender eyes, so soft and moist that I wanted to kiss them closed, and she opened her mouth, but without speaking, as if she dared not utter whatever it was that she wanted to say.

"I must kiss you," I murmured.

She nodded dumbly.

We went outside. In the dimout across the street the aging men who took you on carriage rides through the park and along Fifth Avenue were adjusting the straps on their horses' feedbags and hoisting blankets over their hides to protect them from the chilly evening. I signaled the leader of the line.

Teddy said apprehensively, "This must be terribly expensive."

Without answering, I raised her up into the carriage and climbed in after her. The driver tucked us in with a warm comforter, swung himself aboard behind us, clucked to his horse, and we were off.

Teddy and I turned to each other so precipitately that we bumped foreheads, searching, in the dark of the covered carriage, for each other's lips. We rode on through the lamplit evening, clinging to each other, kissing until the current that flowed between us warmed not only our lips but our cheeks and our hands, our fingers and the tips of our fingers.

"You have been so nice to me, so nice to me," Teddy whispered.

I responded by kissing her into silence. It was only after a long time that she could protest, trembling in my arms and frowning. "You shouldn't kiss me like that."

"Like what?"

"You know. It's not right, that's all."

"Nobody can see."

"Silly! I mean, I think it's for married people, or anyway for engaged couples, and like that."

We weren't engaged or like that — the very thought was enough to frighten me out of my ardor — but I had every intention of our becoming lovers, and the sooner the better. "There's only one way," I whispered into her ear, "for you to stop me."

"What's that?"

"Kiss me back the way I kiss you."

Before she could express her shock, I had stopped her mouth again. We must have been near Seventy-second Street on the west side of the park before we drew apart, panting.

"You know where I'm going to take you to dinner?" I asked.

"Where?"

"Phil and Charlene's. And I'm going to cook it myself. Wait till you taste my soufflé! On the way down we'll pick up a bottle of wine, and —— "

"They're not there, are they?"

"Who?" As if I didn't know.

"Phil and his wife. Because if they're not there, I'm not going. I don't think you ought to take advantage of the fact that you're so attractive, and I'm so weak."

I forced myself to be calm and reasonable. "Teddy, darling, what's so terrible about our being alone together for a while?"

"I don't trust myself. Any more than I trust you." She uttered the phrases with heartfelt emotion, as though she had invented them — as though no one before her had ever even expressed such thoughts. And she looked more ravishing, more flowerlike than I had ever seen her before, her lips fuller than usual, a little swollen perhaps, her eyes staring piteously at me, her hair escaping from her scarf in little tendrils that clung to her forehead.

"Is it so awful," I demanded, "for two people who care about each other to be alone together?"

"But what you care about isn't me, it's getting me alone." Teddy paused, as if to give me time for a fervent denial.

I could say nothing. I was not the noblest or the most honorable twenty-three-year-old left in the United States, but I was incapable of promising engagement rings to young girls in return for their favors. And this much at least Teddy understood about me. The damnable truth was that I couldn't even imagine myself falling in love with, much less marrying, a girl who would make a big issue out of protecting her virtue. And on top of it all, I had been keyed up for what was going to be a triumph. I still wanted Teddy very badly, but it was obvious that I had failed completely.

After a long while she said, "I think I'd better go home."

She wanted me to protest, as with her other assertion that we had left hanging in the air, but I could no more find it in me to protest this time than before. I was too hurt and too shamed.

But so was Teddy, and when we had been brought back in jolting silence to our starting point, she jumped out and began to walk away so swiftly that after I paid the driver I had to run for the better part of a block before I caught up with her.

"Please, if you insist on going, let me see you home."

"There's no need. Really. And I don't want you to think I'm angry with you, because I'm not. I had a perfectly lovely time, you'll never know how much I loved it, every minute of it. I'm just angry with myself, that's all. You and I are very different, and it's my fault, not yours. I should have faced it right at the beginning."

Still dumb, I shook her extended hand and watched her hurry off toward the subway and the Bronx.

Three days later I stood by my bunk staring at a letter from Teddy, incongruously pink and girlish on the coarse blue of my navy blanket. For a moment, immersed almost superstitiously in shame for the way I had messed things up with her, I was afraid to touch it. Finally I tore open the envelope.

It was the letter of a pen pal, jolly and comradely. A friend had given her two tickets to the Columbia-Dartmouth game this coming Saturday (I was learning that when a girl says a friend she means a boy — otherwise she specifies). Wouldn't I please be her guest, so she could repay me just a little for all the fun I'd shown her?

If I had been older, probably I would have said no. But I was desperately lonely in those barracks, graduation time was nearing for my platoon, and I thought, if I say no she'll think I'm still pouting. And besides, hope revived: If I turned her down, how would I ever know for sure that she hadn't changed her mind and was using the football game as an excuse, a means of saying, I'm sorry, I was wrong, you were right, I'll do whatever you want?

So I awaited the weekend as fervently as I had all the others, and to calm myself on the long subway ride up to Baker Field I worked at two crossword puzzles, the easy one in the *Tribune* and the hard one in the *Times*.

Teddy met me by the entrance on the Columbia side, where she had said she would be — but so much more real, so much more beautiful than even my imaginings of her that I could almost have believed I not only wildly wanted her but wildly loved her too.

It was apparent immediately, though, that we were to be pals. Teddy was dressed for late November, and for this last game of the season, in plaid flannel skirt and a heavy mackinaw and little fuzzy earmuffs. She looked adorable. When she arranged her small lap robe across our knees I reached around her waist and hugged her tightly to me, but all I could feel were layers of wool and bulky insulation.

"It's my brother's mackinaw. Can you tell?"

"It looks better on you, I'll bet."

"This stadium must look pretty tiny to you after those Big Ten games with seventy and eighty thousand people in the stands."

It did, it did. I could hardly take any of it seriously, the scrimmages, the end runs, the collisions, the slow roars, the cheerleading. And especially not the athletes, so puny compared to the hulks on football scholarships with whom I had eaten in my Ohio coop. Not when so many other young men my age were burning and drowning, trapped in torpedoed tankers less than a hundred miles from where we sat cheering. But then it was going to be a long war, everyone promised us that, and these boys on the field would get their chance to die, some of them, next year.

As we shoved our way through the crowds onto the street, weaving in and out among the crawling cars, Teddy turned to me, her face glowing. I had never seen her prettier — or happier.

"That was fun, wasn't it?"

"What's next on the program?"

She laughed. "Know anything about bowling?"

"I know what you're up to," I said. "You're doing your best to wear me out."

We went to an alley she knew of in Washington Heights where a young crowd hung out — refined, she said, not bums or low-class. To me they looked like high school graduates waiting to be drafted, and their kid sisters. No doubt their younger brothers were working as pin boys. We drank two Cokes and bowled two games. Teddy was a little clumsy, but I loved watching her strain forward eagerly, frowning over the progress of her ball down the alley.

If only, I thought, if only. But I couldn't even plead with her, not when she was content to be surrounded by dozens of shouting kids her own age. Why keep pushing her, I asked myself, why not leave her to her games and her soft drinks and her soldier pen pals in Greenland, North Africa and Australia?

We had steaks — black market to judge from the price if not the taste — at a restaurant on upper Broadway, and as I chewed I mumbled, "We've had football and we've had bowling, now all we need is swimming to make our day complete."

"The Saint George Hotel pool has mixed swimming. Let's go!"

"I see enough water all week. We have to jump into the damn bay with rubber suits on, and sometimes they dump out a couple barrels of oil and set it on fire to make it more interesting to swim through."

"I didn't think," she said, crestfallen. "Anyway, it's too cold."

Of course when she spoke like that I had to insist we go. We rode the Seventh Avenue subway all the way down to Brooklyn, got off at Clark Street, and went up by elevator straight into the hotel without even setting foot on the street. We parted, for the first time all day, at the lockers, urging each other to hurry.

I got to the pool first. Teddy came in a moment later, a little shy, tugging at the nether parts of her rented tank suit as she stepped forward on the damp tiles, her pink-tinted toes curling gingerly upward. Her body was slight, paler than mine, and vulnerable. Her embarrassment only increased my own; I turned my eyes away, and dived into the water at the deep end. She slipped in and came up beside me, dripping and cheerful.

"Isn't it great? I'll race you down to the shallow end!"

Actually, although Teddy thrashed bravely, she couldn't swim very well. But she splashed me happily, slipping loose from my grasp when I reached out to paddle her. Laughing and gasping, she hauled herself out of the pool and flung herself upon the tiles. She grinned down at me as I hung from the lip of the pool, letting my legs dangle in the water.

"I'm so glad we came. You were sweet to bring me. Isn't this more fun than all that other stuff? You know what I mean."

"No," I said, "it's not."

Teddy's little bosom was rising and falling regularly, and the droplets of water clinging to her bare arms and legs glistened under the lights. I was infinitely touched by the fine golden down on the soft flesh of her legs and forearms. I had never seen her with so little clothing: her body was not only tender and almost childishly graceful, it was so appealing that it was physically painful for me to survey it without being able to touch it, and I shrank down into the water.

"Why?" she asked. "What's wrong?"

"Everything." I reached up and took hold of her ankle. It was so fine that my thumb and forefinger girdled it, nearly, and it seemed to me that I could feel every little interlocking bone as she flexed it in an instinctive frightened withdrawal. "Do you know what I'd be doing now if there was no one in the pool but us?"

Teddy giggled. "There'd still be those people up in the balcony, looking down at us."

"I mean if we had the pool entirely to ourselves. I'd pull you down here into the water," I said desperately, "I'd hold you against me, I'd kiss you —— "

Her grin faded. She drew her foot from my grasp and pulled her knees up tight against her chest, hugging them as if she had taken a sudden chill, or perhaps wanted to hide from me as much of herself as she could.

"Listen," she broke in nervously, "why don't you come up here and sit next to me, and we'll talk about something else?"

"What else is there to talk about?" I knew my voice was too loud, but I didn't care. "What else can I think about? If you'd only grow up a little —— "

Teddy colored all the way down to the base of her throat. She turned her head swiftly, anxiously, in all directions, to see if any of the handful of Saturday-night swimmers, mostly older women, had overheard us.

"Please don't be angry with me," she said. "You know something, there must be other girls you could go out with besides me. You know — I mean, bad girls. Then you and I could just have fun like we did today."

"You're joking."

"No, no, I'm not." She sucked in her breath and laughed jaggedly. "We could have such fun. Couldn't we?"

I didn't know whether to laugh or to cry. All I could think of to say was, "Here I'm telling you that you're adorable, that it's you I want and not some stranger, but nothing registers. It's obvious that you don't care about me, or you wouldn't say such fantastic things."

"No," Teddy muttered, not looking at me, "it's you who don't care for me. Do you think, if you loved me, that we'd — " She broke off with a quick shudder. The little golden hairs were standing upright on her arms and legs. "See," she said sadly, "I'm all goose pimples. I'm going to take a hot shower. We've done enough for one day, haven't we?"

I remained in the barracks after that, brooding, waiting to ship out into the North Atlantic. I made no effort to get in touch with Teddy. Finally, since for the first time in months I had time on my hands and access to a typewriter in the master at arms' office, where I often stood night watch alone, I wrote a short story.

It was a bitter story, of course, about a young serviceman who, because he is denied physical intimacy by a girl who claims to love him, goes recklessly to his death, a snarl upon his lips.

I made two copies. The first went to *The New Yorker*. After debating with myself for a day or so, I wrote across the face of the carbon copy, *Here is the most I can offer you for Christmas, something I made for you myself, from the bottom of my heart.* I signed my name and mailed it to Teddy.

A few days later the original came back from *The New Yorker*. I stuck it into a fresh envelope and shipped it off to *The Atlantic Monthly*, where I knew from experience that it would rest long enough for me to go off to sea under the happy illusion that it was being seriously considered.

I heard nothing at all from Teddy. After a few days I could stand it no longer, and one night I rang her up from the pay phone in the recreation room. She answered, but from her tone, a little frightened when she recognized my voice, and more breathless than usual, I was sure that she was not alone.

"Teddy," I said, "I've been worried by your silence. Are you all right?"

"Yes, I am. Are you?"

"Yes, of course. Is your mother there with you?"

"I don't see what difference that makes." Then she said what her mother must have been coaching her to say, against the moment when I should phone again. "My mother feels I shouldn't see you anymore. And I think she's right."

I was so shocked that I forgot to ask about my story. I stammered, "But all I wanted was to see you one last time before I ship out. Does that seem so unfair? For us just to get together this Saturday afternoon?"

"If you had any respect for my wishes," she said stiffly, "you wouldn't press it any further."

I muttered goodbye and slammed down the receiver. But the next day, after a night spent cursing myself for not having let matters rest with my sardonically inscribed story, I received a note from Teddy.

She apologized for the way she had spoken (I was right, her mother had been listening) and went on to add that if I still wanted to say goodbye she would look for me on Saturday, at one o'clock, in the waiting room of Penn Station. She would tell her mother that she was going shopping at Macy's.

It was Teddy's willingness to deceive her mother that encouraged in me the wild hope that my story had accomplished what my physical presence and my pleading had not. But when I dashed into Penn Station, hurrying about in search of her, Teddy came up to me unexpectedly and offered me only her hand and not her lips. The hand was gloved, but I had the feeling that her fingers would be cold; her lips were pale and bloodless, and she smiled at me tremulously.

"You look well," she said. "I'm sorry I can't stay very long."

People were bumping into us in their anxiety to reach the escalator. The vaulted terminal was bleak, drafty, and to me — at that moment — terrifying.

"Teddy," I said, "you can't just shake my hand and walk away." I pointed to the bag hanging from her left hand. "You've done your Macy's shopping already. That ought to satisfy your mother. Can't we get out of here? Please?"

"If we could just be happy one last time? Like we were for a little while . . ."

"Come with me." I took her by the hand. "I know a good French restaurant near here. While we eat you can talk and I can sit and admire you."

"You'll have to promise that you won't get personal like that."

"Supposing I get personal *not* like that?"

By the time we reached the restaurant we were laughing together; you might have thought we were just getting to know each other. But in a matter of minutes the laughter had faded away, and we were face to face more nakedly than we had ever been before.

We had entered the restaurant and passed through the long narrow bar where three elderly Frenchmen were having their aperitifs, seated ourselves at the last table in the glassed-in garden din-

ing room off the courtyard and ordered our hors d'oeuvres, when
Teddy suddenly pouted, as one does when one remembers a forgotten obligation. Then she reached into her red-and-green, holiday-
decorated shopping bag and handed me back my story.

I stared at her, my spoonful of pickled beets suspended in air.

"Teddy," I said at last, "that was a present. A Christmas present.
You don't give back presents."

"I have to. I just can't accept it."

"But why?"

"It, uh —" Teddy swallowed. "It was insulting, that's why.
Here, take it, please! Then we won't have to talk about it."

"The hell we won't! Do you know how hard I worked on it?
Maybe it's not the greatest story in the world, but it's the best I have
in me, and you might at least have acknowledged it, even if you
didn't like it."

"But I did. I do." Teddy gazed at me in agony. "It's just that
you shouldn't have put down all those intimate details."

"I can't believe that you felt like that when you first read it," I
began, and then I stopped. A suspicion formed in my mind. "Wait
a minute. Did you show that story to anyone else?"

"Well . . . just to my mother."

"I knew it." I was too sickened to be triumphant. "You might
as well give me her literary verdict. I'm sure she had some memorable comment."

"She said it was dirty."

I jumped to my feet and flung down my napkin, knocking a knife
and a fork to the floor. My legs seemed to be entangled with my
half-tipped-over chair. A French family at the next table looked up
in surprise from its pot-au-feu. So did three ladies on the other
side of us.

With her knuckles at her lips, Teddy asked, "Where are you going?"

"I'm leaving. What did you expect?"

Ignoring the tears that were welling from her eyes and dropping
like little jewels onto her artichoke hearts, Teddy whispered,
"Please, please, please, don't go. Don't leave me like this."

Frightened by her tears and by the enormity of what I was about
to do — walk out on a sobbing girl under the disapproving gaze of a
room full of people — I hesitated.

Teddy went on. "I promise not to say anything more to upset you. All I ever wanted was for us to have fun together, without hurting anybody, before you shipped out."

So I sat down. Weeping softly, Teddy told me that I had expected too much of her from the start, that she wasn't like all the other, older girls with whom I had been intimate. (There had only been two, but Teddy imagined scores.)

"I suppose the trouble was," she mused sadly, somewhat more un-der control, "that it was all just a little too cold-blooded. If I had felt that you cared for me . . . I couldn't lie to my mother about that. Don't you see? Maybe she's not so smart, but she's all I've got, she and Stevie, and I have to live the way she expects me to. The way she wants me to."

If before, Teddy had made me enraged, now she was making me squirm. Seeing this, she reached over the *omelette aux fines herbes* with which we had been served, touched me lightly on the arm and added, "Don't ever think I'm not grateful. You can't imagine how much you've done for me."

Mollified, I disclaimed any special virtue, and we left the restau-rant almost as calmly as we had entered it. We strolled up to Forty-second and then east through Times Square to Bryant Park, stop-ping under the movie marquees to study the stills of the Ritz Broth-ers and the Three Stooges, of Lynn Bari and Jean Parker.

We sat on a stone bench under a leafless tree in Bryant Park, dis-cussing books and observing the types on their way into the li-brary. We were careful not to talk about ourselves, or about Christ-mas, or about what the New Year would bring; when we bumped knees, we excused ourselves. But then it began to rain again, the fine but mean rain of a Manhattan December; and as we looked hopelessly at each other and then at the forbidding bulk of the Li-brary, I remembered the movie houses on Forty-second Street.

"Come on," I said, "I'll take you to see *Intermezzo*."

"I really must go home. I'm expected."

"Not yet." I tugged her off the bench. "You yourself told me Ingrid Bergman is the most beautiful girl in the world; you bragged about seeing her in front of Bloomingdale's."

Laughing and protesting, Teddy allowed me to hurry her to the theater. But *Intermezzo* was a mistake. We had to sit through the last hour of an anti-Nazi epic plus a newsreel of Mrs. Thomas E.

Dewey launching a Liberty ship, before we were rewarded with
Leslie Howard making love to Ingrid Bergman. They went off together to celebrate their illicit passion in a sun-kissed Mediterranean
villa, knowing — or at least Ingrid knowing — that it could come
to no good end, and that she would have to tiptoe out of Leslie's life
in order to spare him for his art.

I sat with my arm around Teddy's shoulders, but I might as well
have clasped a statue. She held herself absolutely rigid and stared
fixedly at the screen through the little shell-rimmed glasses about
which she was no longer self-conscious, her elbows tight against
her sides, her fingers locked together in her lap. By the end of the
film I was intoxicated all over again with the odor of Teddy's damp
blond hair and lightly fragrant perfume, and she was biting her
lips, fighting back tears as Ingrid took leave of her unsuspecting
lover. The theme music swelled to a crescendo, and we groped our
way out to the street.

It was almost pitch-dark, and the rain was driving into our faces.
To my astonishment I captured a cab, and we tumbled gratefully
into it, slammed the door behind us, and waved the driver on. The
astonishment was nothing, though, to the shock I felt when Teddy
flung her arms around my neck, held me so tightly I could hardly
breathe, and kissed me as I had taught her to kiss.

My God! I thought (if I thought at all), have I won at the last
possible moment? And when the driver, by now well on the way
across town, called back, "Which way, folks?" I whispered to her,
"Let's go down to the apartment. Now!"

I have thought since then that if I had been more mature, more
masterful, if I had simply directed the driver down to Jane Street,
I might have won out. But I doubt it. For Teddy shook her head
fiercely, even while she continued to caress me, and muttered, "No,
no, no, I'm going home, I'm saying goodbye to you here."

We remained clasped in each other's arms all the way up to the
Bronx. In front of her apartment house while I stood, distraught,
counting bills into the cabdriver's hand, Teddy ran a comb through
her hair and apologized for the expense of the long ride.

"I'm the one who should apologize," I said, "for never taking
you home before. Let's go on up."

In the back of my mind, I suppose, was the final hope that Teddy's mother and brother would be out.

The old red brick building was shabby, with peeling hallways; what was worse, it was a walk-up, and Teddy lived on the top floor. We climbed slowly and awkwardly with our arms around each other's waists, and on the third floor Teddy told me, blushing, that we still had two more flights to go. "The higher you go, see, the cheaper the rent is."

As we moved dreamlike up the last flights, I thought how often she must have flitted up and down all these steps — no wonder she was so slim!

When we reached the top floor she indicated silently the door which was hers: 6B. But before she could say anything I unbuttoned her coat — my pea jacket was already open — and pulled her close to me. As I began to kiss her, she went limp. I was kissing her hair, her ears, her eyelids, her cheeks, but when I pressed my lips to hers she did not respond with the ardor that had so surprised me in the taxi; she remained passive, drooping like a flower deprived of sun, her eyes closed as I raised her unresisting arms and slipped them around my neck.

For some reason this passivity drove me wild and I tore blindly at her woolen dress. Her eyes fluttered, flooded with tears. I could taste them on my tongue as they coursed down her face.

Suddenly I was crying too. "Teddy, Teddy, Teddy," I whispered, and felt her give way in my arms. At that instant the door of 6B swung open, and Teddy's mother flew into the hall like some great bird of prey.

She could have been no older than I am now, but she seemed a dreadful old bag, a harpy, her hair half crammed into a net, her eyes darting venomously out of a craggy face greasy with cold cream. As I released Teddy, she pulled her coat together to cover her gaping dress, and then, yanked forward in her mother's iron grip, stumbled blindly into the sanctuary of their apartment. Her mother flashed me one scornful glance — part rage and part pure triumph — before she slammed the door.

I stood there dripping rain and sweat, too shocked even to be conscious of frustration, and my eye was caught by the Macy's shopping bag, crammed with gaily wrapped Christmas presents, that had fallen from Teddy's hand to the floor. I bent to pick it up, and the door opened again. Without a word Teddy's mother snatched the bag from me, and before I could open my mouth she had slammed the door again.

No doubt it was the shopping bag, decorated with holly and mistletoe, that reminded me of my story, my gift to Teddy. As I made my way slowly down the long flights of steps, pulling myself together to face what had to be faced in the world beyond Teddy, I discovered that I did not have the manuscript she had returned to me. It must have been kicked under the table at the restaurant, and as I swayed out into the dreary street I thought, Well, I'll never see the restaurant, I'll never see the story, I'll never see her. Never again.

I was right, of course; at least in that limited realization I was right, if in nothing else. But a few weeks ago I had to see an editor about a manuscript, and I drove into New York and parked in a West Side lot. It was a raw, wintry day, with the soundless wind rushing papers about the streets to remind one that, beyond the solid brick and stone, nature still strove to do one down. I gave myself an extra moment of my car heater's warmth before braving the cold, and while I was checking the contents of my briefcase and putting on my hat to protect my bald skull, I was overcome by the eerie sensation of having been here once before — in some different incarnation, younger, hatless, without a briefcase. But in an empty lot?

The attendant rapped on the car window with his knuckles. "What do you say, Mac, I haven't got all day. Leave the key in the car."

"Wait a minute," I said. "Do you live around here?"

"I was born exactly two blocks down the street." He was an underslung, argumentative Italian, remarkable only for his long nose, and for his pride in the place of his birth. "Anything you want to know about the neighborhood, ask."

"What used to be here, before the parking lot?"

"Rooming house, like every house on the block. Restaurant on the first floor."

My eyes began to smart. I closed them for a moment. "A French restaurant?"

"French, Italian, what's the difference? A restaurant."

I got out of the car and shuddered in the chill wind as loose sheets of paper plastered themselves against my shins. They were not likely to be pages of the story I had left behind, a story which had surely turned to ashes with the restaurant, and probably long before. The story was gone, so was the little blonde who had sat just here, weeping as she handed it back to me, one of the harshest rejections my work was ever to suffer — and so was I, the would-be writer, pompous but still unsure of his craft and of his magic charm.

We have all three died, as surely as if the war had done us in; but did we really die forever? Teddy still lives in my mind as she was then, whether she has gained the chairmanship of her P.T.A. or not. And I, too, live again in my mind as I was then, whether or not I have won my way to what I dearly desired to be — a celebrant of life in death. Only that well-meant and ill-written story, that rejected gift, deserved to die forever. These lines, called up by the sudden stinging recollection of two young strangers, the boy and girl at the last table of the garden restaurant, yearning for everything but understanding nothing — these lines are the real story for Teddy.

ROBERT PENN WARREN

Have You Seen Sukie?

(FROM THE VIRGINIA QUARTERLY REVIEW)

THE Warden — hundred-and-fifty-dollar, glittering black, custom-made boots, gray pants hanging over and short enough to show the expensive black leather, black frock coat long enough to exaggerate the height of strung-out bone, a bony sepulchral face with a hair-line black mustache and a too neatly clipped graying Vandyke, po-maded hair on which was set as carefully as on a show-window dummy a beautiful and authentic panama hat of enormous brim and delicately pinched-in sides — had received them. The Warden, leaning on his ebony cane with the gold head, said he was sure glad, yes sir, to have the letter from the Commissioner about Mr. Jones. He only wished he could hang around now, he sure did, and do it all personal. Then he gave a thin, conniving smile from under the hairline mustache, the smile appropriate to an obscene, man-to-man confidence, twitched one eye in the high sepulchral face into a wink that gave the abrupt impression of bone winking, and uttered one word: "Politics."

He said he had to go politicking. There was going to be a primary. He had to work for the right man, he said, and again the bone seemed to wink.

He turned them over to Mr. Budd — "Boots" Budd, who was one foot shorter and two feet wider than the Warden. Mr. Budd's square face, rust-red from weathering, was noncommittal in the in-troduction, but his enormous hand was not: it was, quite casually, bone-crushing. Mr. Budd said that he was the Deputy Warden; that he was the officer of discipline and welfare, the word *discipline* be-

ing pronounced with a strong accent on the second syllable; that he
had been a guard, then Yard Lieutenant before the War; that he
had got to be Deputy Warden after he came out of the First Airborne; that long back, ever since he figured out his legs were too
short to ever make world champion heavyweight, he had wanted
to be Deputy Warden and now by God he was; that he ran the pen
clean, hard, and fair, which, he said, is the only way to run a pen
if you don't want steel in you, like the Deputy before him got it;
and that the First Airborne and the pen was all he knew and he was
satisfied and maybe he had rather be Deputy Warden than world
champion heavyweight. His voice moved in a dry, rasping mono-
tone, not loud, and when the words were over one felt, looking at
that rust-red noncommittal face that Mr. Budd was a taciturn man,
that he had made only a minimal utterance, and that the information you had was nothing he had said but something you had heard
long back, from other sources.

They had long since passed the great steel doors. They stood
in the cold light of the cell block, on one side the bare brick wall
lifting twenty feet before the barred windows even began, on the
other side the cages stacked three high, steel catwalks hung along
the front of each level. The cages were empty now. In some there
were pictures gummed to the cement of the back wall, photographs of persons, a magazine beauty, a watercolor of a landscape
or a bulldog done without talent. In some there were bits of carpet
on the cement floor. In one a bit of scrim curtain cozily hung on
each side of the open-barred cell front.

"Some," Mr. Budd said, pointing with his walking stick, "they
try to make it homey."

"Yes," Yasha Jones murmured, studying the scene, "homey."

"It is the nearest thing some of 'em ever had to a home," Mr.
Budd said. Then, after a moment, added: "It is the only one some
will ever have."

He stood there scrutinizing the block.

"But some," he said, "they don't want nothing. They want it
bare. You could fix it up like the Hermitage Hotel in Nashville,
and they would throw it out. Having it bare is the kind of homey
they want. Bare is their kind of homey. They are built like that."

He continued to scrutinize the block.

"It ought to be torn down," he said, glumly. "This block."

"Why?" Yasha Jones said.

"Ain't enough money in half this state to fix a pen like it ought to be, so there ain't much use in asking why. But I'll tell you. An-tee-quated. It is an-tee-quated. This part was the part old Colonel Fiddler built — when he was Governor and made 'em do something for Fiddlersburg. Built their second pen here long back. After the Civil War, I reckin. Got a oil painting of Governor Fiddler downstairs. You can see it."

He nodded toward Brad.

"Git him to tell you," he said to Yasha Jones. "Knows more about them Fiddlers than I do." He meditated a moment. " 'Cept fer one," he said.

"Yes," Brad said. "Except for one."

Mr. Budd moved on, his thick rubber soles making no noise on the cement.

"Are you armed?" Yasha Jones asked.

"Don't allow no guns in," Mr. Budd said. "Guns give somebody the notion of tryen to take a gun off somebody. But heft this," he said, holding out his stick, head foremost.

Yasha took it.

"Hold it by the little end," Mr. Budd continued. "Heft it."

Yasha Jones obeyed. The stem was slightly flexible. The head was a heavy knob. The balance was inviting.

"Bamboo on steel rod," Mr. Budd said, and reached out and retrieved the stick. "Lead in the head. If you can use this here you don't need no gun." He hefted it gently. "They know what it can do," he said. "They stand back. They don't come crowding. I never had to use it but once. Long back."

They moved to the end of the block. "See that pillow?" he demanded pointing to the lower of the two shelf bunks in the last cage.

They nodded.

"They was a head on it one morning," he said. "Setten on the pillow. The eyes was open, and the tongue was hanging out." He paused a moment. "The body was under the bed," he said.

He moved on.

"Gal-boys," he said. "It is hard to keep down trouble in a pen. If I could get shet of these old double cages, then — "

He did not finish. A guard, a harmless looking middle-aged

man, clearly not in good trim, fumbling and clanking his keys, passed them into another section. There three convicts were scrubbing the floor. "Good morning, Mr. Budd — Good morning, Mr. Budd — Good morning, Mr. Budd," they said in voices of identical respect.

"Good morning, Hamlin," Mr. Budd said. "Burrus. Coffey."

His voice was easy, the raspiness thinning almost to a whisper. They moved on. Mr. Budd did not turn his head.

"Do you know all their names?" Yasha Jones asked.

"I know every God-damned name," Mr. Budd said.

Yasha Jones studied the rust-colored stiff neck ahead of him.

"Do you never turn your head?" he asked. "To look back?"

Mr. Budd did not turn his head.

"You get the habit of turning yore head," he said, "and you will soon get the habit of being dead. They will know something is gone rotten in you. If you can't tell all you need to know without turnen yore head, you better git into another line of work. Like shoe-clerken," he said.

He stopped suddenly, and swung on them.

"You know the loudest noise in a pen?" he demanded, leaning at them.

"No," Yasha Jones said.

"Silence," Mr. Budd said.

He turned, and moved on.

They went to the shops ("Good mornen, Mr. Budd — Good mornen, Mr. Budd"). They went to the store, where the souvenirs, made by the convicts on their own time, were for sale ("Yeah, they can save up money, for comen-out time"). They went to the gymnasium, grim and under-equipped, but a gymnasium ("Yeah, when I come in as Deppity, I come to trouble. So I got up a-fore 'em and told 'em. I said, I am runnen this joint. Any man thinks he can, and I will let him put the gloves on for ten rounds, pro referee. If he takes me he will git ice cream for a month. If I take him, it is solitary for a week. Nobody said a word. The Commissioner — he got sore. Made me stop it. Hell, maybe just as well. A man gits older and softens up. But hell, them days I was hard-bellied. You could bark yore knucks on my belly"). They went to the kitchen ("Clean — yeah, clean, hard, and fair is my motto, and I start with clean"). They watched the long lines file into the hall. They saw the two guards quietly pick a man from line ("Look at his face. It is dope. Got it on him now. A stool pigeon tipped us this mornen. You can't run a pen without no stools"). They sat at a table on a platform, visible to all, where they were served by trusties. ("They kin see me eat what they got to eat, no different. One time a day.")

They came out of the mess hall.

"We will go to the hospital," Mr. Budd said. "We runs it. Some of our boys have learned right well. But we got a real pharmacist. Gonna have him a long time. Had him a nice drugstore in Brownsville and killed his wife. She caught him with the soda fountain gal. We are waiten for a real good doctor somewhere in this here state to kill his wife for ketchen him with the nurse."

Mr. Budd paused to laugh.

"A guy gets real sick we got to call in a outside doc," he said. "Not we ain't got a good inside doc. Went to Johns Hopkins. He was a good doc fer us. But he lost confidence. He says he is afraid of doctoren now. Real doctoren. He just sort of piddles around the place. Hell, he'll even empty bedpans, do stuff the nigger orderlies is supposed to do. He helps out, but he has lost confidence."

They went into the hospital and saw the doctor who had lost confidence. He was a tall, thin man with a graceful crest of gray hair above the gray face. He smiled from his infinite distance and had nothing to say to them. So they came out and stood on the gravel in the middle of the inner yard, beside a circular bed of canna lilies, the red of fresh-sliced calf liver, and the sun beat down.

Yasha Jones, thoughtful, lifted his head toward one of the big squat towers that squared the outer walls. Up there a man was leaning on the parapet. Sunlight, far off there, gleamed on what he had in his hand, lying across the parapet.

Mr. Budd followed his gaze.

"That is Lem," Mr. Budd said, "and I'll show you what Lem kin do."

They climbed to the tower and he showed them.

"Show 'em, Lem," Mr. Budd said, when the introductions had been completed, and each, in turn, had grasped, then relinquished, the hand that was offered, offered hanging off a thin wrist, the hand itself long and thin and dry, giving the impression, when touched, of a dried herring hung up by the tail.

Lem stood there, waiting.

"Yonder," Mr. Budd said, "see that sparrow, must be a sparrow, setten on that flagpole?"

The flagpole jutted high, at an angle, above the entrance of the prison. The sparrow sat on the knob. It was a full thirty yards.

"You bust that knob," Mr. Budd said to Lem, "and I'll dock yore pay."

Lem said nothing. The rifle started up slow. Then, suddenly, it was at the shoulder, from the muzzle a wisp of gray smoke threaded, and the sparrow was not on the knob.

Lem turned away, diffident and sad.

"The feller up here a-fore Lem," Mr. Budd said, "he was nigh handy as Lem. But I had to fire him. He lost me a guard. One day a gardener, a trusty, started on that guard with a sickle. Just got grudge-happy and started choppen, with folks standen round watchen, and you know, would you believe it?"

He stopped and stared at them, overwhelmed by the old incredulity.

"Yeah," he said, "and thet feller up here, he ne'er fired a round. Hell, I marched him to look at that-air sickle-work. 'You think you kin shoot,' I said to him. 'All right, why didn't you shoot?' And you know what the son-of-a-bitch said?"

He stopped, again overwhelmed.

"Well, I'll tell you. He said he was afraid of hitten a innocent man. You know what I said to him?"

"No," Yasha Jones finally said.

" 'Jesus Christ,' I said, 'a innocent man! There ain't no innocent man! You are fired.' "

The old rage, the old incredulity, still smouldering, Mr. Budd stared down at the yard where the sickle-work had taken place, where now four gardeners squatted, weeding a pansy border.

"You know," he said, brooding, not looking at them, "if you turned out every guy in the pen tomorrow mornen — yeah, with $1000 apiece — most of 'em would be back in six months. Hell, even them as plans breaks, they don't really want out. They want something but it ain't out. They want in."

He swung suddenly at them.

"You know why they got in in the first place?" he demanded. Then drove on: "It is because they are lonesome. Some folks are born lonesome and they can't stand the lonesomeness out there. It is lonesome in here maybe but it ain't as lonesome when you are with folks that knows they are as lonesome as you are."

"Mr. Budd," Yasha Jones said, "you are a philosopher."

"I am a Deppity Warden," Mr. Budd said.

His gaze roved slowly over the yards, over the reach of wall, back over the yards. He seemed to have forgotten them.

"You ever seen a man come out of solitary?" Mr. Budd asked, not even turning to them.

"No," Brad said.

"Sometimes," Mr. Budd said, "it is like they wanted to lay their head in your lap and cry. They are so grateful to you. Solitary," he continued, "you can't run a pen without it. It is the last lonesomeness. It is the kind of lonesomeness a man can't stand, for he can't stand just being himself."

Mr. Budd stopped. His gaze had never turned on them. It roved the yards, the walls, the roofs.

"Mr. Budd," Yasha Jones said.

"Yeah."

"Mr. Budd, what will happen when the water starts to rise? When the river floods all the land around the prison?"

"Trouble," Mr. Budd said. He paused: "You kin feel it starten now."

"But, Mr. Budd," Yasha Jones said, "if being in is what they want, and the rising of the waters makes them more cut-off from the outside lonesomeness, more in, then — "

"Hell," Mr. Budd said, "I never said the sons-of-bitches knows what they wants."

"Yes," Yasha Jones said, quietly, "yes."

"Let's go see Sukie," Mr. Budd said, rousing himself, it seemed, from meditation.

"What is Sukie?" Brad asked.

"You'll see," Mr. Budd said.

"Wait a minute," Mr. Budd said, "and I'll show you somebody else who is going to see Sukie, and see her soon. Four dollars and ninety-three cents," Mr. Budd continued in that raspy, whispery voice, standing there just inside the steel door. "That was what he chopped her up fer. A old woman runnen a store out in the sticks, late at night. She came in and caught him at the cash register. He really chopped. With a hatchet he picked up. Looked like when he started choppen he couldn't stop. Didn't more'n half try to hide, neither. Stuck his bloody shirt down a privy hole and went to bed. Now all he does is set. Set and maybe make some music on his box. Won't pray or nuthen. The nigger preacher, he comes every day, but he won't pray. You know, folks downtown they done got so they stop the nigger preacher on the street and ask him, 'Has yore boy prayed yit? Has he done cracked yit?' It looks like folks is worked up and got to know."

Mr. Budd paused. "Well," he said then, "he has got three weeks to go. Three weeks a-fore he sees Sukie. You can do a lot of prayen in three weeks."

His rubber soles moved down the corridor, then stopped in front of the cell. The Negro man, a young man, sat on the cot, wearing gray denim pants, no belt, khaki shirt, tennis shoes with no strings. His face was very dark, very smooth. His hands were curled on his lap, as though they, like pets, were adjusted to sleep. He stared fixedly at an invisible spot on the wall opposite him.

Mr. Budd tapped gently on the steel with his cane.

"Pretty-Boy," he said, in his raspy, whispery tone.

The man looked up.

"How you feelen, Pretty-Boy?" Mr. Budd asked.

"All right," the man said.

"Want to make some music?" Mr. Budd said.

The hands on the man's lap stirred. One reached out and lifted the guitar that lay on the cot beside him. He began to sing to the music, low and throaty.

> *Where did you come from?*
> *Where do you go?*
> *Where do you come from,*
> *Cotton-eye Joe?*
>
> *Come fer to see you,*
> *Come fer to sing,*
> *Come fer to show you*
> *My di-mint ring.*

All the while he played, his eyes remained fixed on the invisible spot on the wall. When he had stopped singing, the eyes never moved.

"Thank you, Pretty-Boy," Mr. Budd said. "These gentlemin here — I am sure they 'preciate it."

"I appreciate it," Yasha Jones said.

The man lifted his face toward Yasha Jones, and peered studiously at him. "Thank ye," he said, then.

The eyes returned to the spot on the wall.

Mr. Budd peered assessingly into the cell. After a moment, he said: "Listen, Pretty."

The man turned his head.

"You gonna make it, Pretty," Mr. Budd said, in the raspy whisper, and moved up the corridor, the rubber soles making their silence on the cement.

"You mean he is going to make what?" Brad asked him. "You mean he is going to pray?"

"I mean he is goen to rise up and walk," Mr. Budd said. "When the time comes. He is goen to rise up and walk right down this here corridor. Like a man."

They stood before the door.

"Do most of them make it?" Yasha Jones asked.

"You'd be surprised," Mr. Budd said, "at 'em as can make it. Once a man gits the notion it is his one and only and last chance to be a man. I say to 'em, 'It is yore last chance. It is yore job and nobody can do it fer you.' I say, 'Maybe you never done a decent day's work in yore life, but here is a job you can't pass.' I say, 'I am pullen fer you.' You'd be surprised."

He paused.

"Yeah," he said then, "you take one last year. A real little puke. Time nigh come, he sent fer me. 'Mr. Budd,' he said, 'I means to make it. My legs may give when I come to the door, but I mean to make it. If my legs give, you tell 'em not to carry me to the chair. Tell 'em just to set my feet over the sill. I aim to make it.'"

"Did he make it?" Yasha Jones said.

"He done it," Mr. Budd said.

"Mr. Budd," Yasha Yones said.

"Yeah?"

"Why did you call him Pretty-Boy? The one back there, I mean."

"It is his name," Mr. Budd said. "It is the name his mother give him. It is the name he was tried by. It is the name the doctor will write on the papers when they take out the fried meat. Pretty-Boy."

Mr. Budd looked back down the corridor.

"Look," he said. "There comes the preacher. Brother Pinckney. The nigger preacher, I mean. Maybe he will crack him today."

And then, as the guard arrived to open the door, he said, "Here is Sukie."

He stepped into the room.

Mr. Budd stopped to pat the back of the chair.

"She is waiten here with her arms wide open," he said. "She is waiten and she will take you when you come. She is ever-man's sweetheart. She will give any man a ride. She is the gal with the juice. She will give a man a jerk like he ain't never had. Sukie hugs you once, you ain't never gonna want no other kind of a jerk."

Mr. Budd, with his rubber-soled ease, had swung around, and dropped himself into the chair. "You come in yonder," he said, nodding back toward the door, now closed. "You take a seat. You lean back restful."

He leaned back.

"You lays yore arms on the arms of the chair."

He performed the action, laying his arms on the straps.

"You sets yore legs straight."

He set his feet straight on the floor. The electrodes were there.

"You holds yore head steady and they drops a black cap on."

He adjusted an imaginary cap.

"They pulls the big cap down, the one with the business, and you are ready to ride. Sukie is achen to go. She is groanen with the juice."

He sat there a moment as though the other men were not there, in that moment looking down, it seemed, at his own body in the chair. Suddenly he lifted his head at them with a glint of cold challenge sudden in the pale gray eyes. "You know what I am?" he demanded.

No one answered.

He said: "I am the executioner for this here state. I am the guy that throws the switch."

He picked up his right arm from the arm of the chair where it had been lying on the straps. He scrutinized the hand as though discovering a new interest in the object. He lifted it that others might see better.

"That is what throws the switch," he said. "It has lost count." He studied the hand. "Long a-fore I was Deppity," he said, "it was throwen the switch."

He lost interest in the hand, and again looked at them.

"Twenty bucks a throw," he said. "Same price it was before the War, inflation and all. Yeah," he said, "you used to buy somethen with twenty bucks. Buy a pretty for a gal and maybe grab a piece off'n her, her bein softened up and grateful. Or hell, jist git drunk."

For an instant longer he sat there, then suddenly rose from the chair. He leaned at Brad. "You set there," he commanded.

Brad looked at him, at the sudden cold gray challenge of the glance in that rust-colored face. Then he looked down at the matter-of-factness of old oily sweat-soaked wood and leather and metal, set in the dreary cleanliness of the little room. He thought of how you would come through the little door and would not be able to believe that this was all, that this matter-of-factness, the dreary matter-of-factness of an antiquated dental chair discarded in a junk shop, was all. He thought how, in that instant, a wave of deprivation, of irremediable diminishment, would sweep over you. Was this all? Was everything as inconsequential as this? Just this old chair in a junk shop.

"Won't you kindly set?" Mr. Budd invited, with a courtly gesture.

Brad sat in the chair.

Mr. Budd leaned at him from one side, over him, speaking in his raspy voice. "Listen," Mr. Budd said, not very loud, leaning, "you do one thing now."

"What?" Brad said.

"Think of the worst thing you ever done," Mr. Budd said, whispering, and suddenly peered into Brad's face; then broke into roars of throaty laughter.

When he had conquered his mirth, Mr. Budd slapped Brad on the shoulder, then turned to Yasha Jones. "It is my joke," he said. "It's a joke I pull on folks. Hell, you oughta see some of the faces on some of 'em. Hell, one time a man just pee-ed in the chair."

He turned to Brad, who now stood there, looking down at the chair, and again gave him the brotherly slap of the shoulder. "Hell," he said, "you didn' pee."

"Mr. Budd," Yasha Jones said, "I should like to sit in the chair."

"Sure," Mr. Budd said, "she is ever-man's sweetheart. Sukie — she is waiten fer you."

Yasha Jones took his place, adjusted himself. "I suppose I would spare you the usual haircut," he said, and smiled, a simple smile with no wryness in it.

"Yep," Mr. Budd said, looking at the baldness.

Yasha Jones was still smiling up at Mr. Budd. "Aren't you going to ask me the question?" he said.

Brad stared down at the brown, aquiline face that was smiling there, under the shadow of the heavy leather-and-metal cap, and wondered what was the worst thing that that man — his friend — had ever done. He was wondering this, he knew, because when he himself had sat there under that question, he had been able to think of nothing, nothing at all. He had not pee-ed, but he had been able to think of nothing.

BIOGRAPHICAL NOTES

Biographical Notes

FRIEDA ARKIN was born in Brooklyn, but raised in a small village in upper New York State. She received her B.A. from the University of Chicago and her M.S., in anthropology, from Columbia University. She taught anthropology at Hunter College for seven years before deciding to devote herself thereafter to her husband, two children, and the writing of fiction. Seven of her short stories have been published to date, and she is currently at work on a novel about the small Dutch-founded village in which she grew up.

RICHARD G. BROWN's varied careers have included sailing with the Merchant Marine for two years, working in oil fields in Texas and Louisiana, clerking in an office in Los Angeles, writing advertising copy, and being a mailman. A course in creative writing given by Alice Frances Wright in Long Beach gave him the incentive to begin a writing career. Mr. Brown is now working on a play and a novel about the Merchant Marine.

JOHN STEWART CARTER was born in Chicago where he still lives. He attended Northwestern and Harvard, and received his Ph.D. from the University of Chicago. Except for a four-year stint as a lieutenant in the Navy, one year's research under a Ford Foundation grant and a year's leave as Fulbright Professor of American Literature at the University of Teheran, he has spent all his professional life at Chicago Teachers College, where he is a professor of English. Mr. Carter is married and has two daughters. His poetry appears frequently in literary magazines.

DANIEL CURLEY was born in 1918 in East Bridgewater, Massachusetts. He received his bachelor's and master's degrees from the

University of Alabama and has taught at Syracuse University, State Teachers College at Plattsburg, New York, and since 1955 at the University of Illinois. He was an editor of *Accent* for the last five years of its existence and a Guggenheim Fellow in 1958. *That Marriage Bed of Procrustes*, a collection of stories, appeared in 1957, and in 1958 his novel *How Many Angels?* His stories have appeared widely in the literary quarterlies and a new novel, *A Stone Man, Yes*, was published in the summer of 1964.

MAY DIKEMAN was born in Baldwin, Long Island, majored in painting at New York's High School of Music and Art, and was graduated from Vassar, where she studied under John Malcolm Brinnin. In 1961 she was given the Atlantic First Award for her short story "The Tender Mercies." Other stories have appeared in *Harper's* and an early novel, *The Pike*, was published in 1954. Her story "The Sound of Young Laughter" appeared in the 1963 volume of *The Best American Short Stories*. She lives in New York City with her three children.

WILLIAM EASTLAKE was born in New York City of parents who came from Cornwall, England, but has lived most of his life in the far West. He spent four years in the infantry during World War II. For the past eight years he has been living on a cattle ranch in northern New Mexico. His work has appeared in a great many magazines and reviews and in numerous short story collections and college textbooks. He has published three novels, the latest of which is *Portrait of an Artist with Twenty-six Horses*. A war novel, *The Castle*, is now in progress. Mr. Eastlake's avocations are chasing wild horses and trying to save the West's mountain lions and coyotes from extinction.

WILLIAM GOYEN is well known as a short story writer, novelist and playwright. His stories have appeared in most of the major American magazines and in several editions of *The Best American Short Stories*. His novels include *The House of Breath*, *Ghost and Flesh*, *In a Farther Country*, *The Faces of Blood*, and *The Fair Sister*. Three of Mr. Goyen's plays have been produced and he is Playwright-in-Residence at the Repertory Theatre of Lincoln Center, New York, for 1963-64.

PAUL HORGAN, novelist, short story writer and historian, has received recognition as a ranking American author at every stage of his career, beginning with his Harper prize-winning first novel, *The Fault of Angels*. He is the author of nine other full-length novels and many volumes of short fiction. As a historian, he is perhaps best known for *Great River: The Rio Grande in North American History,* winner of the Pulitzer and Bancroft prizes in history, and *Citizen of New Salem,* a short historical work about the young manhood of Lincoln. His novel *A Distant Trumpet,* published in 1960, received wide acclaim. "Black Snowflakes" is a section from Mr. Horgan's most recent novel, *Things As They Are.* Mr. Horgan is at present a Director of the Center for Advanced Studies at Wesleyan University. He is a member of the National Institute of Arts and Letters.

WILLIAM HUMPHREY was born in Clarksville, Texas, on June 18, 1924. His first book, *The Last Husband and Other Stories,* was published in 1953. His first novel, *Home from the Hill,* appeared in 1958; a second, *Look Away, Look Away* is to be published in the fall of 1964. Mr. Humphrey and his wife now live in Lexington, Virginia.

SHIRLEY JACKSON, who was born in San Francisco and spent most of her early life in California, is now living in Vermont. She is particularly well known for her short stories. Her books include such novels as *Sundial* and *The Bird's Nest,* a nonfiction best seller, *Life Among the Savages,* and *We Have Always Lived in the Castle.*

EDITH KONECKY is a native New Yorker who now lives in Scarsdale. She attended New York University and Columbia. Her stories have been published in *Story, Esquire, The Kenyon Review,* and *The Massachusetts Review.* She is now at work on her first novel.

KIMON LOLOS was born in Salonika, Greece, and received his Ll.B. from the University of Athens. He served in the Greek Army during World War II. Since 1950 Mr. Lolos has lived in the United States and he is now a naturalized citizen. He has studied at the State University of Iowa and at the Carnegie Institute of Technology. Mr. Lolos writes both in Greek and in English; two novels, *Respite* and *Under the Circumstances,* have been published in this country. At present he writes and gives weekly talks on the arts and letters for the Voice of America. He is working on two novellas and a number of short stories. "Mule No. 095" was reprinted in the January 1964 issue of *Short Story International.*

BERNARD MALAMUD was born in Brooklyn and attended CCNY and

Columbia. After college he worked at odd jobs, then began to teach evening school and write during the day. After five years of life in Greenwich Village he moved to Corvallis, Oregon, where he combined teaching at Oregon State College with a writing career. He has been the recipient of several literary awards, the latest being the National Book Award for Fiction in 1959. His short stories have been published in many periodicals and anthologies. "The German Refugee" also appears in *Idiots First,* a recent collection of his stories.

CARSON McCULLERS, with her first extraordinary novel *The Heart Is a Lonely Hunter* (1940), took a secure place in American fiction. She is also the author of the very successful play and motion picture *The Member of the Wedding* (1946) and in 1958 her play *Square Root of Wonderful* was produced. Her most recent novel, on which she worked for nearly fifteen years, was *Clock Without Hands* (1961). She was awarded the International Publishers Prize in 1963 and has won two Guggenheim Fellowships and an award from The American Academy of Arts and Letters.

VIRGINIA MORICONI was born in New York City where she worked in the theatre for Robert Edmond Jones. Her novel *The Distant Trojans* was published in 1948 and in 1962 she translated *The Deserter* by Giuseppe Dessi. Her story "The Maternal Element" appeared in June 1964 in *The Transatlantic Review* and she is now working on another short story. Mrs. Moriconi is married to an Italian painter and lives in Rome.

JOYCE CAROL OATES was born in Lockport, New York, received her B.A. from Syracuse University and her M.A. from the University of Wisconsin. She and her husband live in Detroit, where she is on the faculty of the University of Detroit. She was the winner of the 1959 *Mademoiselle* College Fiction Contest, and her stories have appeared in many magazines, such as *Colorado Quarterly, Prairie Schooner, MSS,* and *Cosmopolitan.* A collection of her stories, *By the North Gate,* was published in 1963.

REYNOLDS PRICE was born in North Carolina in 1933 and received his Bachelor of Arts degree from Duke University. He studied as a Rhodes Scholar for three years at Merton College, Oxford, where he received his Bachelor of Letters. In 1958 he returned to Duke where he teaches in the Department of English. His first novel, *A Long and Happy Life,* published in 1962, received the award of the William Faulkner Foundation for the most notable first novel published by an American in that year. A collection of stories, *The Names and Faces of Heroes,* titled after the story in this collection, appeared in 1964.

VERA RANDAL was born in New York City and attended Connecticut College in New London. She and her husband, four children, and three Siamese cats still live in Manhattan. A novel, *The Inner Room,* is scheduled for publication in September, 1964; a section from it has appeared in *The New Yorker* under the title "Alice Blaine."

HARVEY SWADOS is the author of half a dozen books and the editor of a seventh, an anthology of the muckrakers entitled *Years of Conscience.* His most recent novel, *The Will,* was preceeded by his collected essays, *A Radical's America* (1962), the novel *False Coin* (1960), a book of connected stories entitled *On the Line* (1957), and his first novel, *Out Went the Candle* (1955). Born in Buffalo in 1920, graduate of the University of Michigan in 1940, he has lived for many years with his wife and children in Valley Cottage, New York, where he writes and teaches part time as a member of the faculty of Sarah Lawrence College. He is now at work on a new anthology, a new collection of stories, and a long novel.

ROBERT PENN WARREN, a highly versatile writer, has won wide acclaim for his short stories, poetry and novels. In 1946 he was awarded the Pulitzer Prize for Fiction for *All the King's Men* and in 1958 the Pulitzer Prize for Poetry for *Promises: Poems.* He is co-founder and editor of *The Southern Review* and a member of the Fugitive group of poets. His latest novel, *Flood,* was published in 1964.

THE
YEARBOOK
OF THE
AMERICAN SHORT STORY

January 1 to December 31, 1963

Roll of Honor, 1963

I. *American Authors*

ARKIN, FRIEDA
  The Broomstick on the Porch. Kenyon Review, Summer.

BONGARTZ, ROY
  For Benny . . . Much Loved. New Yorker, September 14.

BRODKY, HAROLD
  The Abundant Dreamer. New Yorker, Nov. 23.

BROWN, RICHARD G.
  Mr. Iscariot. Literary Review, Summer.

BURNHAM, TOM
  The Price. Georgia Review, Summer.

CARTER, JOHN STEWART
  To a Tenor Dying Old. Kenyon Review, Autumn.

CHEEVER, JOHN
  The Embarkment for Cythera. New Yorker, Nov. 16.

CORRINGTON, JOHN WILLIAM
  Reunion. Southwest Review, Summer.

CURLEY, DANIEL
  A Story of Love, Etc. Epoch, Spring.

DIKEMAN, MAY
  The Woman Across the Street. Atlantic, Nov.

EASTLAKE, WILLIAM
  A Long Day's Dying. Virginia Quarterly Review, Winter.

ELY, DAVID
  The Human Factor. Saturday Evening Post, Nov. 16.

FICHTER, ROBERT
  We Listenin': Teach On. Transatlantic Review, Spring.

FLOWERS, LEE WINNIFORD
  Last Night on Fant Hill. Literary Review, Winter.

GALLANT, MAVIS
  The Ice Wagon Going Down the Street. New Yorker, Dec. 14.

GASTER, THEODOR
  ? Literary Review, Winter.

GILBERT, SISTER MARY
  The Bird Watcher. Minnesota Review, Summer.

GIPSON, FRED
  Papa's Straw Hat. Southwest Review, Summer.

GOYEN, WILLIAM
  Figure Over the Town. Saturday Evening Post, April 27.

HORGAN, PAUL
  Black Snowflakes. Saturday Evening Post, March 30.

HUMPHREY, WILLIAM
The Ballad of Jesse Neighbours. Esquire, Sept.
The Pump. Esquire, Dec.

IORIO, JOHN J.
Paradise Acres. University Review, Winter.

JACKSON, SHIRLEY
Birthday Party. Vogue, Jan. 1.
JONES, JAMES
The Valentine. Saturday Evening Post, Feb. 16.

KESSLER, SYDNEY
That Which Was Once a War. Epoch, Fall.
KONECKY, EDITH
The Power. Massachusetts Review, Summer.
KOKJOHN, JOSEPH, E.
Dearly Beloved. Harper's Magazine, Sept.

LA FARGE, OLIVER
Caviar Remembered. Esquire. Oct.
LAURENCE, MARGARET
Mask of Beaten Gold. Tamarack Review, Autumn.
LOLOS, KIMON
Mule No. 095. Carleton Miscellany, Summer.
LUDWIG, JACK
A Woman of Her Age. Quarterly Review of Literature, Vol. XII, No. 3.

MALAMUD, BERNARD
The Refugee. Saturday Evening Post, Sept. 14.
MATHEWS, MARTHIEL
A Region of Time. Hudson Review, Winter.
MORICONI, VIRGINIA
Simple Arithmetic. Transatlantic Review, Spring.
McCORMICK, JAMES
Wunderjude. Kenyon Review, Summer.

McKINLEY, GEORGIA
Shall We Gather at the River? Redbook, August.
McCULLERS, CARSON
Sucker. Saturday Evening Post, Sept. 28.

OATES, JOYCE CAROL
Upon the Sweeping Flood. Southwest Review, Spring.
Stigmata. Colorado Quarterly, Spring.
O'HARA, JOHN
Aunt Anna. Saturday Evening Post, March 23.

PACKER, NANCY HUDDLESTON
Once a Thief. Southwest Review, Summer.
PEDEN, WILLIAM
The Cross Country Dog. University Review, Autumn.
PRICE, REYNOLDS
The Names and Faces of Heroes. Shenandoah, Summer.

RANDAL, VERA
Waiting for Jim. Colorado Quarterly, Summer.
ROTH, ARTHUR J.
The Expatriates. Critic, June-July.
RUGEL, MIRIAM
The Sweet Forever. Saturday Evening Post, June 15.

STERN, RICHARD
Teeth. Partisan Review, Fall.
SWADOS, HARVEY
A Story for Teddy. Saturday Evening Post, Nov. 23.

TAYLOR, PETER
Two Pilgrims. New Yorker, Sept. 7.
TURNER, CLAYTON
Something Lost. Arizona Quarterly, Autumn.

WARREN, ROBERT PENN
Have You Seen Sukie? Virginia Quarterly Review, Autumn.

WEATHERS, WINSTON
The Gifts We Bear. New Mexico
Quarterly, Autumn.
WINDHAM, DONALD
A Leave-Taking. New Yorker, July
13.

WOLF, LEONARD
Fifty-Fifty. Kenyon Review, Autumn.

ZIMPEL, LLOYD
Sleeve. Massachusetts Review, Spring.

II. *Foreign Authors*

CHEKHOV, ANTON
Late-Blooming Flowers. Ladies'
Home Journal, Nov.

DELANEY, SHELAGH
Sweetly Sings the Donkey. Saturday
Evening Post, May 18.

GREENE, GRAHAM
"Dear Dr. Falkenheim." Vogue, Jan.
1.
GRIFFIN, WYNN
A Significant Experience. Saturday
Evening Post, Sept. 21.

KAZAKOV, YURI
Autumn in the Oak Woods. Esquire,
Oct.
On the Island. Esquire, Dec.
KERSH, GERALD
A Bargain with Kashel. Saturday
Evening Post, Apr. 27.

LESSING, DORIS
A Letter from Home. Partisan Review, Summer.

MACINTYRE, THOMAS
Epithalamion. Transatlantic Review,
Spring.

McGAHERN, JOHN
The Barracks. Transatlantic Review,
Spring.
MULISCH, HARRY
The Crown Prince. Transatlantic
Review, Spring.

NAIPAUL, V. S.
The Night Watchman's Occurrence
Book. Saturday Evening Post, Sept.
26.

O'FAOLAIN, SEAN
Too Beautiful, Too Good. Ladies'
Home Journal, Oct.

SILLITOE, ALAN
The Ragman's Daughter. New
Yorker, Aug. 3.

VINCENT, M. G.
The Eye Stopper. Literary Review,
Winter.

WILSON, H. H.
The Firebreak. Literary Review,
Winter.
WUORIO, EVA-LIS
The Singing Silence. Saturday Eve-
ning Post, March 23.

Distinctive Short Stories in American Magazines, 1963

I. *American Authors*

ABBE, GEORGE
Larky. New Mexico Quarterly, Autumn.

ADDINGTON, LUTHER F.
Uncle Waldo and Aunt Mandy. Arizona Quarterly, Spring.
The Old Mullins Place. Arizona Quarterly, Winter.

ALLEN, JOHN HOUGHTON
A Parable. Southwest Review, Summer.

ARKIN, FRIEDA
The Broomstick on the Porch. Kenyon Review, Summer.
Miss Dunphy Is Dead. Georgia Review, Fall.

AUCHINCLOSS, LOUIS
The Deductible Yacht. Harper's Magazine, February.

BARTH, JOHN
Water-Message. Southwest Review, Summer.

BERCOVITCH, REUBEN
Crazy Foal. Literary Review, Winter.

BERGE, WILLIAM
Special Leave for Rest Camp. December, Fall.

BERLAND, ALWYN
The Light at Cobh. Minnesota Review, Spring.

BINGHAM, SALLIE
Going Away. Ladies' Home Journal. Nov.
The Ice Party. Atlantic, Dec.

BINNEY, JAMES
Night of the Shadows. Arizona Quarterly, Summer.

BIRMINGHAM, STEPHEN
The Boy Behind the Door. Saturday Evening Post, Apr. 27.

BONGARTZ, ROY
For Benney . . . Much Loved. New Yorker, Sept. 14.

BRADBURY, RAY
The Life Work of Juan Diaz. Playboy, Sept.

BRENNAN, MAEVE
In and Out of Never-Never Land. New Yorker, July 6.

BRODKY, HAROLD
The Abundant Dreamer. New Yorker, Nov. 23.

BROOKE-ROSE, CHRISTINE
The Chinese Bedspread. Critic, Dec.

BROWN, RICHARD G.
Mr. Iscariot. Literary Review, Summer.

BURNHAM, TOM
The Price. Georgia Review, Summer.

CAIN, EMILY
Cassius' Castle. New Yorker, Nov. 23.

CARTER, JOHN STEWART
To a Tenor Dying Old. Kenyon Review, Autumn.
CARVER, RAYMOND
The Furious Seasons. December, Fall.
CASEY, BILL
The Way We Fish Now. Southwest Review, A··tumn.
CHAY, MARIE
Marriage Is Different. Southwest Review, Spring.
For a While the Gate Was Stuck. Arizona Quarterly, Summer.
CHEEVER, JOHN
An Educated American Woman. New Yorker, Nov. 2.
The Embarkment for Cythera. New Yorker, Nov. 13.
COHEN, FLORENCE
Mrs. Poe. Epoch, Spring.
New Vintage. Prairie Schooner, Winter.
CONANT, LORA M.
Theresa and the Dust Bowl. Arizona Quarterly, Spring.
CONNORS, THOMAS E.
God, the Devil, Etc. Quarterly Review of Literature, Vol. XII, No. 3.
COOK, BRUCE
Weltschmerz Blues. The Critic, Dec.
CORRINGTON, JOHN WILLIAM
Reunion. Southwest Review, Summer.
CURLEY, DANIEL
A Story of Love, Etc. Epoch, Spring.

DAVIDSON, GUSTAV
Joe—and Bartlett's Familiar Quotations. Literary Review, Winter.
DAVIS, CHRISTOPHER
Silence. Saturday Evening Post, Nov. 9.
DEASY, MARY
The Wedding. Virginia Quarterly Review, Spring.
DEJONG, DAVID CORNEL
Narrow Path with Snakes. Southwest Review, Summer.
DE VRIES, PETER
Forever Panting. New Yorker, Sept. 28.

DIKEMAN, MAY
The Woman Across the Street. Atlantic, Nov.
DOBIE, J. FRANK
Hunting Cousin Sally. Southwest Review, Summer.
DORIAN, EDWARD O.
The Silk Tie. Ararat, Winter.

EASTLAKE, WILLIAM
A Long Day's Dying. Virginia Quarterly Review, Winter.
EDWARDS, ARCHIBALD
The Unsigned Sully. University Review, Autumn.
ELKIN, SAM
The Sunny Side. Georgia Review, Spring.
ELY, DAVID
The Human Factor. Saturday Evening Post, Nov. 16.

FAIR, RONALD L.
World of Nothing. Chat Noir Review, Vol. II, No. 1.
FICHTER, ROBERT
We Listenin': Teach On. Transatlantic Review, Spring.
FINNEY, JACK
No Time for Billiard Ball Ballet. Playboy, Oct.
FLOWERS, LEE WINNIFORD
Last Night on Fant Hill. Literary Review, Winter.

GALLANT, MAVIS
Careless Talk. New Yorker, Sept. 28.
An Unmarried Man's Summer. New Yorker, Oct. 12.
The Ice Wagon Going Down the Street. New Yorker, Dec. 14.
GARDNER, JOHN
The Edge of the Woods. Quarterly Review of Literature. Vol. XII, No. 3.
GASTER, THEODOR
? Literary Review, Winter.
GILBERT, SISTER MARY
The Bird Watcher. Minnesota Review, Summer.

GIPSON, FRED
Papa's Straw Hat. Southwest Review,
Summer.
GODFREY, DAVE
It's Going to Be a Grand Summer.
Tamarack Review, Summer.
GREEN, HERB
Interlude. Transatlantic Review,
Spring.
GOYEN, WILLIAM
Figure Over the Town. Saturday
Evening Post, Apr. 27.
GREENBERG, JOANNE
Summering. Hudson Review, Sum-
mer.

HARRIS, MACDONALD
The Cricket Murderer, Prairie
Schooner, Summer.
HART, JANE
The Moth. Georgia Review, Summer.
HAZZARD, SHIRLEY
A Place in the Country. New Yorker,
June 15.
HEISERMAN, ARTHUR
A Shabbas-Goy. Kenyon Review,
Summer.
HEMENWAY, ROBERT
Late Show. New Yorker, Nov. 9.
HIBBIE, LAURIE L.
Third Manassas. Georgia Review,
Fall.
HORGAN, PAUL
Black Snowflakes. Saturday Evening
Post, March 30.
HUMPHREY, WILLIAM
The Ballad of Jesse Neighbours. Es-
quire, Sept.
A Voice from the Woods. Atlantic,
Oct.
The Pump. Esquire, Dec.
HUNTING, CONSTANCE
The New Coat. Western Humanities
Review, Autumn.

INGLER, JAMES
Mr. Bartheld. Southwest Review,
Spring.
IORIO, JOHN J.
Paradise Acres. University Review,
Winter.

JACKSON, SHIRLEY
Birthday Party. Vogue, Jan. 1.
JONES, JAMES
The Valentine. Saturday Evening
Post, Feb. 16.

KAUFMAN, SUE
Mary Pride. Atlantic, June.
KESSLER, SYDNEY
That Which Was Once a War.
Epoch, Fall.
KLEIN, NORMA
Summer Evening. Southwest Review,
Summer.
KOKJOHN, JOSEPH E.
Dearly Beloved. Harper's Magazine,
Sept.
KONECKY, EDITH
The Power. Massachusetts Review,
Summer.

LA FARGE, OLIVER
Caviar Remembered. Esquire, Oct.
LA RUE, ROBERT
The Day of the Rabbit. Arizona
Quarterly, Autumn.
LARSEN, ERLING
The Trout of My Dreams. Antioch
Review, Summer.
LAURENCE, MARGARET
Mask of Beaten Gold. Tamarack Re-
view, Autumn.
LEAHY, JACK THOMAS
The Net-Weavers. Virginia Quar-
terly Review, Spring.
LEVINSON, RICHARD AND WILLIAM LINK
An Afternoon With Harry. Univer-
sity Review, Spring.
LOESER, KATINKA
End of a Season. New Yorker, Sept.
21.
LUDWIG, JACK
A Woman of Her Age. Quarterly Re-
view of Literature, Vol. XII, No. 3.
LUTES, DELLA
Cousin William Comes For Christ-
mas. Woman's Day, Dec.
LYNDS, DENNIS
American Landscape—The City. Lit-
erary Review, Summer.
Freedom Fighter, Literary Review,
Winter.

McCARTHY, MARY
The Hounds of Summer. New Yorker, Sept. 14.
McCORMICK, JAMES
Wunderjude. Kenyon Review, Summer.
McCULLERS, CARSON
Sucker. Saturday Evening Post, Sept. 28.
McGOVERN, THOMAS
The Face at the Window. The Critic, Oct.-Nov.
McKINLEY, GEORGIA
Shall We Gather at the River? Redbook, Aug.
McNIECE, JAMES
A B C. Epoch, Spring.
MADDOW, BEN
Sad Seduction of the Teddy Bear. Hudson Review, Autumn.
On the Square. Hudson Review, Autumn.
MAJOR, T. W., JR.
A Matter of Justice. Prairie Schooner, Summer.
MALAMUD, BERNARD
The Refugee. Saturday Evening Post, Sept. 14.
MARSH, WILLARD
The Vigil. New Mexico Quarterly, Spring.
O Happy Dagger. Western Humanities Review, Spring.
MATHEWS, MARTHIEL
A Region of Time. Hudson Review, Winter.
MAZOR, JULIAN
Washington. New Yorker, Jan. 19.
MILLER, WARREN
Chaos, Disorder and the Late Show. Saturday Evening Post, Oct. 5.
MOORE, HAROLD
Ah, Swimmers! Western Humanities Review, Summer.
MORICONI, VIRGINIA
Simple Arithmetic. Transatlantic Review, Spring.
MORRIS, ROBERT
The Boss. Tamarack Review, Summer.

NATHAN, NORMAN
Embers. University Review, Spring.
NIERENBERG, EDWIN
The Chosen. Southwest Review, Summer.
NISSENSON, HUGH
In the Valley. Harper's Magazine, Oct.
NULLE, S. H.
Decline and Fall. University Review, Spring.

OATES, JOYCE CAROL
Upon the Sweeping Flood. Southwest Review, Spring.
Stigmata. Colorado Quarterly, Spring.
O'HARA, JOHN
Aunt Anna. Saturday Evening Post, March 23.
The Ride from Mauch Chunk. Saturday Evening Post, Apr. 13.
Exterior: With Figure. Saturday Evening Post, June 1.
The Lawbreaker. Saturday Evening Post, Nov. 16.

PACKER, NANCY HUDDLESTON
Once a Thief. Southwest Review, Summer.
PEDEN, WILLIAM
The Boy on the Bed. New Mexico Quarterly Review, Spring.
The Cross Country Dog. University Review, Autumn.
PRICE, REYNOLDS
The Names and Faces of Heroes. Shenandoah, Summer.
PUTZ, MARILYN
The Lesson. University Review, Autumn.

RANDAL, VERA
Waiting for Jim. Colorado Quarterly, Summer.
ROSE, KAREN
Uncle Phil's Death. University Review, Winter.
ROSEN, NORMA
Sister Gertrude. Redbook, Nov.

ROTH, ARTHUR J.
The Expatriates. The Critic, June-July.

RUGEL, MIRIAM
The Sweet Forever. Saturday Evening Post, June 15.

RUSHWORTH, EMILY C.
The Peace Offering. Georgia Review, Fall.

SAYRES, WILLIAM
The Wrong Play. Kenyon Review, Summer.
Combs and Belts and Other Things. Arizona Quarterly, Winter.

SCHWARTZ, JOHN
The Snake and Jack Coker. Genesis West, Fall.

SEGAL, LORE
The Beating of the Girl. Saturday Evening Post, Nov. 23.

SHERWIN, JUDITH JOHNSON
Unity: An Impartial Report. Massachusetts Review, Spring.

SINGER, ISAAC BASHEVIS
Traitl American Judaism, Winter.

STEIN, DAVID LEWIS
Spring Morning. Tamarack Review, Summer.

STERN, RICHARD
Teeth. Partisan Review, Fall.

SWADOS, HARVEY
A Story for Teddy. Saturday Evening Post, Nov. 23.

TAYLOR, PETER
Two Pilgrims. New Yorker, Sept. 7.

TERZIAN, JAMES
The Gift of Summer. Ararat, Winter.

TURNER, CLAYTON
Something Lost. Arizona Quarterly, Autumn.

WARREN, ROBERT PENN
Have You Seen Sukie? Virginia Quarterly Review, Autumn.

WEATHERS, WINSTON
The Gifts We Bear. New Mexico Quarterly, Autumn.

WELLS, JOEL
Second Passing. The Critic, Aug.-Sept.

WHITBREAD, THOMAS
The Way Things Are. Shenandoah, Autumn.
The Magic Hand of Chance. Shenandoah, Autumn.

WHITE, WALLACE
Poulette. New Yorker, Nov. 2.

WINDHAM, DONALD
A Leave-Taking. New Yorker, July 13.

WOLF, LEONARD
Fifty-Fifty. Kenyon Review, Autumn.

WYNNE, CAROLYN
The Communications of Summer. Minnesota Review, Summer.

ZIMPEL, LLOYD
Sleeve. Massachusetts Review, Spring.

ZIVKOVIC, PETER D.
If Pride Holds Tomorrow. Georgia Review, Fall.

II. *Foreign Authors*

BEVIS, ALISON
The Impulse. Transatlantic Review, Spring.

BONHAM, MARGARET
Man in a Corner. Saturday Evening Post, Sept. 7.

BOSCH, JUAN
The Indelible Spot. Saturday Evening Post, Nov. 16.

CHEKHOV, ANTON
Late-Blooming Flowers. Ladies' Home Journal, Nov.

CLARKE, AUSTIN
The Woman with the BBC Voice. Tamarack Review, Spring.

COWAN, PETER
The Voice. Literary Review, Winter.

COWARD, NOËL
Mrs. Capper's Birthday Party. Ladies' Home Journal, Dec.

DELANEY, SHELAGH
Sweetly Sings the Donkey. Saturday Evening Post, May 18.

DITLEV, HANS
The Musk Ox. Saturday Evening Post, Nov. 19.

FORSHAW, THELMA
The Widow. Literary Review, Winter.

FRIEL, BRIAN
Ginger Hero. Saturday Evening Post, May 18.

GARY, ROMAIN
The Fake. Ladies' Home Journal, Nov.

GREENE, GRAHAM
"Dear Dr. Falkenheim." Vogue, Jan. 1.

GRIFFIN, GWYN
Significant Experience. Saturday Evening Post, Sept. 21.

HERBERT, XAVIER
The Black Beast. Literary Review, Winter.

HUNGERFORD, T. A. G.
Remora. Literary Review, Winter.

KAZAKOV, YURI
The Smell of Bread. Esquire, Sept.
Autumn in the Oak Woods. Esquire, Oct.
On the Island. Esquire, Dec.

KELLY, GIVEN
The Killers. Literary Review, Winter.

KERSH, GERALD
A Bargain with Kashel. Saturday Evening Post, Apr. 27.

LESSING, DORIS
A Letter from Home. Partisan Review, Summer.

MACKEN, WALTER
The Kiss. New Yorker, Sept. 7.

MACINTYRE, THOMAS
Epithalamion. Transatlantic Review, Spring.

McGAHERN, JOHN
The Barracks. Transatlantic Review, Spring.
Summer at Strandhill. New Yorker, Sept. 21.

MEHTA, VED
Call Girl. Harper's Magazine, July.
Four Hundred and Twenty. New Yorker, Dec. 7.

MULISCH, HARRY
The Crown Prince. Transatlantic Review, Spring.

NAIPAUL, V. S.
The Night Watchman's Occurrence Book. Saturday Evening Post, Sept. 26.

O'CONNELL, CHARLES C.
Island Teacher. Atlantic, May.

O'FAOLAIN, SEAN
Too Beautiful, Too Good. Ladies' Home Journal, Oct.
One Man, One Boat, One Girl. Saturday Evening Post, Oct. 16.

O'GRADY, DESMOND
Hard Core. Literary Review, Winter.

PE, U WIN
Prelude to Glory. Arizona Quarterly, Winter.

PORTER, HAL
Gretel. Literary Review, Winter.

PRYCE-JONES, DAVID
Last Thing at Night. Transatlantic Review, Spring.

RAU, SANTHA RAMA
The Countess, Ladies' Home Journal, Dec.
Softly. Saturday Evening Post, Dec. 7.

REGE, SANANAND
The Last Day. Arizona Quarterly Review, Summer.

SAVORY, TEO
The Alley Cat and the Laws of Status. Prairie Schooner, Summer.

SENDER, RAMON
The Red Light. Southwest Review, Summer.

SILLITOE, ALAN
The Ragman's Daughter. New Yorker, Aug. 3.

SIMON, SOLOMON
Perpetuum Mobile. Literary Review, Winter.

SINCLAIR, MARIANNE
  Reverse Progress. Transatlantic Review, Spring.
SOLDATI, MARIO
  The Seagull. Transatlantic Review, Spring.
SPENCER, COLIN
  It's Anemones for Mabel. Transatlantic Review, Spring.
STRINDBERG, AUGUST
  Three Stories. Minnesota Review, Spring.

TAYLOR, ELIZABETH
  Mr. Wharton. New Yorker, June 8.

UNGER, LEONARD
  "Deja Vu Etcetera." Minnesota Review, Fall.

VINCENT, M. G.
  The Eye Stopper. Literary Review, Winter.

WARD, PETER
  Mr. Forster's Christmas Party. Literary Review, Winter.
WARNER, SYLVIA TOWNSEND
  Some Effects of a Hat. New Yorker, Nov. 9.
WILSON, H. H.
  The Firebreak. Literary Review, Winter.
  Sunday School Picnic. Literary Review, Winter.
WON, HWANG SOON
  Cranes. Prairie Schooner, Fall.
WUORIO, EVA-LIS
  The Singing Silence. Saturday Evening Post, March 23.

Addresses of American and Canadian Magazines Publishing Short Stories

Antioch Review, 212 Xenia Avenue, Yellow Springs, Ohio
Ararat, 250 Fifth Avenue, New York 1, New York
Arizona Quarterly, University of Arizona, Tucson, Arizona
Atlantic Monthly, 8 Arlington Street, Boston 16, Massachusetts
Audit, Box 92, Hayes Hall, University of Buffalo, Buffalo 14, New York
Between Two Worlds, Inter American University, San Germán, Puerto Rico
Canadian Forum, 30 Front Street West, Toronto, Ontario, Canada
Canadian Home Journal, 71 Richmond Street, Toronto, Ontario, Canada
Carleton Miscellany, Carleton College, Northfield, Minnesota
Carolina Quarterly, P.O. Box 1117, Chapel Hill, North Carolina
Catholic World, 180 Varick Street, New York 14, New York
Charm, Glamour, 420 Lexington Avenue, New York 17, New York
Chat Noir, 1354 N. Sedgwick St. Chicago 10, Ill.
Chicago Review, Reynolds Club, University of Chicago, Chicago, Illinois
Chrysalis, 5700 Third Street, San Francisco, California
Coastlines, 2465 North Beachwood Drive, Hollywood 20, California
Colorado Quarterly, University of Colorado, Boulder, Colorado
Commentary, 165 East 56th Street, New York 22, New York
Commonweal, 386 Park Avenue South, New York 16, New York
Contact, Box 758, Sausalito, California
Contemporary Fiction, Box 1323, Milwaukee, Wisconsin
Critic, 210 West Madison Street, Chicago, Illinois
Descant, Texas Christian University, Fort Worth, Texas
Ellery Queen's Mystery Magazine, 505 Park Avenue, New York 22, New York
Epoch, 252 Goldwin Smith Hall, Cornell University, Ithaca, New York
Esquire, 488 Madison Avenue, New York 22, New York
Evergreen Review, 64 University Place, New York 3, New York
Fantasy and Science Fiction, Box 271, Rockville Centre, New York
Four Quarters, LaSalle College, Philadelphia 43, Pennsylvania
Genesis West, 711 Concord Way, Burlingame, California
Gentleman's Quarterly, 488 Madison Avenue, New York 22, New York
Georgia Review, University of Georgia, Athens, Georgia
Good Housekeeping, 57th Street and Eighth Avenue, New York 19, New York

Harper's Bazaar, 572 Madison Avenue, New York 22, New York
Harper's Magazine, 49 East 33rd Street, New York 16, New York
Holiday, 666 Fifth Avenue, New York, New York
Hudson Review, 65 East 55th Street, New York 22, New York
Husk, Cornell College, Mount Vernon, Iowa
Inland, P.O. Box 685, Salt Lake City, Utah
Kenyon Review, Kenyon College, Gambier, Ohio
Ladies' Home Journal, 666 Fifth Avenue, New York, New York
Literary Review, Fairleigh Dickinson University, Teaneck, New Jersey
McCall's, 230 Park Avenue, New York 17, New York
MacLean's, 481 University Avenue, Toronto, Ontario, Canada
Mademoiselle, 420 Lexington Avenue, New York 22, New York
Mainstream, 832 Broadway, New York 18, New York
Massachusetts Review, University of Massachusetts, Amherst, Massachusetts
Midstream, 515 Park Avenue, New York, New York
Minnesota Review, Box 4068, University Station, Minneapolis, Minnesota
MSS, 670 Fifth Avenue, Chico, California
Mutiny, Box 178, Northport, New York
New Mexico Quarterly, University of New Mexico, Albuquerque, New Mexico
New World Writing, 521 Fifth Avenue, New York 17, New York
New Yorker, 25 West 43rd Street, New York 36, New York
Northwest Review, Erb Memorial Union, University of Oregon, Eugene, Oregon
Paris Review, 45-39 171 Place, Flushing 58, New York
Partisan Review, 22 East 17th Street, New York 3, New York
Perspective, Washington University Post Office, St. Louis, Missouri
Phoenix, Ida Noyes Hall, 1212 East 59th Street, Chicago 37, Illinois
Playboy, 232 East Ohio St. Chicago, Illinois
Prairie Schooner, Andrews Hall, University of Nebraska, Lincoln, Nebraska
Prism, University of British Columbia, Vancouver, British Columbia, Canada
Prism, 250 Park Avenue South, New York 3, New York
Provincetown Quarterly, P.O. Box 473, Provincetown, Massachusetts
Quarterly Review of Literature, Box 287, Bard College, Annandale-on-Hudson, New York
Queens Quarterly, Queens University, Kingston, Ontario, Canada
Redbook, 230 Park Avenue, New York 17, New York
Reflections, Chapel Hill, North Carolina
San Francisco Review, P.O. Box 671, San Francisco 1, California
Saturday Evening Post, 666 Fifth Avenue, New York 19, New York
Seventeen, 320 Park Avenue, New York 22, New York
Sewanee Review, University of the South, Sewanee, Tennessee
Shenandoah, Box 122, Lexington, Virginia
Show, 140 East 57th Street, New York 22, New York
Southwest Review, Southern Methodist University, Dallas, Texas
Tamarack Review, Box 157, Postal Station K, Toronto, Ontario, Canada
Texas Quarterly, Box 7527, University Station, Austin 12, Texas
Transatlantic Review, Box 3348, Grand Central P.O., New York 17, New York
University of Kansas City Review, University of Kansas City, Missouri
Virginia Quarterly Review, 1 West Range, Charlottesville, Virginia
Wagner Literary Magazine, Grymes Hills, Staten Island, New York
Weird Tales, 9 Rockefeller Plaza, New York, New York
Western Humanities Review, Building 41, University of Utah, Salt Lake City, Utah
Yale Review, P.O. Box 1729, New Haven, Connecticut
Yankee, Dublin, New Hampshire